The Young Kingdoms

Dakwinsi Steppe

to Xanardwys

d-Öma

Kwan

The Haghaniin Host

SIGHING DESERT

Mordaga's Castle

The Ragged Pillars

ai

The Teeth of Shenkh

esh

Nishvalni-Oss

Anakhazhan

rn

Quarzhasaat

Valederia

Elwher
ESHMIR

Bas'lk

ilmar

ILMIORA Karlaak

WEEPING WASTE

to PHUM
Yeshpotoom-Kahlai

ORG

Forest of Troos

Gorjhan

to OKARA
CHANG SHAI

Nadsokor Rignariom

Jadmar

IR

Old Hrolmar

Uhaio

STRAITS OF VILMIR

Ma-ha-kil-agra

Menii

The Fortress of the Evening

Utket

ISLE OF THE PURPLE TOWNS

Oi Oi

Ufrch-Sormeer

Chalal

Cha River

THE ROARING ROCKS

repesaz

Raschil

agasaz

FILKHAR

losaz

ARGIMILIAR

Alorasaz

PIKARAYD

The Dead Hills

River

Ryfel

DOREL

For Jim Cawthorn—
The Master Cartographer
of Elric's World

John Collier 2021

THE
ELRIC
SAGA

THE CITADEL
OF FORGOTTEN
MYTHS

THE ELRIC SAGA

THE CITADEL OF FORGOTTEN MYTHS

BY MICHAEL MOORCOCK

SAGA PRESS

LONDON SYDNEY **NEW YORK** TORONTO NEW DELHI

SAGA PRESS

AN IMPRINT OF SIMON & SCHUSTER, INC.

1230 AVENUE OF THE AMERICAS, NEW YORK, NEW YORK 10020

First Saga Press hardcover edition December 2022

SAGA PRESS and colophon are trademarks of Simon & Schuster, Inc.

For information about special discounts for bulk purchases, please contact Simon & Schuster Special Sales at 1-866-506-1949 or business@simonandschuster.com.

The Simon & Schuster Speakers Bureau can bring authors to your live event. For more information or to book an event, contact the Simon & Schuster Speakers Bureau at 1-866-248-3049 or visit our website at www.simonspeakers.com.

Interior design by Kathryn A. Kenney-Peterson

Manufactured in China

1   3   5   7   9   10   8   6   4   2

Library of Congress Cataloging-in-Publication Data is available.

ISBN 978-1-9821-9980-7
ISBN 978-1-9821-9982-1 (ebook)

Another one for my children, and grandchildren. A cool bunch.
Thanks, everybody.

CONTENTS

BOOK ONE

BOOK TWO

BOOK THREE

THE
ELRIC
SAGA

THE CITADEL
OF FORGOTTEN
MYTHS

BOOK ONE

HOW ELRIC PURSUED HIS WEIRD INTO THE FAR WORLD

Elric was to say little of his quest in the short time before the events leading to war between Law and Chaos, but there were many quests, many travels between the many planes of the great multiverse before he discovered the truth of his origins. Meanwhile, his new betrothed, Zarozinia, had demanded that he settle his questions once and for all. With this in mind, he sent a message to Moonglum to meet him at a certain time and place. From there, they set off to see what answers they might find in unknown lands.

> *They followed the tale of Adric Heed*
> *Pirate Venturer once was he.*
> *Forsaking his sister and his fatherland*
> *Fore'er to sail 'tween horizon and the strand.*

> *The Snow White Glaive,*
> St Mary Brookgate's copy, c. 900 AD
> (Aelford's tr.)

ONE

Over the Edge

THE SUN, RIMMED in copper now and bloated as if with blood, settled upon the horizon. It cast long complicated shadows across a strangely wrought ship whose reflective brass flashed like eyes everywhere in the rigging. On deck, two dignified priestesses of Xiombarg, wearing elaborate ceremonial quilted habits with glinting bronze crowns, stood expectantly at the ship's rail as, softly, they called a prayer to their patron and then peered suddenly upwards. There, in the soft depths of the sky, they detected a movement and, bowed in contemplation, listened to the distant hungry roar greeting the coming of darkness with godlike glee.

The priestesses were Lady Andra and Lady Indra of the Temple of Xiombarg in far Ko. The captain understood them to be pledged to some sort of mission on behalf of their patroness, the Queen of the Swords. They began to chant their final evening ritual and now saw a great shadow in the form of a sword-bearing woman, the shape preferred by their deity in Ko, appear in the sky overhead. As they completed their ritual, two men came up from the passenger quarters below. One was short, with a shock of startling red hair, a ruddy complexion, large blue eyes and a wide, smiling mouth. He wore a quilted maroon jacket and deerskin breeks tucked into soft boots. His tall companion was clad in black silk and black leather, hair the colour of milk, skin pale as the thinnest bleached linen. Like his companion he was unarmed. Any casual observer would know that he was not quite human. His long head with its slightly tapering ears and slanting brows was as remarkable as his sharp, glittering ruby-coloured eyes. He frowned. They had been in time to glimpse the last of the apparition.

Lowering their hands, the priestesses turned, surprised to see the men, who bowed politely. The dignified women acknowledged the pair and passed gracefully down the companionway, returning to their cabin belowdecks. The men took the place of the women at the rail. The disc of the sun was halfway below the horizon now, its light cutting a red road across the unbroken surface of the sea.

The tall man was well known in the North and West hemispheres but not well liked. He was Elric, sometimes called Kinslayer, former emperor of un-human Melniboné, until lately the dominant power in the world. The short man was Moonglum from Elwher in the so-called Unmapped East. Since meeting again, they had been travelling companions, with Elric seeking answers to his questions concerning the beginnings of Melniboné and Moonglum seeking knowledge and treasure. They had shared rare adventures. Most recently they had come from Chun, where they had found two more people with complicated reasons for travelling with them, and who this evening had elected to stay below. Now nothing of Xiombarg, rival of Elric's own patron, Arioch, remained.

Moonglum grinned after the disappearing priestesses. "Xiombarg's worshippers are a little more comely in Ko! Our Lady of Weapons picks her women well. I'm beginning to regret that decision I made in the tavern."

A faint smile from his friend. "I'm too closely bound to Xiombarg's fellow Chaos Lord to wish any further entanglement with the Dukes and Duchesses of Entropy. Arioch and Xiombarg have always been at odds. They are over-interested in the sphere of mortals. Some think their struggles will end the worlds. And I think you'll find those two priestesses aren't interested in sharing themselves with anyone but their patron and each other, if my knowledge of their beliefs is correct."

"Ah." Moonglum regarded the empty companionway with disappointment. "Elric, my friend, sometimes I wish you would not proffer your knowledge so freely!"

"I assure you, I'm sharing very little." The albino dropped his gaze to inspect the lapping waters below. Then he looked up for a moment, scanning the darkening horizon as if struck by an unpleasant thought. He did not like to feel Xiombarg's presence so close. The Queen of the Swords was notorious for meddling in mortal affairs.

The albino wondered as usual about his decision to take this journey. Was it nothing more than escape from his fear of giving his love to another woman, or simply a troubled conscience? Surely this was more than a diversion, this restless search for an understanding of his people's ancestral origins, this questing the natural and supernatural worlds for solutions to the mysteries of his and everyone's existence? He had learned all the legends of Melniboné: how a mortal princess had been courted by a dragon of the Phoorn race and how Elric's folk sprang from that supernatural union. His quests on the dream couches of Melniboné, when he was learning his sorcery, had confirmed the truth of that, but explained little else.

Now the sun was almost gone, but the distant roar was louder, as if in triumph. And then the sun went down, leaving the ship in a grey-gold twilight. The scent of brine was stronger. A powerful wind blew suddenly, filling the ship's enormous blue sails as the oarsmen below shipped their long sweeps. Unusually, they drew the oars fully into the body of the ship and stowed them. The two men heard the sound of wood banging against wood, of metal being drawn against metal as the rowlocks were firmly shut.

At this, both men reluctantly left the deck and descended their own companionway to seek their cabins. In the gangway they met the captain's first officer, the plump, pimpled giant Ghatan Tiun, who saluted politely. "Make sure all's watertight within your cabins, masters. We'll be going over just a couple of hours after moonrise. A bell will be sounded in the morning, when it's safe to unbatten."

"If we still live," Moonglum muttered cheerfully.

The mate grinned back at him. "Indeed! Good night, masters. With luck you'll wake in the World Above, as it's known there."

Wishing them both good night, Elric entered his own quarters. From outside came a series of heavy thumps, creaking and the sound of rattling chains as the ship was tightened against the water.

His cabin was filled with a deep orange light from a lantern swinging at the centre of the low ceiling. A seated woman frowned over a small scroll. She looked up and smiled as the albino entered. She was extremely beautiful, the black-haired Princess Nauhaduar of Uyt, who, these days, called herself simply Nauha. Her large, dark eyes reflected the light. Her lips were slightly parted in an intelligent smile. "So we have passed the point of no return, my lord."

"It seems so." Elric began to strip off his shirt, moving towards their wide bunk piled with quilts and furs. His wiry muscles and slender form showed a man of action. His entire appearance denoted the mercenary and treasure-hunter he pretended to be. "Perhaps we'd do well to sleep now, before the real noise begins. Too late for you to consider returning to Uyt."

She shrugged, replacing the scroll in its tubular case. "Never would I wish to miss this experience, my lord. After all, until you convinced me otherwise, I shared the common view of our world as dish-shaped. I believed all other descriptions to be mere fools' tales."

"Aye. It's as well so few believe the ovoid truth, for the reality would surely confuse them." He spoke a little abstractedly, his mind on other matters. "And one's magic becomes more fluid . . ."

"I am," she said, "still confused."

"Well, the actuality will be demonstrated anon." He was naked now, slim and muscular in all his strange, pale beauty. He picked up a pitcher and poured water into a bowl, washing languidly. Once again she noted the sweet, attractive scent of his alien body. Did he seek dragons? Ancestors? The words were similar in his language. Still, she wondered why she confused them.

She, too, began to prepare for bed. Since she had taken up with Elric, the ennui to which she had become reconciled had disappeared or had been absorbed into his. She felt it could never return now. Elric's dreams rarely gave him a full night's sleep, but even if the albino were to abandon her, she would never regret knowing him or, as she suspected of herself, loving him. Womanslayer he was called, but she did not care. Kinslayer and traitor he might be, it had never mattered to her what he was or what she risked. Dark and light were inextricably combined in this strange half-human creature whose ancestors had ruled the world before her own race emerged from the clay of creation, whose terrible sword, now rolled in rough cloth and skin and stowed in the lower locker, seemed possessed of its own dark intelligence. She knew she should be afraid of it, as of him, and part of her re-experienced the horror she had already witnessed once, there in the foothills of the Mountains of Mourning, but the rest of her was drawn by curiosity to know more about the sword's properties and of the moody prince who carried it. She had understood the cost of following him. He had warned her against himself, yet she had insisted she leave her father and twin sister in the lowland city of Nune and accompany him, even though she abandoned all that was familiar to her. Lying beside that hard, wonderful, pale and vibrant body which already slept tense and cool beside her, she listened to the sounds of the ship and the sea as timbers creaked and the thunder from the horizon grew louder. She sensed the galleon's speed increasing, evidently borne on a rapid current. She had some notion of what to expect but wanted to question Elric. He slept, murmuring a little, yet apparently at peace, and she could not rouse him. At the same time she could scarcely believe his lack of concern.

Faintly, from above, a slow bell began to sound. The albino shivered against her, unwaking. The ship reared, rolling her against his body, reared again, sending a vibrant shock through her. *The Paladino* rocked, shuddered, her timbers moaning and straining as her hull dipped one way and then another, rolling from one side to the other so violently that Nauha was forced to wrap her arms around her lover to steady herself. Elric moved as if to resist her, then woke for a moment. "Are we over?"

"Not yet."

He closed his crimson eyes again. For a while they slept. Perhaps for hours, she could not tell.

◎ ◎ ◎

ELRIC HAD RARELY slept in peace since the death of Cymoril, his first betrothed. And now, it appeared, he slept with any fine woman who would distract him from his new love for Zarozinia. He feared, no matter how Moonglum tried to reassure him, that if he committed himself to her, she, too, would die. Every oracle he had consulted on his travels confirmed this. And so he chose to test himself and to forget himself in the arms of any foreign noblewoman he met. Zarozinia, better than Elric, had known what to do. If he returned to her, she knew it would be for as long as they lived.

Nauha awoke to sense the ship's speed increasing. She gasped as they were tossed violently up and down and from the locker below came a deep grumbling out of that sentient blade; but the noise of the water grew into a deafening roar, drowning the complaints of the Black Sword, and bearing them at a steeper and steeper angle of descent:

Towards the edge of the world.

TW○

Strangers at Sea

EARLIER, ELRIC HAD told her where he was going. He had assured her he would leave her at a port from which she could return home. Nauha had asked him if he was tired of her. He was surprised. He had not wanted to put her in danger, he said. Perhaps she imposed her wishes on him?

But she had no intention of parting. The albino fascinated her, as did his obsessions. She had always wondered at the rumours of another world, a kind of mirror of their own. Now she had the chance to experience the truth. She gave herself up to adventure as readily as she had given herself up to this alien adventurer. Now she was to risk her life and her sanity, as she had been warned she must, to discover what lay beyond the edge of the world. Elric had told her of the dangers, from which few voyagers ever returned. While she cared for life, she did not care for a life without risk or excitement. Or so she told herself. Did she regret her decision now?

Still the ship gathered speed, rocking urgently from side to side. Every timber protesting, it dipped at a still steeper angle, rocking wildly, threatening to throw them from the bunk. She clung to the albino, who said *"Cymoril,"* and held her with gentle strength in his arms. She moved against him. This was by no means the first time he had cried out the name of his slain betrothed. In his sleep, he steadied her as the ship bucked again, and then suddenly there was the sensation of falling, falling as the ship plunged over the edge, falling forever, it seemed, until, with a massive, shivering shock, it struck something and must surely break apart, as if on a reef, and began to move rhythmically up and down until she could not stop the long, full-throated scream which burst from her body. Almost certain that they were destroyed, that they were sinking, she prepared herself for death, but Elric's arms tightened a little more, and, when she opened her eyes, she could see through the gloom that he was smiling. Was he, too, accepting their fate?

Then the water was quiet. The ship gentled into an easy forward motion, and overhead she heard men's urgent voices, full of relief, calling orders and responses. Elric swung out of the bunk and began to unscrew the covers over the cabin's only porthole, letting silver light through damp muslin, making his body almost invisible to her. Cool, sweet air flooded through the ship. Was that a seabird she heard?

"Where are we?" she asked, then cursed herself for her inanity. He did not answer but moved away from the porthole, becoming a shadow. A little later, softly, politely enough, he answered.

"We're where you did not expect to be. On the underside of the world. The World Below, as your legends have it."

"You know this world?"

"From my dream-quests, as a youth. On those dream couches you heard about."

"And which you refuse to discuss."

He shrugged. No point. But he added: "We had an easy transition, I think. Easier than I remembered. This captain was well experienced, but in those youthful years I was on a dream-quest, when sensation's often amplified. What some call dreams are merely emphatic confirmations of our realities and instincts." He climbed back into the bunk and supported her head and shoulders on his arm. "There are still several hours to dawn. Best sleep some more."

"I thought you spoke in metaphor." She smiled uncertainly. "But why?"

"Simply? Curiosity."

"About what?"

"About my people. Some of our legends say we settled on this side of the world first. Before we came to the one we now share."

"It is true, then, that you are unhuman."

"We never claimed to be human. Long ago, our women were egg-bearing. Like reptiles. Like our Phoorn cousins. Amongst the refugees, I hear, some still choose to have their offspring by the old methods, but most now prefer live birth as the humans. It is safer. Before that, we're taught, they were lizards. Snakes, if you believe one myth. Among my people it was insulting if humans claimed kinship with us. We have blood in common with ancient saurian, who lived long before we did! We have some means of communicating with them. We were not called *phoornghat* for nothing. The word means 'dragon-made' in our tongue. Perhaps not cold-blooded (though some argue otherwise), we are a species which predated and parallels your own."

He was baffled by her laughter. She shook her long head. "I am surprised you have no insect blood, too!"

He shrugged again. "So much of our history is lost to me. Even my dream-quests failed to reveal all I needed to know. My memory was never entire after an accident on the couches with my cousin, who hoped to trap me in a dream! I doubt that any memory is exact, but mine did not survive my various transitions. There is a story that at least one nation of my race is characteristically almost the opposite of my own and beloved by the humans with whom they shared their world. Others tell of pirates, even more voracious than Pan Tang's raiders."

"They are here?"

"I already know some of them."

"How?"

"I have explained my education," he told her, rolling over. "Dream-quests. Reality experienced on a different plane. Yet those are selective, and they never gave me the answers I hoped to find. Certain legends have been confirmed as having at least some grounding in truth. Yet how could warm-blooded creatures like myself combine with reptiles to give birth? How did Phoorn, the ancestors of dragons, and *phoornghat*, the ancestors of Melnibonéans, procreate? And under what circumstances would those matings take place?"

"Sorcery, of course," she said. "Old-fashioned sorcery."

She was sincere.

He did not answer any more questions. In a moment she realised he was oblivious to her. It took her a little longer to return to sleep.

Later, dozing, she heard a tap at the cabin door, and Moonglum called from the other side. Elric slipped on his shirt and rose to answer, letting her cover herself before opening the door to the red-headed Elwheri who stood there grinning, his arm around the woman he had met in port the night before they embarked. The woman was slender, with black hair and eyes, her dark skin typical of her people. She seemed most relieved of all four. No doubt she too had expected to die as the ship fell. Now she breathed in the sweet, cool air blowing through the ship, and she cocked her head, hearing the oars being unshipped and thrust into choppy water. She heard a sharp snap as the wind took a sail. From somewhere came the smell of frying meat. Overhead, a dozen voices called at once. Everyone aboard seemed astonished by their survival.

When they had bathed and dressed, Elric and Nauha joined the others in the big public galley where passengers and ship's officers took their meals. As well as the two priestesses of Xiombarg and Elric's party, there were six more passengers of the merchant class, all a little shaken and exchanging excited descriptions of their experiences. To Elric's keen eye only one other was not evidently a trader. The mysterious Nihrain Masters were giants from the Forsnei Massif, servants of the Great Balance. They were said to sleep, like Phoorn dragons, awaiting some kind of call. Rumour had it in Chun that the Nihrain and their servants were stirring and might even be abroad again. He sat a little apart from the rest, wrapped up in a dark red sea-cloak, as if against a cold no-one else felt. Saturnine, with deep ebony skin, uncommunicative, he showed only a passing interest in his fellows. His woollen bonnet was stuck with rare feathers, like a motley halo. He had said nothing of substance since boarding, offering no-one his name. This tall, well-bodied man had arrived late on the dock in a chariot containing himself and a driver. The chariot had displayed a complicated and unfamiliar livery in black and yellow. The charioteer, handing his passenger a small travelling bag, turned his massive black stallions and had driven away at a gallop through the crowded traffic.

The previous night the man had eaten quickly and retired without introducing himself, considered rude behaviour in that quarter of the world. His name was on the manifest but impossible to read. One passenger thought "Nihrain," which all the others considered fanciful. The Nihrain, by repute, did not travel by means of earthly ships but on massive horses which travelled on unseen planes. Apart from a heavy red fur wolfskin travelling cloak and boots, the man wore a yellow shirt and black breeches, with doe-leather boots, also a dull yellow. He carried a short sword and apparently no other weapon. Was this uniform or was it individual taste? Unsure if this was a kind of dandyism or not, Moonglum glanced over at the handsome man wondering why he had an air of familiarity, trying to decide if the sailor spoke truth or lied. But Elric, whose interest in humans and their affairs was casual at best, ignored him as thoroughly as he did the rest. He gave his attention only to Moonglum, who had a trick of amusing him, and to Nauhaduar, for whom he had an unusual regard, though the city of Karlaak by the Weeping Wastes and her loving princess were never far from his thoughts.

"And so here we are!" Munching on his bread, Moonglum stared out of the nearest porthole at the calm sea. "I owe you an apology, friend Elric, for I did not wholly believe your assertions of a world on the other side of our own. But now it is demonstrated! Our world is not flat but egg-shaped. And here we are alive to prove it. I was taught much cosmology as a boy. Not all of it appears to equate with certain realities! While I do not understand by what supernatural agency the ocean remains upon the surface of the egg, I have to accept that it does . . ."

A deep-throated laugh from one of the merchants. "And do your folk believe, as some of mine do, that there are other eggs, scattered like pebbles across the ether, of all sizes, some of which resemble our own, Master Elwheri? With people dwelling on them, of commensurate dimensions, perhaps existing within other eggs, those eggs contained within still more eggs and so on?"

"Or perhaps"—another smiled—"you do not believe any of our worlds to be egg-shaped, and are instead round, like the nuts of the *omerhav* tree? What say you, Master Silverskin?"

Refusing to be drawn into the general conversation, Elric shrugged, sipping the yellow breakfast wine which he had brought with him. His only interest in travel was in finding some clue to his own and his people's history. He could not believe he would find much he needed here in this galley. Who were the Phoorn? What had brought their two races here? Had they been driven here as refugees during a cosmic struggle between supernatural powers? Had they come as warriors or as peaceful settlers?

Moonglum, however, was more gregarious and curious. "So some philosophers are convinced, I understand, amongst the intellectuals of my own country. Yet none has yet explained how the waters remain spread so evenly upon the surface of these worlds, nor indeed how ships remain on them. How are we able to stand upon these decks and not float like pollen into the air. Some name Magnetism as the answer, where the iron in our bodies is attracted to iron in the soil. I hear that ancient scholars wrote on all such things in the Melnibonéan Golden Age, before that people determined to become conquerors rather than scholars and entered the madness of the Great Reconstruction, when so many of our histories were destroyed. And from which we never entirely recovered."

The saturnine man raised his head, suddenly alert but, when neither Moonglum nor Elric elaborated, returned his attention to his food.

Moonglum's tavern girl giggled, wiping gleaming juice from her scarlet lips. "My people have known of the sea passage between the two worlds for centuries. They benefitted. There are land passages through the Weeping Waste also, but those are still more dangerous. My folk became wealthy as a result of that knowledge, for we developed ships like this one, able to negotiate Turnaround Falls, where Chaos controls the very weight of things. A few of our forefathers made the road through World's Edge, but the dangers of bringing goods back on mules caused them to give up their journeys."

The captain, seated at the far end of the table, put a cautionary finger to his lips. "Best say no more, girl, or our secrets become common property. We're rich only while most folk believe this side of the world is legend at best. Or impossible to reach. We have persuaded our customers that our goods are acquired through bonds with the great elementals!" He winked. "Both sides believe that lie rather than contemplate the truth!"

"But my companion here has been this way before," declared Moonglum, privately amused by this turn of the conversation. "Which is why I was ready to take the risk of it. And swear that oath, of course, before we set sail."

"I was not aware, sir . . ." The captain raised an enquiring eyebrow at Elric. But the albino did not respond, merely dropping his gaze to look at his own pale hand gripping his wine-cup. "What proposed your first visit, sir, if I might ask?" The captain made cheerful, casual conversation. "Trade? Curiosity?"

For the sake of his companions, Elric made some effort. "I have relatives here."

He had, he thought, been unusually loquacious and egalitarian. The captain did not pursue his theme.

Later, as they took in the fine air on deck, staring over what seemed an infinity of rolling blue white-tipped water, Princess Nauha said to him, "I'm curious to meet these relations. I had no idea Melnibonéans lived elsewhere than the Dragon Isle."

"They are relatives," he told her, "but they are not of Melniboné and never were. Nor wished to be. And, should we discover any, they probably will not welcome us. Had you heard of the Phoorn before?"

When she said she had not, he did not go further.

The ship sailed smoothly on, through unchanging weather, across that undisturbed ocean, beneath strange stars, and Elric, in the days that followed, grew increasingly taciturn.

On the fifth day of wide water the fo'c's'le lookout suddenly cried with some vigour, "'Ware above! 'Ware above!" And pointed into the sky to where a distant, dark shape came flapping towards them and then veered back again. "Dragon! Dragon ho!"

This brought all the passengers but the saturnine merchant up on deck to follow the pointing hand and watch with a murmuring mixture of wonder, terror and disappointment and suddenly draw their attention to where a long shoreline was visible through light mist, soon more clearly revealing a series of deep, sandy beaches on which white waves broke. "Land! Land ho!" The lookout pointed directly forward. The ship was travelling on great breakers, using her special hull to negotiate the treacherous waves. Behind the beaches rose dark green foliage, a dense forest, but no sign of settlements. Not so much as a wisp of smoke.

Later, back in the galley, Moonglum speculated that possibly these woods were an extension of the jungle which they had lately left, wrapping itself across the world, but this was ignored so he fell silent as the ship changed course to follow the new coast.

"Shugg Banat," replied one of the merchants when Moonglum asked what their first port of call would be. "If the pirate slavers spare us."

Moonglum had heard no previous talk of pirates or slavers. "Eh?"

"There are many good bays along this coast offering safe harbour. The pirates use them. They watch for ships coming in from the edge and prey on them. Some are here by accident and are perfect victims. They are therefore unlikely to attack us."

"Why so?"

"We watch for them and are prepared. Fighting us is uneconomical! They tend to know us. Moreover, the chances are we carry comparatively little cargo, while our money's only of use to merchants like ourselves. They place no special value on our silver coinage."

"I'm relieved, sir!" Moonglum was drunk from the strong, unfamiliar beer and also, possibly, the faintly psychedelic turnips he had chosen for his meal. "Like the Happy Ape, who lives on the island of Bjarr. The happier he is, the more he farts, the more he farts, the more people avoid him and the happier he is! The Happy Ape lives exclusively on fruits, roots and vegetables. The Island of the Happy Ape is a paradise with more than enough to sustain the tribe, who live everywhere on the island there is shelter. Although the island is quickly found due to the sepia fog which hangs over her in certain seasons, few visit. The Apes spend their days in philosophical debate and discovering the curative properties of plants. Their diet results in their constant flatulence, so foul it keeps all potential invaders at bay." Whereupon he seemed to fall forward into a silence of his own creation and landed facedown in his faintly glowing turnips.

For the rest of the day the ship held her course, still following the mysterious coast, which changed occasionally from dense woodland to high cliffs. There was little wind, but the water was calm, giving good purchase to their oars, allowing the rowers, all free or indentured sharemen, to keep steady time. Moonglum and his lady friend went below as usual, while Elric and the princess remained on deck. She was grateful for the sweetness of the air, asking if he, too, smelled the forest. Elric smiled. "I have my own theory. This second world has fewer inhabitants. Therefore they expel less foul air . . ." He was not entirely serious. "Therefore we breathe fresher air!"

She thought her paramour continued Moonglum's uncouth behaviour at the breakfast table. She left his side and went to stand on the foredeck, raising her head against the breeze, letting it lift her dark hair and sending it streaming behind her. He stared landward, his thoughts on his past when, lost in a dream-quest, he had first found this world and a city and a people which welcomed him. Would he be welcomed again? he wondered. Had he, for instance, come originally to this world in his past or his future? He knew there could be wide discrepancies.

A wild yell from above. Still on the foredeck Princess Nauha echoed the lookout's voice from the crow's nest. Swiftly over the horizon came a great, grey square sail. Two more. A fourth. But Elric's interest was claimed by a lower, darker hull in the water, the other ships following it in rough formation. The hull had no sails, no oars, yet it slipped through the water like a killer whale, a triangular shape rising from its slender deck like a dorsal fin. The long, sharp prow, crimson as blood, split the light waves, and several spearmen stood on it, leaning forward as it sped towards the merchant. Never had Elric seen a ship move so quickly, darting almost like a fish. He mentioned this to the captain, who kept his eyes on the ships, answering from the corner of his mouth. "First they had the dragons, a century ago or more, who raided with them and made them invulnerable. Then the dragons slowly disappeared, and these strange, supernatural vessels replaced them. Now there is only one left, but so great is their power and impregnable their White Fort that we cannot ever hope to resist them."

Archers were already running to their positions around Elric. Others pulled canvas from the oiled wood of massive catapults. The stink of olives and Chaos Fire filled his nostrils as braziers were lit and throwing jars filled. Black smoke gusted. From below, Moonglum, his twin swords sheathed on left and right hips, came running up the companionway. He carried something large and thoroughly wrapped in his hands and threw it towards Elric, glad to be rid of it. Elric caught it easily, stripping away the cloth and leather wrapping to reveal a heavy scabbard, a hilt with a pulsing dark jewel imbedded in it. He attached the long sword to his belt. The sword moaned for a moment, perhaps anticipating a bloodletting, and then was silent.

"Pirates?" Moonglum asked. "Will they attack?"

"Perhaps." He looked over to where the princess, tying back her hair, approached. "My lady. You had best arm yourself." She had her own blades below.

"They'll fight?" she asked, turning to follow his suggestion.

"Best be ready for the worst." He indicated the crew. "Just as they are."

She went below and reappeared with a slender sword and poignard.

A kind of gasp from the strange, leading ship.

Followed by a loud hissing.

A cloud rose from around the central greyish dorsal. Clad in armour the colour of amber, pale warriors crowded forward. Their long features with slightly slanted eyes peered from their helmets. Moonglum gave a grunt of surprise.

"Melnibonéans!"

Elric said nothing, but his left hand tightened on Stormbringer's hilt.

The ship, still moving towards them, without evident propulsion, was clearly visible now. With its high triple prow, its long sleek decks and elaborately carved rails, it had only seemed smaller than the surrounding ships because it sat so low in the water. One tall man stood on the massive upper deck, his armour more intricate than the rest. His features declared his race, but the ship and armour, even the look of his weapons, had little in common with Melnibonéan artefacts.

Slowly the red hull hove to. The tall captain called out from his poop deck. "Who are you, and where are you bound?" Another great hissing sigh came from the oddly shaped dorsal, ribbed and faintly rosy with reflected light, in the middle deck. "Quickly now!"

"We're *The Paladino*, bound for Selwing Aftra and ports beyond," called back the captain. "Carrying trade goods and passengers from the World Below."

But the strange ship's captain barely acknowledged him, staring straight at Elric and frowning. Elric stared back with equal hauteur.

Then, to Moonglum's astonishment, the pirate captain spoke in liquid High Melnibonéan, addressing the albino. Thinking it to be what he called *Phoornish*, Moonglum understood enough to recognise a different accent.

"You have come from Below? Where do you journey?"

Elric did not reply directly. "Do you mean this ship harm?"

The captain shook his head slowly. "If you mean to sail on." But he remained curious. He switched to Common Tongue, addressing the captain of *The Paladino*. "We're no threat to you or your ship. You're bound for Apho and Selwing Aftra?"

"We are, my lord. And Shugg Banat before that. Then Hizs, where we shall take on provisions, make repairs and give our men some rest before going on to the Snow Islands and taking the warm water via the Silver Coast, then home again."

"And stop at no other ports between here and Hizs?"

"We do not."

"Then go in peace." The pirate frowned, placing slender hands on his railing. He seemed strangely unsettled by his decision.

Moonglum was staring at the tall, pale triangle in the centre of the ship. Under his breath he said, "I'll swear that's flesh . . . Those are scales. Some reptile. Blood? A harnessed monster." Then the ship was backing, clouded water still hissing, obscuring the dorsal, giving out a not unpleasant stink.

There was a dreadful, heavy stillness in the air, as if an attack might yet come. All that could be heard was a creaking of timbers, the heavy slap of fabric in the wind, the sound of water lapping against oars. Moonglum thought he could just hear the sound of breathing nearby.

"They believe our side of the world to be the netherworld," said the first mate, keeping his lips from moving too much. "But I believe that this place is Hell, and we have just met one of Hell's aristocrats."

Elric and the pirate captain continued to stare at each other in fixed fascination until the two ships were far apart. Then, without comment, Elric returned to his cabin, leaving his companions on the upper deck.

"My lord has more relations here than he previously owned," observed the princess dryly. "Has he spoken of that captain to you, Master Moonglum?"

Moonglum shook his head slowly.

"Is that why he is here?" she wondered.

"I think not." Moonglum watched the archers unstringing their bows and replacing them, together with long quivers of arrows, in their oiled wooden cases.

Then, unbuckling his swords, he followed his friend below.

THREE

Ancestral Memories

MOONGLUM HAD NOT expected to find such subtle beauty in the harbour at Hizs, nor such a richness of scents and floral colour. Until now the ports he had seen on this side of the world had looked somewhat gloomy, with massive old fortifications showing they had once fought long defensive battles.

But not Hizs. She was still known as the Fortress of Flowers, the Sweet Port and Summer's Harbour. Her pastel terraces formed slender ziggurats over which poured dark green foliage and all manner of gorgeous flowers, the so-called Singing Flowers which attracted bees and birds with sound rather than scent. On her terraces lounged brightly dressed, brown-skinned citizens, lazing in the warm, easy air, cupping their hands to call down into her streets to vendors and messengers or merchants on their way to inspect the broad-beamed galleon's cargo and greet her traders. Artefacts which were common on his side of the world, the captain had warned them, might be highly valuable to people here and so, should he be offered something for, say, his belt buckle, he should be prepared to spend some time bartering. And hint, perhaps, that his sword had magical properties. Another wink.

The tavern girl, Cita Tine, had brought a whole sack of goods she planned to barter and knew exactly what she planned to trade them for. To his chagrin, Moonglum understood that it was not wholly out of blind passion that she had decided to accompany him to the World Below (or, as the locals preferred, Above). Indeed, almost as soon as they had berthed, Cita had raced down the gangplank to the quay, telling him she would see him back at the ship around suppertime. The last he glimpsed of her was, sack over her shoulder, pushing her way through a crowd of men and women and entering a narrow side street between two warehouses. Clearly, she knew exactly where she wanted to go. Although he was aware her family traded regularly in Hizs, Moonglum rather resented the fact that she had not thought to include him in her confidence.

Once again, they were running out of money. The fare had cost them almost everything they had between them, far more than expected and taking every scrap of platinum and tin they owned. Elric disdained such thoughts, but they needed treasure, not close encounters with pirates. Moonglum watched the group of merchants as they made for a couple of dockside inns and saw the priestesses met by two of their own in a canvas-covered carriage. The saturnine trader signed for a rickshaw to take him up the hill into the city's centre. Then Moonglum glanced at Elric and followed his friend's gaze down to the quay.

Separated from the others, hanging back somewhat in the shadows, stood a tall woman. She was dressed in several shades of green silk, a wide-brimmed green hat hiding the upper part of her face. A small, leather-collared boy held a long-handled parasol, protecting her from the noonday heat, and she rested one slender hand on his shoulder. That hand attracted the Eastlander's attention most. There was a familiar pallor to it. He knew at once that, like his friend, the woman was an albino; and, when she turned to avoid a lumbering merchant anxious to reach the ship ahead of his fellows, the Eastlander's observation was confirmed. Her face was as white as Elric's, her eyes protected by a mask of fine gauze through which, no doubt, she could see, but through which the sun's rays could not entirely penetrate. She had the same languid insouciance in her manner. She could be the albino's sister. Was this Elric's motive for being here? Was Moonglum the only one risking the voyage from simple curiosity? He sighed and began to wonder about the quality of the local wine.

But when Elric, guiding his princess towards the gangplank, indicated that he would be pleased with Moonglum's presence, the little Elwheri hitched his two swords about his waist and went with them, glad, after a moment, to feel solid land beneath his feet, even if he had some slight difficulty in standing upright.

"Another of your Melnibonéan relatives," murmured Nauha, as they approached the green-clad woman. "Is she blind?"

"I don't think so. And she is not Melnibonéan."

The princess frowned, looking up into his face in the hope of learning something more from his expression. "Then—what—?"

Elric might have shrugged, even smiled, as he said: "She's Phoorn."

"Phoorn?"

"At any rate more Phoorn than I am."

"And, again, what is Phoorn?"

For the first time since she had known him, the albino seemed ill at ease. "I told you, madam, that we are closely related. But I am not sure. I don't know if . . ." Now he recalled that this was not the kind of thing his people discussed too frequently, and probably never with humans.

"You don't remember . . . ?" She was sceptical.

"I remember her. From the dream-quest. She might not know me."

He had told her enough about the nature of his dream-quests for her to understand at least the gist of what he said. He might have met this particular woman before or after that moment in time. She might not even be the same woman Elric remembered. Dream-quests usually took place in his plane's past or in utterly alien periods of time; but in the other worlds where his quests had taken him as a youth, lying on the dream couches of Melniboné, time became more flexible, more chaotic, even. Drawing closer, however, it was obvious that this woman knew Elric. She looked up expectantly as he approached. She began to smile.

"Lady—Forentach?" To Nauha's surprise, his voice was again a little hesitant. But the woman smiled and held her fingertips to be touched in that odd Melnibonéan greeting. "Prince Elric," she said. Her voice was unlike Elric's baritone, somewhat sibilant and strangely accented, as if she did not speak a language she used often.

Pushing back his long, white hair, he offered her a respectful bow. "At your service, my lady." He introduced the others. Princess Nauha was a little over-enthusiastic in her response, while Moonglum's bow was blusterous and deep.

"You knew we were coming?" asked the albino. Her swaggering slave, striking at the oncoming crowd with his rolled parasol, led the little party to where a carriage, drawn by two lively but unhappy striped horses, waited for her at the top of the quay.

She answered: "How could I have known?"

He helped first her, then Nauha into the carriage. Moonglum, comparing his traveller's cloak to the fine linen and silk, chose to join the driver on his seat. This clearly gave the driver no particular pleasure.

"Your magic, perhaps?" he answered Lady Forentach, challenging her apparent innocence. She smiled back but was silent on the subject. "Such a crowd today. Ships from your world are so rare. And always welcome." She lifted an elegant cane and tapped the driver on the shoulder.

The narrow streets, bustling with merchants' stalls, led away into less crowded thoroughfares, becoming roads which eventually passed between slender pines and cypresses, giving glimpses of the city below and the glittering sea beyond.

"Your city is lovely," said Princess Nauha, by way of small talk.

"Oh, it is not *mine*!" Lady Forentach laughed. "In fact I have very little communication with it at all. But I suppose it is prettier than most hereabouts."

Thereafter, they travelled mostly in silence, the visitors occasionally remarking on aspects of the city or the bay, which Lady Forentach, as if remembering her manners, now acknowledged gracefully enough. At last they followed a white wall to tall twin pillars. Between the pillars were great bronze gates inscribed in a script they could not read. At a cry from the driver, the gates opened, and they entered a long driveway which took them to the steps of a low, rather simple house, built in marble and glittering quartz.

While a servant indicated the house's appointments, Lady Forentach led them through high, cool rooms, sparsely decorated and furnished, to the far side of the house and a well-landscaped garden surrounded on three sides by a tall wall, offering a view directly ahead. The garden smelled sweetly of flowers and shrubs. Summer insects flew from one to another. On the lawn a low table and couches had been arranged, ready for a meal. The view was gorgeous, looking out for miles over rolling, wooded hills, all the way to the sea.

The architecture and design of the place was radically unlike anything Moonglum remembered from Elric's Imrryr, the Dreaming City. The capital of Melniboné had been designed, through her ten thousand years of evolution, to impress with her aesthetic magnificence, her overwhelming power. In contrast, this house and its garden were meant to soothe and welcome and afford comfortable privacy.

Almost immediately Lady Forentach's servants, all of ordinary human appearance, came to take their outer garments, showing them to guest rooms, helping them to bathe and put on slightly scented fresh, cool robes. Each guest was ascribed at least one servant. Moonglum was only recently used to this. He had yet to tell his friend of his recent service as the Republican shadow dictator of Elwher. He took considerable pleasure in experiencing again the luxury of wealth.

Nauha remarked that the fountains and the walls felt to her, though she could not be sure why, like the work of a desert people. "You must think me naïve!"

Lady Forentach bowed her head, not denying this. "I believe they were from some desert place, yes." She spoke vaguely. "I think my great-great-grandfather said it was very cold and mountainous. Perhaps that way—" Pointing out to sea. "A valley. A city. A fortress where ancestors drank blue mead and sweetened their wine with sapphire-honey." She sighed. "A myth, no doubt."

It was not long, as they took wine prior to dinner, before Moonglum raised the question of the pirates and in particular their king. He laughed. "He did not make his business clear, though at first we thought he might attack and prepared for the worst."

"You were wise to do so, Master Moonglum. Your instincts did not betray you. He is indeed a betrayer, that one! Oh, it's clear enough, I would guess, what Addric Heed does for a living." She laughed, perhaps bitterly. "He is a pirate and a slaver. A creature born to the highest blood of all—of *all*—reducing himself to such filthy work!" Her mood changed as she glared into the middle distance. Dark green-gold stars flickered in the depths of her pale eyes. "A thief, corrupt as any human you'll find here. A betrayer and destroyer of his own kin! A *slaver*! Worse! A *tradesman*. And his crew is still more disreputable? Why even his ship is an evil act of cruelty . . ."

She lifted her long head like an angry beast. "*Phoornechtas!*" Her robes seemed independently agitated, as if animals fought beneath them. She broke off, remembering her manners. "He is—he has—" She drew a long, slow breath. "It's said he has pacts with the Lords of the Balance. Yet why they would trust him or use him I have no idea!" Her voice took on a light dismissive tone. She clapped her hands and ordered another decanter of wine. "Here's one from our own vineyards I hope you'll find palatable."

Moonglum would have asked more about Addric Heed if he could, but no further opportunity came. Then a little later, their hostess saw him yawn discreetly behind his hand. "You'll be my guests here, I hope, while you stay in Hizs? I should have mentioned it sooner how welcome you are at my house." Again, they noted the slightly sibilant accent, the odd insinuation. Not unfriendly.

"You are kind, madam." Before either of the others could answer, Elric accepted for them all.

"I have my lady friend," Moonglum murmured, a little embarrassed. "She—"

"Then, of course, she must be sent for, too. It is so rare for me to receive guests at the best of times. And such rare guests! From so far away. From the exotic World Below!" She gave the servants appropriate orders. They should go with the driver to the ship and bring all their things, as well as Moonglum's lady, back with them.

But when the servants returned with their luggage, it was to report that the wench had indeed been waiting on the ship for Moonglum, but she had chosen to remain on board. She sent a message to Moonglum saying that she was happier there and likely to stay so.

On hearing this, Moonglum flushed and turned away for a moment. Then, bowing to Lady Forentach, said that while he appreciated her invitation he felt he should return to the ship and see to the well-being of his friend.

"I understand," said Lady Forentach. "I do hope she finds our air more agreeable in the morning."

The sun was setting deeper now, and Moonglum thought he saw a tinge of pale scales under her neck. Some disease? It was surely no more than a trick of the light. Somewhat subdued and doing all he could to hide his emotion, the Eastlander climbed into the carriage and left again for the ship he'd hoped not to see for another few days at least. That his wench should take to pouting now was not to be tolerated. A man should discipline a woman who embarrassed him before local royalty! He decided to give her a piece of his mind. And he could not now be wholly certain she wouldn't try to steal something of local value from his luggage. He was in such poor temper that he almost forgot the swords he had left in his chamber above.

With Moonglum's absence, the Princess of Uyt felt a little removed from the company, though Lady Forentach did all that should be expected of her to put her at her ease.

"And how fares my brother?" asked their hostess when they were settled on the couches again. "Has his temper or his attitude towards you improved, my lord?"

Elric shook his head briefly. "The emperor died still voicing disappointment at my failings of moral courage." His voice held a tinge of irony, but was without emotion. "The succession lay between myself and my cousin, you'll recall. Dyvim Yyrkoon, emperor-in-waiting. He could not be trusted, even by Sadric. Sadric knew change must come. My mother had prepared him for it, told him to trust me and fear Yyrkoon. But he could not. How we behaved upon our respective dream-quests would determine who ascended the throne of the Dragon Empire. And who would guide it! I believe I was chosen not from any sense of fitness but because I made fewer mistakes—in Sadric's eyes, at least!" Another faint, sardonic smile.

As the sun came closer to the horizon, the woman removed the gauze visor to reveal eyes of pale green-gold, but, when her milk-white hair fell from below her scarf, it was clearer still that she was also an albino. She noticed Nauha's look of surprise and laughed.

Nauha blurted, "Forgive me, my lady, I had not realised you were related. You are the Emperor Sadric's sister?"

"My sister married him," she answered softly, while Elric frowned at his lover's rather sudden interruption.

Lady Forentach waved away any imagined rudeness but leaned towards the albino. "So, Elric, is Yyrkoon emperor now?"

"I killed him. My father named me his successor, but Yyrkoon was uneasy with the decision. And he disapproved of my betrothal."

"Your betrothed was not high-born?"

"She was his sister. I killed her also."

"You were thorough! You loved her?"

"After a fashion." His expression became unreadable. "I am surprised you had not heard. Most of my world knows the story so well . . ."

"I had not understood you to be such close relatives." There was some relief in Nauha's voice.

"Aye," said Lady Forentach sipping with relish a glass of grey-green wine. "None closer. Blood relatives."

On hearing this, a mysterious expression passed across Princess Nauha's face but was quickly controlled. Elric, noticing this, seemed for a moment amused.

Then, suddenly, the princess felt as if a gate had shut against her. But she followed them up onto the terrace to dine as the moon came out and the marble and alabaster took on a greenish tinge, touched with gold, and even Lady Forentach's features offered a faint reflection of colour, but not, Princess Nauha noticed, Elric's.

As soon Nauha was able, she blamed the change of environment for her tiredness. Then she, too, graciously begged their pardon, saying she was poor company and could see they had much to talk about on family matters. She did not add how the fact that they had increasingly dropped into High

Melnibonéan as the evening grew older had decidedly helped give that impression.

All went according to the best protocol, but afterwards, in her room, the Uyt princess allowed herself one small growl of rage until her maid had gone, and then, weeping, she took hopelessly to her bed and lay upon it, staring at the oddly ornamented ceiling, trying to get control of her hurt feelings, her sudden lack of power. She knew he would not even consider explaining himself when he joined her. She would be lucky, she thought, if she ever saw him again. This took her mind from her own anger and made her recall that she also feared for him.

Princess Nauha had studied the occult under Uyt's wisest scholars and knew a high-ranking witch when she smelled one. She was very glad she had brought her swords with her and that they were, with her armour, in her luggage. She might at least save her own life, she thought, but she was not sure she would be needed to save the albino's. Did the fool realise he was in danger? Or—realisation came suddenly—was she the only visitor in danger here?

Was it coincidence that Elric had brought her with him to Hizs? He had told her nothing of this relative—if relative was all she was—had told her of no plans to visit. Clearly he had known she would be here. He had hinted at something only a short time before they reached the port. Had he some disgusting plan for the three of them? Or did the sorceress mean to bewitch them both? Or had Elric been bewitched since the moment he had decided to take ship for the edge of the world?

Nauha carefully inspected the room and the garden beyond for ways out of the grounds. Then she took out her armour and laid it upon the floor. Then she polished her sword and dagger, ensuring they would slip easily from their scabbards.

Then she lay down again. She controlled her breathing, forcing herself to think as coolly as she could. A little more relaxed, she next began to wonder if the wine had not been overstrong. There was nothing sinister about the night, after all. Indeed it was beautiful, as were the city and the house. Yet why had all the ports they had seen, she wondered, been so heavily fortified? But not this one?

She took a long, deep breath. It was stupid to brood on all this, particularly now her swords were stowed close to hand. She was perfectly well prepared to take on any danger presenting itself. She was certain that clean steel could cope with any ordinary foreign witchery.

F🜂UR

The Phoorn's Bargain

"I HEARD YOU had found the White Sword," Elric said to Lady Forentach as soon as they were alone together.

She laughed easily, with genuine humour. "And that's why you are here?"

He saw no purpose in lying. "You have it? Oh, I see you do. Or know where it is, I'm sure." He spoke ironically. But he could feel intimations of what he most feared: his energy slipping slowly away and little to replenish it save Stormbringer. His patron, Lord Arioch, was slow to respond in this plane. He seemed preoccupied with some power struggle between the aristocrats of the Higher Worlds.

This time she made no reply. She lay back on her couch and stared up at the stars. Then, after a while, she said, "You have heard of the Eyes of the Skaradin?"

"An even vaguer legend than that of the White Sword, Divergent. The Skaradin? Some kraken from your world's inner sea? You have its eyes, too?"

"I know who has them. But you need not win them for me, my lord. They are, however, the price of the blade." She turned suddenly in the moonlight and looked at him, hungry for something. Her eyes had taken on a deeper, harder green, even her voice had changed timbre, was oddly accented. She moved restlessly on her couch. "Blood pearls, they call them, I hear. There are two. Blind Skaradin, they say, flies at night across the world, seeking solace for the betrayal suffered. I desire them . . . I desire. I have a purpose. An honest purpose. Do you remember when we first met, Prince Elric?"

"I remember my dream-quest. I was scarce more than a boy. My father sent me to see you and bring back the jade dagger my mother had missed."

"Oh, Elric, you were a well-made lad. Were you not, when I saw you, surrounded by three of those golden warriors who used to inhabit these parts? From another plane entirely. We drew so much more energy from those alien planes. So much *material* . . . You had no famous sword at that time. I gave you the jade dagger . . ."

"You did not ask me to pay you for it."

"Oh, you paid me. Did you ever discover your father's reason for wanting it?"

"Never. I think it was simply because it had belonged to my mother. But you saved my life. A surprise."

"I saved you for myself. You were ever to my taste." Her mouth seemed to have widened now, revealing rather more teeth than should be there, and they were sharper, too, while her tongue—that tongue . . .

He roused himself. "You will only sell me the White Sword in return for those red pearls?"

"Just so. But, as well as possessing the sword, I know where to find the pearls."

"Lady Forentach, I did not travel this far to bargain. You despise traders. Besides, I know nothing of this world. I could not begin to look for what you want." He wondered if there were some way he could reach his sword. He had come here following a legend, a memory—something he had heard of even before the Black Sword had been placed in his keeping. He remembered one of the first dream-quests on which he'd embarked, of a woman he had met here, on the other side of the world, and whom he had remembered as a friend. But Lady Forentach had changed, or, probably more true, he had been naïve and had not seen her for what she was.

Now, his desire to be rid of the Black Sword was further destroying his judgement. He shivered. He was risking the lives of those who, in their way, had come to love him. He had set off once to travel the world and discover what human love was, what constituted their morality. Somehow he had reached a point where instead he had killed the only one of his own kind he had ever actually loved, while learning almost nothing of the human race. A wave of profound regret swept over him. He sighed, turning away from her.

She rose from the couch, and, as she did so, she seemed to grow larger, her gown taking on greater substance. A heat came out of her, strong enough to burn him, he thought, if he touched her. He remembered those nights. Those terrifying, fascinating nights, when she had introduced him to all the secrets of his ancestors—the real reason, he now remembered, why his father had sent him upon his quest. Or so she had told him. Now she said otherwise. He frowned. Why did she lie to him? Or had she lied to him then? "Madam. I must go. I can't do what you desire of me."

That great, reptilian face glared down at him. The voice was frigid. She hissed, "You are my sister's son. Your sentient acid blood demands you help me! So, succulence, you must feed and I shall feed . . . You come here seeking the White Sword when you already possess the Black. And you did not know there would be a price? Have you forgotten all loyalty to your own, sweet Prince Elric?"

"I did not know what you would demand." He sounded feeble, even to his own ears.

She drew a strong breath and seemed to grow again.

Elric moved nervously on his couch, wishing he had his sword with him now. He felt a need to renew his energy somehow, but he had so little of anything left. He needed to feed Stormbringer, who in turn would refresh him. Her skin was made of delicate scales and was no longer white but had a gold-green sheen to it, while her hair moved almost under its own volition. He feared her in a way he had not when he first came to Hizs, existing in two worlds at the same time—visiting as a courtesy, he thought, the sister of his mother, whom Sadric had loved to distraction. Then Elric had learned more than he had wished to learn of his ancestry. Of the people known as the Phoorn, who even now lived on in Melniboné, who had not been scattered as the others had been scattered, or killed as his cousins and his other relatives had almost all been killed, hunted to extinction after he had brought the sea reavers to destroy Imrryr.

He had loved the Phoorn as he loved them still. He knew they had made alliances when they first discovered this world, coming as exiles to found a civilisation which would be based on notions of empathetic justice until then unknown to most gods or mortals. They had, by some vast supernatural alchemy, interbred. Their offspring usually took one form or the other, not both. It was not always possible to predict what would emerge from a Phoorn egg or, indeed, a human womb. Yet Lady Forentach had told him of the shape-changers, those few who could be what they willed themselves to be and who had, for centuries, continued their race. He owed much to her. He was wrong to begin fearing her now.

"My lady, I would help you if I could, not because you would strike a bargain with me, but for the sake of our old alliances. I came here, after all, to ask a favour. And I would gladly do you a favour in return."

Her great, Phoorn eyes softened. Her speech changed. She sounded affectionate again. "I should not have tried to bargain with you, Elric. But life here has changed a great deal since we last met. It has been many centuries. The world grew corrupt. Wars were fought. Monstrous treacheries were conceived. Such appalling treachery . . ." Her tone became reminiscent. He found himself sympathising with her.

Yet, he was still wary, still unsure. Was she persuading him through her ancient powers of mesmeric sorcery?

"You could not have found a warrior here to help you?"

"No. For none has what you have."

"I will fetch my sword," he said, "and tell Nauha—"

"My servant has already brought it. No need to disturb the Princess of Uyt. It is safe. Well-wrapped." Elric knew she told the truth. If Stormbringer herself had been handled, it was unlikely that handler still lived. And he would have heard.

A darkness was filling the sky as deep clouds sailed in from the south. The night grew colder and the albino shivered, fearing further for Princess Nauha's safety.

"Nobody will harm her," said the Phoorn. "But now I must venture into—"

take more substance—from—the—netherworld . . ." A noise like a whirlpool, running fast in high seas.

He had difficulty seeing her now. His mind was less clear. The table seemed to have disappeared. The house was a black shadow, unlit. A long-drawn squeal, darker than a demon's tortured soul.

The sounds of the night had faded when her voice came again. He turned, peering as if into a void. Above him were two green-gold staring stars: passionless, cold. Her voice was still recognisable, yet hissed like waves on shingle:

"Are you ready to go with me, Elric?"

"I gave you my word." His baritone was steady as his crimson eyes' stare.

Something fell at his feet then. He knew what it was and bent to pick it up, attaching it to his belt. When he straightened, scaled flesh, long and sinuous, stretched down out of the sky, and he looked deeper into those green-gold eyes, knowing them for what and whose they were. At the base of her long, reptilian neck was a natural indentation in which a man might sit. It had not been long since he had taken a Vilmirian *skeffla'a* and placed it in just such an indentation. For the Lady Forentach was a shape-changer of a very specific kind, and while Elric had experienced her gifts before, reliving the first coming together of their respective races, he had never seen her change so rapidly. Nor, in all his adventures and his dreams, had he seen a movement so quick in any shape-changer from mammal to reptile. Subtle and almost silent, there was no melodramatic creaking and cracking and groaning as beloved of human mummers.

This was Phoorn magic, and Phoorn magic was sweet, sophisticated and quiet unless it needed to be otherwise. As he drew invisible energy through his sword, the Phoorn of her kind could draw *matter* from other planes to add to their physical appearance! The Phoorn were not true reptiles, any more than Melnibonéans were true humans. Both had come into being in other worlds under different gods and philosophies. Both had learned the virtues of the other. And then, at last, when auguries and blood were right they had mated, though still in many ways alien one to the other. And this was the folk whom the Dragon Kings of Melniboné claimed as their ancestors. This was not the first time he had seen the truth of this. He had once wondered why in his world their dragons were called brother or sister and treated with such complete respect, each conversing with the other. He knew the beasts lived on altered time, so that it seemed to Melnibonéans that their dragons slept for years or decades, but this did not explain the origins of their long relationship. Part of his current quest was to find answers to those questions.

There were no further traces of the human about the Lady Forentach, a word which meant 'Firetaster' in the old language. She was completely Phoorn and speaking in the ancient language used only between Phoorn and Melnibonéan. Completely Phoorn as she bent that beautiful serrated neck so that he might mount, carefully turning her head so that residues of fiery venom from her mouth-sacs fell bursting upon the tiled terrace and did not harm him.

As if suspicious of pursuit, Firetaster peered this way and that into the night, her great claws clattering on the terra-cotta, her wings stretching, wide, wide as she prepared to lift into the darkness of the night, giving voice with wild, beautiful music to the Phoorn's ancient "Song of Flight." Then springing off the terrace she began to run across the lawn, her sharp senses noting the obstacles as she ran towards the obsidian sea.

And then came a sharp crack. Then another. Then she was aloft.

And Elric, seated astride her gigantic, exquisite body, found himself flinging back his head, letting the cool air stream through his long, white hair as he lifted his own voice to join in that complex melody, as natural to him and his kind as when the Phoorn and his own people first came to this glorious world and determined to take stewardship of it in the name of their ideals. Sweet brothers and sisters of the moon! We came in the night, regardless of our doom!

So long and long ago, when man and woman shared blood and flesh flowed to flesh and creature was prepared for creature by way of four-armed sacrifice. *Meat again and falling. Phoorn loved meat, too.* Once. What had gone wrong in the time when he had enjoyed a long idyll with her and fallen in love in a new way? Then their world had been protected by his people, their faith in the Great Balance translated into so many practical notions of order and justice. Now? Now they had become used to lies, secrecies, political and other bargains. He saw so little difference between his own people and corrupted humanity. Law and Chaos? Corrupted! The whole world was a darker, more threatening place. If he had known this, he would not have had his friends come with him. All the old neutral priesthoods were taking sides! But he was here, and such darkness was familiar to him from his dealings with Yyrkoon's Court, as well as some of the Young Kingdoms. The innocent must not suffer!

Nothing mattered, for he rode a dragon again, bonding through the natural *skeffla'a*, as his genes remembered, with that monstrous *thump-thump* of her great heart, the deep, slow pulse, the long beating of those vast wings and the sweeping from side to side of that long, muscular tail. All he lacked was his heavy black armour and his great dragon spear, through which thoughts were transmitted back and forth, while, behind him, a squadron of Melnibonéan battle dragons took wing against an aggressor. Oh, how he yearned to soar once more at the head of a flying army! Now, all he could tell was that he was heading west, inland of the first coast they had encountered, and, as dawn sunlight streaked the blue-black horizon, he saw that they flew over a forest, spired by great pines, towards a turreted fortress of gold-veined marble and dark green flint, woven in a way to show both artistic elegance and sturdy practicality and also, somehow, a sense of brooding menace. Slowly, slowly turning . . .

Firetaster dived into the depth of the forest, wings close together, claws extended and neck hunched to land perfectly in a glade through which light had yet to penetrate. She allowed him to descend, then spoke to him in Phoorn. "Now we must roost until this afternoon when they begin their tournament. The targets have yet to be chosen and assembled in the castle grounds, within the central bailey." And, cocooning him in her folded wings, she perched on a massive lower branch on one of the tallest trees and went to sleep.

FIVE

A Question of Ancestry

THAT DAY, when the sun was still high enough in the sky to burn a bright purple-orange, Lord Elric and Lady Forentach made their way along a hard beaten red earthen road towards the unsuspected magnificence of the White Fort which rose like a fantastic cloud of clear-edged smoke from the sharp green of the almost impenetrable forest.

Reaching the six-foot-thick ironbound timber of the white-painted barriers, she called out with such authority that the gates swung open almost at once. Huge iron bars rose on some sort of balancing machinery. The oiled runners hardly whispered. The newcomers were recognised by their height, build and race if by nothing else, and this gave them unquestioned admission. The fort was formed by a series of large towers, one inside the other, a model of multiversal planes, to be defended to the death. Each tower had land which could if necessary grow its own food. Elric realised it had been designed on the same principles as Imrryr, built to impress and to be impregnable at the same time.

Elric's people had used an island and an ocean for this. Supernatural blasting and carving with the help of a friendly King Grome, who had once favoured humanity's cause. Addric Heed employed a trackless forest for much the same purpose.

She led him through one walled area after another, through towers and halls and finally up a flight of steps to a short gallery and out into the upper tiers of an amphitheatre, the stone seats arranged to look down onto a long oval green where targets had been arranged for an archery contest. Elric recognised this as something his own ancestors used to play. At Forentach's signal, he sat down with her well above the occupied tiers. She began to tell him again what she planned and what he must do. From the archery green, drifting in on the light, late air, came the distant screams of the targets, the heavy thunk of arrows into bodies and the applause as an archer made a good score in one of the higher marked parts of the slave's body.

Slumped in a tall, carved chair was the slender form of Addric Heed, clad in light yellow robes, an orange scarf swathing his head and shoulders. Unmistakeably, he was Elric's and Forentach's kin. He was surrounded by his captains, of his own kind as well as human, and by some who were lightly armed or bore no weapons at all. Elric recognised one of them as the saturnine trader on the ship. Forentach nodded when he murmured this information to her. "As he has done for two centuries, he raids up and down this coast. The slaves will be sold in Hizs, which almost depends upon the trade for her subsistence. Those traders inspect the stock here and then know roughly what they'll bid when they return to Hizs. They often keep their own bands of soldiers in Hizs, and the odds against us would be even greater there. You know the tower to seek?"

"Aye. On the far side and to the furthest tower."

"He'll expect no attack if I work my Phoorn sorcery, but you must hurry, nephew, for it will be hard for me to keep so many engaged."

Then, as a lull came in the tournament, Lady Forentach rose in her seat and called, "How goes the game, brother?"

And saw Addric Heed's head come up in astonishment as he stopped halfway through a joke with his visitors. He controlled his features, though a question still hovered in his eyes. "Sister! You should have warned me. I'll have rooms prepared! Your entourage is below?"

"Beyond the gates," she said. "I did not know I would be welcome."

"Always, dear sister." Their words were formal and without warmth, but there was no animosity, either. Elric guessed that both had grown used to keeping secrets even from themselves. Addric Heed had no notion of how disgusting his sister found his trade and why for other reasons she should hate him when she and her adopted city should do so well from the business he brought in. Equally, who knew the resentments and greed for vengeance that her brother held for her?

Elric hung back as if in discretion or embarrassment, and Addric had forgotten his manners, his whole attention upon his sister. Elric nodded to the nearest kinfolk and typically ignored their visitors, even the one he knew. He went to loll in a seat some distance away, as if to enjoy on his own the meeting of brother and sister, and many humans observing this would have taken it to mean he relished the taste of incest, not knowing perhaps that incest was not considered even in poor taste by Elric's people. It was how they had come to interbreed their kind, after all, and gain their power. That, and a few well-chosen compacts with the Lords of Chaos.

All attention but Elric's was now on the were-Phoorn as she continued to mesmerise them and none noticed that he was no longer in his seat but had stepped swiftly into the tower. The only light came from a small table of some kind. Rosy light which drew Elric to it immediately. And there they were! Two perfect crimson-coloured pearls of magnificent size, depth and lustre. Was Addric Heed so certain of his power that he could leave such remarkable gems where anyone might pick them up? There came a movement from the corner of the room. A sound like a chuckle. And a voice dry as summer corn spoke. "Good afternoon, stranger. You are an optimist, I see. Another who hoped Lord Addric grows careless. Well, he might do so, but I do not. I only have one task to perform, after all, and take much pleasure in performing it."

Elric felt a sudden exhilaration at this, and his hand flew to his left hip, seized the grip of his sword and began slowly to draw it.

Another chuckle, almost good-humoured and lazy. "My dear mortal, you had best hear who I am before you waste your time unsheathing a weapon. This will give you time to turn and just possibly reach the door before I catch you."

Elric continued to draw the sword, standing his ground, peering into the roseate darkness in the hope of seeing his antagonist. "You are a very assured guard," he said.

"I would perhaps be more modest had I not caught and punished every thief who ever sought to steal these Eyes of Skaradin in the past two hundred and fifty years, ever since my master, Lord Addric Heed, placed them in my safe-keeping."

Then something was rising from the flagstone floor to hover over the crimson pearls which certainly resembled living eyes. They seemed to watch Elric as he continued to draw his black sword from its scabbard. What was it which guarded the Eyes of Skaradin so confidently?

Then Stormbringer was free of the scabbard and writhing like a living thing in its master's two hands and howling with a profound and horrible hunger.

While overhead two black wings spread with a brittle, whispering sound and fluttered up towards the tower room's roof.

"Coward," said Elric. "Do you know who I am now? Do you fear for your life? For your soul, if you have one? Come down and fight me, for it would give me pleasure. I have never fought an Asquinax before."

From above there came a growl; the flying thing opened huge blue eyes, glaring into Elric's face. "You are dead," it said, "in your failure to restore Law to your dissipating world."

"No doubt you are confusing me with another, Sir Asquinax, for when I die, it will not be in the cause of Law, but in my own cause, or that of Chaos." He swung the howling blade this way and that. "Depending on my luck. For I am Elric of Melniboné, and my patron is Arioch of Chaos, one of Entropy's great generals."

"That hero died in another world. He has no power here. And, as for Arioch . . ." But there was puzzlement in the half-seen creature's blue eyes. Then it opened a white mouth, glittering with luminous teeth, each sharp as a dagger. And it licked its oddly shaped lips with a long, red tongue. "As for Arioch . . . Did you not hear? He is indisposed."

"I know not by what crude sorcery your master brought you here and kept you here, but I warn you, petty demon, I am Elric, and the sword I hold was given to me by Duke Arioch. I am the tutored son of Great Sadric, Sorcerer Emperor of Melniboné. What you call the Lost Empire, I believe. This blade is called Stormbringer and is quite as hungry as you are. I am hungry, too."

The demon flapped up towards the roof again and hung there for a moment, its dark blue eyes regarding Elric's own glittering red orbs. It shifted its gaze from Elric's eyes to the pearls it guarded, and it frowned. Again it opened its mouth and licked its teeth, one by one, as if counting them. Then, with a high whistling sound, its long teeth clashing, its eyes glaring, the thing dropped upon him, digging long claws into his back and making it impossible for him to stab at it with any precision. Roaring the name of his patron Duke of Hell, Elric swung the blade back over his left shoulder, and there was a crack as it connected with the demon's bones. It shouted, the noise filling the tower, and one claw came free. A swinging cut over his head and Elric's blade connected again. The demon dragged those claws from Elric's shoulder and flapped back into the shadows. Its white mouth was panting now, and it turned its head, lapping noisily at its own wounds, its blood dripping and splashing.

"You are more powerful than I, it is true," said the demon. "However, I must try to kill you or break my compact with Addric Heed, in which case I should perish all the more terribly."

With evident reluctance the demon flapped down, attempting again to get purchase with its claws in Elric's flesh. This time, however, Elric understood its intent and ducked, throwing up Stormbringer so that the demon fell back, yelling curses in its own tongue. Then Elric leapt forward, stabbing, and the thing flapped further up the tower, trying to work its way around so that it could make another attack on the albino's back, clearly its only manoeuvre. So Elric deliberately turned until he heard the demon begin to drop down, then whirled, swinging the great blade with all its wild momentum and striking the demon in its hip, which cracked and made the Asquinax collapse, still attempting to walk on one leg and constantly screaming.

"*Eeeeeeeeeeeeeeeeeee. Eeeeeeaaaaah. Eeeee!*" A thick mass of ichor gushed from its wound as it turned. Elric dodged it in time. It flooded over the floor, narrowly missing the albino. He leapt, stabbing, the blade slipping through flesh and meeting bone. Now a foul stench began to fill the tower room, and black blood boiled as the demon tried to crawl, its claws reaching desperately for the huge gems! "*Eeeeeeeeeeeeee . . .*" A stuck pig could not sound worse.

And Elric swung Stormbringer again. The sword was screaming now, too! A scream of pleasure as its hunger began to be satiated. Elric felt the dark, supernatural energy flow into him. He shuddered, for the stuff made every nerve tense, every muscle threaten to cramp. He swung at one of the grasping claws and sliced it off so that it began to inch by its own volition towards the red pearls, but failed to reach them. Stormbringer hummed, feasting. The demon flapped up into the air just above the pearls, still struggling to fulfil the duty of its compact, knowing that the penalty of failing was worse than dying. Then Elric chopped off its other hand. "You are a poor wretch of a guardian," he said, "but you are doubtless all that fellow Addric wished to pay for. Sometimes it is best not to believe you have made a successful bargain with a Chaos Lord!"

And when the creature turned its blue, despairing eyes upon him, the long teeth shuddering and clashing in its mouth, the red tongue flicking up and down, it said, "My weird told me I could never be slain by a living mortal. But I did not know I could be killed by a dead man, nor by one as powerful as the thing dwelling in your blade." The last of its energy throbbed out of it, pulsing through the sword, which took its due and passed the rest of the foul stuff on to its master, if, indeed, Elric was the master and not the blade.

The wounds from the demon's claws had burned into him, and though he now had extra energy, he was losing blood. He stumbled to the table and picked up first one heavy pearl and then another, slipping them into his shirt and tightening the lace with one hand. Stormbringer remained unsheathed, which was as well, for the door had already burst open, and there stood the saturnine man from the ship, with about a dozen of his fellow slave-traders, all of them fully armed with a miscellaneous collection of weapons, clearly from their own cultures. They had not expected to find Elric standing, let alone standing over the still-writhing body of the guardian demon.

If the doorway had not been so narrow, they would have backed off, but it was not easily done. Warily, they continued towards the albino, beginning to form a half-circle, intending to close in on him. He smiled, holding Stormbringer almost lazily. He was panting a little, from his exertions with the demon, but otherwise the creature's own energy was still sustaining him, though he could feel the blood moving slowly down his back.

"I am glad to see you gentlemen." The albino offered them a brief bow. "I cannot tell you how famished I have been feeling."

With rather less confidence than they had shown on first entering the chamber, the traders began to circle Elric, their booted feet slipping in the demon's dark blood.

Elric was laughing now. He feinted with his growling blade. The men's eyes narrowed as they pressed in, and he reached out, almost elegantly, and took off the head of the nearest. Suddenly all they wanted to do was escape through the door, but Elric reached behind him and drew it so that only a single bar of light entered the tower room. He feinted again, moving like a herdsman, gathering his flock, and then, when the men were grouped together in the light, he swung the great, moaning broadsword so that its blade sliced into one, cutting him so deeply in the torso that half his body fell backwards. Elric laughed as the energy filled him. He struck again, and two arms flopped in the mess made by the demon's dying. He stabbed, drawing that man's life-force deep into himself, and then, when only the saturnine slave-trader was left, he took his sword and slipped it delicately into the man's chest so that the pumping heart sent energy into the sword and almost instantly into Elric's own glowing body, so the white skin blazed like silver and the red eyes glared in triumph, and he lifted his head, surrounded by its halo of milk-white hair, and laughed—a sound which filled the tower with anguished triumph and which seemed to echo through all the countless worlds of Creation.

So that when Elric stepped out of the door, he saw the amphitheatre filled with startled faces, Addric Heed and his slavers staring up at him in baffled astonishment and Lady Forentach running like the wind towards him, shouting, "The slave quarters! Follow me!"

"The slave quarters? Are we going to free the slaves?"

"That, too, if there's time."

Then, while Addric Heed and his warriors began to absorb what had happened, they dashed down the outer steps of the tower as she led them into the bowels of the White Fort. She had armed herself with a massive battle-axe, which she knew how to wield, and together they cut down any who sought to stop them until they stood in the long corridors which stank of human waste and putrefying flesh and where, shackled in every available space, were the choice men, women and children—the healthiest people Addric Heed had taken from all the cities and ships of the coast to be sold in Hizs in the coming days.

Lady Forentach did not listen to their questions or answer their hope. She was heading for a large marble enclosure at the far end of the furthest corridor, whose bars were set further apart and were four times the thickness of any others. She had dropped the axe, so while she ran on, Elric spared time to strike through chains wherever he could and release as many slaves as possible. He anticipated rapid pursuit from Addric Heed and his slavers. Elric wanted the people fighting for their own interests as possible.

By the time he reached her, she had drawn back heavy bolts from what was little better than a gigantic cage. Within the cage, its empty sockets staring into space, its wings crumpled and awkwardly set, its claws clipped and bound with brass, sat an old Phoorn which might be on the point of death it seemed so frail.

But Lady Forentach was approaching the creature to place gentle hands upon it, to stroke its grey-white leathery scales and croon to it in the ancient language of her people, which Elric understood.

"Father, it is I, *Firetaster*. Here to free you."

"Oh, child, you know I cannot be free. I cannot see to be gone from here. Addric will always keep me prisoner. There is no hope, daughter. You should not have risked him discovering the truth, of knowing what only we two know."

"It is different now, Father."

From the far end of the slave quarters there came shouts and the noise of fighting. Clearly, now they were free, the slaves were not readily going to lose their liberty again. Clashing metal told Elric that some had already seized weapons. But they would not prevail for long against Addric's trained warriors.

With a deep, not unhappy sigh, Elric prepared to do battle with an army.

SIX

The Advantages of
Supernatural Compacts

THE OLD PHOORN was called Skaradin, and he was Lady Forentach's father. "He has been here for over a century," she gasped, "dying to serve my brother's despicable trade."

"Your brother holds his father with his slaves?" Elric considered this bad taste at best.

She was too hurried to answer. "Quickly, the pearls. Give me the pearls!" she demanded.

He slipped them from his shirt, already half guessing what she meant to do. Stroking her father's long snout, she got the old Phoorn to lower his head, then, taking the glowing crimson pearls from Elric's hands, she placed them one by one into the sockets where his eyes had been, all the time crooning a long, melodic spell. And then there came a shout from up ahead, and the battling slaves, protecting their children, began to fall back before Addric's well-armed warriors. And the twin crimson pearls began to glow and pulse.

A deep, distant boom rose from somewhere within the old Phoorn's massive chest. He lifted his head, and the quills, each the height of a tall man, rattled on his scales, while all along his tessellated tail the huge combs rose and stood proud. Even Elric found the transformation astonishing. The booming grew deeper and louder. He rose up on his muscular legs and blinked. From each eye, a drop of blood fell. The face, which regarded first his daughter and then Elric, was benign and profoundly sad, full of bitter wisdom. "With vision comes power," he said in Phoorn. And blinked again. This time it was a gigantic salt tear which fell.

Elric realised that the slaves had dropped back, were running past them, seeking the freedom of the forest. Addric had been brought a mount: a battlehorse, blond and armoured. At his back were more cavalry and fresh infantry, beautiful forest ponies, small and speedy to avoid the low limbs. The slaves had for the most part dropped their weapons, taken up their children and were running out into the light, only to stagger back in, pierced by Addric's arrows. "Like all others, save Hizs, this place was designed for warfare, no matter what the occasion," Skaradin said.

And then, from directly above, came a thunderous excitement, of yelling, terrified voices, a clashing of metal.

"Some fresh sorcery of Addric's no doubt," she said. "That was how he first learned to make slaves of his ancestors and use them to build his power."

"Aye," agreed Skaradin. "We were unsuspecting. When he could not make us fly for him, he took out our eyes and made us swim."

Another roll of thunder. Did it come from the sky? Addric was surprised by it. He reined in his pale stallion, looking upward, staring about him. The slaves had come back to mass around Elric. They seemed to have reached a sudden impasse. Even with the Black Sword they could not defeat such numbers.

Elric considered a parlay with Addric Heed, but the power in him, which filled his mind, his body and his soul, was not a compromising power; it did not apologise for itself for it had no conscience. His human empathy had drawn him to the Young Kingdoms and beyond, to learn of their morality and humility, their curiosity. His Melnibonéan pride had brought him home and assured the destruction of his people, the burning of their towers and the end of a power they had taken for granted. The only power he had now was from Melniboné, his family's sorcery and its history, the pacts which it had, in its moments of crisis, been forced to make with Chaos, where once it had leaned toward Law. His own dream-quests into other planes, including his family's past and present, had taught him all this; he had learned to a degree how to harness and control such power. But not now, not when he was filled with the savage sorcery of his ancestors and the gods with whom they allied themselves.

As Addric's army advanced through the echoing galleries towards them and his archers began assembling at their back, the thunder came again. This time Elric saw a messenger riding through the ranks to address Addric Heed. Addric lifted his hand to stop his men, but not all had noticed and they continued to advance. Elric watched as the pirate led his men back through the slave block and up into the main fortress, the stairways wide enough to allow them to remain mounted through several of the upper galleries.

Soon, the advancing soldiers began to realise they had been deserted. Some turned to follow. Others called out, warning that the fewer their numbers the worse their plight.

Wearily, the slaves bent to pick up abandoned weapons.

Elric led the charge which broke the army, making it think it was already defeated. The warriors were brave enough and well-trained enough, but they were completely demoralised from the moment Elric struck them—a ghost from their own pasts—a whirlwind of black, vampiric death, the howling runeblade an image from their own legends, its blazing crimson eyes haunting all their nightmares. And with their leader gone, and in the certain presence of their own Prince of Chaos, the demon lord Arioch, who was one of their shared pantheon, they had no stomach for fighting their kind. It took the Lady Forentach to speak to him in the High Tongue of the Phoorn, reminding him of who and where he was, for him to lower his sword and look wonderingly around him at the piled corpses, the bodies of all who had gone to feed himself and his sword Stormbringer. And then he knew a kind of grief. But it was not for the dead slavers he was weeping.

There came another wave of the amber-armoured soldiers. This time they were in obvious disarray. Many had lost their weapons and, seeing that their comrades were captured, put themselves at the mercy of their former property, who promptly stripped them of their arms and clapped them in chains. The archers had been called to another part of the fort. Suddenly they could look up and hear the constant rolling thunder moving first towards them, then away from them, while the alabaster walls shook and shivered, and small showers of stone and plaster fell from ceilings and walls.

Leaving the others behind to guard the ancient Phoorn and to organise themselves and their prisoners, Elric and Lady Forentach walked warily to the nearest stair and began to climb. As they reached galleries with windows which looked out on other galleries they could see that all the way to the top of the great fort a terrible fight had been taking place, and dead soldiers in amber armour lay everywhere. The sound of thunder was beginning to subside. And then from above, Elric heard his name being called.

"Elric! My lord! We thought you dead!"

The albino stopped and looked up. At length he saw that through a smashed window in the gallery above a broad, red-headed face looked down. Moonglum!

Slowly the madness deserted Elric, and in something close to joy he ran through the galleries until he found his friend. By now Princess Nauha stood with him and also Cita Tine, the tavern wench. All were armed and bore the familiar panting expressions of wolves who had fought a long, exhilarating fight. And then, as if Insensate Fate could not contain this level of coincidence but must burst it across the multiverse, there appeared the nuns of Xiombarg, smug as nuns are, who have pleased themselves by some deed of virtue, to report that all was settled as justice demanded.

"Our lady answered us, and we reached an agreement," declared one as she straightened her crown. "Be sure that peace will soon come to the Higher Worlds and the Lower Worlds. There shall be no war in heaven!"

"Agreement?" Elric knew that the Gods of the Balance rarely made bargains not to their advantage.

Then Cita Tine was calling out, "Where? The slaves? Are they still in the pens?"

Elric shrugged. "Some are. Others set off through the forest." He was puzzled by her interest.

She sheathed her blades and peered down. Then she moved away in the direction from which Elric and the Lady Forentach had come.

Elric turned enquiring eyes on his friend. Moonglum sighed and scratched his head. "That's why she came with us. Her plan all along was to sell valuables here and use the money to buy her husband back from the traders. He was taken a voyage ago."

Elric frowned. "So—?"

"Aye. She used me, and now she's off to see if her spouse survived." Moonglum sighed. "Still, for a few weeks, I have to say, she was happy to have me as his substitute." He cast a hopeful eye upon one of the acolytes, who moved closer to her colleague. And he sighed again.

"So Xiombarg's the cause of all this destruction?" Elric was enlightened.

"She certainly helped us," said Nauha, stepping closer, "but we enjoyed a little sword-work of our own." She noticed that blood was crusting on both her blades and, glancing around her, saw a useful cloak. Bending, she ripped the garment away from its former owner and began to wipe first one sword and then the other.

"Addric Heed?" asked Forentach looking about her at all the devastation. "Does he live?"

"After a fashion," said the Princess of Uyt. "Knowing your relationship, I begged him spared. But I was almost too late. Xiombarg—"

"Where is Addric Heed?"

Nauha frowned, thinking. "Two floors below and . . ." She shook her head. "Two to the left. His banners and his horse are there. He barely lives, however. Xiombarg was eating him."

Lady Forentach was already running from the hall, seeking the downward staircase.

"There has been a feasting here today." From curiosity, Elric followed her, the others coming in his wake. "Was this Xiombarg's only payment?" He indicated the mounded dead.

Nauha laughed. "I think not. I recruited the priestesses when it became clear the supernatural was involved. Moonglum and his girl came up from the town, ready to defend you, but Forentach had already—already transformed herself. And carried you off."

"You knew where we went?" He moved down a staircase covered in corpses. "How so?"

"Cita Tine knew of Addric's fortress and how to get there."

"But you got here so swiftly!"

"The priestesses summoned Xiombarg to transport us."

"Yet no sacrifice was made?"

"There was something at Forentach's house which Xiombarg valued. All she did, she did for that."

They came upon Forentach then, amongst all that blood and dismembered bodies, amber-coloured armour discarded like the remains of shrimp sucked clean of their shells. She crouched on the marble floor, her shoulders shaking in grief. In her arms she held something ragged and red. Elric saw that it was all that was left of a man. Addric Heed, proud pirate prince and dealer in slaves lay there taking great gasps, making the lifeblood bubble from his chest. Not much was left of his face. His legs and an arm were missing. One side of him looked as if it had been gnawed upon. Xiombarg had been interrupted in her feasting. She had been invited to this plane, doubtless by the idealistic priestesses. The turncoat pirate was trying to speak, but failed. Then he stopped breathing, and no more blood came out of him. Laying him tenderly back upon the floor, Forentach stood up, straightening herself. She saw Elric but stepped away from him, walking to one of the tall, broken windows.

When, after some moments, she turned to stare at the albino, her eyes blazed green and the tongue which flickered across her teeth was not human. "He has paid a fair price for carrying out his despicable trade. His blood and the blood of his followers shall feed the forest, and soon nothing will be seen of his fort. It is all he deserves. But now I am the last of my kind, at least on this side of the world. There is some talk of Phoorn guarding a city on the edge of the world, but I have never spoken to any traveller. In our literature it is called *The Legend of the Blue Honey*. It is very obscure." She let out a deep, hissing breath.

"Anywhere," said Elric. "Today none of us is fully Phoorn and non-Phoorn at once. Few who bridge the history of both races. Few save your father."

"And his father, too," she said, looking toward the fallen pirate. "The father he betrayed and enslaved. Now we are both revenged."

And even as she spoke there came a kind of moan from the surviving slaves, and something began to rise from the clearing below the fortress, beating clumsily into the air at first, its huge wings slapping and snapping in the sunlight, its bulk vast and white as it turned, its massive tail swinging, its long, pale neck stretched out and topped by a massive reptilian head from which blazed two eyes as brilliant and crimson as Elric's own. There were the so-called red pearls, now animated with a new life-force, gazing up into the pale, gold clouds passing high above: The Eyes of Skaradin had returned to the possession of he from whom Addric Heed had stolen them . . .

Skaradin, most ancient of the known Phoorn race, father to both Lady Forentach and the renegade Addric Heed, who had stolen his eyes and forced him underwater to drive the last of the slaver's ships. Skaradin, his voice a deep-throated call of joy and relish at being free again to fly.

"Addric Heed was ever jealous of his father," murmured Lady Forentach. "For years he and his fellow Dukes of the Blood plotted to enslave the true Phoorn who were not Halflings like me. And when the time came, and their eyes were stolen, I lacked the courage or the character to resist. I saw the great runes cast and the great sorcery made, and then the Phoorn were robbed of their eyes and forced into servitude. First they were harnessed to the ships and made to fly just above the water, guided by sharp goads. Then, as they grew old and too feeble for that task, Addric Heed determined how they might have ships built around them, using their wings to drive those vessels at enormous speeds, terrifying and mystifying all they claimed as prey. I could do nothing but help my brother. He swore that if I did not, then he would torture my father to death. I acted between him and the slave merchants of Hizs."

"That is why Hizs is the only unfortified city along this coast," murmured Elric in sudden understanding. "Hizs did not defend herself, because Addric Heed never attacked there. Indeed, he probably only came to prey on ships as his dragon allies died one by one. But his own father! This is treachery even I could not match . . ."

Her smile was tragic. "Few could," she said.

Elric watched the albino dragon twisting and turning high above them, then diving to sail across the tops of the trees, and for a moment he envied the creature, his own ancestor, who had existed for at least as long as the Empire of Melniboné! Who had seen its birth and lived to learn of its end.

He looked back. The two priestesses stood behind himself and the others. They watched the old Phoorn's flight in evident wonder.

"We have to thank you, ladies, for your intervention," said Elric. "Now might I ask what price your patron asked for her help?"

The acolytes of Xiombarg exchanged glances. "It was something not strictly our right to offer her," said one.

"But the needs of the moment seemed to dictate our agreement with her bargain." Nauha stepped forward, the better to watch the wheeling dragon. "She knew it was in your house, Lady Forentach. I knew it was your property . . ."

"It was all she would accept in exchange." The other priestess seemed a little embarrassed. "That said, the Balance has been restored, temporarily at least, Chaos brought back to her rightful place in this plane's grand cosmology! That was the will of Xiombarg. For as you serve Duke Arioch, my lord Elric, so we serve his cousin, while she serves the Balance . . ."

"Ah," said Lady Forentach in quick understanding. "But it was already promised, I think."

"We had no choice."

"It was, I take it, a white sword." Forentach glanced around her at all the destruction.

"Aye." Moonglum was surprised she had guessed so easily. "Divergent. There was nothing else Xiombarg would accept, and time was pressing. My guess is she fights larger battles elsewhere! She lies to both sides in order to manipulate us to do her will! Pause! Consider!"

"There is a certain irony in the matter," agreed the albino.

They were all stunned by the next sound.

Except when Stormbringer was drawn and he was engaged upon his joyful work of destruction, Elric had not been heard to laugh aloud for some years.

BOOK TWO

HOW ELRIC DISCOVERED
AN UNPLEASANT KINSHIP

After a despairing Nauha had left to return aboard a merchant venturer taking the so-called "long passage" home, deeper into the mysterious World of
Below-and-Above the two friends went, driven by curiosity and then the need
for treasure to sustain them on their travels. At last they heard of a city deep
in the jungles of the Midland Continent where dragon and man lived in harmony. Elric persuaded his companion to make the journey with him, so that
one could guard the other's back.

> Gorgeous green those flowers, sick sweet
> Are fed by Melniboné's taxed blood
> So much has sustained that noble stream.
> The Realist's drought but the Romantic's flood

> —Wheldrake,
> *The Apothecary's Ambition*, 1906
> (A Jacobean Pastiche)

SEVEN

The Apothecary in Horse Alley

FROM THE SEA, the city of Nassea-Tiki was a mosaic of vivid colour, fluttering flags, gilded domes, rust-red battlements, a busy market, tiny black figures. The harbour was vast, serving the trade of the entire continent. Foot forward in the prow of the Hizsian cutter, peering ahead as the late-afternoon sun set the great port on fire, Moonglum of Elwher remarked to his friend on the wealth of shining masts which stood at all angles, like the spears of embattled armies, casting a dozen reflections. The sails were furled for the most part, tightly rolled blues and loose-hung russets to match the gargoyles and grim sea-bulls decorating the hulls. These big ships were local. Others, such as their own, favouring black, dark red, white and silver, were from months away.

The ship's captain came to join them, staring ahead. "What a sight!" He drew in a breath, as if inhaling the entire vision. "After Imrryr they say she's the most beautiful city Above *or* Below."

He looked at Moonglum's companion, as if for confirmation.

"After Imrryr," the passenger agreed. "And perhaps Tanelorn."

Throwing back his thick, green cloak Moonglum turned his head, hands around the pommels of his twin sabres. "Who would have thought we'd come upon such a rich metropolis after all those half-civilised villages we've seen on the way here?" He looked back at his friend, whose blazing crimson eyes seemed to find reflection in the effects of the sun. Set in an intensely beautiful face the colour of bone, the eyes were slightly sloping, like the lobes of his ears.

His lips were full. His long hair was like poured milk. His eyes stared into a past and a future of equal tragedy. Yet there was a kind of amusement there, too.

Moonglum's own eyes were troubled as he contemplated his friend. The last emperor of Melniboné was breathing heavily, having difficulty moving along the edge of the deck, holding hard to the rail. He was hampered by the scabbard of the massive broadsword whose hilt was tightly wired to his belt.

Not for the first time, the captain turned away, ostentatiously incurious.

"The drugs are ceasing to work, my friend," whispered Moonglum. "Were they the last?"

The albino shook his head. "Almost," he said.

Elric of Melniboné and his red-headed companion, refreshed to some degree, stepped towards the busy dock while over their heads swung goods of every description. Most eyes were on the cargoes rather than the passengers. Only a few noticed the two disembark. Most had no idea whom they might be.

Nassea-Tiki was not merely busy. The vast port was in celebration. Her very palms seemed to dance. When the two adventurers stopped a passer-by and enquired of the uproar seizing the city, the man said that the old system of peacekeeping had, on that very day, given way to the new. The two men were mystified until a passing ship's captain, dressed up in crisp blue silk and black linen on his way to meet a prospective customer, told them the capital city's notorious private, corrupt police force, who had been Addric Heed's men here, was being replaced by a trained band of municipal employees. These would be free from bribery and arbitrary brutality. "At least in theory," said the displaced Tarkeshite, whose first impression of the albino's identity was now confused and who wanted to be on his way, a desire he indicated by glancing at the gigantic public hourglass of copper and greenish crystal dominating the busy quayside. A little amused, the Elwheri wished him well, and the two allowed him to continue.

Feeble as the young albino had become during his uncomfortable voyage, on Moonglum's arm he was still able to stumble to the blazing metal-and-glass timepiece and reach the inn recommended by Captain Calder Dulk, master of the *Morog Bevonia*, as somewhere to find clean lodgings at little risk of being robbed. As they pressed slowly through the narrow streets, full of men and women enjoying a public holiday, celebrating the death of a pirate who had been feared even this far south, he was noticeably taller and slimmer than the average. Though his cloak's high collar was raised about his face, it was clear by his slightly slanting eyes and ears to which race he belonged. After making sure he was not Addric Heed, the local people paid him no special attention, but those few Young Kingdoms traders from nations closer to his own kept a respectful distance.

Paying for a quiet room, with two hammocks and a window overlooking the inner courtyard, Elric tipped the servant generously when hot water for baths was brought. Moonglum sighed. His friend was too careless with the little money they had remaining. After washing and grooming themselves, they donned fresh linen and went back downstairs. Looking around at the other guests, they judged Dulk's advice reliable. In spite of his recent civic duties in faraway Elwher, Moonglum's thief's eyes brightened with speculation when he saw that the main hall of the inn was full of well-dressed merchant seamen already engaged in the business which brought them half across the world and, in some cases, over the edge. Some men were running impromptu auctions with those who had waited days for ships, delayed by bad weather. Examples of diamonds and other precious jewels were quickly displayed, of strangely wrought spider- and ant-silks, oddly fashioned metals. Elric had travelled widely on dream-quests, experiencing over a hundred thousand years of history and had seen and forgotten much. Even he was surprised by the amounts of money changing hands on speculative bargaining.

They sat together, under a window in the quieter part of the hall, drinking the local wine and studying a map they had bought in Thokora. The albino was having difficulty focusing. He muttered that the livestock the ships had brought was in considerably better health than himself.

"Aren't you at all tempted to untwist those supernaturally intricate lengths of brass and copper which lock your sword to its scabbard?" Moonglum whispered, holding a blank scrap of vellum up to the light because he thought he might confuse a potential observer while he had the chance. Shaking his head, Elric seemed utterly unaware of what two men in a harbour tavern poring over a map might signify to the crazed, treasure-hungry denizens who hung around these merchants like carrion birds. He did not understand his old friend's attempts to distract a potential enemy.

Elric still feared his blade Stormbringer quite as much as any would-be attacker. Indirectly, it was their chief reason for risking this long journey so far away from the few remaining sources of Elric's drugs. In Melniboné's past, before such drugs were discovered, "silverskins" like himself had led short, painful lives usually ending in madness and self-destruction. Only by resorting to the darkest sorcery and trading their souls for supernatural aid could the enfeebled creatures hope to live like others. While the drugs sustained Elric, they did not invigorate him as the sword had. Yet he wished never to draw it again and have more souls pay the terrible price so many had already paid for his own life.

Before leaving Hizs, Moonglum had consulted an oracle, a highly recommended human woman. He had not cared to ask for himself, but for Elric. The oracle had been specific. If Elric wished to cease his dependency on his sword, he must find the legendary *noibuluscus* plant. And that plant grew in one place, it was said, in the jungles beyond distant Nassea-Tiki.

Although feeling permanent sickness and weakness, for the first time in months the pale prince rested. He was reassured that, in Nassea-Tiki, his reputation was no more than a distant legend. Here, the Bright Empire of Melniboné was a faeyrie tale. He himself was no more than a legend at most. Here, there were no further reminders of his past, no-one to recall Cymoril and what they were calling elsewhere the Great Massacre and sometimes the Great Betrayal. He faced his own past, his own unfamiliar guilt, with deeper insight than any of his accusers. He saw nothing noble in his deeds. He believed he deserved all his suffering, physical and spiritual. And as for his health—well, the *noibuluscus* could soon be his. He had bought the book and map in a market; they had been in the middle of a vast pile of manuscripts, any valuable decoration already removed, looted from somewhere by illiterate nomads who brought the stuff to sell only in the faint hope someone would put value on it. He had found a partial map fitting his own, but not the whole thing. Parts were still missing.

Map and herbal had told of the so-called Black Anemonë which grew in a temple's *lunarium* at the centre of an ancient jungle city, upriver of Nassea-Tiki. The plant had all the properties Elric needed to sustain himself. But, another grimoire he had consulted reminded him, the black flower only bloomed once a century, and only in full moonlight. The grimoire featured a so-called hundred-year almanac, predicting phases of the moon, but was itself at least fifty years old. So he had gambled on finding it, taking its seeds and forever protecting himself against the sickness brought by his rare form of albinism, which affected his eyesight as well as his sword-arm.

A dozen dark legends surrounded the Black Anemonë. Some were familiar, occurring in most peoples. Others were rarer, with a hint of reality. Truth could not be told from fable. What all his sources agreed, however, was that the time of the Black Anemonë's blooming grew close. They consulted another seer in Kleif, a city of unnatural pleasures. Here, they were warned to avoid the black flower and to return to their own world. A second philosopher looked into his crystal prisms and began screaming and sobbing, throwing their money back at them. He was a large, indolent-seeming man, but well-respected. When he took his own life shortly after their visit, they had been blamed. He had given them a name. Soom. Their departure from Kleif had been hasty. There had been little time to discover details.

They had at least another part of what they needed. A city, a river, a ruined metropolis. At certain moments, when the seas grew stormy, they feared they would arrive in Nassea-Tiki too late, and Elric would be forced to fall back on any power derived from his sword just to sustain them in food. As it was, the ship docked with only days to spare. Now they had to get upriver to the mysterious city of Soom marked on the map. Ancient Soom was now said to lie in ruins, deserted by its folk. There was every kind of curse upon the place, every doom and weird which ever accumulated around an inaccessible ruin. Men came to avoid such places which, in Elric's experience, were as often as not harmless places reclaimed only by Nature. Yet, harmless or dangerous, neither man had any great desire to visit the abandoned settlement.

Relaxed and wearing the loose silks of Aflitainian gentleman-captains, Elric and Moonglum completed their supper at an inn. Then, with his friend at his side, Moonglum at the bar enquired of his good-natured, corpulent host if he knew the whereabouts of a certain apothecary with the unlikely name of Nashatak Skwett, said to reside in the older part of the port. This brought a broad smile to the landlord's face. "So old Nashatak's found another customer, eh?" Even here, so far from Hizs and her pale queen, they spoke some pidgin form of Low Melnibonéan.

Elric raised a white, enquiring eyebrow.

"Nashatak has a bit of a reputation as a quack in these parts," explained the innkeeper, unconsciously fingering his chest, "though I'll admit I've met a few wise medical men and women from abroad who seem to respect him. And I like him personally, make no mistake. He had a phase of making up poetry, and I got to know him during our old poetry evenings here which got too big for this place and had to move uphill. And you, no doubt, are one of them, sirs. A fellow pair, sirs, of poets! And you're not the thieves he frequently mentions. Who stole his work, sirs. He wrote a much-copied book, I hear. It's often said that local wisdom gets no respect until it's travelled a-ways. He's eccentric, I will tell you. He comes and goes a bit, but when he's here, he's generally to be found at his shop in the Moldigorne. That's the area sometimes called the old fortress. A fortress no longer, of course. It's where the robber-captains who founded Nassea-Tiki built a great stone keep. It grew into a self-sufficient village, then a town, then a greedy city, for eventually the lords of Nassea-Tiki came a-visiting, impatient with their thieving. Long ago, when Soom was still powerful, the lords brought an army downriver. They razed the keep but, having no quarrel with ordinary folk, left the outer walls and the village standing. They became famous botanists, raising rare plants and selling seeds and bulbs to all the surrounding towns, even this one. Anyway, it's in the Moldigorne you'll find him. He visited Soom twice, I hear. Once in temporal and the other in spiritual form. He made no great secret of it. He sought the Black Anemonë.

He knew it would fetch a magnificent price, enabling his own botanical ideas to continue." He smiled. "He's a sweet man, for all his habits."

"Habits?" To Moonglum's further disapproval, Elric put down generous silver. "But Soom, I gather, is itself a ruin. What became of her folk?"

"Nothing pleasant, sir, that's for sure. We must all cater to custom and to customers, sir, as we say in the guild. A few of Soom's lords settled here and rebuilt the harbour. Some members of our present ruling council claim them as ancestors, for they were a learned and brave people according to legend. Others, however, say their blood turned bad with arrogant pride and they took to perverse teachings and strange practices. They mated with serpents, we heard. Superstition, of course! All we do know is that Soom is shunned by wise folk, not because of any supernatural curse upon the place, but because it is occupied by a nomad tribe of cannibals during certain seasons of the year. Scholars disappeared. Then scholars and their mercenary guards. Then two squads of royal cavalry got up there on rafts, and after they did not return, bar a horse or two, no further expeditions were sent. Occasionally a corpse or some odd artefact drifts downriver, but . . . I heard that the King of the Das was the last to go there, seeking some fabled treasure. Neither he nor his men are yet returned. I knew the old hunter, as you could already be aware. Never heard of the old hunter? Well, master, he was tall and silver-crowned, like yourself . . ."

Fearing that his loquacious landlord was about to launch into a series of local stories, Moonglum interrupted gently to ask the way to the apothecary's.

"You're a fascinating man, sir, and I look forward to sharing many evenings with you. Meanwhile, my friend is almost at death's door. Nay, not with the plague, but an ague which attacks only those in his condition. Sir, if you could point us to the apothecary, I'd be ever in your debt." The man seemed to wake up suddenly, raised a finger, then led them back to his nook behind the bar. He reached under a cupboard and unrolled a local map. "There it is—just off Horse Street." He waited patiently while Elric took a piece of charcoal and, borrowing Moonglum's scrap of vellum, made a quick copy of the map. Then, with a promise to return, the exiled prince of Melniboné and his friend left the inn, pushing through still-celebrating crowds packing streets of multicoloured stone and brightly painted wood whose ornate frontages rose eight or ten storeys into the glaring, blue-gold sky. They followed the harbour wall until they found the turning into Moldigorne's darker alleys, where one side leaned toward the other to form a kind of tunnel, and were soon at Horse Alley.

The apothecary's sign was prominent at the far end of the narrow cobbled way, painted on the fading white wall of a tall old house whose black timber beams looked hard as iron. Now that they had at last discovered the apothecary's, the pair found themselves approaching with a certain reluctant caution. For too long Elric's quest across this world for his ailment's remedy had ended in failure. Once or twice there had been a kind of near-success, but the concoctions of plants and herbs soon ran out and were never replicated. Moonglum knew the albino had gambled everything, this time, on what he had read in Nashatak Skwett's *Herbal and Magical Remedies for Rare Diseases and Conditions* and was almost afraid to proceed. What did it matter that a few good folk had died to feed him their energy? After all, most of those his sword killed deserved their fate. But then he remembered his betrothed cousin Cymoril, who had died, albeit accidentally, on the point of that blade. Elric's pace quickened. Slipping his silver-hilted dagger from its sheath, he rapped on the door with its hilt.

The door was almost immediately opened. A pink-skinned, bright-haired child of indeterminate gender opened its mouth in a question.

They gave their names. Moonglum asked for Master Nashatak. The child disappeared, then returned to hold out its warm, moist hands to lead them through ill-lit halls and passages, up flights of crooked stairs. A mixture of smells struck their nostrils—chemicals, animal odours, a sweet stink reminiscent of rotten flesh. But, entering the room at the end of a long, twisting passage, they were impressed by its orderliness and the cleanliness of the relatively young man who rose to greet them. He was rerolling a parchment and set this down as he opened his arms to them. "I have your letter, my lord. Let me tell you how honoured I am to receive one as learned as yourself. And, of course, you too are welcome, Master Moonglum."

"Ah," said Elric, embarrassed, "such learning was commonplace in my homeland, where we absorbed it on our dream couches. I am a stranger in your world. As you can guess, we are novices in the wisdom of the World Above." He was diplomatic. "I can make no claims for myself . . ."

"As you please, prince." Master Nashatak's lank fair hair was pulled back from his lugubrious dark brown face and secured by a fillet of copper. He wore a long velvet gown which had been recently washed but on which the stains remained. He looked curiously at Elric. "We have an acquaintance in common. Doctor Cerlat Vog . . ."

"Who sent you this letter." The walk had tired him. Breathing with some difficulty, Elric reached into his pouch and brought out a sealed packet.

"My old friend! Was he *well?*" Nashatak accepted the letter, breaking the seal. "His teeth?"

Moonglum answered. "They were little better when we left Noothar. But his feet showed some improvement. He enquired after the health of your wife."

Still enough of a Melnibonéan noble to find such pleasantries irritating, Elric disguised his impatience.

"She is well. I thank you, Master Moonglum. Visiting her mother on the other side of the river. This is our child."

They still had no clue as to the little creature's gender. Its large, hazel eyes continued to regard them from the shadows.

Master Nashatak read the letter carefully, holding it close to one of the lamps and occasionally nodding to himself. "So you've heard of the *noibuluscus* by its true name. In your original letter you spoke only of a black flower. And you've come seeking it in the right season of the right year. But I fear there's another searching who has gone ahead of you. Do you know of Tilus Kreek, King of the Das?"

Moonglum shrugged. "We were told he died in Soom seeking a treasure."

"He has not returned, that's so. But I learned from a friend that Tilus, too, sought the *noibuluscus.*"

Elric turned, hearing the child utter a deep, throaty chuckle.

"The *furi* caught him and ate him," it said. "They nibble the genitals. It is quite pleasant at first. Until they start to bite." It licked a slimy lip. "And almost every one of his mercenary army was thus killed. Or, in gratitude, were captured."

Moonglum shivered and swore. "Where did you get such intelligence?"

"The streets. It's common knowledge."

Elric laid his hand on his friend's arm. "Nonetheless, I would go to Soom and find the Black Anemonë. Where can I seek a guide with a boat to take us upriver?"

"I suspect it will be difficult. There are other terrors, they say, in Soom."

"We've dealt with fierce beasts and men in our time, Master Nashatak," Moonglum told him gently. "And supernatural horrors, too."

"I believe you have. You are evidently soldiers of great courage and re-source. And you, Master Elric, have the air of a fellow adept. Indeed, this letter speaks of your bravery and wisdom. You performed Cerlat Vog a considerable service, I gather . . ."

Elric restrained his impatience. "If he says so. I must have that boat and a guide, sir. I have little time remaining."

"If it's true," added Moonglum, "the black flower blooms only once in a century at this season when the moon is full, you will appreciate . . ."

The apothecary shrugged. "Nonetheless, it is unwise to go at this unpre-pared. I myself am curious, as you can imagine, but I could not afford the small army needed . . ."

"Unless you can discover the whereabouts of the Das king's twin daugh-ters and their escorts," murmured the child almost to itself. "I heard . . ."

"Heard? Where?" Its father frowned, and Elric gave the child his concen-trated attention.

"They came this morning, seeking audience with the Council. They met with one of your race, Prince Elric."

"A Melnibonéan?" asked Moonglum.

"Aye. And I heard that some of the same folk were in King Tilus Kreek's band. Dyvim—Something . . ."

"Dyvim simply means 'royal cousin,' " murmured Elric. "Most of my cousins died at the great battle . . ." He was further intrigued.

"How could we find these twin sisters and the others?" Moonglum demanded.

"If the street speaks truth, then they no doubt lodge at the great Council House as guests of the city."

"Where's that?"

The apothecary interrupted. "Prince Elric, I would not have you go to Soom alone. I will write you a letter. My boy will take you to the Council House. Certain members of the Great Council are good customers of mine. You will need to be introduced. But first—" He crossed to one of several tables covered in all kinds of curios, many whose function was completely mysterious. He opened a box of ivory-inlaid cedarwood and took out of it a short string of amber beads which moved like sluggish flames in the lamplight. He handed this to the albino, who, puzzled, turned it over and over in his long-fingered bone-white hands. The amber felt warm, almost like living flesh. It seemed to vibrate as if to the beating of tiny wings.

"You might not need it now, but you might need it some day. It is in acknowledgement of the service you did my old friend. Put it on," said the apothecary. "Place the beads around your neck."

To humour him, Elric did as he was asked.

"Wear it until you have the opportunity to use it," Nashatak told him. And when Elric sighed, he added, "I can tell that you are one who does not value his own life overmuch. But that thing might prove useful to you, for I know you have a destiny and a duty to live. In those moments between conviction and doubt it could enable you to continue. I have no further personal use for the charm. I wish you good fortune, sir, for I suspect you carry a weird which few would envy."

Elric's smile was thin. "My poor folk had lost any sense of sin they might once have had. It was my poor fortune to rediscover it. My destiny is a result of my actions. Nonetheless, I value your goodwill. There are few in this world, I suspect, who share it. I thank you." While Moonglum waited with growing impatience, Nashatak Skwett went to his desk and began to write. Meanwhile, the strange child continued to watch them through those laughing, hazel eyes until its father folded and sealed the letter, handing it to his offspring. "Go in peace, gentlemen." The apothecary made a sign to his child, who again took their hands to lead them from the house.

Outside, the sky had darkened. Looking up, they saw a three-quarter moon above the rooftops and heard a distant sound, like the cawing of a crow. For an instant they saw black wings outlined in the moonlight, then they were gone, and the city, which on their way here had been so raucous, was momentarily completely hushed.

For a moment, in a cobbled alley, the child paused to bend over and spit out a cheekful of mouth-worms, which symbiotically lived in and fed off this people's teeth. The little things wriggled off into a puddle where they would mostly die. The remainder would be farmed for reuse.

Not for the first time, Moonglum wondered how people could call themselves civilised. Especially when it came to their sanitary habits and standards.

EIGHT

Two Princesses: A Pair of Dukes

THE CITY CONTINUED its celebration. The new peacekeepers had not had time to lose the citizens' goodwill. Somewhat cynically, Moonglum reflected on the many times in his journeying through the world when a change of government had been greeted with the same joy only to be followed by disappointment and anger when the new proved no better. "People hate real change." The stocky Eastlander had served in elected office only recently. "And are usually only satisfied with superficial and momentary differences. At least when Law controls the Balance. Remember how the Young Kingdoms, even as they recovered from their own terrible losses, took pleasure in the collapse of your Bright Empire. Now they grumble and curse their own leaders as they once cursed Melniboné. Some even long for the stability they knew under the Sorcerer Emperors. No doubt this republic's satisfaction will last as long."

The child led them deeper and deeper up the twisting, cobbled lanes of the port, away from the sea, until they looked back at the dark, crowded masts below and the glinting water, like ebony, beyond. To their left they followed the silhouettes of warehouses and other buildings on both sides of the river as it wormed under two stout stone bridges, out of sight into the distant jungle, seemingly impenetrably dense. They would have to go to those upriver docks in the morning, either alone or in company, depending on what transpired at the Council House.

The night stank of sour wine, burning wood and moss, of sweating bodies, roasting meat and other less identifiable things. Men and women linked arms and stumbled past singing. Although they had to pause occasionally while Elric rested, the three ignored the crowds and their friendly invitations, walking until the child brought them in sight of the gates of a vast and beautiful building, low and wide, with a tall irregular roof topped by masses of miscellaneous towers, drawbridges and battlements, all in different styles yet strangely unified, each patrolled and guarded.

"There!" The child pointed to tall towers framing glittering gates. "The entrance to the Council House."

They could have found the place by its description: myriad towers, domes, steeples and causeways, some in paint and others in naked native stones of buttery yellow and flawless grey. As they approached, they saw that what they had mistaken for a single decoration was in fact a medley of various sizes of flags and banners which festooned the entrance in turn separated by vivid coats of arms. Again, Moonglum found himself marvelling at the wealth and strength displayed. Before he could call out in Low Melnibonéan, to announce themselves, the child shouted something in the local dialect and instantly received a reply. A further exchange, followed by the slow rising of a great gate. At which point a liveried officer strode forward to receive the letter handed him by the child. The mismatched trio were left to stand in a circle of fluttering brandlight while the officer took the letter away.

A short while later a voice spoke from the darkness, asking their names and business.

"I am ex-Chancellor Moonglum of Elwher, whom some call President, others Duke. This lord's companion. And he is Prince Elric, Sadric's son, of Melniboné. We seek audience with the Republican Council concerning a proposed expedition to the ruins of Soom."

Elric looked up in some surprise. Moonglum had yet to tell him that, among all his many recent exploits, he had briefly served as Chancellor of Elwher, which was again a republic. And Moonglum was forced to explain, as the lords conferred, once more to a frowning albino what exactly a kingdom without a king was and how it might function.

"The king is elected, except he is not really elected, by his subjects?" Elric mused. "I believe I was taught about that. On a dream-quest, of course. In another reality once. Somewhere. Does the name Berleronix mean something?"

"It means a great deal. I have studied ancient Berleronix, of course. The philosopher."

"Then you know of the tale of the blind dragon?

"Not clearly."

"A legend of a blind dragon guarding a string of pearls. The Pearls of Ochnaeia. They gave anyone who wore them the power to see worlds wherever the moonbeam roads led. The entire multiverse laid out on a map for you."

"And Ochnaeia's pearls, I gather, were stolen." Moonglum assumed a bored expression. "And can only be regained by a hero with a heart of purest good and a mind of all-encompassing nobility . . ."

Elric laughed with him. "True, it is a familiar enough tale, but I followed it to these waters."

☉ ☉ ☉

AND THEN THE child had vanished. They were almost at once surrounded by soldiers in rather intricate and impractical armour. Their ornamental, plumed helmets hid all but their disciplined eyes. Refusing to be engaged, the guards led the pair into the depths of the palace. Eventually, without explanation, they allowed themselves to be marched into a great hall. Coloured banners hung everywhere from the ceiling; pampered hounds chewed on discarded bones. Great platters were filled with scraps of meat and vegetables, spoons and glasses.

A celebratory banquet was clearly just ending. Diners fell silent, looking up from their wine as the two entered. The women in particular found them interesting. Male curiosity was warier. Rows of tables bore the remains of the elaborate meal, with plates and forks abandoned and even the wine jugs running dry. Cats and dogs roamed the floors, occasionally risking a tabletop for a half-carved joint. At the head of each table sat a man or a woman wearing identical blue-and-yellow robes. These were evidently members of the Council. A trestle at the far end of the hall was set crosswise to the others. At its middle a tall, substantial man, in the same livery but wearing a conical black cap, rose to greet them. "Good evening, Prince Elric. Forgive our hesitation. We heard you were either a legend or a ghost. We never thought to meet you in the flesh . . . Two such distinguished travellers are most welcome here. I am Admiral Juffa, privileged to be this city's Chief Councillor. Please come and be comfortable at our table. We'll have fresh meat and wine brought. Tonight we are graced with not a few people of high degree. Our nation, being a republic, as yours, Citizen Moonglum, still recognises those of rank. You are not the first of ancient blood to honour us." He spoke as an habitual diplomat.

Two distinguished-looking women, of a darker and more refined appearance, sat to Juffa's right and two equally dignified men to his left. From their clothing, they were clearly visitors. But it was not their dress which impressed the newcomers. For a long moment Elric stared into the face of the stranger furthest on the Chief Councillor's left. The man had risen from his seat, his face pale and his lips pursed, a gleam of hatred in his eyes. From his high cheekbones, slanting eyes and ears, he was clearly of Elric's own unhuman folk.

Elric bowed first to the women, then to the Chief Councillor, then to the golden-bearded black man and lastly to the one who directed a look of terrible intensity towards him then raised a piece of meat on his table dagger. Placing the food in his mouth he began to chew fiercely. He took his time swallowing.

"Greetings, cousin," Elric said. "I did not know you still lived."

The man controlled himself. At that moment he was almost as pale as Elric. He was a duke, Dyvim Marluc, one of the few Dragon Masters to survive Elric's betrayal of their nation to the Young Kingdom reavers. Trained from birth to show no emotion, he barely kept the tremble from his voice. The white feathers about his throat gave him the appearance of an angry eagle.

"Greetings, Prince Elric. Sadly, I survived where my brothers and sisters did not."

"You are countrymen, I take it, from your appearance." The Chief Councillor seemed unaware of any tension. "Well met, eh?" He waved the letter the apothecary had sent with his child. "And with common interests, I gather."

The other male visitor was a man with jet-black skin, with thick blue-black brows, full red lips smiling from within a square, divided black beard, his oiled black curls falling to his shoulders. He stared with some amusement at Elric and then at Dyvim Marluc. Dressed all in martial black leather. He clearly knew more of Melniboné's recent history than did Juffa.

"Forgive me," said Councillor Juffa, rising a little unsteadily. "May I introduce Prince Elric? The Princesses Apparent of Das, Princess Viricias and Princess Semilee." Elric and Moonglum bowed. "And this is Duke Mitcha, Seneschal of the Shanac Pines, also of Das." Bearded Duke Mitcha rose, his palm outward from his forehead in what was clearly the normal gesture of greeting of his people. The two princesses were both of exceptional beauty. Viricias was pale-skinned, with wide black eyes and black hair curling to her shoulders. Semilee was of a rosy complexion, her auburn hair cut short against her oval face. Both were frowning, not quite able to understand what was happening.

Breaking this tension, two huge ginger dogs came to sniff at Elric, growling softly in an almost friendly way and wagging their tails. Elric recognised them as the tall, slender hunting dogs of his people, his mind meeting instantly with theirs. They had come with Duke Dyvim Marluc as a gift for the Councillor. Mitcha turned to Dyvim Marluc and made a joke, but the young man did not respond. His eyes were still fixed on Elric. The dogs, too, looked to him as their natural leader.

Councillor Juffa continued. "The princesses are the twin daughters of Tilus Kreek, King of the Das, and these gentlemen are in their service. Duke Mitcha attached to the late king's household . . ."

"Last king," interrupted the dark-haired princess in low tones. "We have no proof of his death." She stared steadily at Elric from beneath half-closed lids, her full, sensual lips curved in a sardonic half-smile. Her black hair fell over her left brow, and she looked up at him through thick curling lashes. Elric smiled and returned his attention to the Councillor.

The regent bowed his head, acknowledging his mistake.

"We have come because your countrymen failed to protect our father on their recent expedition to Soom," said Duke Mitcha. "We had hoped to recruit other soldiers who might not have his portion of ill luck . . ."

At this, Elric's kinsman turned away, his eyes hardening. He had been insulted. Moonglum noted the various tensions between the Council and visiting nobles, and he was sure it was not differences of political opinion they had been quarrelling about.

Duke Mitcha cleared his throat. "But it seems only Dyvim Marluc's Melnibonéans and a few Lormyrians had the nerve to make the crossing to our side of the world-egg to seek dark, forbidden Soom. In spite of offering generous wages, we have been unable to raise soldiers for a second expedition."

Elric glanced at Dyvim Marluc. His cousin spoke evenly, controlling any anger or confusion he felt. "Hoping to find something of value, I followed a fragment of a map I found in an old library in ancient Za. I lost twenty-six brave Melnibonéans and seven Lormyrian archers, following that map. The jungle around Soom teems with dwarfish cannibals. We suspect more than one tribe has been travelling for weeks to get there. Some kind of gathering. We converged by land and water! They attacked us. One Lormyrian and I escaped in the river, carrying our wounded, who died. I believe some of our men were taken alive. I suspect we were allowed to escape, perhaps as a warning to others not to attempt a further expedition. The Lormyrian is also dead. What brings my kinsman to Nassea-Tiki?" He clearly had some notion of Elric's intentions.

"I seek certain answers concerning our ancestry and a flower said to bloom in Soom once a century. Under the light of the moaning moon."

"You are a botanist, sir?" This from an apparently innocent princess. "My father also studied plants. He, too, spoke of what he called 'the singing sky.' Can they be the same?"

"A curious coincidence." Elric inclined his head. There was still considerable tension in the air. "But what of these savages? I was told the city was deserted."

"So it is." The Chief Councillor was almost amused. "Unfortunately, the surrounding jungle is not. It is full of wily, brutal cannibals thought to be the stunted degenerate descendants of the Soomish people. Perhaps they regard the city as sacred. They appear to have been gathering all this year. We know not why. We suspect it to coincide with the blooming and seeding of the black flower. Usually the individual tribes war amongst themselves and offer us and the river traders no serious danger. But clearly I would fail in my duty if I did not keep all my people here to defend our own city against this horde, should it choose to attack."

"Aye." Elric drew breath to continue but was interrupted by a young man who rose from the end of the table. Like many locals, he had deep brown skin and long black hair. He dressed simply, conservatively in black, while the collar and cuffs of his white shirt were exposed at throat and wrist. He carried a heavy, scabbarded sword of antique design. He had a ready smile, a charming manner.

"I am Hered Dehlian, son of Councillor Menzi of the eighth ward. I have already volunteered to return with the new expedition, no matter how small."

Elric guessed the handsome youth to be enamoured of the sisters. Moonglum did not smile when he enquired, "How many do you command, sir?"

"None." Hered Dehlian sat down again. "But perhaps a few of us can reach Soom where a larger party would be more readily detected."

"True." Elric looked enquiringly at the others. He was the dominating presence, the natural leader, yet more than one there questioned his authority.

"It's as good a logic as any other," said Duke Mitcha. "I'm willing to put it to the test."

Princess Semilee rose suddenly. "Then shall we to our beds, my friends? Will you be ready to begin moving upriver in the morning, Prince Elric, Sir Moonglum?"

Taken aback, but impressed by her decisiveness, Elric smiled. "If there are no objections to my joining your party, my lady, at least until we are all arrived at Soom." Then he looked directly at Dyvim Marluc, who said softly:

"I see no reason why you should betray us on this particular occasion, cousin. We have a good-sized boat in readiness. You will find us at the river harbour soon after sunrise."

Elric bowed his head again. "I look forward to it."

He fought to repress the sense of foreboding which filled him. Not since he had led the attack on his homeland had he felt so unwell. But he had no choice. He would free himself of the Black Sword's power or die in the attempt. Besides, he felt an obscure compulsion to aid his kinsmen if he could. He knew it was guilt that drove him, but this time he would allow his guilt to rule. What if fierce, blind dragons occupied the abandoned ruins? It did not matter a whit. Careless as he was of the opinion of the world, which could not hate him more than he hated himself, he would follow these most un-Melnibonéan urges to their logical and natural conclusion. Could this world's forests be full of dragons, their ancestors and descendants? Part of him was curious to explore such feelings. Moreover, he found Princess Viricias singularly attractive. He guessed that, were he to succeed and choose to take it, the fruit of the black flower would not be his only prize.

As they turned to leave, Princess Viricias's voice came sweet and clear from behind them. "Do you know what they call that black blossom, Prince Elric?"

"I have heard it called by several names, my lady."

"The Blood Flower. They say it yields a sap which can be dried and from which a drink can be distilled that will give a sickly silverskin the strength he naturally lacks."

When Elric looked back at her, he saw that she was smiling directly into his eyes. Again he offered her a brief bow. "I had heard that, too, madam. But, as one wanders the world, one comes across many unlikely tales. A man would be a fool to believe them all."

"And foolish to ignore a few?" she said.

NINE

Upriver

ELRIC AND A grumbling Moonglum arrived at the river dock in the cool air of early morning when dew brightened every uncurling leaf and gaudy piece of wood. Cocks still crowed, and the languid smoke of breakfast fires rose from a thousand chimneys. Carrying a long bundle under his arm, Elric paused in surprise, seeing five figures standing near a big single-masted, scarlet-painted boat anchored between several much larger inland barges which, they had been told, traded between Nassea-Tiki and the interior cities beyond Soom. Normally Soom was easily avoided, the river captains had said, but their traffic had stopped since news of the gathering tribes had come. Now, said the landlord, only fools would risk the journey, or those whose greed outstripped their common sense. When Elric asked him "Why greed?" he replied with some old, familiar tale of lost treasure.

The people waiting to go aboard the vessel, whose only shelter was a small deckhouse set amidships, were Dyvim Marluc, wearing the formal light battle armour of the Dragon Master, but carrying no *skeffla'a* or goad; Duke Mitcha had intricately carved wooden armour which made his body bulky and seemed cleverly designed to protect the wearer from arrows and yet keep him afloat in water; the Councillor's son, Hered Dehlian, had equipped himself in a coat of light brass mail and an elegant conical helmet. To Elric's mild surprise, the two princesses were also present. Their armour was wooden, like their countryman's. Elric greeted them with a bow. Princess Viricias met his gaze with that same almost mocking directness, while her sister dropped her gaze and seemed to blush. They greeted each other and, at a signal from Dyvim Marluc, who was captain by common consent, began to cross the narrow, bouncing gangplank from quay to boat.

"We are grateful for your company, Prince Elric," said Princess Semilee as they boarded.

"We are at your disposal until we reach Soom," he replied. "And from then until the moon turns full. Then we have our own curiosity to follow."

She looked up at him, clearly restraining herself from asking him any further questions.

The tide and wind were in their favour. Within moments Hered Dehlian had freed the boat, and they were carried by the current towards the centre.

As the women watched, the men unshipped oars and set the single sail, following the tide while it ran upstream.

Soon they had rounded a curve, and the city and suburbs were lost from sight behind a curtain of lush palms and thick foliage. The rowing grew harder. The familiar stink of the forest almost clogged their lungs. The air filled with the calls of myriad birds and all the grunts, barks and bellows of the diurnal jungle. The journey to Soom would take several days. None showed the same impatience to reach the city as his cousin, Dyvim Marluc, whose eyes never lost their haunted quality and rarely looked directly at Elric. The titular emperor of Melniboné felt an equal discomfort, though for opposite reasons. Dyvim Marluc hated him for the doom he had brought to Imrryr, a hatred Elric also felt; yet the Dragon Master still knew respect for a name and lineage which had ruled the Bright Empire for ten thousand years.

Dyvim Marluc had no Phoorn to command and was by nature laconic, when not speaking to his dragons. His motives were simpler than Elric's. He, too, had hoped to find his own Melnibonéan people—but still in ascendancy, a kind of Melniboné restored, to help him forget his lost power. Phoorn and Melnibonéans, said the oldest of their histories, had once been of the same race, in a time before time began, and still spoke the same language. But most dragons needed decades of sleep to restore their energy and their powerful venom. Only profound sorcery could restore them again for a short while.

Almost all the dragons had been used in Imrryr's defence, destroying the invaders even as they fled with their booty, and none remained for a Master to command. This, Elric knew, was a further source of Dyvim Marluc's frustration. The dragons slept in their deep caves, beneath the ruins of the city. He had heard of certain arcane summonings and invocations which could wake them before their time. The surviving Dragon Masters, Elric among them, yearned for the moment when they would begin to wake again. The very things which had once bound Elric to his cousin were those which kept them apart. He noticed that Dyvim Marluc also tended to keep his distance from the others, as if he in turn considered himself guilty of betraying those soldiers he had first led to Soom.

In contrast, Duke Mitcha and Hered Dehlian seemed positively loquacious, talking almost to turn their thoughts away from the dangers ahead. Elric and Moonglum sat in the stern, taking the tiller whenever possible, and the two women, when not doing their share of the steering, sat near them. Princess Semilee, as she became used to the company, seemed direct and open compared to her twin, who was full of smouldering, secret humour and enjoyed baiting the men whenever the opportunity came to her.

At noon of the third day, they put up an awning and nets to protect them from insects and reptiles, and they lunched off local meats, breads and wine purchased from a nearby village. Sunlight reflected by dappled water gave the interior strange, agitated shadows. Princess Viricias turned her sardonic stare on Elric: "A question I have been meaning to ask for some time, my lord emperor."

"Lady?"

"I wonder what at the same time brings so many exiles from the Dragon Isle to these shores?"

Elric shrugged. As was common, Moonglum spoke for him. "I would imagine they need employment, my lady, and soldiering is the thing they know best, now they have no empire to defend."

"But the women? Are they soldiers, too?"

At this, Dyvim Marluc growled, "There are few women. I saved my daughters but not my wives or sons. The reavers either slew them or took them as prizes. Then—" He lowered his eyes. "Then our dragons pursued the reaver ships."

"And?" She genuinely did not know the answer. Dyvim Marluc turned away.

"They died aboard those ships?" asked Moonglum.

Then Elric spoke: "My cousin would want you to know that it was as a result of my betrayal. They had sworn they would take only inanimate treasure. I planned to warn the innocent, but I was delayed—

"Perhaps we were all betrayed, one way or another, that day." Instinctively, his hand had gone to his black sword, Stormbringer, so tightly bound to its scabbard. "Their captains had sworn to spare all nobles. My entire remaining kin!"

"We are from the Das, as you know, and have no direct experience of events surrounding your nation's sudden fall, but I heard—a noble woman, was there not, to whom one of your princes was betrothed? I seem to recall a tale . . ."

"I doubt it's a tale my lord the emperor would care to hear retold," interrupted Dyvim Marluc bitterly. And Elric stood up suddenly, finding some work in the bow of the boat. In spite of Moonglum's warning glance, Princess Viricias called after him. "There's a sword involved in that story, too, my lord."

"Too many swords!" He sighed, his eyes clouding as he drew his brows together. "Lady, you'll have heard no doubt that my betrothed died by my own sword . . ."

"Is that why you keep it so thoroughly bound?" With slender fingers, she gestured towards Stormbringer.

"Oh, 'tis best you ask no more questions concerning this sword, Your Highness." He pretended further interest in the boat's equipment. On both distant banks of the river, under the blaze of the afternoon sun, the dark jungle moved slowly by. "Indeed, it is in none of our interests for me to release this sword."

Enquiringly, she looked up directly into his own ruby eyes. "Then why carry it?"

"To placate my own patron, I suppose." His returning gaze was as direct as her own. "Be warned, lady. Few have ever been glad to have such questions fully answered."

At which point Moonglum offered a warning growl, his fingers tensing on the hilt of his own sword.

Viricias made to speak again. Then her twin called from where she sat in the prow. Semilee pointed to their left, to a long sandbar on which several large crocodiles basked. Among them was an object reflecting the sun. Metal washed by the river and polished by the sand. A large piece of armour. As they drew nearer, Moonglum recognised it as a breastplate of Melnibonéan workmanship, similar to that worn by Dyvim Marluc. The two kinsmen turned away, frowning.

"Was it here?" Princess Semilee's voice was sympathetic.

Dyvim Marluc shook his head. "Further upstream. It must have been dragged down this far by the current. And perhaps by those reptiles . . ." He lifted his head and stared into the middle distance.

Duke Mitcha murmured, "I never knew a people so racked by guilt. And yet which never knew a moment's self-doubt before their diaspora." He spoke ostensibly to an embarrassed Hered Dehlian, who pretended to stare down into the water. Duke Mitcha turned away, stroking his beard, his thoughts inturned.

For some little time the party sailed on in silence. The heat had caused the men to discard much of their own armour. The sluggish water was thick with strange leaves, boughs and exotic, brightly coloured blossoms. Occasionally a curious animal broke the surface, stared at them, and left. The two women murmured together, but as evening came and the sun sat atop the silhouetted jungle, the atmosphere aboard became significantly more relaxed. Duke Mitcha and Hered Dehlian fell into a political conversation. The notion of a republic was foreign to the duke. Like Elric, he found it difficult to understand how such a thing functioned. "The body needs a head as well as hands. It is the natural order seen everywhere!"

He was used to the state embodied in the person of a king, reflecting and exemplifying his nation's virtues. A nation run by a set of institutions and elected officials seemed to him to be a strange, even sickly affair, no longer dependent on the virtue and honour of its hereditary leaders, prey to the basest desires of people who would promise any lie to an electorate in order to be placed in high office. "Where, being base beings already, they would enrich themselves! Are such beings fit to rule?"

"As a king and his court?" asked Viricias innocently.

"Ours are exemplary. Just as your great temples to the Goddess of Reason are exemplary."

The princesses, bored with such politics, speculated on the wildlife to be found in the jungles and of the ancient, perhaps unhuman people who had built the city and ruled the land of Soom, occasionally asking Elric or Dyvim Marluc for their opinion.

"The savages, though ugly and stunted, seemed human enough to me," Dyvim Marluc said. "Not Melnibonéan stock. I was hoping—"

"For ancestors?" said his cousin almost savagely.

The women spoke of their father, who had employed the Melnibonéan mercenaries. Tilus Kreek had been obsessed with learning Soom's secrets, they said. He was convinced the city had been the centre of a wise civilisation almost as old as that which had built Hizs and the inland cities of the Kara. Its treasure might have been knowledge or gold, he had not known from his reading. It might even have been the black flower, said to confer power on its kings. Ancient manuscripts had spoken of it in mysterious terms. Whatever form it took, that treasure could have revived his own nation's fortunes. The Das had suffered a great plague, taking a huge proportion of the population, making it weak and liable to being preyed upon by stronger neighbours.

"My father was obsessed with the stories he had heard of Soom," said Semilee almost despairingly. "He believed the older civilisation would save ours. The Soom began like your folk, gaining power by mating with dragons and making compacts with Chaos. We belong to a race of scholars, and it is our wisdom alone which has kept the worst predators at bay, even though we lost a number of our vassal states. Our war-engines are sophisticated, our magic, too, is feared. We have conducted none of the alliances which, by all accounts, made ancient Melniboné great. We believed that the crisis was over, that we had been able to resist the worst of the threats. There were other plans in place which did not depend upon discovering the secrets of Soom . . . But his curiosity, we suspect, began to drive him more than any immediate danger."

"You say he was a botanist, also?" Hered Dehlian asked. "Perhaps this wealth he coveted was in the nature of rare spices? Our own city's fortunes were based upon the spice trade. There is a good trade, too, in rare bulbs, seeds and plants."

"Perhaps." Princess Viricias was looking at Elric, as if to discover his reaction. Her own expression indicated that she did not welcome this suggestion.

Night fell for the third time since they had left Nassea-Tiki. The men again drew an awning over the deckhouse and set up nets against the biting insects, tying their main line to a large tree trunk wedged where the river curved and the current ran slowly. Within it, luminous nightfish hunted, and the nocturnal tree-alligator was known to make these waters terrifying, when it dropped on its victims from above, taking them to the bottom and drowning them by their own body weight. Ignoring the calls and cries of the jungle, which was quieter than in daytime, they all slept soundly through the tropical night, save for the albino, whose occasional groans and mutterings reminded Moonglum that his friend still relived those events surrounding the fall of his great capital.

DAWN CAME AGAIN and they rowed on upstream. By noon the sun was a throbbing, glaring eye gazing pitilessly down on them as they sweated to force their course on a river grown increasingly difficult to navigate, whose bends twisted and snaked, narrowing then widening unpredictably at every turn. And as night fell once more, Dyvim Marluc warned them not to drag their hands in water now seething with poisonous reptiles and giant cephalopods. "And all are hungry for our flesh, or blood, or both." As he spoke, to illustrate his warning, a great coiling serpent leapt from the water to snap at a bird skimming the surface in pursuit of a giant dragonfly. The spineless creature, a monstrous firefly squid changing colour wildly, used its windmilling arms as a kind of parachute to return to the water—occasionally with a captured nightfish or two. The depths of the river were full of flashing, coloured light as the species, mostly nocturnal chromatophores, twisted and turned, spreading colour to the reeds and weeds of the dark river bottom. Nightfish were not true fish, but reptiles which built energy in the day and hunted after sunset. They were not the only strange, almost unnatural species which filled this river's haunted waters.

Moonglum murmured to his friend, "What could have possessed the Das king to leave his country and his daughters and mount an expedition here? You at least have a somewhat better reason for seeking Soom. I have no great interest in my own nomad ancestry, but I understand your curiosity. We look for models, I think. And so, no doubt, does your kinsman. He believes the reality we know is a myth! A myth based on a reality we have witnessed! A nursery-tale which will lead him to a fabled treasure we know to be real, if not here . . ." He grinned. "I know we need as many as we can get for this venture, but is it fair to take advantage of their greed?"

Somehow, they survived yet another day and a night until at last Dyvim Marluc stood up in the boat to point at something the colour of dried blood stretching out into the water. Clearly of sentient manufacture, it had the appearance of a ruined mole, of worn, red sandstone with rusted iron rings still set into slabs casting black shadows on thick, unpleasant water.

Moonglum, half certain that intelligent eyes were watching them from the dark green jungle depths, made to draw one of his curved swords from its sheath. At any moment an arrow or a spear would come flashing out of the shadows and plant itself deep in soft flesh. Then a worse thought came to him—*What if they want us alive?* For what? For bait? In spite of all his experience, he caught himself shuddering. Now he wondered about more sinister projectiles. A net, perhaps? Or a poison dart?

Pulling on his armour, Dyvim Marluc said, "If they act as they did before, they'll wait until we reach the city proper until there is little chance of escape to the river." Buckling his breastplate with the help of a soldier, he turned to

Elric. "Others beside me have noticed how well secured that blade is, cousin. It might be wise to have it more immediately to hand."

Elric reached down and picked up the long bundle he had brought aboard. He raised his eyebrows. "You'd risk that?"

"No choice is palatable, but, having experienced what these savages are capable of, I'd take my chances with Stormbringer. Assuming you plan to remain on our side . . ."

This further stab at his conscience froze Elric's face into a familiar expression of hauteur. "Why, cousin, would you trust my word, even if I gave it?"

While his soldier buckled and knotted, Dyvim Marluc peered into the forest. "Cousin, I trust nothing. But at least I know you . . ." With Moonglum at the tiller, he took an oar and, in unison with his kinsman, began to row towards the overgrown quay, murmuring, "It was no idea of mine to bring women here. But I was allowed no say in the matter. I understand why they want to find their father, but he is a fool. Haste and stupidity led us to that doom. Some of my own men might have survived. I hope to save them. But you, Elric, what do you really seek here?"

"I seek to free myself from the weakness which made Yyrkoon believe he could usurp my power and put his sister, my cousin, into a trance. Which led me to lose my mind and destroy all I cared for, as if doomed to such action over and over and over again, no matter how I sought to find a substitute for my addiction to this damned and damning hellblade!"

Dyvim Marluc nodded, adding, "Which led you to rely upon the stolen souls that black sword harvests."

Elric sighed. "The *noibuluscus* is the five-fingered flower whose petals are the colour of jet. It grows only in Soom. They say that to conquer their vast empire, which preceded our own, Soom's soldiers drank its distilled essence and thus imposed their authority upon the world in a few weeks."

"And do you recall the rest of that story?" his cousin asked.

"There are many versions."

"Most agree that the black flower poisoned the people of Soom, so that they relied upon it merely to survive. They degenerated into creeping, pale things, feasting on their own flesh, quite literally, for in days of famine each member of the tribe contributed a body part to the common pot which, reduced to a thick soup, fed all indiscriminately, prince or pauper!" Moonglum grinned and licked his lips, close to terrifying himself with his own imagination. "They say that, properly spiced, it could be served at any king's table. What if one were his honoured guest? Uck! The dilemma. One cannot even claim vegetarianism, these days."

"I should fear that?" Elric smiled more broadly than he had done for many years. "Sometimes I deeply fear reliance upon a potion rather than upon a sword. Yet, in conscience, I cannot feed upon the souls of my fellows! No longer. Not much longer, at least!"

His cousin shrugged. He could think of no suitable answer.

TEN

Soom

SLOWLY, THE THICK foliage parted to the careful blades of the seven oddly matched men and women, each of whom carried a small, brass-studded shield. Duke Mitcha exclaimed at what they saw. He was still the only one of the company not apparently affected by the atmosphere of danger. Elric unwrapped the long, simple Jharkorian blade he had carried aboard. A thoroughly practical weapon. Dyvim Marluc was disappointed. "I would have preferred a bow or two or perhaps a javelin." If attacked from cover at a distance, they would be unable to reply.

"Gods! What minds designed and built such architecture?" Moonglum peered ahead.

Young Hered Dehlian gasped. "Sorcery was used here. See how the rock is melted and blends together. Not human, whatever they say. Now I truly believe the stories. These buildings were raised even before fabled Tanelorn thrived." He looked to Elric as if for confirmation.

Elric smiled sardonically at this reference to the fabulous nature of a city known to several of his kin over the centuries. The two princesses carried slender scimitars similar to swords of the old Fookai pirates. They were probably trophies, but Elric hated them. They were symbols of the terrible fight which had led to his blinded mind being utterly corrupted by an imagination turned in on itself! He had fought their descendants when employed by the Ilmioran Seawomen's Union.

They stepped onto a weed-grown pavement through which old trees now pushed up trunks, some grown almost as high as the great red ziggurats which stretched before them, carved with bizarre figures and shapes. Elric had some dim memory of this place. Perhaps he had visited it on one of his dream-quests as a youth. But the association was in no way pleasant. On instinct, he turned suddenly to look backward. He saw nothing but the jungle which, as silently as possible, they had trekked for the past few hours.

Duke Mitcha lowered his own longsword and rested his gauntleted hand on the haft of a busily engraved battle-axe of silver-chased steel more commonly associated with cavalry fighting. He allowed a look of scepticism to spread across his bearded face, and he shook back his black head to rid it of the damp locks obscuring his vision. He and Elric, ebony and ivory, might have been opposing pieces in a chess game. He would be an interesting opponent, perhaps on several levels. Dyvim Marluc pointed a slender finger towards the centre of the ruined city and its crumbling pyramids. "That's where we were ambushed—as we entered yonder square overlooked by that ugly building—palace, temple, whatever it is. We had made too much noise, and I think we were followed."

"You say you could not count them. A fair-sized tribe?" Princess Semilee pushed auburn hair back from her damp forehead.

"A party of perhaps a hundred." With his soft doeskin boot, Dyvim Marluc indicated fairly fresh bloodstains on the paving. "Perhaps a few more. We dispatched half that number—"

"Before you let them take you prisoner?" said Princess Viricias sharply.

Dyvim Marluc bridled. "I am a hired mercenary, madam. We followed the king's commands!"

"To do what?" The question was rhetorical. Elric suspected she had heard the answer before.

"As I said, lady, your father was anxious to reach that sandstone pyramid there, the one they have made some crude attempt to restore. He called it a palace, but I think it was some kind of temple. He took the majority of my men forward and left me to protect the rear with some Lormyrian archers, a few lancers and my chief lieutenant, Agric Inricson. You'll recall him from that seminar. The last we saw of the king he had disappeared into the palace. We fought off the savages for several hours until they fell back. Then we moved to try to rejoin the king and the rest of our men. We got as far as yonder house— the one with the walls still intact. A trap. They were waiting for us inside. Fresh warriors. I saw half my men butchered. Most of us were overwhelmed. Then we thought we saw a way free. We got almost to the river before they began shooting at us. We carried the wounded down into the boat. I now think they intended to let us go, maybe as a warning to any other expedition. That is why I think we have not been attacked. They believe no-one else will dare come to Soom."

"Or they have moved deeper into the jungle," said Moonglum, "taking their prisoners with them. Or function on an entirely different system of thought. Or are making it all up as they go along. Our own people blazing their way down the old, forgotten paths . . . Ourselves!" He spread his arms in a massive shrug.

"Or they completed their business in Soom and returned to their tribal homeland further upriver," suggested Duke Mitcha. "I agree it is most likely they would have attacked us by now if they were still in the city."

"Should we try to follow them?" Hered Dehlian did his best to hide his disquiet.

"You may do as you please," replied Elric. "My business is in Soom."

"We need all the swords we can muster." Princess Viricias glared at him.

"Indeed, my lady," Elric acknowledged. "But we agreed to lend you our aid until Soom and the rising of the full moon."

"There is some hope that Melnibonéans are still alive," said Dyvim Marluc softly.

"And I hope to be again at their disposal once the moon has risen," said Elric. "A matter of hours." He reached into his pouch and drew out the crude map he had bought in Thokora. Beside what the king had called a palace was some kind of garden, perhaps the *lunarium*, what Elric's people had called a night garden, judging by the iconography on the map. The *noibuluscus* appeared to have a religious function. Perhaps the black flower had grown there. While the others debated, he marked out the site in his mind. Timing was important. The flower had to be picked at the moment of its blooming. He and Moonglum moved away from the others. "This is where I guess the site to be . . ."

They had gone only a few steps when the brooding air was cut by a terrible sound—a high-pitched wail of agony which was suddenly cut off. The others stopped talking and listened carefully. Elric turned, questioning, into a sickening silence.

"It came from inside," Moonglum said. Duke Mitcha began to cross the square at a run, heading for the huge pyramid, the women behind him.

And then, out of a dark, ragged hole in the pyramid's wall, a scarlet figure came stumbling. Even Elric, versed in the refined tortures of his people, could not disguise his horror.

The figure might once have been a naked man. How it continued to move Elric could not guess, for every inch of skin had been flayed from scalp to feet. The red mouth moved. The throat gurgled with blood. Blue eyes, from which the lids had been removed, stared blindly before it. Every movement must have been a century of agony as it raised bloody hands before it, groping for unseen help.

The party stood stock-still as the flayed man approached. He screamed, trailing thick strings of blood behind him. With the intention of helping the man, Moonglum ran forward. Instantly, an arrow thrummed from somewhere and took him in the shoulder. He descended to his knees, an almost ludicrous expression of surprise on his face. But the arrow had failed to penetrate his mail and fell to the ground even as he raised his hand towards it. He stood up, sheepishly, drawing his long curved swords.

"Form a square!" Elric, Moonglum and Dyvim Marluc took charge, showing the others how to raise their small shields to protect their faces and upper bodies. They began to run. Moonglum ducked and picked up the long barbed arrow, darting a look of enquiry at Dyvim Marluc. He nodded, confirming that it was the same kind of shaft which had killed so many of his men. Then a whole rain of arrows came from the same direction, thudding into their shields.

"I suspect they don't plan to negotiate confrontation," said Moonglum. Elric nodded. "So it seems we're in the stew. As it were."

"They might even have released that flayed prisoner to encourage retreat."

Moonglum was puzzled. "Why, when they clearly outnumber us, would they avoid conflict?"

Still screaming, the flayed man stumbled on.

"Use the Black Sword, Elric! Use it now!" cried Dyvim Marluc.

Everything in the albino told him to do as his cousin demanded, yet still he resisted. His hand fell to the scabbarded blade.

"No!" cried Moonglum. Then he murmured, "At least, not yet."

Dyvim Marluc made to go after the flayed man. Elric stopped him. "No-one can follow him. If we break ranks we are all dead."

"Then use the damned sword!"

Instead, Elric reached down and carefully, by its blade, pulled a spear from his shield without breaking the light shaft. Now he had a more useful weapon. Stormbringer stirred against his thigh. He heard it murmur, but he deafened himself to its voice, to the tones of Arioch, Duke of Chaos, urging him to do as Dyvim Marluc demanded. They were looking to him for leadership, even as the bloody figure, still intermittently screaming, disappeared into a jungle opening like a maw to swallow him.

Duke Mitcha stood trembling, his eyes blank, maybe mad. The acrid stink of the skinned man's bloody flesh was in their nostrils. "Ugh." The duke spat. "I'll never eat again!"

Seeking the best cover, Elric made the small party fall back towards the pyramid and the high-walled annex from which the man had come. He had his own motives for investigating the compound. As they crowded in, one of the women screamed, and the lad fell back retching.

Princess Semilee turned her head away, but her twin sister, pushing black hair from her face, forced herself to stare down at the blood-soaked ground. Laid out on it, like a suit of clothes, was the flayed man's skin, neatly separated from the body by an expert hand, including the hair of the head and the man's private parts. The operation would have taken a long time. Looking at the pelt, they imagined the victim's horror and pain.

Some attentive pupil of his own Doctor Jest? The albino admired the work if not the intent. But Elric saw something else, pushing its way through the dark mud created by the man's blood and urine. He barely resisted falling to his knees and staring at the small, dark shoot exactly the same as the one he had seen in a dozen grimoires and herbals. The *noibuluscus*. The Black Anemonë.

"So your instincts were right." Moonglum spoke so softly only Elric could hear him. They stood in Soom's ancient *lunarium*. From the histories and geographies Elric had read, he had expected something larger. Clearly, the compound, now roofless, had been roofed in crystal, perhaps even a great prism concentrating the moon's rays, used to grow the sacred flower which blossomed once every hundred years. And would bloom tonight, if the scrolls and books he had consulted told the truth. Then Elric was struck by a realisation. The arrival of the savages was no coincidence. "The man's flaying, the draining of his fluids into the ground was a ritual. Those degenerates, doubtless descendants of Soom's ancients, were gathering to witness the black flower's blooming." The shoot was growing before his eyes, a tightly closed bud surrounded by black, spikey leaves. It took a sinuously animal-like shape as it writhed like a prisoner in its strange environment.

Moonglum reached his hand towards it, but his friend stopped him.

"The *noibuluscus* must be plucked at the optimum moment. We must wait until the moon is full. It's not even twilight. We must somehow hold out against the savages until midnight." He had waited so many months, he could feel the last of his strength ebbing out of him. He could think only of his own immediate needs.

Dyvim Marluc stared at his cousin in contempt. The princesses, too, knew what they had found, for their father had spoken of it. He hoped to find it. Perhaps the *noibuluscus* was the treasure their father sought? Even Moonglum was troubled.

Elric cared nothing for the thoughts or opinions of anyone. At last he need depend no longer either on herbs or hellsword. This, in turn, freed him from Arioch, from all those hideous pacts which had led, in his mind, at least, to the death of Cymoril and gave pause to wedding Zarozinia. He knew a deep satisfaction. Everything he had hoped for was coming true. After tonight, his dependence on the supernatural would be over. All he had to do was survive . . .

"We're heavily outnumbered, Elric," Moonglum was reminding him. "We're trapped."

"This place can be readily defended," Elric replied. "The only entrances are that gap in the wall, through which we came, and that smaller doorway or whatever it was—" He pointed to a square, regular opening in the main structure of the great pyramid itself. "It seems to be some sort of outlet, perhaps for water, used in the original construction." The battle-leader he was trained to be, he positioned Dyvim Marluc and Duke Mitcha at the small, regular opening. The others were told to watch for activity beyond the wall. Any attackers could only come through one at a time. The walls themselves were too high to permit spears or arrows to be aimed at them.

When Elric turned to Princess Viricias to explain this, she looked directly into his eyes and said firmly, "We are here to rescue my father, Prince Elric . . ."

"And to save any of my men who survive," Dyvim Marluc added, peering down into the square opening and then leaning to look up, as if it was, indeed, some kind of sluice from above. "If only we could calculate the enemy numbers, we'd be better able to determine our strategy."

Elric ignored them. He had already told them his purpose. While their mutual interests coincided, he would work with them. If they conflicted, he would have to concentrate on the black flower's blossoming.

Moonglum went to stare through the gap in the wall at the horizon. The sun was already setting. He had long since accepted that Elric was driven by his own needs, but he had thought there was another quality in his friend, something which might just possibly on occasion put the greater good above his own. He shook his head, trying to clear it. What made him so capricious, torn by such terrible conflicts? Then he had a new thought. Perhaps the savages, who had already demonstrated their sophisticated strategies, did not want to frighten them from the city at all? Perhaps the party had been deliberately offered this route. He whirled, and as their eyes met, it was clear Elric shared the same suspicion.

Elric cursed his desperation and need. "Is there time for a new strategy?" Hadn't he already found what he had come to Soom to take? Why not do, however, what the mysterious tribesmen least expected and attack the pyramid? Apart from himself, there were only two experienced soldiers amongst them. True, the women were brave and willing, even trained to arms to a degree, yet they were scarcely strong enough for an assault. Not unless most of the defenders were already dead . . .

Suddenly a shout came from above. Elric could not see who it was, but Hered Dehlian, furthest away from the main wall, looked up, and Princess Semilee exclaimed, "Father! We are here to save you!"

A distant voice replied. "Fools! Now we are *all* doomed. Get out of here while you can. You men have brought my daughters into danger!"

"He lives!" Princess Semilee hardly listened to her father's words. "Oh, thank Sirob and Yenob! He lives!" She and her sister stared upward with radiant faces.

"Great king!" cried Duke Mitcha. "If they speak a civilised tongue, tell them we'll pay any ransom they demand."

"Get out of that cursed compound if you can. Now! Get into the jungle. They do not want our gold. They want our flesh—ah!"

"Father!" Princess Viricias was beside herself with emotion. "He's gone. They took him back!"

"He's right. We can't stay here." Dyvim Marluc feared more for his men than for the king. "We must help them, Elric. Draw the sword! You are the greatest sorcerer in our history. You can help them! You owe them that!"

Moonglum said quietly, "Elric. Friend. You must."

"I am losing strength. It's almost gone. My sorcery is all but exhausted. If . . ." But he realised he could not continue as he had. Every instinct was against it. Cruel his people might be, but they had loyalty one to the other.

The last of his herbs were gone. His only hope now was that he could live until the *noibuluscus* bloomed. Even then, there was no certainty. A spell of the kind they wished him to cast would drain any vitality left him. If the spell failed, would he be too weak, then, to help his countrymen? Could he do nothing while another victim was flayed alive? Yet, not for the first time, he had vowed never to draw the Black Sword again . . . He cursed himself for his own weakness.

His cousin was yelling something at him. Beyond the tall, red walls of the ruin the blood-sun was beginning to sink behind the dark jungle foliage. Twilight was coming. In a short while the full moon would rise, and, if Elric's understanding was right, the black flower's petals would open and begin almost instantly to fall. At that point, they must be gathered. He must collect the seeds so he could raise fresh plants somewhere. Or was this red mud the only kind in which the plant would grow . . . ?

Still he hesitated. It would be worse than ironic if, only an hour or so before those petals opened, he lacked the energy to pick them.

"Elric! Do you not owe us *something*?" Dyvim Marluc's bared sword almost threatened his cousin. "Do you want to see your remaining kin slain as—as that poor wretch"—and he pointed at the skin laid out on the wet ground—"was slain?"

Moonglum said nothing. Clearly, he shared the Dragon Master's opinion. Elric lowered his eyes.

"No," he said.

From somewhere above came another prolonged and terrible scream.

The albino drew a deep breath, fingering the necklace he had worn within his linen since receiving it. It had become warmer. Almost hot. Through that strange amber, he was channelling a way to find the sleeping creature. He had not merely learned the casting of spells at the seminar, but spells of defence, also. The beads were communicating something. His eyes stared as if into a vision. His lips began to move, silently forming the words of a tongue more ancient than that of Soom, more ancient than Melniboné's. Words he had learned in a dream-quest, long ago, sleeping upon the dream couches of

Imrryr, when he had forged certain alliances. Aided by the supernatural beads, his mind began to travel out along the strange network of roads that had once taken him through the many dimensions of the multiverse. The necklace was some sort of conduit. He had thought it merely a charm against danger, but it was much more than that.

He lifted his head, his eyes now shining with an alien brightness. And he shouted a word which burst like a blaze of voices upon the agonised ears of all near him. Yet the others could not make sense of the word they heard. They did not recognise the name. Only Elric heard and recognised it. And it drained his life-force from him even as it left his lips.

"*Saaasuurrasssh!*" he said. A passing breath of wind. Hardly a word at all.

ELEVEN

Kalakak

SOMEWHERE under THE river, in a dimension of waters and dank foliage, Elric's voice found a supernatural resonance, stirring the memory of a creature which opened its jaws a fraction and passed a long, leathery tongue between pointed teeth. Its eyes were shut in the sleep of centuries and would not open. The creature's curiosity was not yet aroused. Indeed, it still dreamed dark, sluggish dreams of death, of things devoured and things to be devoured. It was some time before it recognised the word which had awakened it and some further time before it recalled that *Sasuras* was perhaps one of its waking names, though not the name by which it identified itself. That name was Kalakak, and it knew that somewhere it had kindred which spoke to it, called to it. But Kalakak still dreamed that it lay curled in the egg its mother had laid somewhere in the multiverse so many millennia ago. Kalakak lay safely in the mud on the bank of a vast river, whose further bank could not be seen. The world river wound between mud flats, and beyond the mud flats was the rich warmth of mile-high thick-boled trees, branches twisting and curling and full of living things, all of which tempted its appetite.

Kalakak remembered its appetite. It began to salivate. It remembered *Sasuras* . . . that name . . . the name which called it not to feed but to serve, and it was therefore somewhat slower in its response . . .

Saaasuurrasssh

Kalakak's tail twitched. Its limbs began to sting, and its eyes moved beneath heavy lids.

Saaasuurrasssh

Kalakak's nostrils moved and tasted murky, amniotic air. Something flickered in the darkness; veins of red fire, streaks of deep green and blue. And Kalakak took a massive breath.

Elric lay in Moonglum's arms. Dyvim Marluc looked on, almost sympathetic. Somewhere, near the ruined gap in the wall, Hered Dehlian thrashed and groaned and clawed at an arrow which had found a gap between his helmet and his throat. Princess Semilee stood beside him, trying to stop him from moving while she attempted to snap the head of the arrow from the shaft. It stuck out from the side of his neck. She spoke to him as soothingly as she could. Elsewhere Duke Mitcha and Princess Viricias peered around their shield rims. A makeshift brand in her hand cast sputtering light across the compound. Out in the square, shadows shifted, running swiftly here and there, shooting arrows, flinging lances. Only by accident had an arrow struck Hered Dehlian. The young man dropped to one knee, his eyes wide with horror as the princess at last managed to get the shaft out of him and staunch the blood with his own torn shirt. The arrow had not struck the jugular.

Weakly, Elric climbed to his feet, balancing with the spear, the steel sword in his right hand. From above, men's voices were shouting, and it seemed to him that the imprisoned Melnibonéans had broken free and were fighting their captors. Certainly, something was happening up there. He looked over to where the Black Anemonë grew, its tendrils pulsing and lengthening with every passing moment, the flower not yet opened. His mouth was dry; his arms and legs shook. He had difficulty breathing.

"Elric, you're too enfeebled." Moonglum spoke reluctantly. "The spell did not work."

Dyvim Marluc was grim. "There is only the Black Sword now."

Still Elric shook his head. Trembling, he steadied himself with the spear and, sword raised with difficulty, turned to Princess Viricias. "I led us into a trap, I admit. But I promise I will do all I can now . . ."

She cursed a soldier's curse and all but spat in his face. "I thought you, amongst all men, would be the one to help us. Now my father faces dreadful death and your own people, too. You carry an unhappy weird upon you, Elric of Melniboné. Oh, how I wish I had not let you join us . . ."

He managed to respond, his smile ironic, panting. "Madam, you must try to wait until midnight before you condemn me entirely . . ."

Another flight of arrows came pouring through the gap. By now they had taken cover. Hered Dehlian had stopped screaming and sat against a wall breathing rapidly, the rag pressed on his wound which no longer bled badly. Princess Semilee, sword in hand, darted a quick glance around the ragged gap. "I can see little in this blackness. It sounds as if they've gone back into the ruins or the forest."

Then, as if to contradict her, from above several spears rattled down uselessly. The object of both attacks was to demoralise them. Moonglum's attention was on the *noibuluscus*, "It's bigger! Look!" It reached towards the starlit sky now touched by the first faint traces of the rising moon. Even though Elric had studied all there was to study about the plant, its rate of growth astonished him. Was he going to die there, with the object of his quest so close? Watching it go through its entire cycle while unable to make use of its petals?

"Elric! Take the buds!" Moonglum helped his friend to his feet. "That attempted Summoning weakened you too much." Yet still he refused to untangle the wire binding his sword. "Where is Arioch? Is he distracted by events in the Higher Worlds?"

The long stem of the Black Anemonë stretched high towards the night sky and then curled downwards. It was only as it reached out towards the wounded Hered Dehlian that Elric realised the thing seemed to be scenting for something. Questing for fresh blood.

Moonglum cried, "No!" and leapt forward, twin sabres whirling, slashing at the plant, which reared back, hissing.

Blood had encouraged the plant's growth. "It needs more blood! It's feeding." Moonglum's shout alerted the albino, who cursed himself. That was why they had been tricked into entering the compound. They were food for the black flower.

This knowledge seemed to electrify the albino. Shouting an oath, his voice quavering, Elric shook his fist up at the window—to be answered by a haphazard rain of missiles. "Those savages want us wounded but not dead. That's why they took so many prisoners. To feed the plant!" A plant which drank blood and souls as thirstily as his runesword.

Above him scarred, wicked little faces glared down at them. Out in the night the other savages prowled, their only intent being to keep the party inside the compound.

As it had dawned on Dyvim Marluc that they were the intended food of the black plant, he began to whistle an old, complicated Melnibonéan melody: "The Drowned Boy."

"What do you say, cousin?" Elric asked. "Would you wait like a pig in the slaughterhouse? Or would you die fighting these filthy little devils?"

His kinsman darted him a look of approval and began to move towards the ragged gap in the wall.

Before he could reach his object, he drew a startled breath and stepped backwards, staring. Turning sideways on to the plant, Moonglum peered into the gloom.

There was something else out there now. A much larger, heavier shadow. Some kind of beast?

And then Elric collapsed and Duke Mitcha came blundering past them, screaming, to flee into the night. They looked back. "Gods! It's so fast!" Moonglum gasped. He tried to help, but he was already carrying Elric. The plant writhed and shifted on the ground. It had seized poor young Hered Dehlian, who now struggled in its coils. It was squeezing him so that his blood streamed from his orifices to be sucked up by the plant's tapering bud. "Ugh. The poor bastard's dead already!" What had been a thin stem was now a fair-sized trunk, and as they watched, horrified, it thickened visibly, sucking the flesh and blood from the youth's now limp body. Then it dropped back to the ground, slithering into the spread-out skin of the flayed man, filling it.

A travesty of a human creature now swayed before them, its tendrils occupying the skin like legs and arms. And from each branch now, more tendrils sprang, like fingers and toes, reaching towards the five who remained in the compound. The plant, distinctly manlike in form, continued to grow.

And still, as Elric knew, it was not yet moonrise. Still the blood-plant sought more sustenance.

With a yell, Dyvim Marluc now flung himself forward and began to hack at the disgusting limbs. The sisters imitated him, their scimitars flashing in the growing light from the sky. Moonglum tried hard to hold his friend upright. Elric did his best to summon the last of his strength. He fell forward, stabbing at the monstrous thing. Anger and disappointed rage empowered him. He had wanted no more than a normal life of the kind enjoyed by others. But his curiosity about the nature of the world and his origins, how and why his people differed from humans, it had led him towards his death!

Again—and again—he thrust the sword, but he made no impression upon the thing.

A noise behind them. Duke Mitcha came shrieking back into the compound. His armour was pierced in a dozen places by arrows. His helmet had been knocked from his head, which streamed with blood. He gibbered and pointed behind him and then fell to the ground.

They tried to pull him free of the Black Anemonë, but the gigantic plant was too strong. Its tendrils wrapped around the duke's body and dragged him to itself. He gave one last, long perfect yodelling cry as he was lifted into the air, and then suddenly the full moon rose above the high wall and illuminated the scene, the struggling Duke Mitcha, the five figures, weapons in their hands, gathered around the swaying, manlike plant.

Then they turned to see what Duke Mitcha had seen. What had caused him to flee back into the compound.

"Kalakak," said Elric.

And he smiled.

TWELVE

The Black Flower's Blossoming

THE TWO WOMEN stared in horror as the creature Elric called Kalakak pushed its massive bulk against the gap in the compound, breaking down the ancient brick, its cold green eyes glaring, its long snout opening to reveal teeth the length of swords and the thickness of a man's arm. In the moonlight its scales glistened with water. Its massive tail thrashed this way and that, scattering the corpses of the savages who tried to attack it. When it saw Elric, it lumbered towards him, and from its vast, red throat something like language sounded. Only Elric could understand everything it said, but Dyvim Marluc recognised a form of High Melnibonéan which he and the Phoorn dragons spoke between themselves.

The monstrous reptile looked down at Elric, who was again supported on Moonglum's shoulder. Its eyes were full of profound memory, of old wisdom and a new thirst. "You summoned me, old friend?"

"I thought you had not heard me, Lord Kalakak. I called to you in the name of our ancient pact. I presumed you still slept." The thing looked like nothing as much as a gigantic crocodile, but its snout and tail were more slender, its legs and webbed feet longer. Like certain dragons, it had a tall, spiked crest on its neck and head. Its colour was neither green, nor black, nor brown. It was not an earthly colour. As it moved, its scales clashed softly, the sound of wind over drying leather.

"True it will be a millennium or two before I am fully rested. Summoning me has exhausted you! Now I am at your service. At least before sleep claims me again. Unlike our mutual kin, the Phoorn, I need rather more sleep than a mere century or two." The symmetrical jaws clacked and smacked almost as if Kalakak joked. "Remember, I cannot kill for you. Otherwise, you must tell me what you need, before I return to the river below the river and close my eyes. There is a dream I need to continue. There is destruction and recon-struction coming, and if you die, all destiny is doomed to turn askew and eat its own. I do what I can, and my kin can help. A weft here, a woof there. The shuttle must not stop. There is a great tapestry being woven, its materials so subtle they can barely be detected in certain dimensions, and we are part of it, making certain of its accuracy, even as we play the golden Game of Time and continue to quest for Paradise."

As the manlike plant, distracted, began to devour Duke Mitcha, Elric pointed towards the high window. "We need to reach that opening, yonder. Can you help us, cousin?"

"Use my crest to climb." Steadying his scaly bulk with his tail, Kalakak lifted himself on his huge hindquarters, his snout extending to the window from which the Das king, Tilus Kreek, had last called to his daughters. The black flower swayed in the background, unable to assess this new potential danger, as if for all the world a sentient thing. The albino was dangerously weak, but he could still call out instructions to the others. They began to clamber up the reptile's massive back. Below them the black plant thrashed and screeched. Above them the dwarfish cannibals crowded to the window and stared in disbelieving consternation. With a yell as bloodthirsty as any warrior's Princess Viricias led the way through the window, her scimitar tak-ing off a head as smoothly as if she were cutting daisies in a field. Then she disappeared inside, Dyvim Marluc and Princess Semilee behind her.

Elric and Moonglum were the last to reach the window. With a word of thanks to Lord Kalakak, the albino dropped into the room. The princesses and his cousin had already taken their toll of the savages. Bodies lay everywhere.

Red revenge had been taken at last. The remaining savages scrambled into the outer corridors and scattered as fast as they could go. They left their prisoners bound but otherwise unharmed.

Weeping with joy, the princesses ran towards their straight-backed but naked father. As they cut his bonds, he stared at them in astonishment. He, like the captured Melnibonéans, had not expected to survive this night.

Rubbing circulation back into limbs, King Tilus Kreek crossed to a corner of the room where weapons were stacked and found his own sword amongst them, returning it to his scabbard. He was a tall, old man with a short grey beard and long hair. He drew on a padded surcoat over mail and sweated in the heat of the night. Moonlight streamed into the room, showing Moonglum, Elric and Dyvim Marluc the captured warriors, whom they set about releasing. Elric leaned beside the window taking great gasps of air, scarcely able to stand. Below, the ground shuddered. Presumably, Lord Kalakak had dropped back to all four gigantic legs. Looking down, Elric saw that oddly coloured tail disappearing from the compound. Out in the moonlight, the black flower still hissed and slithered and quested for fresh blood.

Swiftly, the released warriors recovered their weapons, then embraced their commander, Dyvim Marluc. To Elric, they offered more formal thanks, clearly surprised by his ruined condition. Some showed concern as he leaned weakly against the window frame, still gasping for breath. The summoning of Kalakak had almost exhausted what was left of his strength, and the climb had taken the rest.

"We owe our lives to our emperor," Dyvim Marluc explained. "Without him, gentlemen, we should all be dead."

The fine-featured Bright Empire soldiers remained reserved in their greetings, but some were prepared to accept the truth of their captain's short speech and bowed briefly to the Prince of Ruins, best known as Kinslayer, whose treachery had destroyed their homeland. Yet their desire for unity and continuity was so great they found themselves following their hereditary emperor. Elric expected nothing from them, save acknowledgement of his rank, for none denied that he was their rightful emperor, named by his dying father as the true inheritor of the Ruby Throne. Being the creatures of habit they were, they were incapable of refusing to follow him.

"How easily can we leave Soom?" said Princess Viricias. "We are still outnumbered by the savages. Has your reptilian ally departed the city, Prince Elric?"

"He was the best I could summon under present conditions. He helped us, but he is forbidden to kill, which is the thing he yearns to do most. Like our Imrryrian dragons, he must sleep a year for every hour or so that he's awake. He is old and large. He will sleep longer. He returns to his rest."

"So we have no other ally against the savages?" asked the princess, glancing significantly at his sword.

"Only our own courage and cunning, my lady." Elric turned again to glance through the window and stumbled suddenly backward. A thick, black tendril appeared. Next moment it was curling through the opening. Moonglum yelled to his companions. "Quickly. Back down the stairs. We'll fight our way through the savages to the river." Already the tendril had come snaking in, as if scenting blood. Elric cocked his head. He could almost hear it sniffing out his remaining life-stuff.

Led by Dyvim Marluc and Tilus Kreek, with the twin princesses following close behind and Elric leaning on his friend, the Melnibonéans poured from the room and down the broad deep winding bloodstained stone steps within the pyramid.

It was almost with a sense of anticlimax that they ran out into the open square to find no enemies. Warily, back to back, they moved slowly out through the alien ruins towards the jungle. Half fainting, entirely dependent on the stocky Eastlander, Elric came last. From the darkness, spears and arrows flew. A Melnibonéan sobbed with pain as an arrow took him in the arm. Without another sound, he pulled the arrow through and discarded it. The remaining Lormyrian archer gathered the arrows for his own quiver. Their shields absorbed the worst of the onslaught, protecting Elric and Moonglum. With a hissed curse, the archer fitted an arrow to his string and sent it back into the invisible pack.

Two more men were lost to enemy spears before they reached the edge of the jungle. In the moonlight they could retrace their original progress from the river. The undergrowth remained dense. With Dyvim Marluc leading, they moved slowly on.

For the first time, the savages made a direct attack. Tattooed faces, white, glaring eyes, ochre skins and an assortment of crude axes, spears, swords and lances suddenly surrounded them. No longer was the strategy to herd them into the compound to become food for the Black Anemonë. Now the cannibals sought only to kill the survivors, so that the man-flower would not devour the degenerate Soomians themselves. Their caution was gone. Moonglum, guarding Elric, who was still barely able to hold his blade, did his best to fight back. Then Princess Viricias took the albino's arm onto her own shoulder and helped defend him as they stumbled on. Mostly, the enemy's weapons fell on shields or were blocked by steel. Every so often one of Elric's party would groan and blood would flow. But they could smell the river now. If the savages had not destroyed their boat, the remains of the two expeditions might still escape.

Then the surviving savages had fallen back. For a moment the jungle was still. No animals called; nothing moved. The brilliant moonlight cast deep shadows. Some of them seemed to shift and curl into alarming shapes. "Maybe," murmured Moonglum, "they've lost their stomach for the fight?" King Tilus Kreek let out a long relieved sigh—just as a huge, manlike shape loomed up behind them. A giant, with long, curling fingers waving as, momentarily unsteady, it balanced itself in their wake. The Black Anemonë lumbered relentlessly after fresh food. Any food so long as it pulsed with human blood. Then, suddenly, a dark arm shot into their ranks. The last Lormyrian archer shrieked and beat at the huge shape as he was lifted into the air.

They watched helplessly. "In some way, we all live by feeding off our own," murmured Moonglum, turning away.

"We are finished," murmured King Tilus. "We cannot defeat that thing. I know its power. I should never have led my men here. Now my daughters will die obscenely, thanks to my folly. You go on. I will stay here and try to slow it . . ." It was clear he had no hope of defeating the hugely bloated manlike tree. Only a few hours before it had been a tiny shoot. Now it came swiftly after them, gaining speed with every kill. Whenever it paused, it plucked another man from the jungle. It was indiscriminate. Savages, too, were lifted kicking and shouting into its maw. They had no chance of reaching the river before they were caught and their life-stuff added to its size, speed and energy.

"We will fight together," said Dyvim Marluc, coming to stand beside the king.

Moonglum drew his twin sabres. "Rest your back on mine, friend Elric. Sadly, we'll die disappointed deaths. Killed by the very treasure we sought."

"No." Elric moved to join his friend in their familiar fighting stance. He sighed. "Get the women and the rest of our fighters to the boat. I will stay to slow its advance . . ." And he readied his blade.

The savages had not fled after all. Realising that they were now also food for the *noibuluscus*, they flung themselves again at the Melnibonéans, perhaps hoping their blood would satisfy the black flower. This time Princess Semilee gasped as a saw-toothed blade slashed her arm. Her father roared his anger, and his sword took the attacker in the throat. Blood spurted. Another black tendril came out of the night and seized the slain savage.

"Go!" cried the albino, almost falling. "All of you! Go!" And his fingers began to fumble at the copper wire securing his sword.

Moonglum gripped his shoulder. "Elric. We may yet . . ."

"No. We'll all be slain. And for what? Take everyone and hold the boat for a little while. I'll try to join you. If not, well then, I'm missed by one friend, at least. And a debt will be partly paid."

Five long fingers, black petals, a hideous, grasping travesty of a massive human hand, reached for his arm. He drew back in horror, his own feeble fingers trying desperately to untie the thongs securing his sword's hilt to his belt.

Moonglum paused and helped the albino to untie the wire. Then he turned and with a shout began to run into the jungle, herding the little party of survivors before him.

The Black Anemonë rose up out of the tangle of silhouetted forest, the full moon outlining its writhing head, while moonlight revealed its broad, waving arms and hands. A thin, terrible whistling noise escaped the cluster of long leaves surrounding what resembled a mouth. From under its feet, a score of savages rose to surround Elric.

For a moment the tattooed cannibals stood there confronting him. The silvery light emphasised the whiteness of his skin. No doubt they saw him as some kind of phantom, the chief source of their plan's failure. With deliberate movements, they began to close in on him, watched by the creature they had created through their barbaric blood sacrifice.

Elric grinned.

Reaching for the great broadsword at his hip, he drew it like silk from its scabbard. So finely balanced was the black blade, he could hold it easily in one hand, almost like a rapier. The sword murmured and whispered in his grasp, and he felt a sudden rush of energy suffuse him. He stroked the hilt, and the blade almost warmed to stroke him back. A thrill of ecstasy that others might feel in love-making.

Then he began his work.

Elric's eyes blazed with red, unholy light, reflecting the flickering runes which ran up and down his blade. He swung Stormbringer first one way and then another, as if to display its power. Pale fire glimmered. Gold fire to brilliant, pulsing scarlet with black runes murmuring, moving restlessly up and down the sword's length. He felt it lurch and writhe, alive in his hands, and then the blade began to croon. *Long and low the runeblade crooned / and all before it fell a-neath his tune.* The albino's lips twisted in crazy delight as he stepped towards the savages, now standing between him and the parasitic monster they had raised. Elric's chest rose and fell with deep, strong breaths. He knew a pleasure he had all but forgotten. And, as that familiar black radiance poured from the blade and its song rose and fell in a melody that to him at least was beautiful, he remembered why the Black Sword had been so hard to put aside. Why his addiction had taken so long to conquer. "*Aaaah!*" Again he swung the blade, but this time it was not in display.

"*Arioch! Arioch! Lord of the Seven Darks! Arioch! Blood and souls for my lord Arioch!*" This time the black, strangely wrought metal sliced into flesh and bone. Heads sprang from necks like so many weeds in a hayfield. Arms flew into the foliage. Legs buckled and torsos were hacked in half. Terrified savages tried to flee but were now trapped between Elric and the Black Anemonë, drunk on the smell of ruined flesh. It was down on the jungle floor, sucking the blood which pumped from the remains of their bodies. It clucked and yelped with dreadful glee. It showed them an appalling travesty of a human face and body. A few men managed to scuttle past the monster they had brought into being, only to be snared by its prescient tendrils.

Elric yelled his mockery at the creature. "Come, Black Flower! Come, beautiful, and drink more rich Melnibonéan blood, sweet as evil! Come to me. My blood is thin, but it is yours if you can take it!"

The *noibuluscus* paused, staring from its strange head, around which great, spiked leaves curled like a living crown. It bent, reaching out its long branches towards this laughing, white-faced, puny little thing of flesh and thin blood which challenged it and which, perhaps, it sensed as the agent of its own frustration.

Voicing the ancient battle-yells of his ancestors, Elric ran at the Black Anemonë. "Arioch! My lord Arioch! Blood and souls for thee and thine! *I present thee with this sacrifice!*" The life-force of all those he had killed seared through his veins, filling him with preternatural energy, with a wonderful lust he had almost forgotten, but always craved. To his surprise, however, the albino felt no answer from his patron Lord of the Higher Worlds . . .

The gleaming tendril hands reached out to seize him. Elric dodged them, hacking at legs like two trunks standing across the path above him. The hands curled down to try to grasp him. A weird shriek escaped the monster as the black blade slashed at the writhing fingers, sending them flying into the undergrowth.

"*Arioch! Blood and souls for my lord Arioch!*" The albino's features were contorted in unhuman delight. Stolen life-force flowed into him, yet Arioch's response was almost feeble.

"Arioch! Save me, Arioch! I bring you fresh souls!"

And from somewhere in the darkness came a low, mocking chuckle, as if Elric's patron demon had always known that he and the sword would feed again.

At last the black flower was down, but still the arms whipped and thrust and grasped for the albino. Still the Black Sword sang. Monstrous branches transformed themselves into snakes, coiling around his body, his arms his legs. But too much energy now pulsed through him. He easily broke free, the blade rising and falling, rising and falling, like a woodsman's axe in the forest. Suddenly, he was tireless. With every blow the albino's energy increased, while the plant weakened. The head darted at Elric, the cluster of long, tough leaves spearing towards his face, trying to suck it from his shoulders, but he dodged it cleverly, still laughing with that wild, maniacal glee, as much in his blade's power as it was in his.

A huge blow. Another. Squealing and chittering, parts of the plant tried to escape now, slithering off into the undergrowth. From head to toe, Elric was covered in black sap, but still he hacked at the thing, finally pausing to reach out and rip the crown of leaves from around the ruined head. To snatch a handful of large seeds, beating like so many hearts, from the centre. He stepped back, panting. His body sang and thrilled with the force pouring through it. He lifted his head in exultation, shouting his mocking triumph at the moon.

"*ARIOCH!*" he growled.

A tendril began to curl itself around his leg. To his horror, he realised that the plant was re-forming itself. He stepped back and with the point of his sword threw the branch as far as it would go. Then he turned and ran towards the river.

BOOK THREE

IN WHICH OUR HEROES DISCOVER A LOST PAST

Turning like baffled lodestones, our two heroes rode this way and that across an alien world in Elric's search for the solutions to mysteries and their own distressing poverty. Their adventure became familiar and boring, and they began to look for differences. Selling their not unskilful or unwanted services and their extraordinary weapons to whoever offered the highest price or most intriguing adventure, until, weary of slaughter and destruction, they sensed new, undefeatable forces gaining power ever since they had arrived in the World Below almost two years before. Disappointed in holding treasure, if not finding it, they rode across this old world with only one ambition remaining—a need to return to the world they had left. But more than one great Lord of the Higher Worlds considered using the pair for their own ends. And from this threat, Elric, too, would have to make a careful defence . . .

O'er the mountains rode Orlando Funk.
From out of Faeyrie-Land came he;
Brother to the swift Nihrain,
Cousin, father, sister, swain.
Mystic spells were his to spend,
And sorcery? Sorcery was his friend.

The Ballad of Orlando Funk
(Æerdri's version, 600 AD)

The Witnesses alone may wake the world
Returning blood to blood and man to man,
For they have seen a pale blade forged
And wait until the sword shall wake again!

Ibid.

THIRTEEN

Knights

THE FULL MOON still brightened the dark waters as they rowed out into midstream and began to follow the current away from Soom. Dyvim Marluc, seven Melnibonéans, the King of the Das, his two daughters and Moonglum. In the stern of the boat, taking no part in the rowing, sat a solitary figure. He was now washed clean of the filth that had covered him. His pale hand rested on the pommel of a scabbarded black broadsword. Crimson, gloomy eyes stared into another world, seeing nothing of the others.

After some time, Tilus Kreek made his way to where Elric sat and placed a hand on his shoulder. "I must thank you, prince, for all you did tonight. I know from your friend and your kinsmen that it was no easy decision. You saved our lives. Perhaps, too, you saved our souls. I can only imagine the cost to you."

Elric turned those brooding eyes upon the Das. He nodded slowly. Then he reached into his purse, feeling what writhed there, almost like human flesh. He drew the stuff out. A bunch of already drying black petals which still moved with a life of their own. A few large pods which also had a fleshy look to them. "Here," he said. "I have no further use for these. I sought an impossible remedy for my condition. I should have known the only real remedy is the one I carry with me." He held the petals and spores of the *noibuluscus* towards the king. But Tilus Kreek shook his ageing head.

"I thank thee, Elric. We both sought to save something by the cultivation of the Black Anemonë. And both of us risked far too much in its pursuit. Perhaps we are lucky to have learned something and still have our lives?"

Dyvim Marluc shook his head when Elric next offered him the petals and pods, but he drew something from his own sleeve, a small scroll secured with thread. "That's the cursed map that brought us here! 'Tis no longer any use to me, but it might help you find your own destiny." And, as Elric reached for it, he laughed and threw the map over the side. "But you will never know, will you, cousin? As I shall never know what became of my wives and children after you betrayed us to the pirates. I doubt I'd envy you that relic or any other emanating from this damned place! But you shall never know. You will soon be as lost in this alien world as I am, without allies or real friends."

"Perhaps." Elric showed no emotion. He turned away as Moonglum leaned over the side to watch the disappearing map. Then, with a sudden movement, the albino took the petals and scattered them overboard onto the murky, glistening water. For a moment they wriggled on the surface, like fish, and then swam out of sight. He threw the pods after them. It was just possible the current would carry them downriver and even out into the sea. One day they might even find fresh soil in which to take root. Whether they would ever again be nurtured by human blood, find form in human skin, however, was unlikely. "It's a relief to see so much gone of that vampiric thing." He appeared to find no irony in his remark.

Turning away, Moonglum smiled. Unlike his friend he was only partly a romantic. The realist in him fingered the petals in his purse as well as a damp scrap of map, for he remembered other romantic gestures his haughty friend had come to regret.

As the king moved discreetly back to join his other daughter amidships, Princess Viricias came to sit beside Elric, her face flushing as she looked boldly up into his dangerous eyes. "And will you seek a substitute for the black flower?" she asked.

Taking her hand, he shook his head. "My lady, the sword will have to serve me for my usual sustenance. Meanwhile, I have other consolations. Though still no real answer to the mysteries of my ancestry."

Yet, even as she responded to his touch, he looked away again, as if hoping to see something familiar in that dense, unpleasant forest.

⊙   ⊙   ⊙

Some two years later

THE RAIN HAD ceased. A low sun pierced clouds of morning mist as two well-armed men, one tall and lean, an albino, the other short and sturdy, a redhead, riding hefty ponies and leading another, left the ruins of Tinak. The once-walled town had until lately been the prize in a long and vicious fight. The sickening stink of burned wood, fired thatch, spilled blood and decaying flesh still hung in the air.

The riders took the trail towards distant snowy peaks rising behind a massive oak forest whose trunks grew so close together they appeared to form a single green-topped wall of darkness.

"Our taciturn host swore this road would take us to the mountains rimming World's Edge. Maybe he merely told us that to be rid of us. He fears this mythical warrior-wizard from the West! Ramada Sabaru, I suspect, is a myth or a fiction of some kind!" Pushing back his russet hood, the redhead raised himself in his stirrups, shading his eyes. His features bore a tired ruggedness they had not possessed when he and Elric met to begin this adventure. "But it looks from here as if the trail stops at the forest. Is he sending us into more trouble?"

The albino seemed to sleep in the saddle, his strange gaze fixed on the horizon. Frustrated, his friend turned to address, with elaborate courtesy, the ruined fields around them.

"Since the Four Cities fell, those scavenging bands spread like spring muck everywhere! The tribes are scattered, living off what little they can. This Western wizard, Lord Ramada Sabaru? Should he or someone else unite them . . ." Turning to his friend. "Can't I persuade you to end our quest and get back to where we can board the ship that brought us here?"

Elric appeared not to hear.

"Aside from that sad coven of starving warlocks and their unfortunate serpent, we have avoided supernatural conflict for over a year," Moonglum pointed out. "The Chaos Lords appear to dispute this region no more. I have remained loyal to the Republican cause wherever it's established, and to the Rule of the Balance. I have sworn fealty neither to Chaos nor to Law. I have adhered to all my principles as, Elric, have you! And now? We are pursued into mountains at wintertime!" He shrugged and shook his head. "Wintertime! Novices!"

"We're as likely to find such a ship as you mean in a port *ahead* of us as behind now for we have crossed, as it were, the egg's central divide and are on our way to the rim again. Your own geographical logic suggests it." Elric continued to stare into the faraway future or perhaps the distant past. "There's no retreat for the likes of us. We've had that truism confirmed a thousand times! When gods debate, men struggle. When gods struggle, men die. Hungry fighting men are everywhere! My advice to them would be to flee this entire continent, as every half-sane creature must! We've a massive wave of deserters behind us, and even my sword tires. Call it sin or virtue, we press on."

"Or are driven," murmured Moonglum. "It's a sin against reason to keep pushing forward, when all sense tells us to go back. Elric, I like not this land of trickery and torment. Each wall hides an assassin, and some disinherited tribesman is behind every tree. The sooner we reach a country not suffering desperate war, the better. There are brigands everywhere. Some have even gone ahead of us. Stories of the Lords of Law and Chaos struggling for ultimate victory! It's as if Chaos toys with us. We can trust these steeds to get us through the forest and over those mountains, but what then? What's there? An ocean? An ice waste? We'll need something larger than a pony, I'd guess, to take us beyond World's Edge. You'll recall the complicated mechanicals of the ship which brought us here?

"Two full winters since then, earning our way with swords and slaughter, have we followed rumours and legends. We got good sport, goodwill, good gold and plenty of gallant remuneration—"

His companion's night had not been restful. He patted his animal's neck, speaking in an effortless baritone. "These fellows are no dragons!" His eyes, red as rubies, glittered in melancholy reminiscence. "But they have courage and strength more than any I've ridden."

He had grown to admire their sturdy little war stallions. He and Moonglum had ridden them across plains and hills all the way from Low Lop'na, on the border with the C'a'asyrisa middle lands, far from the battlefields. The C'a'a tribes were famous for their equine prowess as well as the physical peculiarities and stamina of their ponies. The intelligent pack mare was sand-coloured. She had a scarlet mane, red hoofs and deep-set, red-brown eyes. The stallions were glossy black, with silver hoofs and mane. A kind of friendship had developed between ponies and riders, and these sure-footed animals trusted Elric as he trusted them.

The albino felt a pang as he recalled the still stronger bond he had with the Phoorn. His encounter with his ancient dragon kin had caused him to remember the dragons ridden in his youth when Melniboné had ruled his world. Now he must wait on the will of the Phoorn. Recently, all the dragons he had encountered slept for years after almost any period of waking. He had ridden them when he could and taught his friend many secrets of the *skeffla'a*, but there was a certain sadness to the encounters. He longed for a time when he and Cymoril, the Dark Jewel of Melniboné, had awakened together and gone to the vast Phoorn caves at dawn, singing in their common Phoorn language, half-human, half-dragon, sweeping through tall crags and over forests and rivers; their eery voices blending with their vast beating dragon wings, they seemed to be lifted on music alone. Then he would take his horn and blow a melancholy tune until she slipped it from his hand and blew a sweeter one. Their songs echoed in sunless valleys between tall granite cliffs. Free from gravity and drunk on dragon venom, they sang the wild, crazed, beautiful, sad songs of their common ancestors, when poetry and music combined with airy, free-flying art forms wholly their own, and the air was full of wild colour . . .

Elric remembered how he and his wonderful betrothed had flown on the backs of Flamefang and Fleetway, oldest and wisest of dragons, who had taught them so much and made poignant their sense of loss with his visions of their island nation's past glories. He remembered his homeland's forests of living flowers which had populated a universe, her dream couches, her monumental love stories, her astonishing magics and mathematics, her mystic knowledge and crafts, her malicious wit. Many times he had risen from the dream couches, having crammed a thousand years into a single night, more eager than ever to explore the world they shared. He had woken her in the early morning and whispered the dragons awake, too, as only he could, filling the world with the pungent smell of flowers. They had flown between the black crags of the island's eastern range and high into the clear blue-white skies above the city's slender, oddly shaped spires. Their love had seemed preordained, endless. They spoke of their old age and how they would spend it together. They had talked only of better futures. All would be content in both Young and Old worlds. Melnibonéan and human arts would flourish.

Our beautiful, our exquisite choirs . . . He sighed and twitched the reins to move his pony to the left for Moonglum, who rode up beside him.

The Elwheri was concerned. "Friend Elric! Did you sleep at all? You scarcely look well enough to reach the forest, let alone the mountains."

"You slept too long and now dream." The albino forced a laugh. "But I cannot deny my eyes are growing weaker, my friend, and my limbs, too, it's true. For all her superb balance I can barely hold Stormbringer." The albino laughed again and tried to grasp his friend's arm to reassure him. "I fear Arioch really has deserted us, if only momentarily. You have seen my feeble state! Worse than the time I spent in Soom. The sword feeds, and the sword sucks sustenance from their useless lives. But Arioch neither takes his tithe nor gives power to my sorceries. I require that energy to work the large magics I once depended upon. I feel that he believes that energy is better spent elsewhere. Indeed, I think all gods and demigods have deserted us since we reached this ruined land. The sword no longer sends me strength. I fear she'll turn on one of us for sustenance. She needs souls before she'll transmit me more energy. I drank my last sustaining tea before we saddled our animals. Possibly I'll find the herbs I need in the forest, though this climate is not ideal for them. If we're to reach our goal, both of us need to revive ourselves. Maybe old Grome himself lives among these earthy roots. I'll be better when that bloody stink has gone from my nose! By Kas Kowljupit's sticky fingers, I believe I still smell it!"

"I, too. Death clings to us as others cling to life. Was it worth all that to escape to all this? To lose our lives—and souls if we still have 'em—in this foreign wilderness. And for what? A tattered shred of legend which speaks of a cave reaching to the other side of the world? Purchased seven thousand miles from here or further! Oh, what wonders the old romance promises! A flying cat. A magic horse. A tunnel carpeted with roses, through which we stroll home—or anyway to somewhere we are not completely unwelcome! You discovered pieces of your people's history. I have been near death six times and haven't a copper coin to show for it. And as for bloody revolution—why, I've seen more autocracies established since we arrived than tyrannies torn down! Our adventures are educational, old friend, but they are not profitable." Displaying his familiar grin, the stocky Elwheri leaned back in his saddle to arrange something there.

He sighed. "I have blood-grubbing trouble with your obsession, my friend. You'll agree the tale's flimsy and fantastical at best."

"We've followed flimsier tales and found a truth in them! Indeed, I've reason to trust our fresh scrap of vellum, matching the first. Which cost us our last gold wheel. And turned us into starveling mercenaries, no better than those brutal Amahkian 'knights,' who did the worst of what you saw back there! Those animals joined Jin-kharda's cause because he announced the Great War won and himself king."

Elric's smile was thin and tired. "Are we much better men than they? Even as they cheered the supposed victor, Parnivas the Unclean had breached the walls and slain Jin-kharda Kax as he ascended the steps to a throne nobody really wanted—a symbol of a collapsing collection of city-states they called a nation."

"We were right to leave that night, Elric. For all we had to abandon our loot!"

"Poor payment at best for so much cruel bloodletting." The albino let his lids close over introspective crimson eyes. Then he dropped the other pony's lead-rein into Moonglum's responsive hand, spurred his mount and cantered ahead. Without objection Moonglum let him go. He knew his friend too well to ask the cause of his state of mind. Almost as much as for his own, he feared for Elric's soul as he no longer feared for their lives. They would both feel deep regret if the sword struck them down when it had no more souls to feed upon . . .

They ate a little at noon, keeping their mounts to a walk, feeding with nosebags, taking two more rests on the hoof, continuing to eat while they rested. Soon the woodlands came into clear sight over another low, rounded hill. Moonglum cleared his throat as he often did before going into battle. The sun was beginning to drop and turn to a glowing rust by the time they took the last upward road into the woods.

Perhaps Moonglum's concern communicated itself to the ponies, growing uneasy in the twilight.

⊙   ⊙   ⊙

THEY REACHED THE oak wood. The taverner had not lied. A narrow trail wound through trunks growing larger, the deeper into the wood they went. Ducking below branches, letting his stallion pick its way along the path between the thick-boled trees, Elric's mood had changed again. Moonglum took no comfort in that. The Prince of Ruins now had an air of supercilious arrogance. He wore it like armour. Armour more impregnable than the black steel he carried in the pack on the third pony, where even the Actorios pommel pulsed weakly through its covering of hessian and silk. Elric was facing an unimaginable death, probably at his own hand. Moonglum yearned to lift his strange friend's melancholy.

When Elric was in this mood, his friend hated to talk to him. Sighing, he followed the albino through the increasingly dense woods. Once, a strong shaft of late and sudden sunlight pierced the canopy, bringing Elric's white skin and hair into sharp relief. Moonglum had never seen the albino appear so unwell and so alone.

After half an hour of following the trail through the trees it became obvious to Moonglum that Elric was failing rapidly. As was the day. Should he light a dark lantern? A torch? Twice, Elric had slumped in the saddle, barely righting himself. The Elwheri restrained an impulse to assist his friend. He knew what response he would get.

And so Elric rode doggedly on into the darkness.

At last Moonglum's conscience forced him to speak. "Elric. Now I wish we'd made that taverner throw in a flask or two of his sour *potcheen*! Let us rest, my friend! Perhaps I can scout about and find something from which to make a restorative?"

"We should not divide. I'd be ill at ease drinking untried drugs or sleeping in this foul-smelling wood." Barely a mumble.

"You slept so badly in that foul-smelling town! You'll sleep longer tonight, at any rate!" Moonglum reached into his belt pouch. Taking out flint and tinder, he drew a rush torch carried under his pack. The surrounding forest was suddenly alive with shadows. "There!"

Elric shrugged. "Any who'd rob us will see or hear us well enough. The more confident we are, the stronger a party we shall seem."

Moonglum turned, but, before he could reply, they heard an unlikely sound approaching along the unseen road. The horribly unmellifluous mixture of throaty warbling, cheeps and short, staccato yaps, grew louder. Possibly one voice, probably two. One was probably not human. Here and there in the trees it seemed a firefly flew towards them. Elric and Moonglum prepared for battle.

At last, around a bend in the narrow trail, his way lit by a lantern swinging on a bamboo cane over his head, appeared a skinny grey mule of extraordinary height, caparisoned in faded, tattered brocade, with tarnished and cracked horse-furniture brass and leather. Swaying a little in the mule's saddle, looking about him with startled, pale blue eyes, sat a lanky individual in fantastic finery as faded as the rest of him. He stopped his noise on a squeak which would have done justice to a bagpipe. He lifted his bushy scarlet-and-silver eyebrows in surprise.

Apart from the upturn of his mouth, which gave him the appearance of bemused intelligence, his features were lugubrious above a long neck partially hidden by a straggling red-and-grey beard topped by a burgundy velvet be-feathered bonnet. There was something familiar about him, even though they would swear they were unacquainted. His body was scrawny and tall, his slender legs stretched the length of his well-rubbed stirrups, his bones threatening to pierce his stockings. His only flat bones were his shoulders and his hips, clearly outlined. Somewhat awkwardly he reined in his mount, exclaiming in a voice partially drowned by the enquiring bray of his mule, which, to Moonglum's surprise, was answered by an agreeable whickering from their mare. "Woe, Munch, my girl! You are an aristocrat, sweet lady, and always remember the old ballad. *She has hoisted her kelt of green linen, her petticoat up tae the knee, And she's gone wi' Laird Ranal MacRanal, his pride and his darlin' tae be!*" Doffing his bonnet with a dangerous sweep of his arm. "*Noblesse oblige*, dear sir!" The man had a drunkard's sway. "Forgive 'em, dear sirs, but old Munch here is a rare brood mule. She would call more winsomely had not her voice been damaged honourably enough, in battle. Are you unwell?" He peered at the pair as if trying to remember them. "Forgive me, sir. Your pallor reminds me . . ."

All these voices brought the albino back into the world. He raised his head, settling his simple battle-helm.

"By Grimm, sir!" cried the newcomer. "You'll be Elric the White and his faithful companion Morninglass the Red! I had not expected to find such as yourself in this rather ordinary old forest! Is it so?"

"Moonglum," said the Elwheri, a little peeved. "Though I suppose my friend is better known, even on this side of the world."

With a flourish the man on the mule doffed his cap and bowed, allowing a lock of his dyed black-and-blond hair to fall over his face. He swept it behind his head with a dramatic gesture, tucking it under his bonnet, "I believe we have not yet met. I am Orlando Funk, sirs." A quizzing look, a moment's disappointment when unrecognised. "I am upon a quest, as no doubt you are, too! Your quest, of course, far more portentous than my own! In comparison I am a mere minor questling!" Fitting unhesitatingly into a slightly different persona, then another, shifting features across an intersection of timelines. Then, all colours for a second in vivid contrast, so that for a moment his hair almost blinded them. Then it settled to more natural colours. He became what they had first seen, his grotesque features perpetually amused. He mumbled apologies. Was he some kind of astral projection?

"We are *returning* from a quest, sir," declared Moonglum. "Now all we seek is a road home."

"To Melniboné, no doubt, with the Horn of Fate?" Orlando Funk spoke brightly and offered them a tiny wink, as one who bonds in whispered gossip and thinks it wisdom. Then, perceiving their expressions, apologised. "Forgive me." He fished in a doublet's pocket, brought out a piece of papyrus. "I specialise in the laws of romance, you might say, but should you need me . . ."

Moonglum was impressed by the man's ability to stay on his lanky steed. He held the scrap of papyrus without reading it.

Funk carried on. "I am upon a piece of business now. You are missing one, I believe. A lawyer and a negotiator. Primarily allow me . . ." He waved it into the Elwheri's possession. "Small confidential matters. Hills not always what they seem, eh? Questions of equilibrium. Comfort. Without compassion or any sentiment I am but a mere interpreter of myth and faeyrie lore, sirs. Also, of sorts, a sister. Also a poet. I end with poet lest folk should assume me a false troubadour, a mere mummer." He made all these statements in an apologetic manner. "I am a musician! Ha! I remember. Your instrument! Legitimate, thorough and professionally executed. The whole point of the adventure! Also a playwright. I am, what I fear you observe so clear: A seeker after experience! A dilettante who wanders a baffling tangle of moonbeam roads. I rely on the goodwill of a few friends . . ."

"Those roads"—Elric searched his memory—"are the very ones I trod in my youth, when receiving my education. Do you know of such a road nearby likely to bear us back to the Young Kingdoms?"

"I've searched for one myself, sir, without success. Or a guide, even! But you are weary, Prince Elric!" From his ragged plaid, he pulled out a black, squat bottle. "Revive yourself, my lord, if you will."

Ignoring his friend's evident suspicion, Elric reached out a white hand to take the bottle, held it for a moment to his own chest while torchlight lapped across it, then drank off a swift draft. The stuff was a vivid blue. The taste was hauntingly familiar, yet elusive. So sweet! Masked by other, complex flavours. He did indeed seem somewhat recovered, but Moonglum suspected the effect to be momentary. In less than an hour, his friend would be no better. However, when the albino handed the bottle across to him, he did not refuse. Apples? Fermented pomegranate. Vanilla. Moonglum enjoyed the delicious brandy, which was like no brandy he knew. Just as he was about to identify the taste, it slipped away from him. Its powerful bite brought him fully alert and energised. Relaxed and confident. Extraordinary stuff!

In a voice mellowed by the wine, Elric thanked the stranger. "And for our part, Sir Orlando, how can we be of service?"

"All I seek for now is a roof and a bed." He reached to secure his bottle. "And those I'll not find with you gentlemen, I can see!"

Moonglum returned the bottle reluctantly. He was anxious to be on their way before the light gave out. "You'll find a tavern about a daytime's ride back there, Master Funk. I would not normally recommend it, but in this war-ravaged world there's little choice in what was saved from siege and counter-siege. Keep riding. Don't stop. Look out for roving brigands, sir. They'll claim to be knights but have neither religion nor integrity. And this road, sir? Will it carry us into the mountains?"

"I believe so, should you be lucky. But there are dangers, mark you. Were it not for certain minor magical skills of mine, it's likely you'd find my bleeding corpse a mile or two ahead of you. These woods are cursed. Renegades and bandits have always hidden in 'em. They shelter cruel animals, too, and pitiless cannibals. And whole armies of starving degenerates. And believe me, sir, in my time I have dined with comrades more bestial than the beasts!"

Carefully, a little anxiously, he felt for his hidden bottle, rearranging his rags. "Now I trust gentle manners no better than bad ones." He allowed a prim expression to disfigure his ancient features. "I warn you, we must not be found dawdling."

Instead of succumbing, Elric dismissed his vague threats and promises. "Were you never a child and not curious about Chaos? Never have the will to explore? You are clearly much-travelled. Do you journey from the mountains? Know something of the World's Edge? Have you been charmed by Chaos or enlisted by Law?"

"True. I accept your irony. Those were not the means by which I lately entered your plane, prince." The gawky traveller shuddered fastidiously. "But neither did Law, Chaos nor the servants of a higher power until lately. I know a few roads, I have a little magic. A small number of archaic spells and incantations." He looked around him at the various accessories dangling from his saddle. "An axe somewhere here—for firewood, d'ye see?" He shook the big thing then returned it. "Not the mighty wizardry of your people, as I've heard, my lord. But enough to keep me invisible to those who would murder me for my few rags and books. Torture me for secrets I do not possess. And worse, since I have affection for her and a natural concern for her well-being, slaughter my faithful mule Munch, whom they'd kill for food or treat cruelly. You will note, sir, that I carry a sharp fish-spear." He reached down and proudly drew something from his saddle-holster. A short trident. Almost a toasting fork. "But with my chopper and spear I am well-armed, am I not? I see you consider it a poor defence against desperate men. But with their aid I've eaten many a tasty coney. One day you must join me; I cook to suit most tastes."

His head cocked suddenly. His voice dropped. "Or is it you, my lord, who prefers to dine on friends?"

Elric sniffed the air, turning his head. Feeling the chill. His baritone became a murmur. "That stink grows stronger. It no doubt plans encirclement, means to slay us." The stallions whickered and folded their ears back while the mule snarled, stamped its legs and followed their example. Moonglum was the first to hear hissing voices in the forest depths; he grew alert: saplings and ferns were stealthily trodden down.

Swiftly, the Elwheri drew his curved swords from the twin scabbards crossed over his spine. This was the signal for Elric, his senses muddled, to reach into a hefty bundle on the pony's back and, with some effort, drag out his long, black broadsword. The sword appeared to be dying. They could almost hear its thin panting. The shagreen-bound handle was topped by a feebly pulsing Actorios. The sword's guard was made from two down-turning dragons' claws. Within the dull steel, faint red runes writhed. It was too long since their last battle. Chaos sent no aid. Stormbringer was dying.

A yelp. His forehead tightly wrinkled, Orlando Funk stared at the ebony blade in horrified recognition. He mumbled some spell, drew a long-fingered magician's pass or two over himself and the mule. "No! Oh, dear! We are too late! Or too early?" In a second he made himself and his mount almost invisible against the oaks. "Forgive my manners, prince!" His voice vibrant with terror, he cried, "I know of that blade and would not be in its vicinity once the bloodletting begins! I wish you all supernatural assistance and the blessing of old Bran's brood! Lud be with you!"

Taking a last swig from his black bottle, clattering, kicking and calling out his spells, he fled away from them, almost instantly disappearing into the forest background, squeaking, "*You'll not need my help yet, my lords! So for the moment I make my adieux!*" And was gone, leaving the weary albino and his red-headed companion to face the coming danger. "Light another torch, my lords, or you are most certainly gone!"

Moonglum scowled. He had a distrust of men or women with hair redder than his own, especially those able to make themselves invisible.

Elric sniffed again. "*Aha! That stink!*"

And then, their dark lanterns suddenly uncovered to reveal their numbers, if not their comeliness, the "Amahkian Knights" stepped out of the forest.

Living only to eat, their filthy skins spotted with a variety of horrible plagues, they were scrawny, unkempt individuals of every race, dressed in layers of indescribably filthy rags, their dreams of wealth and power long since lost to them. A stinking rabble of wretched, maimed degenerates, barely distinguishable one from another, man from woman, they had almost lost the power of speech. In their drooling hunger, they saw all that lived as food.

Cautiously, they began to close the circle. They made anticipatory noises as if they already satiated their own greed.

Under different circumstances, Moonglum would sympathise with some of the scavengers. War and human folly had infected them across half a continent. Leaderless, but each believing themselves a leader, they were the hopeless remnants of landless peasants. Recruited, with tempting promises of gold and aristocratic titles, into the recent and spurious Order of Amahkian Knighthood, they had left impoverished homelands to join the Kax's victorious army. There was no honour in defeating them. In eleven years of brutal fighting they had become too cruel to care, too proud to live, too self-despising to die. They were armoured in ill-matched collections of rusty chain and battered plate. Armed to their few remaining teeth with equally unkempt blades and a half-wound crossbow, as ruined as the rest, the mob emerged on three sides, closing in.

Moonglum glanced anxiously toward his friend and was surprised to see an expression of amusement on Elric's gaunt, handsome features. A moment since and he could not hold a blade steady. Now the opportunity for familiar action, together with the invigorating brandy, had given the albino an unexpected respite from his debilitating ennui.

Astonished, Moonglum was much relieved.

Elric drew himself up in his saddle.

"Gentlemen!" A brief, mocking bow. "Which of you would die first for the common good? My hellsword here must *feed*!"

By extraordinary effort he lifted the blade, seeming to gain strength with every second. Stormbringer gave a growl of anticipation. Life stirred within the sorcerous steel!

Now the brigands began to wonder if they had considered the right strategy. The firelight showed them two they recognised on battlefields from "Ilinfa'as" to Misellcnii Bridge. The ones who had seen them fight were always survivors of some hideous massacre of which they were a rare witness. These were fated never to know a night's sleep, fearing to close their eyes, lest those images return. Yet young mercenaries dyed their hair to look like them and had lifeless weapons forged so they'd be mistaken for Stormbringer, as harmless insects have learned to replicate the appearance of predators. None ever claimed the pair's fights to be unfair. The sword was said to hear whatever was said of it.

Meanwhile, Moonglum asked himself how the albino was finding this new energy. Urging his black-and-silver pony swiftly forward, Elric made a movement with his sword, driving it, or driven by it, directly downward into the crossbowman's face and, through fountaining blood, cracked his breastbone.

The sword hissed with relish as it drained the corpse's life-stuff. It began to moan and keen, and the sound turned into a howl of the same pitch, growing louder and louder as Elric cantered towards his next antagonist. And the next. And red blood splashed onto milk-white skin. And those he slew heard the whispered words. "*It's so good to be killing again.*"

Thinking his friend spoke to him, Moonglum glanced briefly at Elric but saw no irony in his eyes.

FOURTEEN

The Empress Melaré

THE TWO WORKED together, as they had worked since they fought the Dharzi devil-dogs in the first hour of their meeting. They worked instinctively, as a single entity. They were now as skilled as acrobatic-dancers, an astonishing killing creature, barely distinguishable as individuals. One by one and two by two, the ill-matched companions whirled back to back and kicked and struck like cobras, snapped their attackers and flung corpses from one to the other, ducking the cuts, dodging the thrusts, piling body on body.

Moonglum sliced with neat economy. Elric stabbed, screaming in psychic agony as he stole other men's souls. His pale, wiry arms tensing like cords, he brought his howling runesword down on his antagonists until, understanding too late who the pair were, the Amahkians began to back around the massive tree trunks, attempting to escape that infamous albino and his notorious El-wheri companion. The new-made knights were learning to fear for their souls. Elric's and Moonglum's reputation had spread quickly since their arrival on this continent. The scavengers realised they had stupidly preyed on demigods. They faced death with a mixture of fear, fatalism and fascination. They could no longer in any way control themselves. They profoundly understood and re-gretted the price of the choices they had made which led to this moment when their souls were drawn into the albino's greedy sword.

"Arioch! Blood and souls for my lord Arioch!"

The sword rose and fell, spreading a tide of red ruin around him. And, while Elric wielded that battle-blade, it seemed Stormbringer hissed her triumph and spoke to him in her own uncanny voice, while black light flickered the length and breadth of the forest gallery. It illuminated that entire scene as a hundred stinking ghouls advanced and Elric's eyes glared again with ruby fire and again he snarled his hideous battle-cry. Lord Arioch? Had he withdrawn his help?

"*Blood and souls!*" He decided for the moment to waste no breath on Arioch. His familiar war-cry usually served to frighten his enemies, to ensure they recognised who and what he was and what his sword would do to them!

"*Blood and souls!*" Moonglum took up the shout. He fervently hoped they could continue without Arioch.

Together the pair chased the Amahkians all the way back to their hidden camp. Not so well hidden! Their swaying sentry lamps betrayed it. In panic the starvelings trampled their pathetic shelters under their own feet, all the survivors making frightened paths of escape through the gloom of the twilit forest. Then, for a moment, the whole world was silent.

As they stood panting among corpses, Elric and Moonglum heard a faint voice, a female voice. They were half-deafened by crepuscular carrion eaters calling siblings to the unexpected feast. Big ravens croaked over bloody corpses, flapping, resettling and flapping off again. Eyes searching the shadowy ground, the albino moved cautiously, arm lifting his torch high sending the half-dead and the worse-than-dead home to Hell. Meanwhile, the contented crows flapped back to their caves and nests, leaving the two men alone in that stinking rookery.

Here, the wretched little army had lived for a time, clearly using the place as a base. "They had horses at some point. Doubtless making raids on the surrounding country. Ate them. Skin for blankets, boiled bones. Not exactly planning for the future, were they?" Moonglum shrugged. Five great nations had been raped, and the only law now came from local warlords defending their tiny parishes against roving bands.

Seeking the source of that tiny voice, Elric and his friend pursued a few of the wretched camp-followers out of their shadowy settlement. The sights and smell outraged every sense. They held makeshift masks against the stench, scattering rough tents and huts as they went. They sent cur dogs, starveling camp-followers, and sickly, underfed children into the darkness until all had disappeared among the trees. They were unlikely to regroup. The pair looked over the smouldering remains of moss fires, the ruins of camp kitchens, lean-to shacks and the worthless rubble of war. Now that the knights themselves were dispersed, their followers could not live as they had, like the detritus which collected around the hull of a ship and only progressed as she progressed. A few might creep shivering back for fire or a blanket, but they would soon become wholly feral, foraging for grubs, roots, berries and small vermin until they became prey themselves.

Elric had seen many miserable landscapes in his journeys through all the planes of the multiverse. He had ridden the moonbeam roads. He had witnessed apocalypse from a distant star. He had been shown the hells of the Thousand Worlds and knew the bleakness of utter Law, the formless fecundity of utter Chaos, when no Balance ruled. This reminded him of what he had seen in limbo with all hope denied. This was a world on course for disaster.

Bright colour! Catching sight of a shimmering piece of blue silk lit by his torch, Elric pointed to it. Moonglum nodded. They moved forward. Just then a voice called out more loudly. A few words in the local pidgin lingua franca. "*Swine! Swine! Oh, how you will die once I'm free.*" This seemed unlikely to persuade a captor to release it. It was almost immediately followed by an astonishing stanza of melancholic and slightly Classical Melnibonéan, the beautiful language of those symbiotic brethren, the Phoorn, fled to fresh conquests in a world above (or below) the world. A world his branch of the family had come to rule more cruelly, and evidently more thoroughly, than this. How many other settlements had lost touch with their dragons, even their sorcerous pacts with the great Lords and Ladies of Chaos? Was that voice an individual explorer from another settlement, halfway across the World Below? Or was it yet another link to his ancestral roots?

For how many aeons had his ancestors continued to spread through a multitude of planes of this universe? Planes among which adepts might walk as casually as a metropolitan traveller strolls a city lane! Planes like this, rich in resources and natural beauty, all in exquisite balance? With their powerful supernatural patrons and profound metaphysical alliances, Elric's had always been a dominant culture. In the World Below, however, none appeared to have had the success of Melniboné. His ancestral empire cast a heavy shadow over its entire world. There had been no continental domination here and only a certain amount of local conquests by the decadent folk he had left in Hizs a year or more ago and an ocean away.

Yet the voice could only be from the lips of his own folk. High Melnibonéan, especially in baroque classical forms, could only be sung by one who had spoken it since childhood.

It was in an elated and hopeful mood that he continued his search.

He cared little that so many ruined men had died to fill his system with energy. They had sent their own victims to fates as bad. But Chaos and Law did not choose between good and evil. He considered those dedicated souls necessary tribute to his patron Lord of Chaos. Perhaps he had never needed Arioch's help more? Revived, he might reach World's Edge and begin to search for the cave connecting one half of this plane to the other. Yet still he felt the absence of his demon lord Arioch's presence. Surely the Dukes of Entropy did not demand more from him? *So many souls!*

Stormbringer needed nothing but human life-stuff to feed upon, transferring much of that to its wielder in the vampiric relationship they had always known and of which he had always thought Duke Arioch a part. He was deeply puzzled.

With all his vast supernatural training, his soul and sword forged and reforged, tempered and retempered by gods and demons, Elric could not fathom why his metaphysical allies were absent. There had always been some who came to his help. He had carried Stormbringer into a thousand decisive battles, sacrificing countless souls to Arioch! Chosen Stormbringer over his own passions. How did Lord Arioch become as hard to satisfy as his albino servant? Elric had always believed his patron demon lord, like himself, to be the slave of a craving which ultimately no-one and nothing could satisfy. Was he dead?

Exiled? Were the old supernatural alliances crumbling? Where were the other demons who served Arioch? Where were the Lord of Entropy's fellows from the Higher Worlds—Xiombarg? Mabelode the Faceless? Even Miggea of Law? None was usually slow to pick up arms. And no sense of the powerful earth spirits who served neither Law nor Chaos. And where was Law? Did all prepare for the great battle they knew was coming? He could guess why existence itself was crumbling. When Gods grow weary and so tired that the brutal language of war is all that's left to them, Men are manipulated by unlikely temptations. They grow tired of safety and tired of thinking, as the country people say, and the Earth herself grows barren for want of mouths to feed, and Death herself has no enemy save gorgeous Life, no destiny save that determined by her contradictions, and destiny determined merely by the needs of the black blade.

For the moment the pair's lives seemed safe enough. Their legend as soldiers had grown larger by the instant. They were the most famous swordsmen alive! A reputation spread rapidly through the fantastic gossip of roaming military men. In such circumstances it was best to leave mysteriously, but, now, chiefly from curiosity, they stumbled toward a flash of soft, blue lapis lazuli that contrasted so vividly with the filthy rags around it. And then there was the voice. Then the words in complex Melnibonéan.

Moonglum guarded his friend's back as Elric followed the dying song and that slip of colour to their origins. At length, peeling back foul straw, a plank of rotten timber, a sheet of ragged canvas and something which had probably been a carpet, Elric revealed a glaring young woman, taller than Moonglum by a head, ethereally beautiful and astonishingly white, both shackled and tied to a fallen tent pole with which she struggled, hoping to make it a weapon.

As well as her torn blue dress, with edgings in darker blues and white gold, she had a full-length hooded cloak of merging greens, countless shades, subtler than a peacock's fan, she wore a steel-and-silver diadem, sideways on her long ivory hair, her lashes shone like icicles, and her eyes burned a lustrous crimson. Her ornaments and her armour were ebony and filigree silver. She did not speak as he got her upright. She could not know Elric's legend. No doubt she supposed the pair to be of the same ilk as the men they had just killed. She gazed upward. Elric gazed down. Moonglum dared not look at her at all. His expression was altogether baffled. With a start the albino fell back, bile rising in his throat. He felt suddenly weak again. He rubbed at his eyes and cursed quietly. His senses were confused; his stomach churned. He should have been dead by now. Instead he was looking at a female version of himself! Another female not only of his race, but a silverskin, like himself! He faced another mirror image! He collected his wits in a few moments as he sought about for a key, found one on a nearby corpse, and got it free. After a few moments he had undone the locks, then settled for separating the broken pole from the chains while Moonglum severed ropes with one of his many knives. With awkward dignity she stooped to pick up a scimitar, a war-helm, and to adjust her crooked diadem, doubtless put on her head when making fun of their valuable captive. Then she turned, looked them up and down and offered them a haughty moue of surprise. They controlled themselves. They were patient. Their long survival as soldiers of fortune had prepared them for the daily rescuing of Ladies of Quality.

Once, some version of her melancholy song had been heard everywhere in Melniboné. Only at that moment, as she stood free, challenging his motives with a hard crimson glare, did he begin to realise the significance of her appearance! She was an albino of the same rare type known in Melnibonéan history as "silverskins" or, less flatteringly, as "leper-kings." They were certainly of royal blood. Their world was created around them, and leprosy, like human albinism, was unknown among the Dragon Princes. How could they be twins, save through some offensive meddling of the gods? They were Elric's direct royal bloodline. Yet that line ended when he inherited the Ruby Throne then installed his cousin as regent, to begin a journey which he hoped would teach him the secret of humanity. He had gained some wisdom from that experiment. Now, however, he cursed himself for a fool for thinking he could change a society by force of arms. Or—he laughed aloud—by moral persuasion and exemplary lessons.

Where was she from, this sweet-voiced twin? He wiped brains and blood from his face and watched the silver-armoured girl, who might have been a younger sister, search the rubble for her slender weapons and armour, all of the same silvery blue. She was different from him, however. She was somehow more vital, in spite of her recent experiences. Her energy carried a promise that his dream could be revived. A false, naïve promise he had come to believe. He had once hoped for a world where his people partnered with an emergent human race to bring just governance to their mutual benefit. Was an idealism he had thought dead reviving in him?

Then all this, too, was set aside as he saw in her expression no gratitude for her release. Instead she began to speak in that pure, thrilling High Melnibonéan he had first heard her sing. Ornate as it was, for High Melnibonéan it was deeply aggressive and direct.

"Damn you to damnation!" Her eyes were red-hot steel. "How long must my hawk fly to reach the squadron? Or does it take Shirizha that long to read my message? By Xiombarg, I'd feed you to the lizards myself if I didn't—and they didn't . . . Ach, there's a level of insult to which vegetarianism cannot rise!" She peered more closely up into his face. She frowned. "By Olish Hief! And you're disgusting."

He stared back. "You must forgive me, madam. I believe—"

"You are no exception! I have seen you with your perverse adam's apple. I want nothing tricky from an ally! I will not have dirty limbs or visages near me. Or are you rival barbarians and would sell me to the highest bidder?! Criminals! That is punishable by instant death. Release me! Do you not recognise your empress? I am the Empress Melaré?"

"Empress?"

"Indeed!"

"My apologies, Your Royal Highness! I was under the impression that I was—"

"You are impertinent! Deluded. And mannish!"

Another bow. "We have yet to be introduced. It is some time since I ruled Melniboné."

She frowned, unsure if she detected sarcasm. She looked for his meaning in his face. "I do not know you. Where are my guards?"

Moonglum said, "She seems to be complaining, my lord! Shall we bind her up again?"

Smiling, the pale prince took another step back. "She'd probably thank us gracefully." And he spoke to her in their shared tongue:

"My name is Prince Elric, and I, too, was once an emperor." He regarded her with some amusement. "I believe we are related," he added.

It was her turn to show surprise. "You also have a mannish voice. Outlaw costume. Yet you are too old and too tall to have been in my guard without my knowing."

"We are travellers who set off some two years ago from—"

"I do not know you. Is it—? Travellers? You *are* a man! I heard rumours. A half-human race of air pirates, threatening their prey with swimming dragons."

"Of sorts." He smiled again.

She showed no reciprocal amusement. She was puzzled. "We've had none such as you since mythical times. Not in Kirinmoir. Here most males not born 'true' are born dead or rarely survive into early childhood. They are always pathetic runts. It is our infamous curse. There are stories, of course, of ancient warrior-sorcerers of enormous power, but—" Her voice hardened with suspicion. "No real evidence. And my family have lived here for thousands of years."

"I know of no Kirinmoir. It's a nearby town?"

"Sir, it is a great city. *There have been no greater since ancient times!* Our capital. She is no secret. Every imaginative being across the plane seeks the Second Tanelorn."

Elric found her deluded and self-important like many petty monarchs and conjurors.

"There is none more exquisite. Many songs are inspired by her. Some say she's sweet Tanelorn herself, since peace has ruled there for so long. Kirinmoir is the City-of-the-Well-at-the-Centre-of-the-World. She began as a fortress. Then our dragons departed. It was almost as if they left us the honey as a gift. Merchant-adventurers risk much from wild tribes and heavy taxes and travel many miles across hard country to trade rare and exquisite goods with us! And to experience our glorious arts, especially our music." Smiling, Melaré began to sing in a high, sweet voice: "*From the Forest on the Edge rises the Island at the Centre. From the Island at the Centre, Kirinmoir points proud towers.*"

Elric found himself close to tears for a moment. Cymoril had once sung that song, which, in ironic counterpoint alone, baffled human ears when accompanied on subtle multiplicities of reed tubes.

From what Melaré told them, in manner and body language as well as her native tongue, these other Melnibonéans seemed to maintain their power through honest commerce with a world outside, which, at least until now, had offered good trading partners. She quoted a couplet which could never be truly translated from the lovely, complex language of their common ancestors.

"And how is your city reached, my lady?" Elric's voice was softer now. "By a well-worn road?"

"Of course it is. It is the Blue Road, our Sweet Road. The only road which leads all the way through the mountains to Kirinmoir and the Quarantine Park. One road comes in, and the same one goes out. Meanwhile we tax the traders and rent them sleep and sell them food. A caravan came here once from the icy wastes beyond World's Edge. They remained here and became part of our world. We understand how attractive our way of life is, but we cannot have settlers destroying it from inside. We keep aggressive borders, yet those who remain within them are kindly treated, and we can provide all their needs from birth to death, for they are short-lived poor things. Few live much beyond a century. There are normally more guards, but, as you know, they were lured away!"

"The ones who—"

"I rode too far ahead of my guard. It has always been safe. No-one has ever attacked us here. Not since the Banishing. Why should they? We trade fairly and set a high example. They could not possibly wish to overthrow us. We are famous for brokering lasting peace between cities. They barely tried to keep pace with me. Knowing the road to our city is no mystery. We are merchant farmers in a small way. Trading in specialised crops chiefly. As I said, we only have one road in and the same one out! Our problem for centuries has been brigands and passing nomads. There are always some, ignorant of our defences, who think they can succeed where all others fail! Our most sought-after crop is our honey. It is our secret and our strength. There is no secret to the road itself. If you know not our mazes, even our own go mad! There is a central maze at the middle of the mountain, which doubly protects us from outsiders! The song in my palace is preserved on vellum. It is said to contain every detail of the route to the World Between the Worlds and from there takes us to another maze, and there is a map of the maze in the Temple. The only one, it's said."

"*There is always a map.*" Elric was cynical. What was the Banishing, and from where were they banished! He reached inside his mail and pulled out a piece of vellum. "This is a fraud, no doubt, and you have the real part! We have no money to buy another map." He was tired. Moonglum began to fear for his friend's sanity.

Since he could remember, Elric had known the function of maps in the so-called Tall Romances of ancient High Melniboné. Even Elwheris had studied them. Did their map match his own? He needed to see it. This ballad referred to the Seven Lost Songs, when his people had divided and were sent into exile. Geraldt of Dexorex, the chief protagonist, was the hero of his favourite Tall Romance as a boy. "The Ballad of the Three Kings" had been sung by many of the so-called jugadors, professional gamblers he met on the moonbeam roads. They had taught him a few of its many verses. Collected, the epic was also known as *The Romance of the Roads* or *Therbin's Saga*. Could their map match the vellum torn from the original he had spent the remains of their fortune on?

"The map to World's Edge is presumably mysteriously lost?" He expected to hear a familiar story of the map's theft and so on. She surprised him.

"Oh, no! We display the map in our Temple!"

Elric had become used to false trails and trickery in this long quest. How-ever, he now knew a sudden surge of hope. If his scrap matched their map, he was certain he had found the road home. Whatever magic was in that map was replicated in miniature on his vellum scrap. He would, without a shadow of doubt, be following the path of their mutual ancestors, two branches of which reached the World Below, while his ancestors went on to the World Above. During what he now knew to be a massive disaster, what had caused Melnibonéans to settle here in particular? He knew of at least four strands of his kind which had spread to different planes of the multiverse.

This was the second time in the World Below that Elric had stumbled on proof that his race, in common with the Phoorn dragons, had suffered a diaspora, perhaps several, more than a million years since, often small bands of refugees, sometimes whole civilisations, spreading along the moonbeam roads, settling in the Nine Planes, some perhaps spreading to the Fifteen Planes or beyond. Sometimes identified as faeyrie folk, they were as much scientists, philosophers, doctors, alchemists or astrologers as wizards. Like him, but unlike most of his contemporaries, these ancestors were filled with curiosity and imagination. For good or ill, they seemed to flee or had followed enemies away from *Klay-ara*, a distant home which barely existed any longer. Somehow whole worlds or series of worlds had begun to vanish, forcing the Phoorn and Melnibonéans, by now completely interdependent, out onto the dangerous and unmapped moonbeam roads, familiar only to those who used the ancient dream couches, so long ago.

And now he remembered one of those very dreams! Dreams that so frequently broke his sleep and sometimes his waking time. All who loved him loathed those dreams. He saw pools of blood, tasting of honey. He was bloated with soiled souls, squatting like a supernaturally sustained toad on the Ruby Throne of his ancestors. Blood and ichor flowed from it, making the steps to the throne slippery. Brooding on his inability to understand men or women of his own, or of human, kind, he was lost in thought. He shared empathy with neither. He probably never would know any meeting of minds. The great connection with a multiversal mind taking physical shape in mushrooms, truffles, toadstools and fungi of every kind. He could not become one with humanity without renouncing all his learning, all his power.

He had begun to accept the cold, simple truth: while he was born to serve Arioch, Arioch no longer acknowledged him. And had somehow formed a pact to refuse him access to any and all supernatural power. His work was proving subtler than he had imagined.

Wading through corpses and camp ordure he stepped into a small clearing to where a ray of moonlight somehow pierced the trees, illuminating his white, battle-scarred body, his head bowed amidst a curtain of hair. He stopped there, sword lowered, head deep on his chest. Still staring at the ground, he walked away from them, trying to clear his troubled mind.

He heard her haughty voice addressing Moonglum as he himself had once addressed servants, and he wheeled urgently to stop this condescension. "Madam! I introduce Duke Moonglum, Chancellor of Elwher, Ambassador at Large, my beloved old friend." With a curt apology, she modified her language. Elric knew that Moonglum would never have let her know the truth if it embarrassed his old friend. Nor would he be patronised, thought Elric. Nor did Moonglum usually declare a title, nor did he admire those who judged their fellows according to rank. Elric had never fully understood the notion of a republic. "Duke of a province" was the nearest he had come to "Representative of a constituency." Moonglum, if he cared to, could settle his score in his own way.

Their ponies whinnied and kicked. They could hear mounted soldiers somewhere behind them. Lord Ramada Sabaru himself could be upon them? Keeping his sword at his hip, Elric helped the Empress Melaré into the pack saddle and prepared to defend her to the death.

"We'll sleep after we pass them," he said. "I will try to ask for help."

He did not sound hopeful.

FIFTEEN

The Road to Kirinmoir

ELRIC BEGAN A half-forgotten incantation. Again, Arioch did not respond. The albino attempted to call King Grome, the earth spirit. Grome would not answer. Neither would Trayalash, Lord of the Oaks, respond, nor any brother or sister of theirs. He called wind spirits to him, but they resisted. Water-sprites? A mist giant's fog of invisibility? Few of these entities held allegiance to Law or Chaos. They made only temporary pacts. To hold the Balance.

For a moment the albino felt a cold understanding. His secret words were suddenly deprived of power. This momentarily alarmed the albino. Moonglum, too, began to feel fear as a physical pain. Even at Elric's weakest, he had never known Elric so helpless. Perhaps hoping for reassurance, he mentioned it at last.

"I have always had magic," admitted Elric. "I have always had great authority. From the earliest age my education was extensive and profound. I was, after all, the emperor-in-waiting. My people made clear-eyed pacts with the supernatural, which I have never dishonoured. Now some force—perhaps an arbitrary one—seems to have broken or rewritten those pacts. At last I am learning what it is to be deprived truly of power."

Moonglum was prepared to admit to himself that he was nervous. And not a bit reassured. Save for a cursed runesword and an immoderately cursing young woman, they had precious little comfort. At that moment, to his relief, the oak wood began to thin out a little, and soon the travellers could see a near-full moon rising above the mountains.

"Now we sleep," said Moonglum.

They still heard the pursuing riders. The cavalry halted for a while, and then they turned about and were riding in their direction. "They sound like elephants!" Moonglum started to laugh. "And fast ones at that! It's almost a *polasad*." He named a quick "dash," a dance he had learned at Court as a boy.

On seeing Melaré's strange expression, he stopped himself and, with a sigh, rode on.

"We'll sleep in the saddle today and hope to find shelter somewhere in the foothills." Elric dismounted to make changes to their loads.

"If my guards were with me, we'd turn and fight," Melaré declared.

"What happened to them?" Elric asked.

"Aye." Moonglum nodded. "What happened to them?"

"We were separated chasing a gang of bandits who entered our city claiming to be merchant traders. They stole a small part of our most precious resource. We discovered they planned to show the flask to the other tribes, claiming we have endless supply. They know nothing of our ways or how the resource is produced! They planned to return with the tribes, take it all and leave us dying in our chambers. Or control our resource themselves. Either way, we'd be dead or enslaved. That's all our torturers could discover."

"Your resource? Gold, eh? Or silver? You have mines?"

"Honey," she said. "We have a honey mine. Or well." She was merry. "Or whatever you choose to call it. You are indeed a stranger! Yes, it is our gods-given wealth. No, not hives. It's, however, hard to gather from our aggressive blue bees. They can become excitable."

"You have no defence against the bees? No spell? No incantation? Surely—"

"We have precious little magic now. We gather the honey regularly, at some small risk the year round, to trade with the barbarians beyond Andrejotya Punt."

"I knew it," said Elric.

"Once some traders in their cups betrayed the secret of their wealth, we knew we should have to marshal new and better defences. Have you never heard of the *bewissett voolc*?"

"*The Mead of Eternity?* The elixir of eternal youth in the faeyrie tale?" Elric had known it as a child and had heard about it more recently. "An epic fragment. My ancestors spoke of it. Such stories always arise in times of uncertainty. I thought that mead was a version of our infamous yellow wine?"

"*That* is Hizsian absinthe. From hemlock. It blinds. Our mead is distill'd into wines, of great quality, savoured everywhere people of taste meet! Distilled it transcends the Heavens. It is euphoria in a sip! The clear deep purple *ofript* honey goes through more distilling processes. Traders use the term. We do not. We have always called it 'blue honey.' We owe our long lives to it. Most of it is naturally blue. But we do not make it from the blood of dragons, as the tales no doubt have it!" She laughed a little, delicate, brittle trill. "We owe it to our well! The hive is housed below our Temple. The bees have always lived there, and we cohabit with ease. Our Well of Strength, my lord! Our Blue Honey, the secret whereabouts known to every merchant trader and generally pretty well kept! What they do not know is how to treat the bees and their authorities. The Lore itself is sacred."

"*The Bee Divine!*" Elric referred to a legend from his people's Gaaneecea Chronicle.

Moonglum grimaced, to humour what was perhaps a joke. "And no doubt is the power of your legend."

"To be, or to become, a legend is to own great power, for a legend is the sum of a people's desires." Was the empress flirting with him? "The responsibility must be overwhelming."

"Indeed," said Moonglum, leaning in to his pony's neck, "and let's not speak of its dangers."

She scanned the foothills and the mountains beyond. "What can have happened to my guards?"

As the day wore on, the pursuit behind them almost caught up more than once, but still Elric kept them ahead, pressing through the tall grass, then across a few miles of marshy ground which stank of stagnant water, a series of insect-infested bayous in which long dark shapes moved. Perhaps pike? Teeth bright as their glaring eyes. The sound of big, slithering swamp snakes. The locals said to "pay 'em no mind" and would only speak to her about the fizzing rainbow pools they found here and there and were some sort of reservoir. They called the contents *coleur*, but not one of them was careless about where they let their ponies put their feet.

After that they climbed low-rising hills and were relieved to discover a valley and a village built around a deep tor with good people more than willing to find a crust or two to feed them, for these were surely the faeyrie folk who honoured them. They always repaid kindness with kindness. In the winter they would receive a bottle of thick blue honey to be diluted in brandy and used by them for their health and well-being through the year. That was the version given them by the empress.

"They came by," said a villager, "and they will come by again, my lady. Where the sun rises *westwardwildishanks*. Those would turn against you, like the warthog in the story. You trust too easily, kind masters."

"When will they come again?"

"When they do not find you in front of them. Then. And then all the tribes will flow into the valley."

"They are behind us now," said Moonglum. "Hiding is the best recourse!"

"Let them pass us again." Elric looked back. "By then, I think, they'll have learned our trick."

"By then, my friend, they'll be tired. Then we attack!"

"I've known few to reject that logic. Few who live!"

He shrugged. "By then they'll have reached the snowline. A full moon. Dawn behind us. The shale and the snow should blind them by the time they are here. We sleep now and then take positions on the high ground. We attack when they come below our ridge, there." He pointed. "We'll be fresh, and they will not be." As he buckled and tested his war-harness which would help him stay mounted, Elric was not disappointed to be discussing strategy again.

Next night they shared a large cellar, their beds arranged feet first around a blazing log-and-peat fire. They had no wish to disturb their three ancient hosts, who were friendly and hospitable, even garrulous. In the firelight their faces had the bright aspect of pickled oranges. Elric and his companions were tired to the marrow. They found it difficult to remain attentive, especially since they understood almost nothing of what was said. "Call out *an ye ki* afoud grand old yarn, Bayantree, wouldn't ye say, maister!"

"Oh, indeed! At that time of night, any rate, A'un. So would ye pick up the full bottle until ye throw their cloaks and hats over to all as waits and Gods bless you, the Baron's ostlers and journeymen all, domestic- and tinker-built they are and so ye'll see, with your unwitch'd eyes, the bringing down of the Demon King and May Mayflower's ascent to grace, to love us, save us and elect old Father Remkin their king. This, we'll drink to in the name of the *Auld King's Ballad* and the last of her enemies. What d'ye say?"

Elric said that, begging their pardon and thanking them most gratefully for their generosity, but there was to be a battle coming, and they were rather weary . . .

"We're in for a short stay, I can tell it. Sure, let's us near the Llud's Crest. Pray they will not bring our houses down."

"We'll choose the ground so that the village will not become a battlefield," Moonglum reassured them.

"Well," said one villager turning over, "battles are inevitable now the tribes are gathering. I'm sure we'll be up in time to see the three of you defeat that army."

In the firelight he hardly saw Moonglum grin. "Don't wear your special smocks, gentlemen!" Then, having made what a city lad thought a subtle witticism, the Elwheri closed his eyes and fell instantly into a self-satisfied slumber.

They were up after a while. The old men still slept. They left the darkened village, creeping along the wide overhang. Then they positioned themselves in high grass. Moonglum had strung his bow and methodically withdrew an arrow. His curved swords were now worn on each hip, to accommodate the lacquered quiver of several rare woods which held long-fletched arrows. The steel of each arrowhead glistened from sharpening. The redhead had his new war armour on. Made for him by Zaokhiss, master armourer to the Ghan-Ghan Commune, occupying the faraway coasts of the continent. Layers of leather and bronze protected his head, limbs and torso. Similarly, Elric was clad in his own light but strong battle armour, with swept dragon helm's wings, intricate visor and every simple curve designed to deflect a blow away from the wearer. They had shields, too, for their nearby ponies. Between them stood the slight, beautiful figure of Melaré, Empress of Kirinmoir, in her light blue and silver armour, her blue cloak and her weapons, also of silver-blue, with her borrowed pony beside her.

They saw the rainbow frost first. It was glorious! It sprayed into the ice-white sky, one curve after another. Colour upon colour was thrown up by the approaching riders. Sparkling swathes of brilliant reds, golds and green. A wash of pale yellow. They made the spectrum swirl and scatter in the brilliant sun. Shadows of blue and silver followed them.

Now they began to see flashes of green, blue and silver within the frost and its aura. Surely a livery. Some real riders at last! In the night it had sounded like an army, but now it looked like a single squadron of cavalry. Perhaps fifteen or twenty riders.

"Easily taken." Moonglum pursed his lips and drew back the bowstring. He was about to let fly when Melaré cried out "Stop!" and threw up her arm, sending his arrow erratically skyward.

Elric turned, red eyes blazing. "What treachery—"

"Not treachery—unless it's mine. I am a fool. My guard has searched for me as I have run away from them!" Melaré clutched at Elric's arm. "These are *friends*, brother! Friends who will help us *defeat* the Amahkian Knights!"

No matter how tired they had all become, even the albino smiled a little when he realised they had been hiding from their own allies.

"They sounded so many more," muttered Moonglum, less amused than the others.

A moment later he gasped when he saw the reason why that cavalry had seemed such a massive force. "By Assi'd! Not war-mammoths! But—"

In her relief, she laughed as heartily as she ever would. "War *lizards*!" she cried. "Where in the whole omniverse does any other nation possess such loyal and affectionate saurian cavalry?"

By certain characteristics and colourings, Elric recognised the animals as cousins or descendants of the Phoorn, but with more rounded features and no wings. These, too, were not hollow-boned so did not secrete venom in their sinus regions. Although inclined to drop to all fours at speed by the look of them, they now stood on two powerful back legs, their mouths bearing harnesses of the same coloured motifs as their riders.

There was no doubt about the pride, indeed loving affection, the woman felt as she hailed her guards and was merrily cheered in turn. Nor of the expressions of sheer shock on the faces of the two mercenaries. The most bizarre cavalry they had ever seen were seated on bright green reptiles, their toes protected by a kind of glove, reminding Elric and Moonglum of huge, ancient saurians from before the time of Man. They had long slender bodies, their snouts were closer to a cayman's, but they had a habit of the chameleon, standing there with their long tongues licking their eyes and moving restlessly over their heads. Their forelegs and protected toes stamped ground that was already frozen and broken to create that multicoloured cloud! Their tails close to the ground, they had a tendency to waddle, even at speed, and Moonglum noted a sprung swivelled saddle which allowed them to be ridden in awkward comfort. As he slowly took in the scene he was disbelieving.

"Affectionate?" Moonglum asked.

"They are our children." Melaré smiled softly.

Elric and Moonglum responded without the enthusiasm she plainly expected. They had travelled more widely and harder than she over many years. "Children, indeed!" cursed Moonglum, looking back on the disrupted village, thinking of unnecessary miles. Now, when they needed to be at their most alert, they came close to exhaustion thanks to this young empress's failure to recognise her own forces.

The Elwheri guessed that horses were rare in her homelands, where, for some reason, giant lizards could be domesticated. The riders were all dressed in the same blue and silver, armed with long lances and sabres. They had few other weapons apart from bows and quivers. They were young, judging by their figures, and Moonglum was surprised to see no obvious veterans among them.

An officer at the forefront was leading another mount which had already recognised Melaré.

As the two companies came together, Melaré jumped from her pony's pack saddle and ran with relief to her dismounting captain.

"Shirizha!" She embraced the captain as she might a brother, gaily explaining her mistake. Moonglum was still disgusted and no longer cared if it showed, but Elric displayed nothing of his feelings, in spite of his growing exhaustion. The Elwheri listened as they fell in behind the lizard riders, hearing Melaré laugh again as she explained to Captain Shirizha how she had ridden too hard after a thief she had spotted, but once among the trees her animal grew clumsy and the men she pursued became her pursuers. In fighting them off she was dismounted. They planned to keep her captive and trade her for a large amount of blue honey. They had mistaken Elric and Moonglum for her soldiers and planned their ambush accordingly, panicking as Elric and his friend approached. Had they seen her falcon? Her mount? Shirizha had seen neither. If they were still gone, they would be meat by now. Many of these invaders had a particular taste for horsemeat.

Plainly the "Knights of Amahkia" had been recruited from tribes spread wide across the world. Even to its edge. Word was they had found allies controlling powerful sorcery.

Before Moonglum could mention this to his friend, his gaze travelled idly along the backs of the waddling beasts before them, and he laughed suddenly. "I am a fool!"

And in answer to Elric's enquiring eye, he said, "Women!"

He added: "Her entire guard are women!"

Elric smiled. "I thought you understood that. Clearly the complexities of High Melnibonéan gender-nouns have defeated you more than you knew!"

Moonglum felt his own spirits rising. Elric's humour had returned. This offered the prospect of his friend finding at least a temporary antidote for his terrible condition. And perhaps a passing flirtation or two for them both!

For this alone he was deeply grateful. He thanked the small, dark gods of his people, in whom he had little faith, for the blessing.

Since Arioch had presumably abandoned his friend, those unpleasant little grimlings were the only supernatural beings he could look to for help.

The women had soon explained the whole story, which Melaré had not been in a mood to tell. Here was the other piece of the story. In their reminiscences, her guards explained what had happened to bring them out of their hidden city. When they reached the city of Kirinmoir, the "knights" had represented themselves as friends. Then they had waylaid a blind worker at evening and stolen a flagon of blue honey.

Stealing honey was the only capital crime in the region. No-one was entirely sure how it had happened, it was such a rare event. But there was also the question, in Moonglum's mind, of how Funk obtained blue honey? Either the soldiers had traded a little to Orlando Funk for something they valued, or else Funk had somehow obtained it directly from the Empress Melaré! Who was the deceiver, who the deceived? Another thought—Funk could have stolen it from the knights who had stolen it from her. When attacked, they were almost certainly planning to trade her living body for more.

Elric ached in every bone and nerve. He had heard fragments of legend, but had come upon not a single history recording the existence of Melaré's people. Where did her ancestors, with their strange manners and ambitions, come from? Had he been dosed with their stolen potion and unwittingly volunteered to serve them in battle? He was growing weary of trickery. Assuming it *was* trickery! And he knew he was becoming confused, he had been in the saddle for so long.

They had confirmed that on the far side of their valley was another mountain range. Beyond that was an ice waste and beyond that the World Below-and-Above. They decided that they would ask her for enough strong blue mead to strengthen himself and Moonglum and to buy time until the runesword could feed him fresh life-stuff. With a little more of that, he and Moonglum could continue on, using the whole map, copied from their own pieces and that held in Kirinmoir. Provisioned and with refreshed ponies, they could make their way through the wasteland between the worlds.

Their visit to the World Below had been in some ways disappointing.

Neither had found what they hoped for. A glance at Moonglum and Elric knew the Elwheri was thinking the same. Yet he would, should he ever dictate his whole history to Moonglum, let the Elwheri embellish it. The scholar-swordsman often begged a tale from him during their considerable *longueurs* of wartime, swapping spells and tips on hunting. Perhaps, for all Elric knew, his friend kept a speculative journal. He was writing some sort of manuscript and would not let it be read or indeed glanced at until all named parties were dead. (Moonglum had no title for what he was calling the *Journal of the Black Blade*, and as he finished a scroll or book, he would send them by a courier to his Library at Pnetochnic University in the Zcvvv, Scholar-City of Hoolin, where his papers awaited his old age and where copies were made. In the event of his own death, Hoolin would determine who would publish the chronicle. But published it certainly would be, for Moonglum now saw his friend as more than a somewhat moody wandering mercenary with a talent for magic.)

Instinctively and rationally, Elric and his friend decided it would be wise to make allies of these unusual women. They could be of considerable help in reaching home. He saw the sense, as Moonglum did, of maintaining friend-ship with them. Moonglum wondered if, at some point, the empress would remember her debt to them. She continued to obsess about her lost honey. She was almost compulsive in her search. She did not seem ungenerous, merely thoughtless. Elric noticed this quality of single-mindedness in all of them. They were all of about the same age as their empress and her captain and, most of the time, if not under orders, were friendly, relaxed and flirtatious in an un-sophisticated way which made Moonglum feel protective rather than lustful.

Meanwhile, stopping to camp, a bottle of blue honey wine was passed around until even Elric lost his usual habits of vigilance and safety. And, in their cups, these pretty women admitted that every trader who took his first sip of the season was influenced by their blushing taste. The two men found this description oddly unsuited to the women's delicate beauty and were inhib-ited, embarrassed. It did, however, go a little way to oiling the social wheels, until the women's conversation was so circuitous it was all that even they could do to join in. And they displayed a rare naïveté for women of their age. Elric wondered at this odd kind of innocence.

He refused to think ill of them. Indeed he grew nostalgic for those evenings in his youth when he had heard the ancients conversing about old times in Imrryr. And Moonglum, on the other side of a flickering peat fire, looked across to where Elric, a lonely figure, sat brooding against a pale rock.

After a moment his eyes rested on the sword Elric still carried at his side. And he wondered if the runeblade and the demon Lord of Chaos were the same entity. Or did Arioch only in certain circumstances now choose to haunt the sword? Or had Arioch left Stormbringer forever? If so, what was the character of the blade itself. Was a sword merely its choice of form, and was Elric merely an extension of its being?

Soon, such anxieties were far from Moonglum's head as he caroused with his lady and her loves.

And meanwhile an enormous struggle for ultimate power was taking place in the highest worlds between Law and Chaos, whose struggles define us all.

SIXTEEN

Dreams as Experience

MELARÉ WAS AT last prepared to thank the men for their help. She appeared to have reached this decision after heated debate with the evidently more diplomatic Captain Shirizha.

Elric and Moonglum, aware that their new hosts could help them reach at least an important stage in their quest for World's Edge, were glad to be diplomats and ride towards the mountains with people familiar with the terrain, though even Elric struggled with a few meanings of their archaic High Melnibonéan. Sometimes he rode in the vanguard, sometimes with the albino empress, asking her many questions about her people's culture and history. Offering stories of his own branch of Phoorn. The name for their city, *Kirinmoir*, their "honey-well temple" and the bees, *kareenm*, appeared almost identical and had subtle differences in their grammar.

She readily accepted his account of Melniboné being a colony of the Phoorn, an old collective name of both his people and the dragon folk, on the far side of the world. She was pleased to hear of others like them. "It is in our history how we compromised to give your people time to escape and start a better civilisation."

"I wonder if we both were not tricked," said Elric thoughtfully.

These women seemed to give birth to few if any male peers. Did they copulate at all? wondered Moonglum. Every word had a maternal root. Ancestry was measured in mothers. In formal language they called themselves *the Keepers of the Bees* and *Protectors of the Hive*.

Her immediate class in their society was the Empress's Guard. For her true peers were only the women of her personal clan, each of whom was addressed as Princess by their social inferiors, the officer class, whose function was to be the immediate rulers and soldiers of the hoi polloi. "Should the empress be killed or otherwise indisposed, her Captain of the Guard shall appoint a new captain and shall assume her functions and powers in an instant."

"A very orderly society," Elric murmured when she told him this.

"Or a boring one." She smiled. "All to a good purpose, you'll agree. We do not lack for immediate heirs."

"The purpose?"

"To make one's people safe."

"Their purpose?"

"To preserve their culture, which will inform and preserve others."

"You are merely conservative? You have no desires, no destiny?"

"We conserve the best, I think. We exist so that our children shall know their ancestral lessons!" She flared (though enjoying their argument).

"You are not merely a reactionary?" He smiled. "Perhaps your only response to innovations is uncertainty and fear! Do you fear new things you cannot control? Must you always silence new voices, not by reason but by threats? Maybe you show no respect for ancestral wisdom, yet you fear the new? It is in the nature of those who follow Law. Your language has an authoritarian slant."

She recognised the direction of his argument, nodding. "So you follow the Way of the Balance? A multiverse of moderation? Are you a theologian, perhaps?"

"Ah!" said the albino, almost amused. "I am an immoderate being, of immoderate appetites and passions. But I keep moderate views."

"I see that you speak true. So? The Balance? Law? Chaos?"

"I am disposed to serve Chaos, even though she sometimes is indisposed to serve me. Indeed we have always served Chaos, and been well served in return. It is a tradition in my family, but I find most settled ways of life dull—and dangerous for you."

This certainly surprised her. "How so?"

"You know I am by nature an outlaw, madam, even though once an emperor. I am made to live in the margins. I challenge and test the law if nothing else. I also trust Paradox. Not the court jesters' pretty paradox, or those of the *ybseed*, that paradox for its own sake, but that paradox which describes the truth. Which lies beyond wall after wall of this omniverse!"

She thought on this briefly. "Ultimately, I suppose I trust Law's certainties and those who trust it. Law, however, also gambles. It believes in the certainty and constancy of systems and also of the altruism that exists in every creature." She frowned. "But there is a great enemy marching against us, and I hardly know a strategy to resist them. If you can do something to help us"—she spoke quietly into his ear—"we'll pay any price."

After listening gravely, he said, "Madam, I must warn you. I live a life of torment, rarely able to sleep through a night. I am a fratricide. I killed my beloved. I question the nature of gods and men. I wake up screaming in words perhaps only your folk and the eldest Phoorn know! Few others do. The secrets I possess are shameful. There is no forgiving them. The sword I carry is a living being, taking the life-force of others and feeding it to me. I survive on death, madam. Without death I cannot live!"

"True of all," she said, unmoved.

"I steal the souls of others!"

"As do we all in some way."

"I could not survive without drugs or the life-force of others, madam. Without them I cannot live! If I told you all I'd done, you would be disgusted. As vampires live by stolen blood, I survive by stealing the souls of others."

She had listened patiently.

"I have told you what I want," she said. "And, if you do not value it, I value it the more."

"Very well," he said. He was surprised by her calm as well as by her request. "But it must be when I'm leaving and after you have shown us your map and how to reach World's Edge and the way to our own sphere."

Her grin was suddenly boyish. "You are a true Melnibonéan aristocrat, my lord. As in our picture-scrolls and the magic cubes they bring out for children on Vanothdane. We have been told of the heroes who once rode on Phoorn across these valleys."

He saw no reason not to let her charm him. He still had enough of his curiosity left to be interested in the unfolding situation.

Thus, independently, the two adventurers came to the decision to guest with the saurian riders while there was something to be gained.

Moonglum did not ask his friend what he had agreed. Elric would tell him in his own time, if he told Moonglum anything at all. The Elwheri was always discreet. If he spoke his inner thoughts to anyone, it was generally to his only friend, the doomed albino. For now, he would mind his own business.

They were below the snowline at last, and the strange, swaying motion of the saurians sent up even brighter rainbow sprays, covering their blue and silver riders like thousands of tiny diamonds.

"We could have come this far without their company," muttered the redhead when he and Elric again rode side by side. "Though without the speed of certainty. There's a guarded cave. You can see the trail the knights made in getting here and the trail they made coming back, burdened, it now appears, with stolen honey. They had some horses then. Cattle? Moving as quickly as possible and pursued by the Kirinmoiri. Their lizards made those serpentine tracks back and forth. They seem malleable beasts, their mounts. Surprisingly swift."

"They do. Easily trained by those who are familiar with them, it seems."

"I prefer a pony or a good warhorse. They do not tire like ordinary horses."

Elric paused. "I, too," he said absently. Why did his thoughts keep returning to his past? He was thinking not of lizards or horseflesh, nor indeed his human princess Zarozinia, but of Cymoril, his beloved cousin, singing the wild song of their Phoorn dragon cousins who carried them into the tumultuous skies, among the towering spires and crags of old Melniboné. *The worst lie is the one you believe and defend with such intensity yourself. The lie you tell the world when you feel at your most irresolute.* He remembered the last time they were together, blending their voices in the odd, complex harmonies they loved. Before Imrryr the Beautiful fell, betrayed. And now all were gone. Most were dead. The dragons slept a long while. They had to renew their venom, dissipated by the raids he had led, and the dragons must get closer to the furnaces at the heart of the world. The Phoorn, who required centuries of rest, but could not go without heat for too long.

Heads lifted to scent their way ahead, tongues licking at eyes, ears picking up faraway sounds, their amiable expressions and gait making them seem friendly, gregarious and comical, like curious children on a journey, the saurians slowed down, suddenly more alert. They changed only when they sensed danger, and their huge pink mouths, powerful as crocodiles', opened wide and hissed a deafening warning. They lacked teeth, but razor edges of white bone stretched from nose to throat, above and below.

At their next rest, drinking a few drops of the sweet liquid, Moonglum blew frosty breath into the air and slapped his arms against his waist. "Did you hear that?"

"I caught a deer call somewhere, but I've seen no herd. Maybe a huntsman's horn to his family. Or perhaps a Melnibonéan intonation even you do not recognise, Master Philologist?" Elric winked and gathered up the reins.

"I fear we face increasing danger. Respect me, Elric!"

"You think they intend to lure us to our deaths? Lead us into an ambush? Bring deaths and dreams, as in the old ballad?" Mocking him. "*Oh free was he at twenty-three and dead he was at thirty.*"

"Did not the Faraway speak of this to you? In that dream? Was there a point to our detour to the Inarondu Oracle?"

"You make impossible structures upon unbelievable alliances! Why should our food providers fawn and flatter, eh? Your power wanes; it was never enough forever to listen to our circulating melodies. The variations accumulate. No dream has one meaning! What dream?" For a moment it seemed he thought this a dream. Their blue brandy had confused them.

"Your death dream. I promised to prepare you for it! The other night, long before we found the village." Moonglum was in a mood to remind his friend of this.

"I am not yet ready to take that step," the albino said, slightly mishearing.

"I must tell you, old friend, that I will warn you when I am. I have a premonition. 'Tis all! You shall always have the choice. I have even prepared for a special fate, and I am full of confidence."

"We live in a world of melancholy death and sad wizardry." Moonglum, reconciled to his friend's vagueness, did not do Elric the discourtesy of touching him. He turned away. For a while, after the twilight drew in under the shadowy walls of granite, the pair rode ahead of the women, wondering ultimately if they were to be hindered or helped to find World's Edge, the one friend counselling the other.

His memories of Cymoril returned with an almost overwhelming rush. Physical and spiritual disgust filled him. He remembered her strong hands behind her back as she led him along the ragged path between vegetables and legumes, a servant's patch, as was the habit of their people to bestow on favourites. She had paused only to pluck a few marigolds from a flower bed and plait them into a golden coronet which glowed like a halo in her raven hair. How he had loved her! He had grown up surrounded by beautiful women, yet no-one was like Cymoril.

Cymoril, whom, in his pride and arrogance, he had murdered when he returned to claim her. He had been a fool to show such pride. And all that he had learned, he had learned too late. Too late to save Imrryr the Beautiful with all her history going back long before the coming of Man.

Elric was about to ask where and how they would spend the night when the steep incline levelled out for a little, and they saw a sandy road leading into the yawning black mouth of a massive cave. Was this where their hosts stored food and water? Their ponies snorted and whinnied, pawing the light yellow sand, evidently disturbed . . .

"I can imagine the size of the animal which makes that their home," said Moonglum with a shudder. "Pray to all our gods it is only one. I heard of a bear living in our own far north, that would choose a little house of that capacity. The *unf'th* or Immoveable Bear. It would not have to bend to enter that cave." It remained obvious to Elric that nobody, including Moonglum, really expected the cave to be occupied by bats, let alone by a giant bear, but the albino proceeded cautiously, knowing the only supernatural aid he might call on came from his own failing energies and his unresponsive blade.

The cave would be good to sleep in before they continued their journey, which was proving a fairly long one.

Their ponies suddenly began to stamp in alarm. Something shocked them! Elric realised they had ridden ahead too far. A chilling high-pitched whistling came from the twilight. The ponies were well-disciplined and brought themselves under control, shaking their long, bright manes as if admonishing themselves. There, in the lengthening shadows, blocking the path, stood five massive, broad-shouldered, broad-headed buffalo with sharp, brass-bound pointed horns over two metres apart, snorting through their flabbering brown and pink nostrils, stamping hoofs wider than war-shields against the echoing rock and glaring through huge round trencher eyes rimmed with bloody white streaks. Belligerent, if a little confused, lifting their mighty heads again as the whistle sounded and Captain Shirizha came riding up.

"Easy boys, easy!" A snort of recognition. The bulls grew a little calmer. They knew and trusted her.

The men of the far Ehsmiri plains bred wild to domestic animals to make self-sufficient grazing cattle that needed only protection from the worst of the environment or predators. Elric admired the ferocious beasts. He had seen them thrive in many harsh circumstances. The herders expected food and warmth from her. She got reliable meat and war-animals from them.

The lizards and the bulls appeared to be familiars. They mingled, nuzzling, with obvious pleasure at their reunion. The cavalrywomen found collapsible buckets and, riding ahead to the cliff face, returned with food and water for the animals. They began feeding the beasts more or less indiscriminately, laughing and joking and telling the events of the recent past over and over again. They were, however, surprised by how far the other cattle had strayed. Even with food, all the animals still seemed pretty restless. The massive buffalo were mild-tempered enough, once they recognised the women, but they seemed nervous of something nearby.

Another shrill whistle. After a little hesitation, the cattle formed a line and trotted into the cave like old milk cows into a familiar barn.

"We must warm our poor lizards," said Shirizha, "as we must ourselves. There are fires within that we can kindle. Not long and you'll be in sight of our City of the Well. Some say she is legendary Tanelorn. If so, Tanelorn must have been a wonderful city indeed."

"Indeed," said Elric, with a hint of nostalgia. He was the only mortal he knew who had found Tanelorn and voluntarily left her. He blinked as he entered the cave's gloomy entrance.

The inner walls were in blackness. The first metre or two were barely visible. Long-used but unguarded troughs, urns and storage racks were dwarfed by the cave's vast entrance. Here, it was warmed by three dormant fires springing to life almost immediately as they were nursed by the brands of the cavalrywomen. More bovine snorts of satisfaction. Firelight deepened the shivering shadows, and it was impossible to see into them. The cave was at least as high as it was long. *Is this a cave at all?* Moonglum wondered. *Could this be the mythical tunnel into the World Above? Oh, I am sure there is danger here. I smell it, mixed with our salvation!*

Sudden consternation among the cavalry! Noisy snorts. The stamping of hoofs. Loud shouts! Something was lost. Brands were lit as soldiers ran into the depths. Melaré called after them, was not obeyed and followed reluctantly. Black shadows against pale red rock. Elric hesitated to join a fray when he did not know whose interest it served.

Horrible shouts and screams. A confusion of sounds. Metal meeting metal.

Someone called in lilting, silvery Melnibonéan, *"They have the rest of the cattle back here, drugged or slaughtered. It's a filthy ambush!"*

Shouting a few confused words about civilisation and freedom, Moonglum disappeared into the darkness.

And so, with a shrug, Elric went to join him.

Now he heard hard breathing, groans, sudden screams. He made out bloodied helmets, faces sweating in torchlight, weapons clashing and sparking. Men and women struggled in full armour, grim, teeth grating. More scavengers, used to slaughter, these were Amahkians, too. Ruthless, quick, efficient killers. "They outnumber us five to one!" cried Melaré.

"If you count the shadows!" Laughing heartily, Moonglum waded into the battle he could barely see.

The Amahkian knights or brigand tribesmen had taken the party's measure as it advanced unknowingly and hidden their horses, waiting in the upper galleries, crouched behind the carcasses they had been stealing before the unexpected arrival of the women who used their buffalo as incidental guards. The silver and blue women herders of these massive buffalo usually grazed them elsewhere. They were doubtless out there with their throats cut. This time Elric and the others had been equally careless. At a time when hungry tribes and mercenaries were massing, it was sloppy soldiering on everyone's part not to have done more scouting and more defending. Elric's contempt for himself was, if anything, greater than it was for these wolfish opportunists. Cursing them and their unsavoury calling, noting his sword's almost sluggish performance, Elric continued taking his harvest of souls. But his sword-arm grew more tired than usual, and he began to despair for all who would fall to Chaos.

To Moonglum, himself reinvigorated on blue wine, it seemed that the albino's body gathered strength with every graceful movement until suddenly he seemed weightless as he flew among the savage warriors, clearing a path for the one they called "swift ghost" in Elwher, and together they slew with an elegant, practised precision any surgeon would envy. Not a single enemy was wounded. Every one was efficiently killed as the pair, usually with a quick slash to the jugular, unless Stormbringer paused briefly to feed deep, with Melaré close beside them, fought a path to the blue-armoured warriors surrounded by hardened, habitually cruel Amahkian soldiers.

They fought only by firelight now, unable to make out anything but the most obvious details of their antagonists. The "knights" were cutting down too many. The women were brave but inexperienced, unused to such brutal fighting. Soon the remains of the squadron as well as Melaré, Elric, Shirizha, and Moonglum, had their backs to the rocks as the scavengers slowly drove them into a small, shallow cave off the main one.

They could see almost nothing as Melaré and Shirizha suddenly began to sing a song together, a beautiful, thrilling song, new even to Elric, who knew what it was. The women were spell-weaving. Every part of Elric wanted to join them, but he did not know the song well enough. He was surprised to sense the levels of magic in it. As their song echoed through the caves, the rock rattled gently. Then it rattled again, louder, stronger. A silence. A soft grumbling reverberated through newly opening fissures. At the command of the women they backed as far as possible into the small cave. All they could see now was firelight, the occasional guttering torch.

And, though for the moment Elric, Moonglum and the two women were somehow keeping the Amahkians back, they remained enormously outnumbered. There was no escape for them.

Then the song grew louder, becoming a strange, lilting buzz, and rose until it was painful before it sank into a murderous grumble, thankfully out of sight. Through the flickering light Elric saw what at first seemed to be a funnel of black smoke. It slowly rose upright until it resembled a nearing tornado. The noise grew louder, an almost deafening buzz, and louder, the same brief tune over and over. As it blackened the air before them, they could see that it was made up of hundreds and thousands of large bees with yellow and blue stripes and prominent stingers. Coming closer, they were massive, some the size of voles or mice. Some, perhaps the wing-leaders, were as large as rats. They seemed almost to lead raids against the hives. Many landed on the defenders but did not sting. The Amahkians began to moan, to slap and scratch at themselves, swords and axes forgotten as the bees struck with bloodstained natural swords, over and over, never losing those bloody stingers, but continuing to sting so hard that men's faces and limbs began to swell.

More bees formed a kind of armour on Elric, Moonglum and the women of Kirinmoir. They clustered thickly. Everyone on their side was almost completely engulfed. Under a mysterious compulsion, the bees did not sting the Kirinmoir defenders! Some appeared to be more aggressive, but not towards the women and those they befriended.

Elric soon grew used to monstrous faceted eyes caressing him as purely protective bees crawled all over him. Their hard carapaces, covered in yellow and black patterns which in places seemed to shade to blue, scraped against his skin, while their spindly legs itched and made him want to scratch. He was aware of a vivid, alien intelligence, a sense of bonding. He forced himself not to respond. They soon began to leave, slowly at first, then in clouds, still attacking the Amahkians, flying, it seemed, to defend their fellows.

Elric was astonished. As far as he and his companions were concerned, the bees were benign! He had never seen bees like them. The warrior women clearly controlled them with those murmured melodies! The air continued to carry a dying note of calm as the bees re-formed and drove like drills at the astonished soldiers. The armoured men and women were terrified as the bees crawled into the chinks between the metal. They turned and ran, rattling and clanking and falling over their own arms and badly strapped greaves. Then, as the men and their mounts struggled out of the main cave, the song grew shriller and seemed to bite into the rock—slicing it into layered shale which slowly slipped inch by inch towards the battling tribesmen, who only noticed too late when the shale gathered momentum and fell with a crash, sending choking dust everywhere.

The stuff stung their eyes, but, to their elation, the mortals and bees together had put a barrier between themselves and their enemies which would take days or weeks to clear and give them time to prepare the city for any attack. Elric turned, looking for Moonglum, as, suddenly, another shower of slate slid and crashed to the cave floor, adding a massive wall through which a ferret could not crawl. He saw his friend stagger out of the mist, roaring with laughter and holding up some horrid trophy, identifiable by the blood and hair as being of animal origin. Moonglum rarely took a scalp unless he hoped to make use of it. The old Eastern fighters had always taken scalps, but Elwheri made a fetish of it. He saw Elric and yelled mysteriously, "In case the ladies need a hand!" and put whatever it was into his shoulder bag with the other superstitious totems of his people.

Elric was still unsure if the ladies needed any kind of help from them. Moonglum had a wild, reckless air about him, and it was possible he had lost his fighting focus. Exposure even to the smallest manifestations of the supernatural was inclined to alarm mortals. Sometimes warriors like themselves experienced light-headedness and disorientation from the exhilaration of the fight.

Panting and coughing in the dusty air, Moonglum lowered his swords. A brief bow. "Magic! By Oillis, ladies, I wish you'd embraced it sooner!" He picked up a flickering brand. "I thought you were helpless against them." He bowed to both. "In the nick of time, eh?"

No-one shared his enthusiasm. None had been excited by a success which had exhausted their metaphysic and depleted their spirits. They watched in silence as the bees flew erratically back up the tunnel again and were quickly out of sight.

"We had a little power left over," Melaré said: "We can only use it for self-defence. We would have no power over the rock spirits did they not choose to help us." She took a scarf from her captain and wiped her face and hands. The whiteness of her skin was almost luminous in that imperfect light. "The bees and the rockslide spent, as it were, our credit! We have given all we dare. Here. But time cannot be wasted. We must get to Kirinmoir as quickly as we can. Bring out all our troops together. If we have to. That rabble's too lazy to follow now. If they did, the maze would soon turn them mad. None can solve that mystery logically for it was done by nature and magic in unison and follows no logic. The few who do solve those mysteries or the occasional band which makes it across the mountains must then cross country to reach our fortified city of silver Kirinmoir."

Elric was wondering to himself if mazes were an instinctive defence of all his ancestors!

"Just as well, Prince Elric, that you are with us," Empress Melaré called over her shoulder, her voice echoing a little in the wide tunnel. "There are marauding bands all over the outside world. We were fools to follow those honey-thieves, but there was a principle at stake, and if one band steals with impunity, others will try the same. So we pursued them. For fifty thousand and fifty years or more we did business with the outside world and were on good terms with all our neighbours beyond the mountains. That they considered us gods for much of that time made it, of course, fairly easy to dissuade them from violence against us. A few still come to worship at the rock on which our Temple and our ancient city is built. We lived in tranquillity for so long." She took a deep breath and let it out as a sigh.

"We lived in some delusion until, we heard, the Amahkians attacked and killed two of our own last winter. Two more in spring and five up to now. What is this killing which follows not the contracts of Law or Chaos? They kill peasants under our protection! They had spoken of you and of our own Ahmi, who considered seeking you out on the moonbeam roads and begging for help. Oh, not as kin. We had all heard of a demon with white hair who resembled us in appearance. I had not then understood you to be of our blood! I felt we were at our full strength as cavalry and infantry does not pursue. Though we fought off the few raids that came then, I knew our defences had stood for too long unstrengthened. I still felt we could defend our city, but not the countryside of our valley. I pray all our mountaineers are home. They guard the difficult overhead ways into us for it is a long and deadly climb through those gloomy crags. In containing the tribes, we have seriously dissipated our cavalry. All our defences are under considerable pressure. We are expecting them in strength next spring. Most of our soldiers were recalled to duty about two weeks ago! Why those disguised brigands pretended to be merchants and acted independently I know not! I am baffled by many recent incidents. Maybe they have exhausted their desire to survive. I am serious. There is a point in battle when a fatigued man suddenly loses the will to fight or indeed to live. Hunger, maybe, is driving these degenerates? Fresh leaders with new ideas? We'll know soon enough."

"As you travel across those ruined lands, you find wretched refugee camps. Soldiers, civilians, rich and poor, aristocrats and commoners, they are refugees, all of them thin as skeletons," said Moonglum. "Slums made of every city still standing. Hordes of homeless people. Recruitment with the united tribes is inevitable. They offer a way out and up. One last mad embrace! Before we left the Four Cities we noted one name growing louder amongst the squawking carrion eaters of the slums. Ramada Sabaru, the Golden Lord?"

Shirizha shook her head, frowning. "A name on the wind, that's all . . . says the story. I only know it's a half-forgotten companion tale from Old Alun's Faeyrie Republic. Another bloody lullaby to poison our sleep and ill prepare our people for the bloody war to come! Oh, Kirinmoir, Kirinmoir! I have already prayed for you in earnest until I hadn't a howling rag dry. This outlander? This Westerner? A faded suit of clothes. Perhaps? Why so? That the reason for his name? He sounds no proper or improper bells. A powerful war-lord, you say, bellowing of Order and Discipline because they are terrified all the knowledge in their heads, all the crimes upon their conscience, will mingle and explode. Well, that can't harm our Kirinmoir!"

"Maybe it was nothing. Just a little familiar, maybe. A children's adventure tale. A wanky witcher who went to the bad! A name I heard in some coarse foreign tongue. The tale about a tailor who would become king. Ramada Sabaru . . . ? Who knows how to marshal men? Or the archer and the pikeman? None better than our philosopher-generals! Not to mention ancient compacts which protect us.

"You have already encountered two of the smaller bands. The few camps in the forest are the remnants of much larger bands, as I'm sure you know, my lord duke. They have raided and even *eaten* rivals. We saw the evidence. But now these cannibals turn their hungry eyes towards Kirinmoir.

"Surely you did not ignore—"

"We heard the name, and it meant little until now. The mercenaries, the invaders and the once-peaceful tribes, some of whom are still trading with us, as you saw, came and went, knowing us to be invulnerable. That particular band of Amahkian Knights will be driven now to follow him. They are hungry. He offers free food. They are angry. He offers new swords and armour. Ramada Sabaru's Chaos banner is raised as a result of the wars we helped wage? They say Chaos aids him already! Villagers, tribesmen, anyone from the far side of the mountain! They have all become raiders with only one simple goal—the fabled City of the Hive." She shrugged. "To become rich and rule the ruins! Someone is bringing them together. Inspiring them with feats of daring and eloquence. We see the type wherever Fate sends us."

Where had he heard the name?

"Perhaps it was not Ramada Sabaru. I have no proof that this Ramada Sabaru is even a real man or demigod or an obvious charlatan. How does he get war-weary men to fight again? What can he be promising that has not been promised?"

Shirizha agreed. "Stupid men change their leaders rather than their ambitions. Our spies confirm what you say. Some tribes have long dreamed of conquering our wealthy fortress, of controlling our Great Well, taking over the honey trade and thereby, as they see it, the world. But can we build better defences quickly enough?"

"I doubt it."

"You're pessimistic?"

"Your defences are good, but we have a saying in Elwher: the stronger the citadel, the weaker are those it shelters. You have grown to trust your defences too much. While you have known tranquillity, your enemies have almost certainly been testing the very things giving you that tranquillity." Moonglum raised an eyebrow.

"It's true." Her smile was rueful. "The only clear path to our valley and the Citadel of the Well is through our great cave system. Our cattle helped defend those tunnels. They know the way through by instinct. Perhaps if a skilled hunter followed a steer they could plot a course through." She became quickly aware that her speculation might hold some truth. "I do know that wild tribes began assembling near the caverns some while before the last civil war brought down the Four Cities and so gave them many more recruits. They have sorcery, we hear, and the engineering skills to sink a new tunnel if they wish."

"We have probably seen fragments of more than one tribe," he said. "They are greedy and worse, hungry! Roaming individuals who have no food might strip another man of his own flesh. Now what I have heard is confirmed. These are warbands made up of many tribes seeking prey. Stealing from others if necessary."

"They have in turn joined larger bands, and so it goes. Now this army has joined forces with this charismatic leader. Its ranks are further swelled by fleeing rebels, scholars, musicians and whatnot trash. Trade has been reduced to theft and defence. Other spies and turncoats say the Amahkians have fresh allies from the West, possibly this Golden Ramada Sabaru, who are persuading the alien intruders who do not belong here. We have been here for millennia! We brought them the very idea of civilisation! But they are mighty jealous!

"A Holy War! What better than righteous piety to disguise over-reaching greed?" Moonglum watched her face as she continued. "Even now Amahkian scouts ride to bring many, many more here. Your information confirms what we have seen. Others, who waited to hear the victory before applauding, will take a day or less to reach their camps! They plan to raid, possibly conquer and occupy, our beautiful city. They would take our Great Citadel and the Dragon Well. It is Kirinmoir and all she shelters, all she serves and who serve her, whom we defend! And shall always defend! That was why we were out here originally. When we learned of riders, posing as merchants, who had stolen some honey, it made sense to pursue them. Blue honey! Stolen honey! They must know that's a stupid idea. Stealing from us! We will make them pay dear when we exact our revenge. Lord Elric! Join our leadership!"

Elric shrugged. "We are bound to aid thee, madam. And so we shall, as we agreed. But we have a notion to return home. I have been an aristocrat. My people ruled the world. I lost all for revenge. My present status suits me!"

"Oh, join us here as equals!" cried Melaré, half jesting. "You have told us your story. Here is the empire you could have ruled, Prince Elric! The empire you should have ruled! An empire founded on the idea of bringing peace to all nations! We can begin a new dynasty, mingling the blood of two ancient families. We certainly have similarities of blood! Join us where you are not an outcast. Forget your supposed destiny. Stay and keep safe and then lead our armies into battle! Become Lord of the Hives! It is a noble cause! Our priestesses will welcome you, I know, as their natural saviour. They have given so much of themselves to us and to keeping our destined course! Through their wise counsel we have followed the ways of Law. We have built and never destroyed! Help us drive the barbarians back and establish our peaceful empire across a world crying out for stability and certainty! Join us here. Once the battle is won, we shall oversee an empire where love, understanding and peace rule forever! We shall pacify the world as we once pacified this valley. And you agree it is peaceful, do you not? To build the New Tanelorn! The City of the Balance."

Moonglum glanced at his friend with quizzical irony. "In a land where neither Law nor Chaos appears to have much power are not these words dangerous? I sense it has reached no verdict." Elric ghosted a smile but said nothing.

She looked from one to the other. "You would have your places in the Annals of Destiny . . ."

They remained untempted.

"Land, should you desire to accept a title?"

Elric said, "We wish, as we said, to find our way to a region known as World's Edge, a waste of ice, we hear, where the Upper and Lower worlds meet. We have a map fragment. We heard you had its partner. A trail is shown both to and from your city, so we know we must carry on through the valley and into the Far Wilderness. In that wilderness, also known as the *Weltesmarchen*, anyone with enough will can cross into the other world. They are usually disappointed, however. Or so we believe. Personally, we know of none who has returned!"

"So I understand."

"We have no high expectations of any world, Sir Moonglum and myself, and only a few moderate ones of our own. How do we reach World's Edge?"

"As I promised. You shall learn. Once our bargain's sealed."

"And that is all you desire of me? The world? It's difficult, my lady, to believe."

"Oh, once I wanted more than that," she said, "but until now the goddess was not in our favour. Now, since this world is dragging us into conflict, why not use our superior resources to tear down the old and build a world of harmony under one great Law?"

"If you could impose harmony on the world, my dear empress"—Elric felt a rising of his old interests—"then it would be putting yourself above the Gods and the Balance! Would they not object?"

"Of course. We are still negotiating an agreement?"

"With whom?"

Instead of telling him, she grinned. "I'm sure you can guess!" And she goaded her unwieldy beast to another part of the line, to give instruction to one of her party.

Elric's physical feelings disturbed him. His own sense of danger was warning him. Death was in the air. He feared for the worst.

SEVENTEEN

Revelations in a Rose Garden

THE CAVE STRETCHED for miles under the mountains. The deeper they penetrated, the colder it became. Their way was lit only by the torches they carried and by the few others they found still fixed to brackets in the cold limestone. Every few hundred metres were well-appointed posts, deserted as the guards went to the empress's aid. As the hours progressed, the lizards felt it worst of all and grew steadily more sluggish. Their riders were forced to bring the torches in closer and to beat their mount's extremities, to warm their heavy reptilian bodies.

At a signal from Empress Melaré, the party came to a stop in a high-roofed cathedral-like intersection from which six other tunnels branched. She murmured a few words to Shirizha, who agreed, and they started down one of the tunnels without further debate. Some of the cattle were already ahead, lumbering down this tunnel.

Melaré laughed. "They are more anxious to get home than we are!"

When Moonglum asked Shirizha where the other tunnels led, he was told simply, "To a maze," with skimpy elaboration. "They'll not manage the maze without help from one of us or powerful magic that will probably not work. That is the nature of affirmation. Magic is very weak here. I believe they'll hold off beginning any other attack until spring. Thanks to this maze those predatory dogs cannot follow us, even if they wished to."

"This is the only safe road through the mountains," Melaré told him. "The unsafe ones which are above are mere trails and are very treacherous. They can only be crossed on foot. This is known as the Honey Road. Traders use it every year. Usually they are met by our people and are blindfolded before continuing. Our city is rich, thanks to our Great Well." She told him how they and their Phoorn allies had fled from the Cold Hunters, the Fhoimoor Elder Gods who proudly called themselves Snake-slayers. "They sought to kill all our reptiles. They hated them, called them demons, including the Phoorn, who were not true reptiles at all, but a species of their own. They were driven by the Cold Hunters into this realm, discovering a way through the rock to the next plane. We, too, were lucky, building our city during a lull in the interminable battling, and able to resist and ultimately defeat the Fhoimoor when they came again into this plane. We found a spring in a fissure in the rock. Around this and another spring we built our impregnable city, fed by the twin springs, one of which became a well and the other remained the spring which feeds our mighty moat! The hill contained a deep crater at its centre, and around this we built up our city and the Temple at her heart. Before Kirinmoir and its Temple were complete, the Cold Hunters came after us again. The Phoorn fled into the Temple and down deep under the city's foundations and were trapped there. Eventually they died. We stood our ground. After many years, we succeeded in making alliances and winning battles until at last Kirinmoir grew as strong as she was beautiful. Now we no longer fear visitors. We welcome them."

Today no human from beyond the mountains considered themselves civilised until they had visited the blue, silver and green towers, the glittering fortifications and the Temple of the Great Well, her museums which told the story of the ancient Eldren and what they had gained and lost in their long migration, her grand art galleries where so much of their wealth was for the public, the libraries and auditoria, theatres and arenas. Her undulating viaducts and her distilleries and breweries will be guarded by the empress's unsleeping soldiers.

"Our honey was discovered a century or so after we settled in the shade of the Witnesses, those gigantic sheltering boulders amongst which Kirinmoir settled and grew. Where we were safe. Just in time for us, for we were smaller in numbers than the dominant humans."

"But you prevailed."

"At some cost," she replied, closing the conversation.

Soon the air grew a little warmer and the great lizards less sluggish. Another hour and the riders felt almost uncomfortably hot. They began to loosen their clothing as the cavern roof lowered overhead, and at last they saw bright sunshine ahead! The animals snorted with pleasure. Their great clawed feet scratched at the rocky ground. Even their huge eyes glowed with renewed energy, golden in the fresh morning light! The long-horned buffalo were uncertain in their movements, since most were rarely driven so far. The leader eventually took charge, and they followed him. Only as they scented the fresh air did they become aware of the almost overwhelming stink of cattle.

The ponies whickered, brightening in the dewy atmosphere, growing increasingly nervous. The riders had more difficulty controlling them, fighting against the beasts' natural desire to break into a run and reach the sweet-smelling air ahead. But the riders all managed their mounts well. They had them under rein by the time they broke into a gorgeous stretch of rolling grassland, broken by little copses of birch, pine, poplar and oak. Unfearing deer grazed, looking up with passing curiosity as the riders began to emerge from the cavern entrance.

The grassland ahead, gentle green drumlins rolling to the horizon with spreading oaks against a bright blue sky, had a quiet sense of long-settled peace. Drystone walls ran up and down the fields grazed by ruminants, broken by spinneys and streams, with the sound of rushing rivers and waterfalls, fresh hay lifted into stacks and white, easy smoke rising from some yeoman's chimney. It was perhaps the most peaceful rural paradise either had ever seen or imagined.

They passed through a series of wickets, overseen by more of the women soldiers, until at last the mountain pass was behind them and Melaré explained that only one group of traders, already waiting there, could pass through at a time. Elric could not help considering the parallels with the island capital of Imrryr, City of the Dragon Masters, and wish he could show her his own home. Was it an instinct in his people to find safety in such places?

The surrounding country was indeed a paradise, with a wonderfully temperate climate and rich earth in which all kinds of fruits, legumes, vegetables, tubers and gorgeous flowers were tended, mostly in market gardens, seen above the low walls of cottage allotments. There were larger fields where wheat, maize, semolina and other crops were ripening. The empress told her guests that they could raise two full crops a year, with harvest soon to come. And, in the far, far distance, pastel shades of clouds rose with the sun into a pale blue sky framing mountains almost identical to those they had just passed through.

Moonglum was astonished. "This climate is perfect, lying as it does in an ideal configuration. It supports a wealth of food. The women are comely." With a gallant flourish. "And close enough to mortals to make mates. What sane man would truly not wish to settle here? I can see how farming people would find it attractive. Yet the land seems fairly sparsely populated."

"There are clear laws regarding population extremism. The people can reproduce themselves just once." Shirizha laughed. "Two generally prove enough!"

"And should they have three?"

"Then one is removed. Parent or child. 'Four's a family, five's a crime,' as they say in our kindergartens." She laughed again. "That rarely happens. Lots of 'fosters' of course, but we turn a blind eye. If the numbers don't change, we don't punish."

"And who administers such laws?"

"District governors."

"Elected?"

"Appointed."

"By whom?"

"By the priestesses through our empress." She darted a quick, puzzled smile. "Who else?"

"The governors are your people?"

"Of course."

"You rule them. As Melniboné ruled the Young Kingdoms?"

"We protect them from marauders, both animal and their own kind. They trade us their produce for our honey. We have no need of prominent manifestations of Law and Chaos here. All is in balance."

Moonglum felt like someone questioning a child's innocence. He shrugged and rode beside her in silence for a while. It could be difficult for an ex-Chancellor of Elwher's Republican parliament (what Elric translated as "a duke") to understand what he was hearing at times. He had travelled from his homeland to discover for himself what strange ideas of civilisation other cultures could teach him. In that the Elwheri resembled Elric. Their ideas, however, were sometimes so far apart neither could follow the other's logic.

"Did they also defend themselves once?" he asked at last.

"They lost that power when Pronal Rinde drove the malevolent spirits from the valley and took upon himself the task of defence, both spiritual and temporal."

"They were not disappointed?"

"They expressed none. When the priestesses elected to serve the public good, we saw no conflict, for they called on the Justice of the Runestaff. There is none fairer. Our enemies could no longer bring supernatural allies against us," she said, "and we are now stronger than any human force. We have plenty of means of defeating these local tribes from the mountains. We have been threatened on occasion. We protect the people who farm these lands, and in turn they feed us well and help us when needed. The priestesses maintain our parliamentary law!"

"The people fight for you?"

"When needed, yes!"

"Your currency, even your whole economy, is based on blue honey. They live such contented lives. Are they good fighters?"

"When they drink their mead!" And she smiled.

That afternoon they stopped at a pleasant village where a friendly hostelry found food for the dozen or so of their party remaining. It was an ideal place to rest, sitting on the crest of a valley, looking over a slate- and thatch-roofed village towards rosewood trees, a pretty river, willows and soft grass. The locals had fenced off with cedar-weave palettes a part of the river so that the young women could bathe naked while they also washed down their saurian steeds. Moonglum suggested to Elric that he found it interesting how these strange young women could enjoy the respect of their peasants who could, by their own reckoning, be turned into ravening and savage fighters, capable of killing with cruelty and without remorse all who threatened this idyllic way of life. Merely with a sip of blue wine.

"It is the essence of feudalism at its best." Again there seemed to be no irony in Elric's response. Moonglum looked at the albino's face, wondering if he really did see approval there! He shrugged and sat down to look at the gentle countryside rolling away into the distance. His friend would forever continue to surprise him.

"How can we ever be certain that we are nearing World's Edge? Is it really so easily reached?"

"It's not the reaching it, it's the strength of mind of remaining in it and of moving forward once you get there." Elric smiled.

"You are not suggesting all this and World's Edge are simply states of mind?"

"I consider it a reasonable possibility, *Duke* Moonglum!"

It took the Republican a moment to understand that Elric was joking with that ridiculous nom de guerre. "Soon you'll be telling me that the moonbeam roads are nothing more than metaphor!" His mouth curling in exasperation, the Elwheri turned away with a sigh.

Methodically, and with great concentration, Elric sat and cleaned blood and filth from hissing black metal. Deep in the sword and possibly not of its dimension, faint red runes writhed in the iron.

Moonglum remained seated for a time.

Then he got up and saw to their ponies. Later, as others of their party relaxed in the evening sun and ate, he wandered down towards a thatched farmhouse surrounded by tall hedges but separated from them by a long gravel path. He entered the gate and found himself almost overwhelmed by the scent of roses. It made him stagger, and he fought against being completely drugged, against that over-comforting glory of soft pink, scarlet and subtle yellow petals falling softly around him, embracing him, forming a clinging blanket of flowers. *Magic! And Melaré had sworn almost all magic was driven out of Kirinmoir.* The scent was drowning him. He could not breathe . . .

Moonglum turned to call a warning! Tripped. And fell over the Empress of Kirinmoir's Captain of the Guard, who was laughing helplessly on the lawn beside him. As he fell, he heard the scream of a young hawk and reflected that spring had come early here.

The hawk circled for a few moments before flying away to the west.

"What?" Moonglum rolled on his back in alarm, hands on the hilts of his twin swords. "Do you entrance me, madam?"

Again she laughed. "Sir, this is a very earthly magic. You are in a rose plantation. The farmer grows them to sweeten our food! Our bees suckle them and turn their homes into honey. Which we steal, always leaving them enough. They sweeten our latrines. Our stables. It is true that they are intoxicating, but naturally so."

Laughing with her, he sat up on the soft grass. "The traders do not only want honey," she said. "They give fine woven goods and good-quality cloth for our seasonings, flavours and perfumes. Our potions and our poisons are valued almost as much as our honey wines. On the southern flank of the valley we also have vineyards."

"It is a rich and contented country, indeed."

"I think so," she said.

He would forever recall that first kiss and how it drowned him in the scent of roses. His political questions forgotten, he only had one other question to ask her.

"Why is your skin so cold?"

EIGHTEEN

The Ingredients of Power

ANOTHER DAY AND Kirinmoir came in sight. She was built upon a central hill surrounded by five others. As if to protect her from something, she was built within six massive granite boulders, covered in lichen, almost human in their rounded contours, big enough to shade the entire city at certain hours, clutching at the sky like monstrous fingers. One huge fissure cradled the old town, which spread around the great rock and outwards. Moonglum recalled that mathematically there was something considered especially benign in the number six. Many old cities were built thus, across a number of drumlins of roughly equal size with a larger city dominant at the centre. An outer wall surrounded every part of the city. Another, moated, wall defended the most ancient part of Kirinmoir. A good omen, perhaps. Not all imperial seats reflected the harmonious marriage of so much wisdom and architecture. Soft rolling hills rose and fell, and the road led up through well-established farms and ancient manor houses and down through pretty villages. The city was not always visible, but came closer and closer. They saw the great grey pointing boulders more frequently. The turrets, the towers, a blue blaze crowning the topmost building. "They have protected Kirinmoir since long before our people came here, pursued by their enemies!" They were like the skulls of giants, thought Moonglum aloud. His new love gasped at his poetic turn.

The saurian riders offered no harm to the human settlements but treated everyone affectionately and well. Indeed, many villagers cheered them as they went by. A contented land. A land in which the Balance thrived and ruled without supernatural aid, for the benefit of all.

Moonglum, relatively recently a Republican, was a little uneasy with the politics of this institution. The world was becoming a whirlpool of ideas as if Law and Chaos debated and questioned every truism under the sun. He was sure there was more than his poor mind could take in. Still, there was a music to Elric's voice that made it easy to listen to, even when the words were sometimes a little obscure. Sooner or later he would say something which made sense most of the time, and that was good enough for Moonglum.

The world was beautiful under a warm, cloudless sky, and little clumps of young trees stood out sharply on hilltops against the blue. The city itself was easily seen now, rising from its moated walls, its towers and keeps. It radiated a comfortable power, its suburbs of low cottages and market gardens, some with their own beehives, spreading across the six surrounding hills, every one sheltering a prosperous village.

The empress explained that the many hives were for an entirely different species of bee to those which had come to their rescue. They commonly called this the cooking bee. A much smaller bee. She laughed at their surprise. "That is the honey we use for baking and sweets for the children."

Moonglum once again felt like a parvenu when the Melnibonéans began what he considered to be high-flown chat he could barely follow. It was on such occasions that he constrained himself from starting a fight in order to relieve his boredom. Determined to be fair, Moonglum reminded himself that he took ideas for granted that Elric could barely grasp.

And now they were on the last wide brick-paved road to Kirinmoir. Trading caravans moved with stately pace, back and forth. Her walls began to tower above her great moat and outer bailey, a city almost as impressive as ruined Imrryr the Beautiful, the Dreaming City, Elric's birthplace, where his love had died on his own sword.

The city was indeed a wonderful thing to behold. Save for Tanelorn, no city exuded such an air of peace. Save for Imrryr, Elric had never seen a more prosperous metropolis, with orderly red, green and yellow roofs, her streets rising one by one up to a domed building of blue columns and white walls and the silver dome crowning everything. Pewter, gold, polished copper, bronze and glittering quartz ornamented everything. The green and turquoise roof tiles of the surrounding whitewashed buildings sparkled in the sun. The multicoloured awnings of market stalls gave an air of festival to the entire city.

From out of a well-built granite tunnel at the base of the hill, a river, so blue it seemed artificial, rushed into the valley. Where it wound on, it powered grain mills and saw mills and supplied water to every settlement along its winding course. As if the city literally poured its wealth and security over the surrounding countryside.

Why should these happy people not wish their contentment and peace to last for always?

They ascended the last hill before the final one. The sandy road ran below piney ledges and walled villas with extraordinary views. Trees were in full leaf, about to turn, summer roses were in final bloom and magnificent scent. Autumn flowers were emerging. The faint, lush scents of autumn spread up from the forest floor and gave a sharpness to the water. Both travellers enjoyed these nostalgic scents, almost synonymous with safety and happiness. Now they were level with the city proper and could see it clearly. It was glorious, soaring into the air with a profusion of towers and turrets, silk flags and sparkling, crenellated marble, all rising in impressive harmony to be crowned by the deep reflective blue and gold of the dome, one of the most beautiful architectural creations either Moonglum or Elric had seen in their combined travels.

Moonglum congratulated them on the glorious building at the peak. Such structures were rarely seen on this continent. Was it a monument?

"Austere yet impressive," he said, noting the exceptional craftsmanship and architectural skill. "It could be an example for public building across the world."

He went on, keeping their attention. To the ones who understood the city's exceptional position it was surely the source of their power and their security! He spoke to pleased ears, and the women purred with pleasure.

As professional soldiers, Elric and Moonglum immediately understood the citadel's strengths. It was pretty much impervious to human attack. It would require a cunning and probably supernatural force to take the fort, given the health and cleverness of the defenders. Her many lush little parks could be enough for livestock and vegetables, even fruit! Nothing known could take her, from any direction. In the way she was built she could even withstand attacks from the air. Her hard-tiled roofs had formed a barrier against the hideously destructive venom of their own war dragons. In those days war dragons had lived in common with Elric's kin, sleeping in intervals to ensure some were always in readiness, and been instruments of political policy.

The newer settlers, pursued by powerful enemies, separated from their own kind, hid in the woods, trying not to make any noise. This was how they had lasted for millennia. Then they used their ancient pacts with earth elementals to build a fort. This river was the reason for the fort's success in those times, resisting siege after siege. It started as a spring somewhere under the monument at the top and wound down the hill until it spilled boisterously, dancing blue and white, into the sunlight and ran rapidly along the valley floor, with weirs and bridges and channels and all the other industries depending on it. Shirizha carried tiny droplets of the element making the waters blue. This honey was carefully sieved, captured and successfully resold all down the valley, for insomnia and listlessness. A liquid which men would die or betray their loved ones for, which could be traded for a fortune with the coastal merchants or with the woodland tribes. Shirizha was proud of their heritage. She showed him a bottle it was sold in. Dark blue smoky jade.

"It is a wonderful design," Moonglum murmured. He was overwhelmed by a sense of melancholy, and he openly took her hand. She was puzzled, smiling, but he did not have words for her unspoken question. All he felt was sadness. He had seen so many beautiful, proud old cities put to the torch, leaving nothing but ruins, their populations raped, killed or left dying, their learning and their wisdom destroyed and forgotten except for a few muddy legends married to faeyrie stories and folktales and informing only children. The old legends were warped. Moonglum had already remarked the exaggerated stories families so frequently told about themselves and their ancestry.

He understood the power of myth and how legends were created, why small bands fled without wishing to die before those three whirling swords. Especially the black one. The thirsty one. The howling one. He grinned at himself and his own fancy. He felt a certain almost proprietorial affection for that terrible blade, sometimes taking a brotherly pride in its ability to spread terror. And that, no doubt, was why, he recalled, he had taken himself back to Elwher but from there run like a fox back to his pack-leader as soon as he called.

Moonglum hardly cared. He lived for action and exploration, and Elric was in so many ways his perfect companion. Besides, he admitted, he was almost as addicted to following the albino as Elric was symbiotically addicted to his sword.

As they approached the great gate, it seemed the whole city erupted into colour and noise. Banners waved from every hand. Flowers floated through the joyful air, and our local heroes (of which the pair appeared to be included) crossed first one drawbridge and then another, and then a third, until at last they rode into a city where Melnibonéans mingled with humans apparently as equals. This was at first shocking and then oddly comforting to Moonglum, always conscious of the way in which most of the old world perceived his relationship.

Elric and Moonglum saw a storm of white and blue, black and orange, green and white as the banners of the valley's principalities fluttered around them. They had no idea what was being asked of them, save what they had been told. They were too tired to make any requests of their friends. But it was a wearying business for them, and they longed for their beds.

After a while, too, they began to hear a faint but persistent murmuring. Did it come from underground? Elric imagined the sound of a great mechanical construction behind the valley and the city, creating this vision of peace and prosperity. They soon became used to the sound and continued on their way. The empress's palace was relatively modest compared to the tall temple above it at the top of the hill and also reached by a long set of stone stairs. They were warned not to climb those temple steps without the empress or her guard captain with them for every second. "Your own safety, you do understand. And everyone's. Our honey springs are well guarded." She had heard enough of their tale. They were to stay with her as guests until she would personally put them on the road home. All Kirinmoir approved this. And he had sworn to do as bidden before he left. The pale walls, pastel greens, greys and blues, the dark reds of the interior were restful. The entire building was designed to soothe. Even Elric could not resist the sense of tranquillity received from the comfortable palace. He let it calm the questions that continued to crowd his mind.

He and Moonglum were shown through room after room, on floor after floor of the palace until they reached the quarters set aside for their use. Both men had the idea that Empress Melaré wished to impress them, with not only the luxuries of her palace's interior, but also her exquisite gardens. The view in all directions was peaceful and picturesque. Moonglum continued to praise the architecture and planning of the city's builders. Even Elric felt bound to nod his agreement regarding the aesthetic charms of Kirinmoir and the palace's excellent views, for they were almost unreal in their restful beauty. Melniboné's greatest artists could not match their exquisite craftsmanship. He thought to ask about the odd buzzing which seemed to rise from the bowels of their beautiful city. She began another subject and he did not find a fresh opportunity.

She remembered when Lady Grivaan'sew had been forced to give up her angelic horn and never played again. "Now some of our greatest sons lie dead on cobbled streets," she said. She spoke of an old city-state near his homeland, and she sympathised with him that there had been a need for them to destroy it.

Their spacious chambers were connected, with windows and balconies overlooking the city and a lake, in a park filled with cedars and poplars fast becoming silhouettes in the red setting sun. Soon Elric was bathed and sleeping. Moonglum, returned late from entertaining Shirizha, was snoring quietly in the next room.

Elric's dreams contrasted violently from one to another. He recalled the many battles he had fought when he travelled in the Dream of a Thousand Years, walking the moonbeam roads, following the Melnibonéans from city to city and finding that not all his kind were monsters. How many pasts had he had?

He dreamed again. First he dreamed that he strolled between the high hedges of a formal garden, such as the Miltharians favoured but was fashionable in Melniboné for a while. He smelled pineapple foxgloves and heard ethereal string music. He could still not find the officer in charge of the guard. Stormbringer was in his hand, but, when a Beiakan bear confronted him, the sword remained insentient. The bear raised up suddenly, red jaws dripping. All magic was lost to him! He was weak, maybe feverish. He had known many moments when Arioch sulked, forbade all his minions and allies to be responsive to the White Wolf. He was helpless without his sword and his patron. Now he dreamed he rode a Nihrainian steed, twice the size of a warhorse and able to gallop upon roads whose bedrock lay in another sphere! Did this mean that his magic was returning to him? He felt it growing. For how long? The dog was still with him, following over thin air, across a landscape only the horse could sense. Below, mighty armies massed. He looked and saw that he rode a mule. Several tall black men with nodding yellow plumes, armed with long-bladed spears and black cowhide shields encircled him, either protecting him or threatening him. Cymoril was still there. This was the dream! This was the dream. "*Zarozinia!*" He was confused. "*Melaré!*" Why had he left on this last, dangerous adventure? What led him to ruin all he cared for? What could he learn? He fell back, screaming and sweating, but not waking. There was a nervous, edgy force to Cymoril. She had been unable to speak to him, not since all became numb and muddy with her in death. She would have stayed at his side, helping him rule as a Melnibonéan must. She had understood his dilemma far better than most. They had bonded as he and his beloved Zarozinia never could. Brother and sister. Blood cousins. What fey children they might have had. Scholars and politicians, emperors and empresses to raise Melniboné to her former glory!

"*Zarozinia!*" His latest love. Human. Whom he hardly knew. She had been patient with his dreams, which had proven too much for most of the women he had travelled with. They had parted ways at her suggestion. She would wait for him. She freed him to move across the world until he was satisfied she was what he wanted in a woman. She had left him unencumbered to practise his familiar killing trade as well as find another woman. This one made him feel different. Of course he and Cymoril were of the same blood, and this created a great bond between them. He remembered giving his word to Zarozinia, unasked, that, whatever he did, he would not declare his love for anyone while he was gone. Perhaps it was merely fantasy, an infatuation?

Was this an omen? There was no telling. At least he could trust the veterans of those dreadful psychic wars to come together with him as fellow survivors.

And then what? He began to feel he had a forgotten obligation. He recalled how, a few months since, a defeated noble's slaves came to him, putting their fate, as was proper, in his hands. Rather than Elric killing them, too, he set a price on his captives. When they heard this, he recalled, some had relations who would not pay the price. Some could not. Some came to him, saying, "You are known to be generous, master! Why are we so worthless? We need your help, master. You are clearly fond of your slaves and are vexed by our sentence, which is one of death. We are useless to you but good for those we are separated from. Will you say what you must to unite us with our families? And let us pay you in instalments, perhaps? Please do not sacrifice us, master. We are mere tradesmen and craftsmen. I beg thee, master, do not give us to Lord Arioch. We are ordinary men and not rich enough for you!"

And the albino had grinned at this and let them go as perhaps he had let too many go of late. Was Arioch punishing him for that? Was the Chaos Lord angry because not enough souls were being harvested and sacrificed? He sensed in this reverie that Arioch had changed loyalties and was ready to lend the forces of Chaos to these human tribes and their young totems. New gods were being created! That, however, did not explain the loss of all his powers such as those over wind and fire, over water and earth, through his many pacts with the elementals. He sought an entrance to the moonbeam roads, but he was helpless. What if they did build a ship? What then? Revolutions necessarily create chaos. Has Kirinmoir slipped too far into complacent Law?

And Chaos prized the peaceful valley and its potent honey, wishing to disrupt one and acquire the other. Arioch's work, then? Or even his rival's? Xiombarg, torturing her terrifying armour into forbidden shapes, who appeared and disappeared. Our side? Or hers? Now she understood her colleagues better.

So from his musings he came to believe that it was true and he had spared too many enemies, letting living prisoners go and not pursuing the so-called knights and their allies. He had admittedly lost some taste for killing merely to feed his patron, but he felt he killed enough in the ordinary course of things. Since he had arrived in Kirinmoir, it had seemed to him that he heard the sounds of the city almost as a whispering swarm constantly reminding him of his own mortality. He made love to Melaré, but he thought often of Cymoril and the days of their courtship in dreaming Imrryr. It seemed so long ago. He felt no guilt towards Zarozinia for his dalliances. He made only specific promises and made it clear he sought a goal which they could not share.

As for Moonglum, he was simply enjoying his romance, as Shirizha showed him all the sights but one. They could hardly hear over the steady, mechanical hum. The long flight of steps to the domed temple was strictly guarded to the hill's very top. Only Melaré and her captain would let them go, but then only if they were accompanied by one of the women. And they could not go armed. Strengthened by a liberally diluted blue honey, Elric felt some normality. He was warned that his need for the blue wine would gradually become too demanding and then he must wean himself off it, little by little, until his addicted body no longer screamed for it. By then he would know if Stormbringer and Arioch still served him. Why did the Chaos Lord seem so *absent*?

Nothing much had changed for the city, either. It was clear from the carts and their contents that they were storing food and arms inside the palace. Their animals were well-treated but, increasingly, stabled within the walls. Elric and General Mulxer Gash, the empress's rather baffled major-domo, one of the few men in the palace, disagreed about the sense of this. Like the few other males Elric had seen, Gash was unhealthy and weak. As brown and wrinkled as a sun-sucked plum, he was far from stupid. Apparently his fellows had all been born sickly. What few males of their kind there were in Kirinmoir all resembled him. Their life-spans were short and they were prone to disease. In an attempt to be on good terms with Mulxer Gash, Moonglum asked if he had any children in the guard. The major-domo had snorted derisively and made some remark about that being impossible!

Moonglum had the impression that males and females hardly ever mated, and when he, in the privacy of the bedchamber they now shared, asked how their people reproduced, Shirizha evaded the question and told him it was not a subject for polite conversation. She was so open on so many subjects that the ex-Chancellor found her response untypically shy. Was there some sort of artificial means of reproduction involved between the sexes, which to them was shameful or distasteful? Some cultures found the sexual act disgusting. No doubt she would choose to let him know. He was not prepared to waste too much time on the subject. He had no intention of settling in Kirinmoir.

Mulxer Gash was completely unforthcoming. He was neither easy to approach nor to question. He strutted with the help of two imperious canes which gave him, at a distance, the appearance of one of their own upright saurians. Elric had expected it to hiss and curl its tongue at him.

Yet Gash assumed an air of kindly wisdom which intimidated his colleagues, so they rarely questioned him. He had led only well-armed soldiers against a rabble of raiders and driven them off, but they were resilient foemen. In discussing military strategy, Gash clearly understood a great deal.

Faintly reptilian down to his greenish-grey scaly skin, with the face of an angry newt, Gash would always, eventually, elect to change nothing, even for the defence of the valley. He was the same with people of his own race as with humans. Moonglum was unimpressed. They willed their security and assured it with words alone. If Ramada Sabaru were coming to the valley and was as powerful as they had heard, the Golden Wizard would destroy Kirinmoir, even to the last bone! Only the old ways were to be trusted. Revivifying wisdom, he thought, was nonsense. Jokes were disgusting either to taste, sensibility, gravitas or all of them. Nothing was funny to Mulxer Gash. Almost everything was a threat. He wished to hear only the old ways of the world. It was as if he had built a granite wall around his mind. A wall without windows or gates. Too many like him in Kirinmoir controlled far too much, thought Moonglum. But Elric held his peace and remained on cordial terms. There was no reason to think the women might change their minds and give up their defence plans. On the other hand, argued Mulxer Gash, Elric and his friend might even betray them, if it were in their self-interest. He was right to fear those things. Should the fight be impossible to win, and giving up the city became inevitable, then the two mercenaries could leave and deliver Kirinmoir to the ragtag but battle-hardened army of Ramada Sabaru and his sadistic commanders.

Elric knew this was true and said nothing to deny the charge.

NINETEEN

The Coming Impossibility

MEANWHILE, AS THE weeks passed, Elric began to notice a change in the nature of the city and the small country they had agreed to help defend. Perhaps because their surroundings were pretty much as they had always been, the empress and her circle were less aware of this. Like so many who took civilisation for granted, they could not conceive of it ending.

To Moonglum, Elric and several of the human generals, the world on the other side of the mountain was becoming increasingly dangerous, precisely because the barbarians beyond the pass were no longer fighting amongst themselves. Many more invaders had been found in the wild mountain passes. It meant the roving warbands, which usually came to blows, were talking instead. Talking mostly of an armistice, of joining a powerful warlord giving great rewards to those who followed him, so many of those men had drifted this far believing blue honey to be only an old wives' tale. Discovering the reality of the rare blue mead and perhaps even tasting a little, their opinion had changed. Knowing the price men were ready to pay for a few drops, they became eager to get some. Roving soldiers had already begun to focus on fabled Kirinmoir as a prize but considered taking her too costly in blood and resources. What had changed their minds? The answer appeared to be a charismatic leader, perhaps with great magical powers, some named the Golden Warlord. Many had it on good authority that he was a Lord of Chaos. Many named him a god banished by the Runestaff millennia ago.

Elric and his friend cared for one outcome—the security of the little nation they had agreed to help protect. At least they would stay long enough for her inhabitants to show them the way back to the lands that were home to them. Empress Melaré had agreed to this, yet there was still a little ambiguity in the bargain. Did she really mean to take them to World's Edge? And, both men wondered, why had the Blue Priestesses, who counselled and effectively ruled through the empress and were known to be benign and just, continued to refuse the visitors an audience? "I feel we are not welcomed by those women the way the others do. Their mysteries include records of the past, and their Temple houses the map you would copy in order to complete your journey home."

As weeks became months, the fact that all the warbands were not fighting each other confirmed to Elric and Moonglum that something or someone was uniting them! They were slowly gathering information from their own spies and those outlanders they were able to interrogate. Large parts of the outer wall had been allowed to weaken, and Moonglum made it his particular task to have them strengthened.

Elric grew increasingly concerned about this warlord approaching from the West. He was gathering power and allies, including the infamous Kop, gigantic war-mammoths on one of which Ramada Sabaru, the Golden Warlord, rode at the core of his army, visible for all to see. He was rumoured to command a million or more infantry alone.

Elric trained outriders to search the passes and caves of the guarding mountains and spy without being seen. For all he was involved in tiny disagreements with Mulxer Gash, the empress's leading general, he came to respect the birdlike little man. Gash had read many obscure works on the art of warfare and had an instinct for strategy. He had an intelligent grasp of defensive and a more theoretical understanding of offensive. He disputed many small points, but they were in surprising agreement on larger issues. He could debate the abstracts for hours, but his experience had never included fighting a superior or supernatural invading force. The Golden Warlord was said to travel with a caged demon as a pet. Yet the women insisted that powerful supernatural beings had been banished from the valley long, long ago, after some terrible war in pursuit of their own folk. Melaré's stories of that time, lost in the mists of myth, seemed to Elric to be wholly without any grounding in reality. Yet it was clear, from more recent histories, that for centuries the Kirinmoir Valley had remained secure from supernatural attack. If not a god, then some much greater power than a locally successful warlord was at work. That power was easily capable of moulding the scattered remains of several armies into one, under a single persuasive leader. Even then, a mighty prize was necessary to whet the appetites of men already weary, cynical and ready to tear anyone limb from limb who spoke any longer of "prizes." It could be blue honey, but Elric suspected the goal to be even richer now, and he became still more uneasy.

The two friends understood the general import of this. The captured spies were eloquent if not especially informative. They were not directly followers of the Golden Warlord, had only heard of him from those closer to him. This power from the West was coming towards the mountains with no intention of being stopped. A power commanding a tremendous reservoir of supernatural lore, suggesting an alliance with at least one major Lord of the Higher Worlds, possibly Arioch of Chaos. Were they denying the power of a device even Elric barely believed to exist? Which would explain their own lack of supernatural aid.

And they had nothing as powerful. Nothing more than the sting of an aggressive and odd-looking bee. Could Arioch have changed his loyalties altogether? Did he lead Elric's enemies now? Elric would not have been surprised to learn of Arioch's change of loyalties! And if Arioch called, would Elric be bound to answer his summons and turn against the people of Kirinmoir and the peaceful valley folk?

Elric and Moonglum were agreed that this was one of the few places in this world not populated by one form or another of the ancient Phoorn. The semi-reptilian beasts did not appear to favour the local climate. Perhaps, as mythological but real, they were drained just as Elric felt drained of all his own magical powers. To have any real chance of defeating that enemy they would have to become a disciplined and savage fighting force not reliant on magic. To make such a force out of that generally pacific group of women and a few thousand peaceful farmers was, if not an opium dream, a faint hope, even with possession of the blue honey. They would never be a disciplined army.

Elric could plan all he wished and train all he could, but there would be overwhelming numbers and a mysterious force against them, thought Moonglum. It would not be enough to fill a handful of peasants with fiery blue wine. They would be cut down, however brave, sliced like overbaked hamshanks until they no longer resembled living creatures.

The two adventurers had become restless, speaking of an attack which would never come, of Kirinmoir clearly more than able to defend herself, of Ramada Sabaru, the Golden Warlord, being no more than a whisper on the west wind which could not do harm to anyone he loved. And Elric, cool and self-perceptive as he was and seeing this to be little more than a piece of sophistry of the worst kind, which is logic designed to prepare the way for the worst betrayal, which was self-betrayal.

One day, news came of a massing in ruined Tinak, where Elric and Moonglum had rested months earlier. Because of the good-sized river and its ford, warbands and small armies were setting up a huge camp there. A charismatic leader was on his way to address them. Some said she was female, Lady Terhali of Chaos, invited to the mortal realm by Mamkin the warlord of Thair, who had changed sides so many times that his head was on permanent swivel. To join Ramada, he was coming from the West at the head of an entirely fresh army. As well as his monstrous war-mammoths, the Warlord had savage man-eating great-cats and dire wolves, grotesques and shape-shifters in his entourage.

Elric quizzed his human informants, including the women of the guard, about Orlando Funk. He suspected the old chattering drunkard might know a deal more than he appeared to about the invader. A Chaos god in disguise? How long did he reside in Kirinmoir? What had he said before he set off on the Tinak road? Elric asked among some townsfolk, who knew the man slightly, if they had any news of Orlando Funk. Had he said anything of note?

But Funk had set off from the city soon after the human raiders had stolen the mead. "Within a day if not within the ten-hour, my lord!"

"He was here for no more than that, my lord," insisted a nearby publican, pulling up his boards. Hearing the story of honey-theft and the thieves' escape, the gossip amongst townsfolk when he arrived, Funk apparently set off after Melaré and the others who pursued the thieves. After that, the pair knew, he appeared to have retrieved the wine and, escaping both the thieves as well as the original owners, left their leader in the savages' hands. From what the spies said, he had left Tinak just ahead of the various warlords' emissaries. At first Funk appeared to be riding south early, no doubt on the Four Cities road. Apparently Funk had said and done nothing especially meaningful in Kirinmoir nor before setting off for the West in Tinak. On leaving, he had placed some luggage at his hostelry, saying he hoped to claim it before the snow set in. So he had planned to return! Was he on the way back? Elric felt a sudden lurch. At the head of an unholy army? This could be the "powerful sorcerer" of which some spoke. Ramada Sabaru? Some other fabled or supernatural creature? Coming from still another direction! Were they to be inundated from every point of the compass? Were the Lords of the Higher Worlds—for impossible to understand reasons—riding upon them with the intention of crushing them utterly?

And what, he asked himself, was he doing here with only the potent blue mead to give him the power to draw the Black Sword, which seemed to take fewer souls and feed him less power every time he wrapped his hand around its shagreen hilt?

When Elric asked if they knew any more about Funk, most townspeople seemed not to have heard of him at all. Only one or two villagers were even slightly familiar with his name from folk stories: Of times when the whole world was inhabited with friendly supernatural folk from Faeyrie-Land.

In Kirinmoir Valley, *Faeyrie-Land* was vaguely where most local humans thought all supernatural creatures lived, somehow side by side with their own people, but visible only in tiny versions of this world, if world it were. Giants had been sighted, too, but these lived in their own land and were sometimes thought *too* big to see, for they seemed insubstantial. Local wise women dealt in small magic and lucky charms, not the summoning of gods and elementals. Even the most powerful of magical aspirants had never brought itself to full appearance, fleshly and fierce, in this side of the Great Egg, as the priests of the Four Old Cities had believed.

That cult had a few followers in the valley. Their High Priest apparently maintained that food and wine would fall from the skies as soon as this beastly deity were proclaimed to mankind. The deity, *N'Jiross B'Onon*, as far as they could pronounce it, some kind of giant reptile, had always been marginal and his disciples mocked. The Blue Priestesses had been forever the spiritual guides of Kirinmoir. In the way of these things, however, the cult had struck a chord in that part of the public that is its fearful, unreasoning, greedy heart. Most folk of wisdom and experience could tell "when the giant reptile was rising" was nonsense, describing the motion of a minor earthquake. As far as Elric could see, the reptile personified a few thousands of ordinary, dissatis-fied, hopeless, dreaming souls of which some evil, greedy creature had taken charge, pointing them in any direction it desired, needing to destroy all they had previously loved and respected.

Elric brooded on this, knowing it was too late to use diplomacy to per-suade the army gathering against them to turn back. They had committed themselves to reckless action, the tearing down of their world's ikons in the hope that this would somehow give them power over history. The best they could hope was to change the narrative a little, he thought. He was at least not identified here as a supernatural "aelf." On this side of the world, Elric, to his great disgust, was often mistaken for a larger than usual *aelf*, making himself visible to the world. He always felt insulted, yet had no real idea what an *aelf* was meant to be. He had always thought humans used that word for a sprite or pixie who sat under the shade of a mushroom, dispensing little spells for domestic use and good for entertaining children. He hoped one day to meet an *aelfin* man or woman to whom, according to folk wisdom, he appeared to be related. As for Orlando Funk himself, Elric gathered that most local people who knew him at all had a poor opinion of him as a drunken adventurer of the familiar kind. They thought that Funk, whoever he actually was, was little more than a clever thief and conjuror who had or had not stolen a bottle of medium-strength blue mead. If any theft had taken place, then Funk was not the minor folktale character whose name he claimed. The hero of a popular sequence of trickster tales, the strange drunkard had stolen his persona from the story, not the other way round. A common thief, said most. A petty deceiver. Violent, even.

"We've known him and his kind forever," one tailor told Elric. "They survive on simple conjurors' tricks and lies for a living. I would happily have cut him out a new suit of clothes, but he preferred his old raiment. Perhaps he thought he appeared more authentic in his threadbare rags. If he took the mead from the men who had stolen it from the city, then he was more or less in his rights. Maybe he had intended to return it?" If he had stolen it from Kirinmoir, then there would be more to discuss if he came this way again. "And the same," a local vintner said, and smiled, "goes for his poetry. And if he uses our blue mead too liberally, he'll come crawling back for more. There's only a few folk of Kirinmoir who know that craving, as well as the *power*, of blue honey . . ."

That stuff, the townsfolk told Elric, turned good, calm, honest farmers into mad killers, delighting in death. A baker was in emphatic agreement. His wife had died of it, he said. "Blue wine can't give uneducated people more general intelligence. I wish it could!" A chin-stroking chandler had added, "I have long since come to the cynical conclusion that half the folk in the world are incapable of imagination. Half of the rest are utterly self-serving, and the remainder are altruistic. Depending on the power and leadership of the first fifty percent, the rhetoric of altruism, or of selfishness, ruled at any given time. The rhetoric of leaders was therefore important to the led." While Elric, in his own experience, was inclined to agree with them all, he could still not fathom whether the valley people knew something more significant of that apparently harmless lanky spouter of rhetoric.

Moonglum remained unsure if the erratic poet they had met on the road was friend or foe. Funk had, after all, not only warned them of danger coming but strengthened them in time to meet it, granting them with much-needed refreshment in the form of blue mead, providing them with the means of defence against that danger. "I wonder to myself—was he real or unreal? Is he one of those half-mortals, those demigods who can project an astral version of themselves from one place to another. Some sort of *djenii*, as my people call them. A spirit which can become a projection of our own worst terrors. They're as real as can be when you first meet and then begin to fade as the effort of maintaining the illusion takes their strength from them. Do we know whether he's wholly real? Of flesh and bone? Or actually a whole deception of air and runes."

He paced a good deal in those days. "Runes, I'm sure. Though runes weaken here . . ."

And in whose interests did Funk work? Elric guessed they were entirely Funk's. He and his friend Moonglum would have enjoyed time with the old man, but in the end they had to separate for everyone's sake. Or so he had wanted them to think. Had he been on his way to meet his master in the West, having spied on Kirinmoir and discovered the city's weaknesses?

"Think you he'll return again, Elric? At the head of an invading army?"

The raids were becoming battles as more barbarians pushed their way into the valley. Whenever they and their soldiers sighted a band, the two friends would try to engage it, but the invaders fled as soon as they recognised Moonglum and the white-haired albino. Stormbringer still served her turn!

From captives, they learned that they were defeated by strangers who resembled Melnibonéans, a people with a terrible and ancient power over dragons, with whom they had an unthinkable bond. How they had come to share ancestry with the reptiles nobody fully knew, though he had been inducted into some such secrets during the dream-quests which were part of all Melnibonéan princelings' education on the couches of those ancients, where he and his cousins lived their people's long, long history almost day for day.

As he and Moonglum patrolled a landscape becoming increasingly dangerous, Elric had time to reflect on the mysterious origins of his people who had once been glorious, arrogant and beautiful. Some had marched and flown and founded colonies where old human cities had fallen. At first they enslaved the humans and then settled into some version of feudalism which appeared to suit them all. As feudalism became no longer possible to maintain in the face of a growing merchant class, civil wars broke out, and these were what the mercenaries depended upon. But here, the civilisation was not based on conquest or injustice, and the only ones who objected were those who received their raison d'être from being righteous. Feudalism, when functioning best, required everyone's self-interest to be considered. Overtaxing or lawless plundering were understood to be sides of the same coin and worthless as plans for any kind of peaceful solution to common problems. People without the promise of hope would not labour thanklessly forever, nor would what they produced be of any great quality.

For a moment he was immensely homesick for his youth, his love, his dreams and his optimism. He turned his eyes from the rounded, grey boulders cupping the city as if to defend it. He was growing too tired. He thought he had seen movement. He knew the signs in himself. He was beginning to impose his own need for action onto the landscape.

"Where our own world meets another," Melaré told him one night, "there are shadows. You can slip into them sometimes. They are doors between those worlds." She had no other reason not to love this handsome cousin to her own race. She was in love with the tall newcomer, but she might have fallen in love with any virile member of Elric's race. Perhaps some day, thought the albino, another will come, one who does not have to return to a loving, albeit understanding, woman.

Melaré reached a pale hand to caress his milk-white hair, so like her own. He was handsome, in the manner of his people, as she was beautiful. Both were in excellent health and general strength. She felt not only was she making love to a man as well as to one of her own sex. This pulsing blood was an extra bond bringing them closer. They discussed such things frequently.

Elric reflected how common human solutions were so often simplistic. As if life and thought could actually be reduced to what a fool might understand. Life was complex, and simple solutions only produced further complications. Human beings really were oddly made. Incredibly unpredictable. One of them could change history for millions, while another could not change the course of their own life by an iota. And all the while Elric understood how unlike they were, one from another. An altruist here, a miser there. Their range was far wider than any Melnibonéan imagination, save his, and was perhaps an explanation for their survival and his own. He wondered frequently at the nature of these people. He hoped that on this occasion he was allied with some of the intelligent ones.

Suddenly he was overwhelmed by an appalling sense of melancholy, and he looked out at the great, grey elephantine bodies of the six granite boulders, arranged so that they appeared to cradle Kirinmoir from any danger. A wonderful sense of security returned quickly. It seemed to him that all felt it, and yet it was an illusion, as the two friends knew from long experience. So many aspirations! He could not ride away from here. Kirinmoir could not fall.

He began to walk back towards his allies. He was anxious for the tension to break. This was a most dangerous time during warfare. Yet there might never be war at all if the makeshift wall and the mazes held. They had stood the test of centuries. Melaré and her people insisted upon it. Elric became conscious of the constant murmuring rising and falling from within and underlying all the other sounds of the city.

THE SNOW BEGAN to appear, a few flakes at first but increasing day by day. It never settled in the valley, but it soon lay thick upon the flanks of the mountains, and a grey cloud began to obscure the blue sky and the mountain peaks, a little at a time. The sporadic attacks from bandits invading the valley became more frequent and then slowed a little. And, with the lowering grey, there came a brooding silence.

Although they had seen none in the city proper, it was obvious to Elric and Moonglum that those from the other side of the mountain also sent their spies. Which meant that they knew the maze-route through the tunnels or that they knew another route through the mountains. It was not difficult to confirm this. Elric had expertly used some of the refined interrogation techniques of his ancient and very cruel people to coax the nuances of truth from those who pretended ignorance.

He was proud of how little he had to do before they were weepingly grateful to let him know every ounce of whatever information he could need. Any pleasure he took in their pain was almost wholly abstract and soon faded. Longer lasting were the dreams that followed. Also it was the ease of those methods to extract what was needed that bored Elric deeply. He knew these men had special powers of some kind and could negotiate the mazes, but he was unable to call on any supernatural agency to help him discover any further information. Moreover, he lacked the sheer pleasure and artistry in inflicting pain common to most of his people.

Perverse as it was, he extracted more pleasure from assisting the human world to inform and educate itself. He had, he now admitted, been perhaps a little idealistic, a trifle optimistic, imposing what he hoped to find on the reality that was. Yet he still saw something he valued in humankind. Few quite rarely trusted him, and he in turn had learned that only the rare human— Smiorgan, Moonglum and so on—could themselves be trusted, not always in their best interests.

Yet Melaré also trusted him almost without reservation. He had said little of Zarozinia, but he sensed that even if he told Melaré that he was betrothed, she would not recognise what he said and would draw him even closer. Yet she was troubled herself, and the albino wondered if she had a secret commitment of her own. Occasionally he would see something in her eyes which seemed to reflect his own uncertain and unsleeping mind.

She told Elric that he was the first stranger ever allowed to see and hear the story of the Great Well, the source of their wealth and also, she insisted, their wisdom. Or at least part of it. Without asking, she knew Elric's opinion of her major-domo and shared it. She told him that Mulxer Gash was appointed by her predecessor, and she hadn't the heart to dismiss him.

"There was little need until now," she said. "And now we have you."

Elric was disturbed by this but did not mention it. His own respect for the general had grown, and he looked to the sickly little man as a chief advisor in a world which was alien to him. The days grew a little cooler but still nothing like as cold as it should have been this far north. He did not wish to make her suspicious of him, but he eventually succeeded in ensuring it clear he *must* have some proof that a map back to the Weeping Waste existed. He also wished to be assured that the benign Blue Priestesses existed and that they existed for the general good. Thanks to them the supply of mead was endless. They kept the entire valley at peace, or had until now. The occasional attacks had been invigorating. He had at last persuaded them that he was no longer an interloper and to let him visit the beautiful dome of the Temple and the wise women who lived there. "And I would look at your map, which will show me the road home."

"You still intend to leave?" she asked.

"After I have kept my word," he said. "Was that not our agreement?"

"Of course." She lowered her eyes. "I will speak to the women and ask if they will grant us an audience in the next day or so."

He thanked her.

"And you will leave?" She put it to him again. "Should you defeat our foes?"

"I should like to see your map now," he said, "so that I can compare it against these—" And he took two fragments of vellum from within his shirt, where he was used to keeping them, and showed them to her.

She did not speak as she took them from him and studied them. She nodded and handed them back to him. "It is certainly similar, my lord." She turned her face from him. "Very similar!"

Elric slipped the scraps of vellum into his inner pocket. Together, saying nothing else, they returned to her bed and looked for oblivion in each other's embrace.

In the morning he left her early. He had his defences to attend to. Later that day he was supervising the mechanisms which would allow ten warriors at a time to operate five or even six troughs of water, in turn operating the cogs and winches of the city's defences. Systems of pulleys and ropes helped the city-machine operate her own ballistae, catapults and other engines. A soldier came to him while he was testing the ballistae. Melaré wished to see him later that afternoon.

When he was finished he met Melaré, and they climbed the wide limestone steps side by side passing a line of strong women in heavy work-clothes and with yokes over their shoulders, which milk-sellers used to carry their wares. These held buckets, however, which glowed a ghastly blue and dripped viscous, sticky stuff. It did not take the albino long to realise that every one of those sturdy, human women was blind.

Again, Elric diplomatically ignored the buckets as they continued upwards on his right or downwards on his left. The limestone was covered in the stuff, dried to a duller colour. The steps themselves almost glowed, worn by millions of feet climbing up and down for millennia. Brasswork had been eroded to a radiant lime-green. Melaré offered nothing more, allowing the scene to speak for itself. If she did not then wish to discuss the matter of the Well or explain a scene which was really self-evident, then he would respect that.

But again she answered an unspoken question. "The bucketeers are all blind from birth. They work five hours a day. Our secret is kept as much as it needs to be. They are paid very well, and their whole family benefits."

Again, the Prince of Ruins chose to remain silent, and she said little more save to point out some of the familiar buildings he had visited earlier. And still he said nothing.

Soon the rest of the city was far below. She did not have to tell him where they were. The entire settlement could be seen from where they stood just before the carved granite stairway which curved up towards the dome. At last they reached the Temple, and massive blue-jade doors swung back, opened by sighted young women, evidently acolytes in modest blue robes. The Temple was cool and soothing. On the other side of the shadowy chamber Elric saw daylight and silhouetted figures reclining or sitting around the rim of what he identified as a large limestone-finished well, its wall embellished with copper figuring rising three or four feet from the surface of the paved floor, all in semi-darkness. On the winches (for there were several) hung large copper buckets streaked with blue. He glanced around, wondering where the blind bucketeers had gone. Then he realised that the faintly murmuring swarm, which had been a constant since his arrival here, had faded. Save for a more familiar sound, of wandering "kitchen" bees, there was perfect silence!

"Stopped for the evening, so that we can meet," said Melaré with a smile. Her light red-tinged brown eyes met his. Rubies seething with profound emotion. She told him how their earlier allies, the "defender" bees, had expended their available energy for a while and had disappeared back to their deep hives about their regular business. "It will be some time before their defences are activated again," she said, and stirred a memory in the back of his mind. His eyes, always a little weak, became used to the contrasts. Outside was a garden, with mature hives for the kitchen bees. Inside was cool and the pace slow yet alive with energy. He followed the empress around the Well. She did not acknowledge the women who first greeted her, staring with open speculation at Elric. She did greet, however, the women who sat in the flower garden outside.

"Sisters! I bring you our Champion, our Cousin Emperor, our Hero of the Hour, Prince Elric, from far Melniboné. He is an ambassador to our realm from the underworld. He is here with his fellow cavalier to help us defeat the enemies who would steal our honey. All he seeks in return is that we share all our scholarly knowledge of this great egg of ours. He will also engage in at least one symposium with our philosophers."

"Then you are welcome, Lord Elric. You are from beyond our borders. Yet you have come to help us. Are you driven to visit us by the Lords of the Higher Worlds? Are you their emissary, or might you be the champion our religion predicts?"

"I believe that I could be, lady." He saw no reason to deny their expectations. Doubtless, believing him an anticipated hero would strengthen the general morale. Somewhat cynically, he reasoned that most cultures had a returning hero in their legends. He had been seen as such more than once.

These senior priestesses were all in their mature years, with the same delicate beauty of their kind. Their figures were slender, and they moved with leisured grace. Their white hair floated around their fine-boned white faces like haloes, silver in that soft light. Their lustrous red-brown eyes were full of a profound mixture of wisdom and melancholy. And, he thought, perhaps a touch of anxiety. These women had apparently lived for aeons in the Temple, perhaps waiting for the moment when their legendary champion would visit at a time when they most needed help. According to all, whether human or Kirinmoiri, their rule had been benign, for they were sworn to protect the city and her prosperity. Now they needed a legendary hero. Elric had heard of heroes with fate-driven destinies chiefly in his people's epic romances. He had no difficulty ignoring the fact that he was not heroic, nor destined to save this valley. However, in reality, he reflected that if by doing so he and his friend got what they desired, then he might as well let them believe what they liked.

"You are from those of our cousins escaped with the rest of our people into the darkness of the underworld?"

"From what I have seen, we would have been wise to have remained in Kirinmoir," he said, by way of a compliment. "But our underworld is not dark. It has a sun similar to your own." He saw little point in offering further enlightenment unless it was desired.

All the women wore heavy blue silk robes embroidered with what seemed badges of rank. Clearly these priestesses were attached to whatever religious variant was dominant here. Like most Melnibonéans, he was tolerant of the polytheistic religions. Some of them, after all, were on familiar terms with those they worshipped. He hoped only that he was not expected to take part in any rituals, any sacrifices, human or otherwise.

"He is a warrior and an honourable one. And he is of our ancient blood. He fulfils the prophecy, which speaks of one called the Champion Eternal who will come to us with help, as his ancestors helped in ancient times, in the days of our exodus. As the Runestaff came to Kirinmoir's aid in the first days of that ancient diaspora. One of our own blood, he will return and bring hope to our besieged city, to fight our enemies and all who would bring destruction to Holy Kirinmoir." Melaré took Elric into the garden. He was almost surprised to see the sun again and the red, green and white roofs densely packed, forming the narrow winding streets of the city below.

These women were beautiful in age. They relaxed on their cushions, smiling and confident, sipping cool drinks, bidding him welcome.

Addressing them with all the old courtesies of his people, Elric bowed and took hands, kissed them one by one, exchanging murmured pleasantries. He was highly impressed. These were not the vulgar theatricalities and exaggerated manners he had found on his return to his cousin Yyrkoon's Court after his first self-imposed exile when he had hoped his cousin might learn good governance from his experience of ruling.

He recognised his hostesses as ladies of great dignity and authority. Had she not died giving birth to him, one of these women might have been his mother. And if she had not died, his father would not have hated Elric all his life. For the crime, as brooding Sadric saw it, of matricide. In his eyes, Elric had killed his mother. Sadric had remained distant and allowed his son to be properly educated on the dream couches of Melniboné. But he had always favoured Yyrkoon and would have made him emperor if he had not respected tradition more than his own temperament.

Elric's bows were low, his attitude respectful. He could not fail to charm, though not deceive, these extraordinary dowagers of the city. Virtue all but radiated from them.

"The sisters are our Holy Advisors," Melaré told him. "Their function is to decide upon our moral and self-interested actions. They weigh, if you like, our sins. Once they have judged the actions and weighed them, they determine the further actions needed to remedy the matter. They have kept our lore and practised our laws for many thousands of years. Our valley owes its peace to them. They are the so-called Witches of Kirinmoir. Their wisest and oldest is called Xastera. They are named to frighten would-be invaders. You'll have heard of them."

Elric had not heard of them. But he continued to be careful to acknowledge what authority they represented here and to show them appropriate respect. When they were all seated, Melaré reminded them of what Elric had told her. It was possible they faced an enemy like none any of them could imagine, one capable of easily crossing the mountains and bringing a conquering army to the gates of Kirinmoir.

"What?" One of the women became suddenly alert. "Has it happened? Is she keeping her oath?"

Another woman hissed, "Xiombarg!"

"She made a bargain, took an oath by the Staff. Whatever battles she fights, it cannot apply to Kirinmoir or ourselves. That oath can only be broken by permission of the servants of the Staff and they have not suggested such a thing! She'll doom us all!"

As they talked, Elric continued to feel that there was another, unseen, presence in the place, one that could readily be sensed the longer he remained. Something almost familiar and which he associated with the mead he had first drunk as well as that murmuring swarm. He could not tell if they felt it also. Did a spy of some kind hide here? If the others were aware of it, they showed nothing in their beautiful, marble faces. They might have been wonderfully dressed statues.

"You have knowledge of this alleged demigod?" Xastera asked him. "Is that why you help us?"

"I know no more than anyone here," said the albino. "I have questioned prisoners. They knew little save what you just repeated, my lady. Ramada Sabaru has promised everyone a share of your blue honey." Smiling a little sardonically, Elric glanced towards the Well. "He tells his soldiers that you have no supernatural allies. Some believe he has sworn loyalty himself with Mabelode the Faceless or perhaps another Lord of Chaos. Others say that Miggea of Law has promised her aid to this. She is known to be ruthless and reckless in her desire to impose the reign of Law by the sword. Her followers call her the Roofer and are sworn to resist her plans to raise one great dome over the whole of her sphere. She defies even my own reluctant patron Arioch, perhaps! He could only help, I now realise, if that oath were broken. He in particular is known for his desire to come and go as he pleases upon our plane."

"He wants physical territory? Our planes?"

"He does, Lady Xastera. They all do. But as you know, they can only come to our plane by invitation and then cannot stay. Mortals must invoke them. Generally, they do not, for a bargain between us must be made for even the smallest service. I have a sword which has certain useful properties, and my comrade Moonglum is perhaps the finest swordsman I know. But those, our reputations and our considerable experience of warfare is all we bring you! I help you because we are of the same blood. And because your empress has promised to show me a map that will help us return to our own sphere. I keep my bargains if the Lords of Entropy do not!"

"I can vouch for Elric's work," Melaré said with a smile. "He and his compatriot destroyed an entire bandit clan between them, as I told you. And saved me."

With slight amusement, Elric saw two of the women appear to shudder. He wondered again if perhaps some of these priestesses preferred the majordomo's notion of compromise with the enemy and secretly aided them. But he bowed in answer to a presumed courtesy. "In other circumstances I rely upon a patron Lord of Chaos and my sword, but lately a sip or two of your mead helped me. As I hope it will again."

"Thank you, Prince Elric," the priestess said sincerely. "I believe that once we were, indeed, the same people. Tell me, are the Phoorn still flying in Melniboné?"

"Not of late, lady. They sleep."

She smiled. "Like cats. It is what dragons do best!"

"But I have seen the Phoorn here, in your world. Far across the Sapphire Sea. And their ancestor, too, exists here. Do you know of them?"

Xastera nodded.

"At least two branches of our people came through when we were defeated at the Battle of Smimnal-Jrang. You recall your history lessons? Our people were divided, Sadric the Sixth had five dragons not utterly exhausted and about four others who had not yet fallen into slumber. We had three Dragon Masters still alive. Four, with Sadric. His cousin G'nilwab Sirob (Sirob the Bad) was for taking the moonbeam roads as far as possible, even as they became blocked to us by Law's sorcery. He hoped the encroaching Chaos Lords would fail to follow him. Sadric believed in making a stand in this very valley. G'nilwab refused to join him and fled. Where he went remains unknown. Sadric was defeated and forced to agree to a compromise with Chaos, accepting an alliance which gave Sadric powerful friends and the opportunity to build an empire. He is no doubt your ancestor!"

"It's a common enough name," said Elric. "My father, for instance . . ."

"Indeed. And now, after century upon century has passed, we at last know your fates! And you know ours, Prince Elric. Our ways and our histories diverged and now converge again. All those prophecies we dismissed as the creation of despair! You have fulfilled them and made them real." The High Priestess Xastera was clearly unsympathetic.

"I think our race divided into more than two or even three," said Elric. He spoke of this and his adventure in the Jade Man's eyes several years earlier and he mentioned other adventures on the dream couches of Imrryr.

He had explored the ancestral home of the ancient Phoorn, where his people had first settled before they made their way to Imrryr, naming the city which became the capital of Melniboné, naming the island after their original home from which they had been driven millennia before. There, Elric had learned a little more of his people's history, just as he had learned of their ancestral beginnings from his several dream-quests. On that island Arioch had begun his alliance with Melniboné, though the Chaos Lord was still only able to be on their plane at their summoning. They had argued and threatened mightily to maintain this agreement with all the Lords of the Higher Worlds, but not with the elementals or the mysterious people known as the Nihrain, whom some said were as powerful as gods, though they never revealed their power to humankind or Melnibonéans . . .

What Melaré and the Witches of Kirinmoir told Elric had added to his wisdom, yet he remained mystified. He kept secret how he believed his patron Duke of Hell refused to aid him. Had Arioch changed loyalties on a whim? The events he recollected had happened before he had met Moonglum, when he had travelled on fate's seas with his long-dead friend Smiorgan Baldhead of the Purple Towns, who had died after the raid on Imrryr, unwittingly murdered by the last emperor himself, his friend Elric. Too many tragic memories. He tried to drive them from his mind. What was this other disturbing feeling which came upon him on occasion and which Moonglum suggested might be "remorse"? He associated it with so many memories. So many. He sighed to himself and turned to look at the Well.

A sense of being in familiar presences puzzled Elric. It was as if he heard distant voices, just out of earshot. Intimate voices, whose words he could almost determine. He moved closer to the great well, which over the centuries had been decorated and embellished by skilful craftspeople and was covered by a great bronze plate which could be lowered by a similar winch to those used to raise the blue honey tubs from the Well.

"Do the bees continue to produce after the warlike efforts we witnessed at the cavern?" asked the albino, resting his hands respectfully on the bronze. He felt a soft shivering of the metal. Could he smell smoke? Did he sense the bees dreaming? That soft buzzing he now heard suggested the voice of a sleeping monster. Was there a further mystery here? A threat, even? What did bees dream of? Roses? Wisteria? Lavender? He found he recalled the lavender fields which filled so much of his home island. As a boy he had loved to dream amongst the tall lavender bushes, so sweet-smelling, instilling in him, however briefly, a sense of order and calm. Blood?

"Less than usual," Xastera the High Priestess told him. "Our workers are exhausted, and their queens sleep. It took what little magic we had to use them to save you."

"Do all sleep?"

Xastera frowned, studying his face closely. "Why do you ask?"

"Idle curiosity," said Elric, and felt a faint movement under his hands that might have been a massive beating heart. "Something—I don't know—almost familiar, though familiarity is to be expected in our circumstances. Tell me again, madam—would you do anything for peace?"

"We are sworn to keep the valley's peace since the time of the Great Interference, when all living beings or their representatives among elementals made an oath to preserve Kirinmoir Valley as a place of neutrality, where sorcery is weak at best."

"Then preserve your sanity, madam, and allow us to keep the peace as I know best."

A further suggestion of a shudder. "We cannot allow our peace to be disturbed. We have sworn to these girls, also. To everyone. The responsibility for the peace of Kirinmoir is forever ours."

The albino bowed again. "I shall take that as your blessing!"

"We have sacrificed everything for peace and kept to the old, secure ways. Why then should we let this war begin?"

"I believe you can no longer choose. The size and power of the force coming against us is considerable."

"But that breaks the witnessed oaths!"

"Is it not inevitable, lady, that oaths shall ultimately be broken?"

Melaré came suddenly towards him, hands outstretched. "We must leave our wise women to their rest," she said. The sun had begun to set, sending a lattice of shadows across both the Temple and its gardens. "Come. Would you see the map I mentioned?"

Elric had thought about that map more than once and had put it to the back of his mind, lest they deem him too eager. "Is it here?"

"It is a floor or two below."

Bidding their respects to the women, they left the Temple, descended some steps and entered a spiral-floored interior, apparently winding its way down around the Temple's outer core. Melaré seemed to think the priestesses were pleased with the albino. Elric continued to consider the strangeness of the Well and what it contained. It was clear to him that his questions were in some way unwelcome. Elric understood how they might be reluctant to reveal too much about the bees. They were after all the source of Kirinmoir's wealth and security. Ironically, they might also be the source of the legend bringing the barbarians and their possibly supernatural allies down upon the ancient city and wells.

They walked down the gradually descending corridor and did not see one of the women. Where had they all gone?

"Why, to their homes and families!" she answered, laughing. "Their job is considered pretty much the most honoured position our young women seek out. They are a direct part of the distillation process which refines our honey for its various uses. One day I'll show you our stills and refineries. But I would guess it is the map you would rather see now!"

They entered a high-ceilinged circular room with an inner wall that was also circular. They must have been more than halfway from the first door until he saw a second, quite small and discrete. They passed through this, and Elric realised it was a simple maze. These people loved mazes and labyrinths as much as Melnibonéans elsewhere had always done. After a few of these turns they emerged into a small, well-lit room. The only object at the centre of the maze hung upon the wall farthest from the door. A large framed page of writing with a smaller frame beside it—and in it, Elric saw with rising hope, was a detailed cartographic drawing. Closer—a map! Closer—showing the features of the valley. A trail through the far mountains to—not the edge of this world but the beginnings of another! His own! The elongated outline of a world he imagined to be a kind of extended egg with his familiar lands on one side and these upon another. And there it was. The far mountains eventually came together on the edge as did the oceans, and even the Weeping Waste was indicated. He studied it eagerly, recognising some landmarks of the world he had come from all those months and years before.

She was smiling. "Is it what you expected?"

His hand almost trembled as he reached toward the map. "It *is*, my lady. It is!" And, in an unanticipated rush of emotion, he turned and took her in his arms.

TWENTY

Intimations of War

PREPARATIONS CONTINUED, WITH the clashes between armed men getting more frequent. Elric had seen an increasing number of spies in the city. After letting them be trailed to find more of their associates, the albino would have them seized. Under his command the humans were becoming skilled spies and outriders, rarely seen by the invading scouts.

He had seen several men he recognised as experienced mercenaries, coming and going in the city as spies for Ramada Sabaru. They were usually disguised as honey-brokers, bringing next year's orders back from the outside world, having allowed themselves to be led, traditionally blindfolded, through the maze at the mountain's heart. Seeing that some of the men carried spy hawks under their cloaks, Elric thought this another sign of Kirinmoir placing too much faith in ancient defences.

The spies were usually picked up and quietly killed in the manner of Melnibonéan practice, which taught that a squadron with prisoners travels too slowly. Economically it made no sense to keep men and women alive whom you could not use. Instead of complaining or arguing the value of their lives, the prisoners took their deaths without much distress. Their own people would do exactly the same to spies they caught.

So far as Elric knew, the general rules of engagement remained the same. Battlefields would be agreed, together with the conventions of combat. On a normal battlefield, if challenged for breaking a rule by the Chivalric Heralds, they would pen a strong note to the Officer in Charge of Archives and Restitutions. Their commander would write back promising the act would not to be repeated and for any wounded to be restored, all of which would be ignored, one soldier being much like another in their utter refusal to remember their war-oaths. This, all Melnibonéans understood as a decadent corruption of their own ancient Code of Chivalry. Few followed the old practices in anything but the most casual appearance of seriousness. Moonglum was unfamiliar with the codes and so was not shocked. Elric, on the other hand, had grown up learning them and was baffled by the casualness with which all fighters but a very few treated the notions of chivalry. Such rejections of convention depressed the albino prince.

Today, as in so many days, the defenders lounged at ease outside, in their own city neighbourhoods, gossiping, preparing for an attack which, with luck and a little will, would not reach them. Elric was unable to convince the ranks of their considerable danger. Seeing nothing, they could imagine nothing. Danger would be stopped at the maze. Because it had always been stopped at the maze. It is very hard, Elric reflected, for the unimaginative to imagine what they have never experienced. Even General Gash understood what was going on and what terrible jeopardy they faced! It is equally hard to get them to see their own looming demise until it is too late, he thought bitterly.

Supplies were plentiful and well-hidden, stacked in cool caves on the islet of Omicooro with a strong guard, within the outer bailey. Armourers had worked the clock round to furnish a plenitude of weapons. Then came the waiting and wondering when and where the main attack would come. This waiting and its tensions were what Elric and Moonglum were used to. The women responded well, however, and the adventurers were impressed by their self-discipline.

A warm winter came and went and the two men enjoyed the company of the empress and her captain, women who made love urgently, as if they expected to be snatched away to battle at any moment.

The chief enemy of most soldiers at that moment was that prolonged inactivity and wondering, the sudden trumpeting of heralds, another pause and then the reverberating clash of action as two armies located one another!

Bloody steel and the rise and fall of red hands would be a release from those tensions as they gave themselves up to savage battle. The empress's previous allies, the bees, had expended their available energy and had long since disappeared back to their hives to recuperate their strength.

The first few attacks came upon their earliest defences, the entrance to the tunnel in what was known as the Cave of the Cattle, and were relatively minor. The generals were jubilant when it appeared the enemy retreated, but Elric and Moonglum knew what was happening. The enemy tested Kirinmoir Valley's strength and resources. Both sides gathered information from those sallies. No magic was employed on either side, save for Elric's greedy runesword howling for sustenance. Apparently, Arioch no longer channelled the sword's energies, which required more and more effort to tap. Even Elric, symbiotically dependent upon Stormbringer, did not completely understand his blade, nor the forces which had combined to create it. All he knew was that he needed the blue mead before he gained the strength to steal the souls of his enemies.

Through the following days and weeks the enemy began to bring up greater numbers, a horde of hungry, hating, battle-hardened brutes which flung itself again and again into all the maze's tunnels, exhausting themselves with every attack! But little by little the power of Kirinmoir was tested, and her outer defences of the mountains slowly eroded.

Mulxer Gash had no faith at all in their ability to defend themselves and had originally argued for "negotiation" with Ramada Sabaru, an enemy whose face or form none had yet seen, but whose strength was attested by their own spies. An unprecedented army of enormous size was marching to join the invaders. Prisoners knew little about him except that the Golden Warlord had united the tribes and promised them as much blue mead as they could guzzle. The wizened major-domo fussed about on the fringes of things, forever in the way, increasingly unneeded. Moonglum almost felt sorry for him. It was a simple case, as the Elwheri saw it, of the more dynamic force taking over a decadent one. Elric was more thoughtful. He had learned much of politics since settling in Karlaak. He probably would have stayed had not Zarozinia encouraged him to go on this one last adventure, to seek the sources of his demons as well as his questions and if possible be done with them at last. He had not thought it would take so long. Would she even have waited? She had explained why he should take what female company he could.

"You are usually at your best when you have a woman nearby," she had said. His friendships with women had been fulfilling, and on that score he considered the adventure to have broadened his perspectives. But, while he had resisted admitting it to himself, his feelings for Melaré had become stronger. He was falling in love with her. She brought back complicated emotions. She reminded him too much of Cymoril. This place was not Tanelorn, and he was not certain whether Kirinmoir would survive the coming war. He was foolish to debate a future he might never see. And his loyalty to Zarozinia was powerful. If Zarozinia were nearby, perhaps he would not have these emotions. Since leaving her, he had been unable to communicate by any means and would only be able to do so when he had reached the edge of his own world, if then. She had offered, "for good luck," her locket. He had accepted it not knowing the custom. He had never thought to open it and find the portrait within. It was hidden amongst his other valuables, in a small pouch within his shirt. He kept all this to himself.

Phlegmatically, Moonglum decided that his friend's changed manner was due to the burden of leadership. He did not feel that burden much but saw the position as a chance to serve his own interest as well as the city's. He continued to enjoy his friendship with the Captain of the Empress's Guard.

Elric found the human generals surprisingly quick to pick up ideas. It gave him some notion of the fine education available to the valley people. They had no experience of the outside world but had read every treatise on warfare and strategy available. Elric found them easy to talk to, but sometimes, when their books clashed with his experience, there were disagreements. The makeshift wall created by the bees had not done enough to stop the invaders, and, better co-ordinated than before, they had quickly cleared a way through it and sent men with lines through the various tunnels to map them thoroughly.

The roads were now all open to the invaders, who were coming in larger numbers. Their old defences were no longer of use and their new defences looked increasingly inadequate. They were getting messages from the front, which now extended across much of the inner valley. There was no part of the undefended valley not overrun by mounted bandits. Every inhabitant sought the shelter of Kirinmoir. Melaré and her generals rode tirelessly up and down the valley, rallying troops whose berserkers gulped blue mead, spat blue foam and glared blood-rage from eyes almost as red as Elric's own. But they were met by experienced aggressors who were heartless, without courage or chivalry. They were, indeed, the scurvy remnants of two massive armies. Lust for blue mead was not the only force uniting them. Something more powerful than blue honey had made them stop bickering and become a disciplined force. A force moving at extraordinary speed to occupy the mountains and valley and move towards the city, which had no escape routes. A force that carried malice as well as ambition.

Elric was now convinced that something was behind that force. Something inconceivably powerful.

TWENTY-ONE

Ramada Sabaru

THE FOLLOWING EVENING the invaders sent their outriders into the low-lying hills, scattering the few sheep which had avoided the roundup, to look across at Kirinmoir and her sparkling moat. In ancient times sight of the city had been enough to make barbarians turn their engines and troops and war-animals and go back to tell their kinsmen that Kirinmoir was invincible. Not now.

Now the army marched confidently and rapidly towards its goal. Never had there been, even in olden times, an army as powerful as this. They had all anticipated it. But they could not have guessed its disciplined speed, or its size and glory!

Elric, returning to his balcony on the high watchtower as the sun began its passage, knew a rare form of despair. He had the will to fight, but not the means. Stormbringer barely served him. He could kill with it, yet drain almost no life-stuff from his enemies. Blue mead presently sustained him, but only for brief bursts of power. Enough for a short, efficient battle. Not sufficient for a long siege. The evil being that haunted the sword did so at Arioch's bidding and might even be Arioch himself. Only at his death, it was said, would Elric know the truth.

For the moment, at any rate, Elric decided to give up relying on the old pacts with even the earth spirits and unresponsive gods and godlings, whether of Chaos or of Law. He had seen and recognised the enemy coming against Kirinmoir. He knew now that his patron Duke of Chaos was unlikely to answer his desperate calls for help! They must fight the oncoming army with conventional means, and it was unlikely that they could win such a fight. Already, no doubt exaggerated, reports spoke of even more monstrous supernatural allies. If the numbers were halved, the aggressors would still outnumber the defenders tenfold at least. Elric was clear about one thing. Melniboné had been confident that Imrryr's dreaming towers would stand forever. The city had fallen in less than two days. To treachery from within! His own. Again he thought of the two tired sisters of Xiombarg who had no doubt perished in this world of their own innocence.

Elric put his mind to the problem once more. There had to be a way of using those bees again, or at least their honey! In all the squares of the city preparations were made to supply adults with enough mead to keep them fighting. Would there be enough? There was only one certain way to discover if there was.

They must mount an expedition. Ignoring the warnings and objections of the priestesses and whatever dangers they might be hiding from their own people. Very soon, he decided, he would insist. His most recent requests had been dismissed. The hive was sacred. The interior of the mountain and the bees and the honey they produced. All were sacred. The Blue Priestesses had given him permission to defend the city. They had not permitted him to plumb that city's secrets.

He demanded a further audience. Somehow those bees must become weapons. An audience was refused. Again. Again refused.

Meanwhile Moonglum, Melaré and Shirizha paced the battlements far below the slender, domed Tower of the Well. They debated endlessly until talk drove them too into silence. Above them the ancient priestesses slept and dreamed of all the terrors which must soon visit Kirinmoir. They had three times rejected Elric's appeals, even with Melaré and Shirizha at his back. The priestesses remained adamant.

Elric, barely able to control his temper, now paced alone, black silk rippling, red eyes glittering, fearing he would quarrel with his friends. The bees were Kirinmoir's only powerful help against an overwhelming army almost certainly possessed of supernatural help! And those priestesses, stuck almost literally in the past, refused to let him observe "secrets" which had almost certainly been dead for centuries! Millennia! How could he save them if they refused him their resources?

And the humans living below them, those who had retreated within the walls with their families and their livestock, reassured one another that there was nothing left to fear now that Elric the Albino and Duke Moonglum of Elwher were here to take charge of the armies of the empress, while Kirinmoir herself, as all of course knew, was invulnerable. Tomorrow they would laugh and drink mead and watch the armies of Ramada Sabaru the Golden run away back to their barbaric wastelands! But once their children slept, the adults lay awake wondering when the moment might come when they would drink blue mead and pick up their sharp tools to defend all they loved until they too were killed. They slept long and late, for the waters were even there tinged with some substance used to let men gather strength for a coming struggle. They rose at noon to learn that another army was gathering behind the first, while the first ranks had advanced. And they knew the time was soon coming when they would drink their ration of mead.

Reports came from the few returning spies. This new invading army was uniformed, more disciplined, marching in phalanx, the widest parts of those guarding fifteen war-mammoths of massive height, with long curling tusks sharpened to razors, bound with copper and gold. They marched in ranks of five, each rank defended by infantry. On the backs of the elephants were four archers at each corner of a howdah and in front of them an armoured mahout also armed with a bow.

The spies had turned mad with the sights. They returned raving of mammoths and men marching in tune to blaring instruments of brass and booming sheepgut, their faces covered by bronze half-masks, protecting the eyes. Their faces were painted with hideous expressions designed to make an enemy tremble. The howdahs were filled with green-fletched arrows whose thin shafts would drive deep into an enemy's body and work their way through the mor-

tal organs! They had javelins of a similar design, with thin breakable shafts
which could rarely be flung back at them. They shouldered bows, while at
their belts were swords, knives and other weaponry of more personal and vulgar design. Armoured infantry poured up and over the hills like a murderous
morning mist. More and more of them came, pushing the invaders closer to
the great boulders enfolding the hill of Kirinmoir topped by the Blue Temple;
then came cavalry, such proud, fresh, high-stepping cavalry, ready to gallop
towards the defenders until the hoofs of their horses reverberated deep into
the ground, to bring the walls of Kirinmoir down! A pulse of gold within their
ranks, a distant cloud which roared and flashed yet could not be seen, suggested that the Golden Warlord himself now rode with his men.

And then came the supernatural monstrosities they had hoped not to see.
The half-apes, the bird-legged men, the brutes with backs bent any unnatural
way at the whim of their masters, the tusked men and the five-eyed women
and the hairy men bearing clubs shaped liked monstrous phalluses; Cercil-
inine renegades, carrying their characteristic "pickle-pokers" in their weirdly
shaped claws. Stinking, deformed, glorious and beautiful minor aristocrats
of the Higher Worlds! First were the petty lordlings, the semigods, the demigods, the disranked mothers and fathers of older gods, rolling or walking,
or floating or flying just above the ground, each one armed with a powerful
weapon of choice. Yet none powerful enough to defy Stormbringer or long-
lost Mournblade save one. That, they knew, had been bargained for and then
bestowed as a gift of peace by Lady Andra and Lady Indra, the High Priestesses of Xiombarg, upon their patron Queen of the Swords. The Ivory Blade
they called Divergent . . .

And here he came at last, bursting like a comet from amongst his own
ranks, and Elric recognised him immediately! Idramadahan Sanfgt Iru Iru
Sab'n in the formal language of the Western Fabor who had adopted him and
made him their chief, the Golden Lord of War, the Conqueror Come Again!
And here he was, according to yet another ancient prophecy—Ramada Sabaru, the Golden Warlord—riding on a mammoth twice the size of his other
war-pachyderms. Its trunk and tusks were festooned with delicately made

enamelled flowers with petals of precious gems and lifelike vines snaking and flashing like the eyes of the passionate women who now gathered, fascinated, at the battlements of Kirinmoir to catch a glimpse of their would-be destroyer.

Seeing him from a distance, Elric puzzled. Those aquiline features were familiar to him, and not as the face of an enemy! He risked a further glimpse over the battlements, half-expecting an arrow storm to come howling up from behind the halberdiers. The Warlord's face had vanished. They were moving to surround the city on three sides, making themselves exposed to archers and spear-throwers Elric had positioned in the enclosing giant boulders which effectively protected them. It was possible to shelter in especially hollowed-out crevices should any airborne enemy fly over. Beyond the turrets the Golden Battle-Lord moved among his men, dispensing largesse and triumphalism, while adoringly cheered. Elric had seen him in very different circumstances and not two years since. It was certainly one he thought either gone back to the upper world or dead. Then he was again absorbed into the swirling golden cloud.

The Warlord's animals, all trained for specific lethal and warlike purposes, were armoured in iron and brass, silver and jade, with caparisons of jewel-stitched scarlet, blue and deep green. Jingling harnesses, spurs and mascots; swords and javelins, spears and lances, all but the heavier clank of hard-beaten iron against edged steel.

He made up his mind. He must find Moonglum. He sent a soldier to find his friends, guarding the northern flank. He needed to speak to his friend. He needed his old ally with him in case one were needed to guard the other. But Moonglum had no doubt decided to take advantage of the few brief hours left and was resting or with Shirizha. So Elric dozed.

He awoke to the sound of a wild and massive shout. The first of the war-mammoths had reached an outer wall and, with muscles straining, was pushing its huge armoured head against the groaning gateway, which barely held. He heard the stone and timbers resist the mammoths, who then retreated to make way for another wave of the mighty beasts. Against conventional siege weapons, the walls could hold forever, but against the Golden Warlord's forces, they would be lucky if they lasted a day!

In a few moments General Mulxer Gash hurried into the chamber pleading with Elric for orders.

Elric said, "Reinforce the gate."

His plan had little to do with generalship.

TWENTY-TWO

Into the Hive

JUST AFTER DAWN, there came a commotion in the besiegers' ranks. Some of their own people shouted. A Kirinmoiri guard urgently pointed upward.

Everyone moved cautiously to the keep's tall, open window and looked out at an extraordinary sight! Three riders on massive black mounts appeared to canter over an invisible road to follow a path of uneven light down towards the four gathered in that castle room, where, like the sun's sudden shaft, the radiance spread to illuminate everything. The shadows of the distant, momentarily rearing, mounts filled the large room, and there was a stink of ozone in the air which Elric recognised. Magic. Another supernatural enemy? A pause. The riders were suddenly invisible, as if they entered a tunnel.

Then, once again the three were galloping down the sky, apparently on thin air: dark riders all swathed in heavy travelling cloaks. Their mounts' hoofs seemed to strike sparks from the misting dawn as, on prancing war-beasts, they reared up at the eastern gate of the town, and, after much shouting, then whispered agreement, the narrow sidebridge between massive buttresses was lowered across the moat and the small party entered the town. The riders were demanding an audience with the empress and her captains even before the bridge was drawn up again. Within seconds before it closed a trained enemy spy hawk had flown in through the gate at enormous speed and was shot down by a vigilant archer. There was a pause in the shouting.

All that could be heard was the faint humming of the mountain, the stirring murmur of the enemy outside the city walls and the sound of water running into the city's reservoir.

With a crack, two great black and yellow banners appeared above a ripple in the sharp morning sky. They flapped heavily against their poles, which bent into fractured shards and then quarters, then they were one again, the banners unfurling with the Sign of the Balance. Steam poured off the horses' flanks, their red tongues curled from between their huge white teeth, their eyes flashed gold and ebony, silver hoofs striking rock now to send shivering slivers of granite flying wherever those terrible hoofs touched their shared earth! And suddenly, once they had presented themselves to Kirinmoir's guards, they turned their mounts and rode *up* the sky towards the tower.

Moonglum's mouth flew open. He recognised them. They were the battle-mounts of legend, the stallions which travelled on the invisible time and space exclusive to the moonbeam roads. Spoken of but never seen. From their grazing fields of the Botu-Pinnian Alps in the high Vovin Marches, serving only one small group of masters, the Nihrain, mysterious supreme justices of the Higher Worlds, the two leading battlehorses were enormous, shaggy stallions whose shoulders were higher than Elric's head. These great mounts, their black coats, caparisoned in gleaming jet and gold, barely bore a trace of sweat, though they steamed like quenched iron and their hearts could be seen and heard pounding.

Elric and Moonglum immediately recognised the women and then the man, who brought his own great beast of a half-stallion, a *gynn* mule, to a halt before them. He was a handsome redhead with a green felt bonnet on the side of his head and a belted plaid across his shoulder, the belt bearing a collection of sharp, edged weapons; a big man in his forties, with a proud yet humorous bearing, who clearly had affection for his handsome and whimsical-looking *gynn* mule. Orlando Funk it was! Looking much younger.

"You've been to the Fountain of Youth, I see, Sir Orlando!" Elric's voice was something of a challenge.

For a moment Funk was puzzled, then he fingered his chin and was enlightened. He carried a great double-bladed axe on his shoulder and had a long trident on his back, a good-sized sword at his belt, as well as two poignards and a pigskin purse. Funk looked altogether stronger, healthier and less vulnerable than the man they had met a year or more earlier on the oak-wood road. He was clean-shaven, save for his greying red muttonchop whiskers, and he was grinning merrily at their astonishment. "I brought them to ye, man!" he roared at Elric. "How's that for a barbarian poet and an Orkney one at that?" He licked his red lips, winking. "I still have a little o' yon mead if ye need it . . ."

"I'm not sure, Master Funk, that I'll have need in the night of another stimulant." Elric spoke lightly and smiled, but he was suspicious of a man he still guessed to be guilty of directing them into an ambush. He realised that he spoke arrogantly and modified his baritone. He could not afford more enemies. Anxious to maintain any alliance at that stage, he said, "I am grateful, sir. You have arrived at an opportune time. I hope, Master Funk, that you bring supernatural help of some kind."

"I hope I bring you wisdom, at least, which you'll find useful, sir." Funk drew a red, gold-stamped book from his pocket and began to read. Elric and his friend looked at the exhausted women as they were helped down from their great chargers. Why had Funk brought them with him to Kirinmoir? Indeed, why had any of them come here to Kirinmoir?

Elric looked from him to the weary women and back again. "Surely . . . ?"

There was no reply. Why was the man so many years younger now? Like his clothing and weapons. His mule, too, had become if anything larger and blacker than a royal warhorse, looking mildly down at the albino still standing by the keep's window. Orlando Funk had an altogether different manner than when they had last encountered him. Was he playing a part? If anything, his manner was even more pleasant. He smiled at Elric. "I'll begin afresh wi' 'Good morning, young master! I trust ye're well.' I believe you and these ladies are already acquainted. Please call me an ill-mannered lout from King James's notoriously slovenly Court, but I strive to fit in, you know, and come up, as 'twere, to expectations."

Elric's courtesy did not allow him to interrogate such tired souls. He felt he had heard doubt in the tone of the strange traveller in plaid. Was this petty wizard to fail him, also? Were the horses stolen from the great Nihrain? Did Funk have nothing more to offer than mysterious words when information was what the albino and his fighting friends needed to defeat an army many thousands of times larger and better-equipped than their own? An army which, with little need of *geeds* and *izrads* or any other misbegotten halfling from some foul *Book of Devils and Monstrous Disguises, Dispositions and Materialisations*, which could, no doubt, crush them in an hour of consistent battling.

"Nonetheless, to save enough slaves for the needs of even the most demanding economy, you must, of course, spare as many lives as possible." Funk appeared to continue reading. "Creating a rapidly decaying economy, an illusory power which falls at a tap—" And he tapped with his axe haft at the crumbling woodwork and flaking paint of the keep's interior. "Of course, if you have already enslaved your own, what need you of more? But, as we soon discover, this is terrible economics in the long run. It takes a slightly subtler system to retain labour pools in seasonal work! Believe me, the economics of magic is a discipline in itself. That's where the feudal system is superior . . ." He seemed to have entered a melancholy trauma.

"May we speak to you in private," murmured Elric, not at all sure that Funk was entirely functioning on a common plane.

"Ye do not know what I have discovered? Something which might possibly be to our advantage?"

"I do," said the albino. "But first you must help us with our urgent plan to escape our dilemma."

"And leave the poor lassies helpless?"

"I am a little suspicious of them. They serve Xiombarg and therefore Chaos . . ."

"However, the situation is subtle. Should they stay or—"

"Only if they prefer to stay with this situation this long! I am pretty sure you knew much of what was happening here before you left! Good enough, Master Funk?!" This from a furious Moonglum who was not so much worrying about his death as he was of once again making no profit from his adventure. "Is this a situation at least partly of your creation, Master Funk?"

Orlando Funk shrugged. "Very well, gentlemen, since we have a few hours before the main battle, and the Golden Warlord has yet to arrive, then I suggest we embark on what you insist is a remarkable and useful adventure. You know, of course, by now that I serve the Nihrain, from whom these horses are borrowed? You know that I tricked you to a degree when we met in the oak wood?"

"Tricked us, indeed! You knowingly sent us to our deaths! Why, you let us enter a den of wolves with barely any warning and no help!"

"Merely offering a little restoring mead . . . ," pointed out Funk, "which I believe was of some use to you in the fight which helped you release the Empress Melaré. Which in turn . . ."

"Well, the mead was thin . . . ," grunted Moonglum.

An acceptance which somehow resembled an anticlimax to Elric.

Moonglum and Funk, now dismounted, at his side, Elric asked that the priestesses Andra and Indra speak to him alone. They received this request with some consternation.

"I assure you, ladies, that I mean you no ill will and accept that you mean us none, for your tale's too thin to be incredible. I hope that in trusting you I show greater wisdom than I have shown in the past." And, at length, they agreed when they had exchanged certain confidences, and he ordered that the women be refreshed and rested and asked to offer any intelligence they had to the empress. Moonglum was speechless at his friend's display of a naïveté he believed he had at last overcome!

Next the albino informed their hosts that they needed again to check all the city's defences. A desperate plan was forming. He reassured the disconcerted male generals that he would be back long before they were needed. Privately, he guessed the enemy would continue its strategic movement so that the city was completely surrounded. That would probably take the rest of the day. If his plan failed, he would be dead before he knew it.

"Fear not," he said to Melaré. "I know that I shall again find myself at odds with your High Priestess, but I have to persuade her that she no longer acts for the common good. I need to test her word against her deeds!"

"I will come with you!"

"You must lead your people. I will return to ride into battle at your side."

Elric was a little uncomfortable with telling this half-lie to his fellow defenders. He had decided he must take the initiative. If they continued to trust Kirinmoir's General Gash and the other ancient, frail cautious male generals and unsure priestesses, with only tradition as their law, who advised already conservative women, it was ensuring, he was certain, the city's collapse still more swiftly before the Warlord's might! It was just possible, however, that in that mysterious hive they might find some unknown method of diverting their enemies' attention long enough for Elric to find a means of recruiting Lord Arioch back to his cause. A wild and unlikely hope, a risk worth taking while his sword remained dormant. Something which had been undreamed of in all the millennia of its story in all the years of its telling. Not a trace of it remaining. But stories, he remembered, could be forgotten as well as created. A tree could be planted and uprooted. And planted again. He turned with a shrug, preparing to go back into the heart of the city and investigate the great Temple!

Elric remained somewhat irritated by Funk's avuncular air. The Orkney-man affected the manner of a relative humouring children, but again, as long as the albino received practical help from the self-called Brother to the Nihrain, that mysterious sect said to serve the Cosmic Balance, he would not complain. He was used to secrets and used to living with secrets. He knew there were secrets locked in the hive, and that, in spite of the High Priestess's warnings, the bees would reveal theirs to adventurers intrepid enough to explore their complex home and fortress. Surely it was possible to communicate with the hive-as-a-whole and inform it of its danger? For it *was* in danger! He must find a way to help it defend itself. There again, Elric found it hard to imagine that those sentient creatures somehow did not already know they were under threat.

Making through the crowded, anxious streets of the city, ignoring all the desperate questioners, they reached the main steps to the Temple. The square was packed with more citizens begging them for news, for hope of any kind.

From here, it was possible to see the mighty army marching over those undulating hills to surround Kirinmoir, the City of Singing Flowers, the City Everlasting. Grimly, they pushed on through. A scream.

They turned. They looked back towards the winding road to the dark tunnel through the barely seen mountains. Half-blinded by the glare and glory that was Ramada Sabaru and—

Elric and the others shielded their eyes.

And then here *she* came. Not simply a golden radiance. Not merely a glaring force with all the power of the sun! Here was a goddess, a supernatural presence which forced men to bow their heads as she advanced: a pulsing, blazing, fearsome, shrieking furious giantess with a thousand shimmering ivory arms! No! *Four* mighty arms which bore one ivory sword! A long, vibrating, curving sword cut from a single huge mammoth tusk and chased with red-gold, platinum and copper, sending streamers of light into the darkening noonday. A sword named Divergent.

Xiombarg! Queen of the Swords. Princess of Blades and Bloodshed. Lady of Locusts and Lavender, of Grain and Gold and ungorged greed, giggling at him in mockery from a dozen leagues distant! Even Elric found himself instinctively raising his shield against the glaring eyes of a goddess.

Xiombarg! Who now bore the Ivory Blade, Divergent, which was four blades united or one blade divided, depending upon the entity carrying her. The Divider and the Uniter. Under her, people fought against people until they were too exhausted to fight further, at which moment they willingly gave themselves up to her rule. Divergent did not serve Chaos or Law but her own interest. She diverted and divided to rule. She came together to punish and tyrannise. She was the enemy of the Great Balance, for the Balance maintained the equilibrium of reality.

"The Ivory Sword," Orlando Funk said, "in serving herself alone, seeks to destroy reality altogether, to return the multiverse to her natural state, as they see it, before matter was born and mind alone existed in a solitary state. The White Sword, symbol of Mind Alone, of a static reality, without Time, Matter or any kind of movement, metaphysical or physical. And now a population which fears too much to resist the very threat of Divergent, that it might abolish Time and Space forever, to occupy the same unchanging moment forever."

"But why?"

"Because they are mad," said Funk seriously, and he shrugged. "Why do women murder their beloved children or sons kill their loving parents?"

"The White Sword!" Moonglum swore. "Those women serve her! They must do or they would not have made the sword their price and then given it to her! They have betrayed us! As they intended all along! That was her price! What bargain did you make with them, Elric? You cannot trust them. They gave Divergent to Xiombarg so she could begin this war. She needed the White Sword to conquer those resistant amongst her own people. To bring traitors and outlaws into her sphere. Before she could conquer Law, she must capture Chaos."

Even as Moonglum spoke, Elric remembered Xiombarg and, closing his eyes, he could see her now, beckoning to him from the battlefield, doing all she could to call him to her. What *could* she want from him? And why would her archrival Arioch not come to Elric's aid?

"Do not be deceived again, Elric."

Elric frowned. And all this while, since he had first glimpsed her from the ship and admired her, she had sought him out. For what? Or was it Elric himself she sought?

Divergent! He had, of course, read the name in the grimoires he had studied as a youth, even before he had come to the long dream-quests on the ancient dream couches. He knew what she was, he thought!

Elric closed his eyes beneath the distant goddess's shining, disapproving gaze. Was it only him, after all, that Xiombarg sought out? Because he had eluded her for so long? Arioch? Had the Lord of the Seven Darks somehow been taken by his great rival? And was Elric her real prey and the rape of Kirinmoir merely the price she paid his cousin, Dyvim Marluc? She helped him destroy Kirinmoir simply to gain Elric as her slave? Elric remained his own creature, and, though they moved like automata, the people still thought only of resisting her. She wanted him, but she also wanted to add blue honey to her tools of persuasion! All speculation, but for one thing.

It was clear to him at last that Xiombarg had trapped Arioch when he was weak. Arioch refused to join forces with any but the minor gods and goddesses of his chosen earthly realm, for which he felt a paternal ownership as a farmer for his slaves, even though he had the power of life and death over them. Did she hate him for that relationship, which was certainly reciprocated . . . ? Arioch frequently addressed Elric with caressing affection, almost as an edible delicacy. *Oh, sweetest of my slaves* . . . True, the Lords and Ladies of the Higher Realms could be petty, but usually not quite so petty as to crush a city from spite!

No, if Xiombarg had added her power to Ramada Sabaru's exceptional army, then Xiombarg had a greater motive than mere revenge. And if Idrama-dahan Sanfgt Iru Iru Sab'n was to share power with a Queen of Chaos, she, too, must have struck a bargain amounting to more than one petty motive.

There is a War Amongst the Angels, thought Moonglum, the Elwheri real-ist, *and it is not only on this plane. The antagonists exist on every plane of the multiverse and flow along the moonbeam roads. Elric knows this in his bones, as do others here. We must choose sides very soon . . . Many resist the truth of this. We do not fight Good or Evil, but to decide what logic rules the coming Millennia, the Times To Be and the Times that Shall Be . . .*

As they moved quickly through the city, frightened citizens tried to follow the three, but Moonglum, responding to his own revelation, waved them back into their shops and apartments. He told them not to be afraid, though his face changed colour to ashen. He told them that help was coming against the forces of Chaos and that even now he and his comrades went to find more. But it was becoming hard to hold them back. These people had known tranquillity all of their lives and had it snatched away suddenly. Barely able to move or think for the shock of it, they reverted to herd panic, blind prejudice and aggression.

Then, at last, Elric moved to join Moonglum. Funk was far ahead, axe unlimbered, gesturing urgently to his companions and pointing ahead as he ran up the steps of Blue Jade Temple of the Forty Winds in the eery stillness of a suddenly overcast day. Had the place been abandoned by humanity as well as the sun itself?

The majority of the priestesses in their beautiful costumes were gone. Below, in the square, clusters of gawping citizens emerged again, ignoring all threats. Far away across the valley, and at the centre of the invader's army, was the blazing light of the White Sword, Divergent! Soon, Xiombarg and Ramada would give their orders, and within a few hours Kirinmoir and her legends and epics would be obliterated forever. Without stories there was no culture, no memory, no forward march into a future, for Time was truly obliterated if one destroyed Space so thoroughly. Or so it was thought in those days.

The albino was not quite ready to witness or create such a disastrous experiment. He tried to make out details of those scarlet and yellow flames. They showed Elric Xiombarg's menacing passage across the valley. Would he know when she decided to strike? Did she mean to destroy Kirinmoir with one massive blow or stifle them to death slowly as a baby-extinguisher performs her profession with a sack and a pillow? To starve them into surrender might prove impossible. There was room to feed and raise livestock. Even if the flow were stopped, it would take many years before the city's reservoirs were drained of their honey. The sources of the spring, over which the Well was built, were deep below the surface, impossible to find by any known magic or natural science.

Perhaps the invaders meant the hive to continue? The honey might be a crucial resource, needed before Xiombarg began a next stage in her conquest. Maybe the priestesses of the Well were gone, having already turned renegade and given Xiombarg their apiarian secrets in return for their lives, until she herself became the only Queen of the Blue Hive! Elric understood the choices offered by tyrants. No doubt, as Xiombarg's slaves learned all that was needed to maintain the Well and her crossbred bees, the priestesses would be killed or allowed to die until Xiombarg herself would alone own the secret. They would be defended as the Queen of the Swords intended! As it was always intended the Well should be. To the priestesses, perhaps, the longevity of the Well had become more important than the city it sustained.

This was not to be the traditionally played-out, honourable fight the forces of humanity had taught their Phoorn allies, but a complete destruction, in a matter of moments of everything they cared for. Now Elric was certain of the face he had seen approaching Kirinmoir!

He knew that the original name of the Golden Warlord was neither Idramadahan Sanfgt Iru Iru Sab'n, nor was it Ramada Sabaru.

But most shocking to the albino—and he really should not have been shocked—was the figure of Xiombarg's chief ally displaying himself to his vast army. He had seen the man once and refused to accept it, but that ally was indeed Dyvim Marluc. Dyvim Marluc, who had been last seen in pursuit of the Black Anemonë. Elric's own cousin. Dyvim Marluc, who had travelled beyond the Edge of the World! Like Elric, he was an exile, hated by all in the Young Kingdoms who had ever heard of Melniboné. An exile, whom Elric had created by betraying his own people! He had made Dyvim Marluc a Dragon Master without his dragon!

And at last Dyvim Marluc had determined how best to pay the albino and the whole non-Melnibonéan world back in kind. He was betraying Elric. Sweet revenge! And what a vast and monstrous betrayal it would be, surpassing both Yyrkoon's and Elric's own. Since they had separated, Dyvim Marluc, Elric's mother's younger sister's son, was no threat to that useless throne. He had nothing to inherit. Elric had known his cousin to consider occasionally the validity of arguments favourable to Yyrkoon when the mood took him, but he had proven loyal enough to the traditional institutions. And then Elric rewarded his cousin Marluc's loyalty with treachery and barely even an apology.

No doubt any embittered Melnibonéan would repay treachery with the same kind of treachery, if he could. It had taken the affair of the black blossoms to bring this to fruition, no doubt. Or had Xiombarg found Dyvim Marluc first? Phoornling in the past had often rewarded Phoornling with worse, more painful treachery, executed through the power of any one of the three most prominent Chaos Lords, Arioch, Mabelode and Xiombarg, in all the countless planes and worlds of the multiverse! So this was the vengeance Dyvim Marluc plotted while his strangely innocent cousin continued to search for the origins of his race.

He sighed, staring gloomily across the uniformed ranks of that well-disciplined army. He had never seen quite such uniform armour before and marvelled at its workmanship. It lacked the baroque impracticality of the elaborate ceremonial Melnibonéan armour and was designed to deflect every kind of weapon. Elric reflected wryly that even sorcerers occasionally required more practical armour than his own magnificent battledress, designed more to impress and identify than to deflect and protect, as if its wearer dared an attacker to strike.

And then Moonglum was speaking to him from the top of the temple steps.

"Quickly, Elric! Quickly! The guards and workers are gone! The acolytes, too! Only the women priests remain!"

Elric joined him at the top of the steps, where the huge copper cauldrons had been put away for the night. Orlando Funk was ahead of Moonglum, cautiously advancing into the Temple's sunken garden, at the centre of which was the Temple Well, smeared with pulsing blue stuff which had dried there as the blind porters had carried their great bronze buckets up and down, up and down, monotonously for centuries.

And then, from their couches, those beautiful ancient blue-robed women rose up, converging on the three strangely assorted men; the tall, slender albino, a bearded giant and a short redhead.

Elric was prepared to kill the women. The High Priestess Xastera understood that also, for she stopped her women with a sharp gesture and a murmured "Go! Do as I told you! Go!" And the priestesses, all of the highest rank, dispersed like mist, unheard and unseen. Xastera, with whom Elric had spent so long in argument, raised her hand, palm outward, and said to him:

"Lord Elric of Melniboné! You came as our friend, and I know you still wish to be our friend. However, I must remind you of the consequences of what will happen if you continue in your intentions! If the Well is invaded, the prophecy must follow. The Kirinmoir secret will be known and her future unassured! In short, our prosperity and good fortune shall be in hard jeopardy! Barbarian gods shall desecrate and ultimately destroy our Temple, which shall provide no more honey!

"Elric, betrayer of your race, do you think I am ignorant of your dilemma? Deserted by your patron, you need our honey to live! So now you attempt to break our most sacred Law! It is forbidden for men to descend into the Great Well. To do so is to violate all history and to break an ancient and profound compact. If the compact is violated, the original witnesses to it will be invoked to punish all. Those who were there when the Treaty was made swore to sustain that compact until the end of time. To ignore the Treaty could mean that the end is summoned! The destruction of everything we respect and love is imminent! Be aware—if you enter the forbidden hive, your mind shall be damaged forever. Your coming doom will be assured, inevitable. Your future will hold nothing but the death and betrayal of all you most cherish. I know you for a troubled Phoornling, Elric of the Dream Realms! Elric, of an impossible union and an inescapable birthright! I know your life has been much-troubled and shall be more troubled in times to come. Do not do this thing, Lord Elric. Do not betray our trust. Keep the compact!"

Elric spoke with stubborn certainty. "I am a soldier who once possessed a sorcerer's power! Now I am only a soldier, with a soldier's power. I am sworn to protect your city, my lady, in the best way I know. I must follow my own judgement alone!"

"Unimaginable doom shall come to your world should you follow this road. Please, Lord Elric, consider—"

"My lady, I act as a soldier must. I swore to you, who gave us this task of defeating your enemies and saving this city, that I would do all I could to achieve that. I promised to do this. I promised your empress, whom I believe takes precedence over you and the others—"

"*SHE DOES NOT!*" Flushed and desperate the High Priestess Xastera looked wildly around her, as if for help, or even a weapon. But she had already dismissed her women. "Xiombarg is more powerful and thus more able to keep a promise. If she promises us and our charges invulnerability, she can give it!"

Elric glanced into the shadows beneath the pillars but saw nothing. Where had the rest of the women gone? For help? For shelter? Or to join the attackers? Did they, too, serve Xiombarg now?

"We have always had precedence in this matter," said High Priestess Xastera. "Our ancestors drew up that agreement, and it was duly witnessed! You will bring destruction down on Kirinmoir, Silverskin! Our ancestors have protected our great secret for millennia upon millennia. Xiombarg promises to continue to defend—"

"She lies!" called Moonglum. "She lies always! Lies are the very bread and wine of Chaos! And Xiombarg gorges herself on lies! Xastera! You serve Xiombarg now! I can smell it!"

High Priestess Xastera was radiant in her outrage. "I will remind you of our oracular warnings! If the Well is invaded and its secret revealed, it will mean that our ancient compact is broken. Those sworn to stand guard upon our honour shall make judgement. That, in turn, will signal the end of our civilisation. All we have ever meant to the world will be destroyed!"

The albino raised a sardonic eyebrow. "All you have *meant*? All your people and mine *mean*! What, I pray, do you think we *mean*, my lady?" His tone became mocking, bitter. "Everything we understand as civilisation will have disappeared within hours if I fail to do what I must!"

With a helpless gesture, shaking her handsome head, she fell back. A constrained murmur and she leaned against a baroque pillar which was so naturally carved it might have embraced her.

There was no time to continue the argument.

Elric reached for one of the sturdy chains holding a large honey-stained copper cauldron. It was wide and deep enough to take two people, but a kind of saddle set either side of the decorated rim suggested that the blind women rode on the outside of the vessel after filling it with honey and bringing it to the top, where it was transferred into the yoked buckets. For overhead protection—though Elric could not see why it would be needed—a large, stained and pitted, copper "roof" protected the occupants' heads. There was ample space for someone to enter the cauldron under the "roof." The controls were operated according to a fairly simple system of cogs, levers, chains, counterweights and wires which Elric and Moonglum had already inspected.

Elric turned and spoke into the shadows. "If they have not already done so, my lady, your sisters may disperse. They might wish to witness our destruction in one of several futures they no doubt foresee. I apologise for our interruption!" A short bow. "No harm will come to you, should you be restrained, my lady, I promise! There is no other way to save your city, your civilisation or the lives of your people!"

Her voice lowered. "Your arrogance is unbelievable! Oh, indeed! You are known in our legends, Elric of Melniboné. We knew you must at some time come, and we prayed we could persuade you to our cause. I doubt it, as I know you do, but your powers of sorcery are said to be as great as any god's. In some of those tales the gods themselves consider you an equal. Others say you were not Sadric's son at all, but Arioch's! Some are said to be jealous of your power and would destroy you as a rival. Many value it, and would have you as an ally. You carry a *geas* within you. Its aura is unmistakeable. Your coming was predicted. And now the White Sword is here! Divergent is here to bring the first conflict back to Kirinmoir in over a million years! As predicted. You are not the Champion Predicted but the so-called Great Destroyer! The signs were ever confusing! But some of us saw you are also somehow the Great Creator! Thus, we think you are the Great Divider! And you, it is, who brings the sword Divergent to our realm!"

Elric was now certain the High Priestess was mad. He could think of no other answer to her words and actions! Xastera continued in a voice shaking with emotion. "Every oracle ever consulted in the World Above or the World Below confuses us. The White Wolf, whom many lesser creatures claim to be, is destined to destroy Creation. You, Elric Silverskin, are destined to bring down everything for which our civilisation ever stood. You are also known as the—"

"Lady, I am fully aware of my many soubriquets . . ."

He looked at the Well. The carved stone and complicated metal of its facing was superbly structured and very sturdy. A sophisticated technology, versed in both natural and supernatural worlds, had risen and fallen to leave behind such beautiful and practical artefacts. Could he smell faint smoke?

Were the attackers bringing fire against them? He rapped on the exposed tiles and listened carefully. He began further to see why the soldier bees did not sting their keepers. The blue, viscous stuff stuck to them all over their limbs and torsos, so that their skin took on a pale blue colour, almost a radiance! As he had guessed earlier, this presented the humans as bees belonging to that hive and meant the bees would not be aggressive. Clearly the blind women were thoroughly protected. But what protected him and his companions?

Elric signalled to Funk and Moonglum to be ready to winch themselves down by pulling back on the levers controlling the simple gears. Gravity and counterweights did the rest. There was simple machinery under the dome's smooth surface. No doubt sorcery had played its part in the hive's bizarre and monumental, half-natural, half-carved construction with the strangest and most lavish architecture even Elric had seen! Now, he thought, only that relatively crude mechanical system controlled its cauldrons.

The others, too, were peering down into misty chambers that echoed and re-echoed through the asymmetric depths. There was a constant dripping sound at different pitches. Their curiosity defeated the smell, which was occasionally repellent, sometimes sickeningly sweet. Certainly smoke of some sort. After his initial response, Orlando Funk grinned, inhaling the fumes with apparent relish.

The High Priestess had not yet gone. Still leaning against the carved pillar, she had closed her eyes and appeared to be praying. When she did occasionally open her eyes, she continued to glare at the men.

In some embarrassment Funk seemed to apologise: "I do, my lady, it is true, fulfil the ambition of years and descend into the heart of this well. I have wanted to know the secrets of the Blue Hive much of my long, adult life. How do the bees create such powerful stuff, distilling it from the gentle scented flowers and herbs of the fields to become a nourishing mead which, undiluted, turns folk mad and makes them lust to kill and kill again? If I were a dull scholar, I'd take some kind of comfort from the various paradoxes they provide. Do busy workers create decadent addictions? Is there a moral lesson to be gained? They are taking pollen from a particular plant, yet we still know not precisely which one. Are they the same flower or different ones, petals or pine-blossom, to turn it from a treat for the table into a distilled wine that makes peaceful traders into berserkers? Near or far? Few adventurers who hear of them do not dream of exploring and profiting from your Holy Well's mysterious depths! Here the honey is distilled and becomes the sweetest, most powerful potion known to Alchemists and Natural Scientists alike? Why is it blue and not red or yellow? Do bees or humans dye it? We spoke of all this earlier, last year, I think. I found you a tad unforthcoming. Whereupon it became necessary to bid you farewell. Without observable knowledge from trusted people, we cannot proceed as a species! We seek that knowledge together. Do we not?"

The High Priestess drew herself to her full height. "I know you, too, Orlando Funk, by all your demonish multiplicity of names! Do not attempt to get your will or my acceptance by cajolery and flattery, bastard of human and Nihrain. I know your sad and sordid ancestry in that horrid, poverty-wasted island! Cunning witch and thief. I knew your mother and her brothers, so you cannot deceive me with your subtleties! All witches and all thieves of hope, for there's precious little silver in Orkney. She's rich only in dull Northern Sorceries and those frightful petty conjurors who scare the people so! It is insulting to us both."

She lifted a hand to point at the albino. "Hide that grim runeblade beneath your cloak if you will. Are you a child? Am I blind? I know you are bound to it, for no other may carry it, now your cousin Yyrkoon is gone to slave in Hell with his fellow demons! I have forbidden you three times, Elric of Melniboné. Three times I forbade you to carry your black hellsword into this holy place! Three times you have appeared to respect my authority. Three times, you have in reality shown contempt and returned! Three times and no more I have indulged you."

"I assure you, madam, I had no intention—"

"*Again* I am insulted! Of course you intended your actions! You are *here*! Had you not intended, sir, you would not have returned! Yet now you gather armed men to you and insist on raping your way to our secret store!" She raised her voice until it rang with controlled anger. "You disobey the warnings of the Balance. Trust nothing that disfrock'd Nihrain tells you!"

She turned her anger on them all.

"You three—mortals of very different blood—contradict the ancient charters which bind all in this plane! Charters made in all our names beneath the authority, the very presence, of the Grand Balance, of which you and your hirelings stand in defiance! Mortal or god, beast or hero, all are bound by that agreement made here when, weary and exhausted, the Lords of the Higher Worlds, the great spirits, the Elementals, the undying spirits, the Essentials, the worlds Higher and the worlds Lower, came to the Compact. The ending of the great War of the Moonbeam Roads was witnessed and signed. The Balance was restored. And, we learned, would remain so until that compact was broken! Without certain strict protocols, the Lords of the Higher Worlds could only materialise here with mortal help. They could aid an adept, but not control an adept, and in this valley, where the Compact was agreed, no mortal or supernatural intelligence might attempt to rule by force of arms. There were few Phoorn here who had not been slain as they slept, not every great elemental had come, but the six greatest Lords of the Higher Worlds—Arioch, Xiombarg and Mabelode of Chaos—Miggea, Arkyn and Donblas of Law—in grotesque disguises, male and female, beast and vegetation or, in the case of Arkyn, she was made wholly of pale, evening light."

"She? I understood—" began Moonglum, also to be silenced by Xastera.

"Has nobody explained how our Lords of the Higher Worlds adopt male or female—sometimes both—guises at will? The punishment? You know that, too! Your soul is consigned to oblivion!"

"Madam, I fear not—" Elric's smile was crooked, cynical.

"Enough of your infantile self-reference, Silverskin! I can say no more to you. On your heads, gentlemen, comes the curse of the Balance so you will hang in limbo, between Law and Chaos forever! Desperate as you are, you disobey all that is great and holy!" She sneered. "In your egotistical arrogance you believe you seek to save us. You cannot! I know that now, though at first I hoped . . . You or others in your name gave your word to the charter signed in all our names—gods, Phoorn, our people—yours and mine when we were one—humans and sentient mortals, as we were then, with honour and dignity and enshrined in Time, by so many millennia passed and witnessed and tested in Law. Between all the forces of the Higher Worlds that compact was made, during the birth of worlds, and it was meant to stand for eternity! You break the Law that governs equally Law and Chaos, the Law of the Balance! This is sin and nothing but sin! Without mitigation!" Her voice rose until it resonated within the dome of the Blue Temple. "I call to the Witnesses! I call to the Witnesses, who saw the Compact made! I call to the stern old Beings who drew up the Compact! It is predicted how the wolf would come and what he would look like. How he would walk on two legs and have hands like a man, carrying a black, runecarved blade and be white as driven snow, with rubies for eyes. Some would call him White Raven and others Winter Wolf or the witch-wolf. How we should fear him! Elric, Sister-Slayer, renegade! Continue and you will be the instrument of this great city's fall!"

And, with considerable hauteur, she disappeared, leaving the Temple to the barbarians.

Whereupon with a shrug Moonglum shoved his swords behind him and, clattering, climbed into a swaying, ornate bucket, removed a wedge and placed it into the cogs above the handle, looping a knot. With considerable expertise, he began to lower himself into the faintly glowing darkness of the Well.

Very shortly afterwards Elric and Orlando Funk followed. The intense stink of the syrup grew almost overpowering after they had breathed even a little of it. But gradually both Moonglum and Funk thought it improved their senses. Another observer might think otherwise. Elric, a little more familiar with powerful drugs, had rather different ideas and remained sober, peering carefully down. Eventually it appeared that a fine spray of blue rain fell from a point *below* the darkness and mingled with something which curled like ordinary, fairly thick, smoke. Soon he was glad to see and smell with a fair amount of clarity.

The great cavern extended much deeper and wider than he had guessed. There were chambers, holes and sudden chasms, sharp elongated spurs of volcanic rock. There appeared to be different degrees of darkness. The stink was still familiar, partly sulphur and partly other gasses, some weaker. Very occasionally, an exceptionally large drowsy bee blundered by, causing someone to start.

As the buckets swayed downwards, Elric continued to be unamused by Moonglum's childish jokes, which were even less funny when they came to the albino through the blue-tinged gloom.

Soon the aperture through which they had passed looked very small above, and Moonglum's puns remained painful even to him. Their descent was very slow. They guessed the blind women were much more skilful at navigating their cauldrons up and down.

For some reason the three continued to whisper to one another as they descended foot by foot into the hollow volcano which had been active, Moonglum suggested, several million years before. He had seen mountains like these, either blowing bubbling rock ("Like a landscape created by Chaos!") or they had cooled, usually leaving only a crater rich in forest growth. "But there is a city not far from Tenk, in Urryes, built entirely within one of the highest peaks in the Withergon Mountains, not far from where I would visit my aunt in the religious holidays."

Funk was having trouble now with the lever lowering or raising his baroque nectar-container. Elric coughed, peering downward. More smoke? Surely the interior was not still active? His companions imitated him, noting his movement rather than the sound. The three paused in their drop, waiting as the long chains swayed gently back and forth, clanking and rattling a little. "It's Mad John Martin's vision of Hell!" Funk murmured. There were jutting, spiked spurs of rock everywhere, richly coloured ochres and greens, even wide patterns of gold, copper and silver all in the same rock. Still curling around them was a thick, grey-blue mist which made seeing far almost impossible. And, below, the vapour had thickened, any of them would have sworn!

For no reason evident to the three of them the chains began to move, sliding almost silently downward, carrying the three closer and closer to a hoped-for solution to the mystery.

Then, with shocking suddenness, the cauldrons came to a swinging stop. Silence followed infinite silence. Next they heard a long-drawn-out sigh which grew to a sharp grunt, then a rumbling half-groan they all recognised from their own experience. Yet, recognise it though they did, their rational minds refused to accept what their senses told them.

They had heard the voice of a sleeping dragon which dreams it is in peril. They recognised it as nothing else. The time between that dragon's dreaming then its waking, then its attack—and so rarely its flight—could be, depending on the dragon's type and age, almost a minute.

And they had it on good authority that the dragons guarding this well had been dead of old age centuries before!

Peering around very cautiously, their reason continuing to deny their experience, they reached up to reverse their descent.

A second passed. Then another.

Elric's sight was generally weak. Gingerly, he leaned over the side as he reached up, feeling for the lever with his hand. He was fairly sure he had no way of seeing all the way to the bottom of this hollowed-out mountain. Kirinmoir city was built upon its sturdy surface when different gods with different, wilder powers had fought in the blazing depths of the earth and darkness of the higher sky. She was, as the more prosaically educated Moonglum noted, actually a volcanic mountain, full of spurs, stalactites and stalagmites, caverns, causeways and tunnels, not to mention the lacelike structures wherein these strange insects—if that was what they truly were—had made an almost infinite system of huge, open nests whose contents could not clearly be seen. Occasionally the shadow of a huge bee staggered upwards in the mist and fell back again. Elric wondered now if this was not another creature which imitated the bee, as was sometimes found in other species, such as their own Melnibonéan *ernig*, the saurian which so resembled a civet cat.

Orlando Funk's soft brogue sounded casually from nearby. "A rare strand of apian, eh? Extraordinary how these caverns amplify their voices, is it not . . . ? We once, in Orkney, called big things like 'em, by coincidence, *dragon*-bees. They swarmed in caves. In spaces like this they can sound like gigantic dragons! The old Phoorn themselves, even? How legends are sustained, eh? Perhaps it is those we hear. They only exist on the marches at the World's Edge. Like many of their fellows, they also have excellent eyes and communicate through complicated dances, as your own dragons also once danced, did they not? I have heard other legends . . ."

Elric was certain in his bones he had not mistaken a bee for a dragon, though Funk was persuasive. There were odd acoustics everywhere within the mountain. It was easier to believe tales of Kirinmoir's haunting now that he saw what the old city was built upon. The city of the bees was also the city of men. Both were interdependent.

He knew, from his adventures among them on his youthful educational quests, that many bees could see well, too, but needed light to communicate the position of sources of food or where to site fresh hives. He had seen the bees dance, when they found a location and needed to tell the others. Yet he still half-expected to see tiny dragons moving about sluggishly together with the bees, for there were also tales of such tiny Phoorn. If he inspected the fields outside, would he discover dragon-bees on the flowers or gathering on the battlements to protect their lives and wealth? He caught himself before his mind went into further abstractions. That sound again.

Now it came from above as again they sank deeper into the region of blue mist and grey smoke. He kept peering through the soft rain but without seeing the small blue dragons he thought must be there. Even the smell was familiar. That taste! What he was reminded of—that delicate hint of—dragon venom? Not quite the same, which was why he had been deceived. Elric was tired, growing anxious at the time they were losing as the supernatural army gathered at their walls! He was, unusually, easily distracted. He put his pale tongue upon pale lips. This tasted a little smokier and nuttier. Did tiny dragons and huge bees live in complicated symbiotic harmony here, a gestalt of some kind created to make the strange, blue honey which in turn gave the people of Kirinmoir their strength? And did the dragons sustain themselves by drinking what was, at root, the pollen of millions of delicate flowers? Elric enjoyed the metaphor for a moment. He shrugged. It made no difference. Without the *skeffla'a*, the symbiotic riding saddle and translator which facilitated communication between Elric's kind and the Phoorn, usually needed before Dragon Master and dragon could communicate, he could not explain to any large, or indeed small, Phoorn *how* they might act in the hive's defence.

Was the blue mist below a sorcerous one? As they swung in their cauldrons, trying not to be heard, back and forth very slowly, peering into the swirling shaft of dangerous semi-darkness, desperate to see and not to be seen, they could just make out the others' forms moving slowly. Who knew what guarded the valuable blue stuff down here, or even what form it took? Did it guard treasure? Gold? Ghostly soldiers of some kind? Elric grinned momentarily at his childish speculation. What guarded it? What still fed off it? And what could make the amplified sound of a disturbed dragon? He would know if small dragons lurked amongst the makers of blue honey, or at least he would have heard of such creatures. A kind of flying minnow. The only dragons he had ever experienced grew to considerable size, like the ones he had seen since he arrived in this underworld and travelled to Hizs, or that wingless dragon they had found in the jungle, where they had last been with treacherous Dyvim Marluc. He remembered, with something of a pang, those old friends he had left sleeping in Melniboné, recovering from their destruction of the pirate fleet, when he betrayed first his own folk, then his betrothed and then his best friend. If larger dragons protected the hive, Xastera, the High Priestess, would have summoned them to defend against the three men slowly descending into the murky vastness of the hollow mountain. Nonetheless, Elric grew warier as he lowered himself metre by metre in the swaying bucket, his friends showing, like him, an unfortunate lack of skill in moving the ratchets and levers.

Yet down they went, nevertheless, in juddering steps, until Elric realised why blind women had always worked the hives. They understood little of their surroundings, save sounds! Had they even perhaps been bred or deliberately blinded for this work?

Elric's first thought was: How would they avoid the bees?

But then he remembered their first encounter in the tunnel. *Those bees are not blind. They need light to guide them, as surely as do we! For their dances, which served them as speech. Light for those daily gatherings of pollen—daily until this moment, at any rate, when they appear to have become dormant, since there had been only bees of the ordinary variety seen creeping about the flowers of that much beflowered city. They simply avoided the gatherers whom they understood to be part of their process.*

Again Elric tried to peer through the mist, which for the moment had taken on a golden tone deepening to pale green-yellow. At last he saw movement of darker shapes against the soft blue of that mist and far, far below, as the mist cleared like clouds in a sky, could make out bodies moving sluggishly. The bodies not, as Elric had half-expected, of tiny dragonlings crawling from distinctive stone-coloured, irregularly shaped eggs, but of the strangely articulated bodies of the same massive bees which had attacked the invaders in the tunnel.

There was suddenly too much movement!

Increasingly, shadows flitted past him, spots of azure and cinnamon and jet. He heard Orlando Funk gasp; then Moonglum echoed his exclamation. Something struck his cheek. He turned his head, white locks swirling, to follow its movement.

Elric looked up! A light blow struck him suddenly across the face. He cried out at this! His cheeks were stinging painfully. A whip? A herder's slapstick? He fell back a little, losing his footing. Did he hear a grunt, like the first? He was pretty sure he did. He touched his swollen cheek and looked for the pain's source. But momentarily, only for a second. A snake slithered swiftly across his face and then had slipped away. Into his jerkin? Another illusion?

Nothing there. He took charge of himself. Automatically, he felt for Stormbringer. Moonglum saw the gesture, hoping to hear at least a murmur, but if the sword spoke, he did not hear her, not even an echo of the dragon voice. Moonglum now knew that if the sword were silent, then they must probably die.

Slowly the pain subsided to be replaced by an unpleasant, acidic stink which clung to Elric's skin like thin oil! No bee, surely? One of those small dragons, perhaps, of the kind he believed he had seen? A dragonfly, even, or a creature he would never encounter again? It was as though he fell deeper and deeper into an hallucinatory abyss providing him with many more mysteries buzzing in his head, almost mocking him with their multitude of forms and sounds until suddenly they were gone.

The three of them hung in luminous blue darkness, adrift upon paradoxes and contradictions. On the edge of madness.

And then, closer now, the dragon grunted.

Elric turned, his cauldron swinging wildly to strike against Funk's. Then it recoiled to swing with a clank against Moonglum's until the things rang like bells and Elric, Moonglum and Funk were little more than the clappers striking against their sides! They were all bruised, winded, but otherwise unhurt.

They were about to congratulate one another on their survival when the blue mist cleared for a moment.

That great, red-streaked eye, blue as a cat's, blinked blearily through the mist, no less surprised to see the mortals perhaps than they were shocked to see it! A great, curving dragon's eye measuring a tall man in length, sunken into a blue-green scaled socket above a red mouth armed with glinting ivory daggers in various states of disrepair. And the stink was the familiar stink of the dragon's breath bubbling at her lips in a dark blue foam, the colour of dragon's blood which dripped, dripped from her scarlet and pink gradually opening jaws. No miniature dragon-bee this, no half-insect, but a monster from Elric's ancestry, the great, long, living head of a fully fledged Phoorn, larger than those he had flown above Imrryr, from whom both dragons and silverskins had sprung in the long, long ago of the world. A Phoorn with a forked fleshy tongue flickering between curved white teeth, each as tall as a man!

And with a yell, Orlando Funk had done something to his lever and his long clacketing chain went snaking and disappearing deep into the abyss below, causing Moonglum unspontaneously to follow with a wild Elwheri whine, so Elric, having received no time to parley with the monster, went spinning after his friend, his hands grabbing fiercely for anything of wood or metal on which to take purchase and at least slow his descent!

Clutching at the air, at the chafing chain ripping the skin from his fingers, Elric went spinning downwards, trying desperately to stop the cauldron's rapid descent while the other two chains tangled and untangled wildly, sickeningly. Until, quite suddenly, Funk's, then Elric's, then Moonglum's chains came to a slow jerking halt. At last when they opened fearful eyes to see what waited below, they regretted it. To a man, they closed them again! When next they came to spare themselves a sight of what writhed and crawled and slithered below, they were first astonished, then disgusted. And then fascinated.

Only a few metres underneath them lay what seemed mile after mile of symmetrical honeycombs, illuminated by a blue glow which came from that odd mist falling constantly upon their own roofed cauldrons and into combs from above. It fell on all observers. It fell on the worker bees which crawled everywhere over the combs, which would fly back and forth to make repairs, which used their legs and feelers to shore up the walls of the combs, forever moving, forever working, forever striving to create their fabulous blue honey from the gold they produced daily. Monstrous insects, some as large as cats, working to create more and more honey for more and more bees whose residual mixture blended with the waters of the springs below, which fed the river and in turn, the hidden valley of Kirinmoir, hidden no more. Hidden no more, at least, from Xiombarg, Our Lady of the Locusts! But where were the queens?

What Elric would not allow himself to see, until he had gathered his mental strength, was a queen. She disgusted him, this wingless, stingless, bloated, mindless egg-producing reproductive system, mother of millions, without intelligence or purpose. Or, if she had any purpose whatsoever, it was to lie pulsing at the centre of her hive, perhaps her empire of hives, endlessly producing larvae, which in turn produced more queens producing more larvae from the same hideous, white living corpses crowned by that travesty of mortal beauty. Meanwhile, as mindlessly, the workers collected the pollen which blended with the dripping residual venom from above to produce the magical source of Kirinmoir's wealth and strength! Blue honey.

For those bodies had once seemed human, and the beautiful pale faces with staring eyes were twin to that of the woman he had agreed to fertilise, the Empress Melaré of Kirinmoir.

Those pale, living machines, gorging, bulbous queens, had no purpose but to create more workers, more soldiers, more queens and more infirm males, some of which, a little stronger than the others, continued in the same purposeless existence while, equally purposelessly, human locusts ate first the planet, then the core and then themselves.

And what made Elric's flesh crawl was remembering the bargain he had struck with Melaré. He must lie with her and whatever her body was now, to begin the creation of a stronger strain of those poor, feeble crawling things down there. He had sworn it! Yet surely she had tricked him? He could not remain true to his word. There was still time to escape. The odds were too great, the task too disgusting. Melaré was a mother of her kind—except her kind, to Elric's horror, were the workers and the soldiers, resembling Melaré, Shirizha and perhaps the other lizard guards making up the empress's crack troops. Was Xastera, the High Priestess, equally pale and bulbous beneath a gown which seemed to hide a shapely figure? Or would Melaré's first pregnancy reveal her nature? He had been persuaded to spawn a swarm. Were they all born resembling what he saw below—grown from the same writhing white larvae to become and die a brainless squirter of pupae into the world? An ever-sleeping mind forever fearing consciousness. For consciousness brought a knowledge of what it had become. The drones were nearly identical to the generals he had seen on the surface—weak, enfeebled, near-eunuchs. Sickly rejections from the working hive and good enough only to reproduce the occasional new queen!

Elric forced himself to control his disgust. This, surely, was why the priestesses made this well a forbidden secret, a legend designed to disguise a more elaborate truth! The Honey Well could be an integral part of their life cycle. Who knew what a mortal like Melaré suffered before and after she became a breeding queen? A secret judged by their ancestors too terrible for anyone to keep. Dragons above, the bees below. Surplus venom, bubbling in the dragons' lips, fell as misty rain onto the hives where the specialised bees worked unknowingly to produce the honey distilled eventually into blue mead consumed by dragon and man alike, adulterating the waters of the spring. Now, shuddering, his mind confused and racing, he understood the real truth of the bargain he had struck with Melaré, the beautiful and delicate Empress of Kirinmoir!

Below, at the centre of the great comb, thousands upon thousands of enlarged insects crawled over the swollen abdomen of their queen. She existed only to reproduce, laying millions of eggs which workers carried away to be stored and hatched. The albino had never seen a sight so appalling to his nature. The Queen was nothing but abdomen and a human head. A beautiful human head, the twin of Melaré's, so like all the women both he and his grieving, jealous rival, his own father, loved so intensely. With her alabaster skin and milk-white hair, her ruby eyes and that gorgeous, wonderful, intellectual beauty, Melaré reminded Elric so much of his own mother, and of his sweet, murdered love, Cymoril, Laughing Cymoril of ancient Melniboné, his own betrothed who loved him more than she loved the rich earth and all its wonders, more than he ever loved himself!

And this was what Melaré had made him promise: that he would lie with her but once with his seed within her. A reasonable enough way to pay his debt. But now he understood better, he considered the action required of him all but impossible! She asked him for this thing only once. To infuse her with seed more vital than anything her sisters had known for perhaps millennia. Once, before she went to meet her destiny and he continued home, to his: she to become another Queen of the Great Kirinmoir Hive! Or was she a queen among many? And if so—? Elric turned his head away. She had been born, after all, one of those larvae and was born to reproduce that same larvae over and over again until she in turn would be replaced. Again and again a woman who resembled and might even be Cymoril, his most profound love, would be consigned to a disgusting fate! Everything which made her glad to live was eroded, then died, and all she could become or ever expect to become was another breeding queen, her fate made more poignant by the fact that intelligence, relish of the world and its beauty, everything she had possessed to the full, was now extinguished so that she do what her race had done and would always do. For survival. For continuation.

As Orlando Funk had no doubt been considering, if her economy died, would Kirinmoir surely die, too? That was the secret that High Priestess Xastera and her sisters kept with such apparently naïve, uninformed piety. It seemed they had been told a profound lie, making them its fiercest protectors, even willing to die for this falsehood, this faith which maintained its believers' credulity first by making them uncertain of the truth, then fierce defenders of a simpler, substituted lie. No doubt it had taken less than a century to confuse this secret and protect the tranquillity of the city and the valley.

They had come to believe that spiritual purity was what they stewarded. All they *really* served were the economic forces keeping their whole decaying culture alive forever. Like his own city, Kirinmoir had survived long past any civilisation's natural span in one state. The city was like an inexperienced, ageless child, attractive but artificially maintained in an unnatural state. Truly, that was a quality natural only to Tanelorn. The piety of her priestesses masked their self-interest in maintaining a completely unnatural tranquillity. Her traditions had been twisted and abused to represent the opposite of their intentions. Mortal idealism served the horrible greed of the mad immortals of the Higher Worlds. Innocent folk had been bred as dogs were bred, to behave obediently, selflessly, for the good of their masters. Every act of self-destruction produced in them the warmest gratification and sense of worth. Xastera must have known this and had trained them all to believe they were acting for the common good. A more cynical reason to use blind women. The bees—even the guardian dragons—even the blind women had helped in her deception and manipulations. They were the hardest enemy to fight, for they had so little consciousness of their part in this great illusion! They were innocents. Deceived by the priestesses for so long, they believed theirs was the natural order, not the outside world's. The evil was a subtle one. Tranquillity enforced through a form of slavery.

Elric knew no real precedent for what went on here. The dragons, now awake above them and blocking their return, could no doubt only regenerate flows of venom by sleeping long periods. Or, of course, by powerful sorcery, if there were warlocks to wake them. Beyond Elric at present. They were usually kept sleeping longer than was natural by their masters, usually feeding them soporifics in animal blood. That was how they once kept their fighting dragons asleep in Melniboné, waking them through sorcery when they weren't needed for war or wisdom.

That excess venom was not as powerful as the stuff concentrated in sacs which they could direct in flaming jets as it mixed with air. The mist was created in their venom glands, falling from a great height on the complex of hives below. This was a multilevel hive, perhaps occupying many planes, which could only be safely harvested by those already coated with the viscous stuff. And only by mating with the few enfeebled humanlike citizens of Kirinmoir could the Queen normally expect to breed. Until of course, a stronger mortal, of the fine old stock, had drifted into an empress's sphere of influence and, in this case, was prepared to bargain for something she owned.

And that was the price she had demanded for the last piece of the map. The map he and Moonglum required to take them home to the World Above from the World Below.

He was grateful for his poor sight! He wished that his memory were as bad. He could not bear to look at that beautiful face on the pallid pink pulsing body perpetually squeezing out those horrible white-grey larvae and pupae, every one of which bore a tiny human face peering unseeingly through a thin film of jelly and every one bearing the face of the Empress of Kirinmoir resembling not those other beautiful women willing to die in defence of Kirinmoir, but of his greatest love, his first true love, his own exquisite Cymoril. Cymoril the Beautiful. Cymoril, who had died on the runecarved steel of his own black battle-blade, Stormbringer: the Stealer of Souls, his doom and his salvation. He had entered a bitter reverie, aided by the gently swaying cauldron.

"Elric?" Moonglum whispered from his own perch. "Are you awake?"

The albino had begun to drift in his memory, back to days when he had known something which, in spite of his troubled questions, he remembered as being happy. Had he inhaled more blue mist than he had guessed? It had affected him! Again, here was apparent danger lurking in apparent tranquillity.

Elric struggled, half-trapped by the chain, trying to free himself from his entangling sword, a sword which now threatened to wrench itself from his grasp and plunge down into that hive where the Queen's disgusting offspring went through their life cycle more swiftly than any insects he had studied in his boyhood years. Might Stormbringer actually be regenerated here?

He forced himself to look down again! Disgusting the larvae might be, but they reproduced with extraordinary rapidity. They were able to replicate themselves with far greater speed than any mammal or reptile and therefore to supply an army with much greater numbers within hours. But to what purpose? Elric wondered. He looked across at his comrades, clearly feeling equal horror at the sight beneath them.

He could tell that they all thought the same thing: Why were these unnatural, sorcerous mutations created?

He attempted to rally the realities at his disposal. Moonglum had shown him how to see events from an economic point of view. He was looking down on Kirinmoir's wealth. Her secret, kept through tradition and superstition, had not been betrayed for thousands of years! For millennia it had been built over and around what was effectively one gigantic hive and a massive deception by omission and obfuscation. Above, judging by his own studies, half slept at least one ancient Emerald Phoorn, according to tradition, their common ancestor. If dragons had remained hidden for so long, some deception must be intended, for even the ancient Emerald Phoorn did not naturally sleep so long. The beast above them had slept intermittently for what, even for a Phoorn, must have been an exceptionally long time. Below him were the wild bees which had, over the centuries, adapted (or been encouraged to adapt) by a kind of old alchemical sorcery Elric still cherished to create the mutation of reptile-mammal-insect on which the wealth and survival of this balanced, most ancient and peaceful illusion depended.

Down the years the bees had also supplied enough aggressive protection to drive away an enemy of ordinary strength. If Elric's suspicions were accurate, the symbiosis between kinds no doubt went further to sustain the Phoorn. It could be that the bees had gradually somehow replaced her corporeal being, bringing about the desired melding over the centuries.

What he had seen overhead was not an illusion. Or, if it were, the thing was an illusion they all shared. Below they had seen an interdependent, co-operative, mutually nourishing quasi-species, which was, Elric thought, a marvel of Nature, a coming together, via the forces of Chaos, if not of Law, to create a perfect combination of living things—and yet everything in Elric, the product of both Law and Chaos, of cold- and warm-blooded creatures, revolted against what was, after all, merely another step in the great Blending, a rehearsal for the Beyond they spoke of, an alchemical marriage, a meeting and unifying of the minds, so long the goal of human wizards and so much despised as vulgar conjury by Elric's people, though he himself remained fascinated. His people rejected vulgar experiment, having determined that there was no metaphysical wisdom to be gained from it. Elric and the haughty, scholarly soldiers of his blood found such greedy pursuits worse than wasteful of their consideration.

There had been, however, merit to learning a language older still than High Melnibonéan, the tongue-torturing language of the Phoorn, ancestors to both Melnibonéan and all the other related peoples he had investigated on his many adventures, questing for the origins of peoples and ideas. Learning Phoorn had helped him with other ancient tongues. He had no idea of the probability of his forming an alliance with any green-blue, long-snouted, snag-tooth'd ancestors of his! He had no *skeffla'a* with which to communicate mentally with, and so direct, the dragon. The bond between them was not merely useless; his lack of it could define him as an interloper! Neither did he know what motive they might have to help him. Or indeed hinder him should they instead be the creatures *directing* the priestesses! What could they win from an alliance save revenge?

Yet, thought Elric looking up at the fine blue rain now falling on the copper roofs over his head and the heads of his comrades, it was perhaps just possible that they had found a means, after all, of resisting the Lady Xiombarg and her Melnibonéan ally, or at very least save the sweet and dangerous horrors of Kirinmoir from the other horrors now threatening them. Ancient science and modern sorcery, perhaps, had created these bizarre mutations, but Elric was determined they would not destroy him or those he cared for.

Not for the first or for the last time in his life did he hope that, through some sort of blood memory, he could bring a great dragon cousin back into his life. But could he reason with a monster with an eye the size he had seen? Could he speak well enough and carry authority enough to recruit its aid against the youngling wolves beyond the walls who were already pledged to follow his cousin and destroy Elric and his people? Their kind and its allies, doubtless even now, could be snarling and sniffing among the weak shoots for scent of friends and relatives. Did more than one huge green-blue long-snout continue to live in some form, even in the World Below? The priestesses of Xiombarg had doubtless gone with their sisters, either into hiding or, more likely, to join the golden stranger, the Lord of the Last, whose blazing, vengeful light must soon bring perpetual night to this fertile valley, darken it forever and teach many the consequences of actions taken in the heat of blind emotion.

TWENTY-THREE

Phoorn

THEY HUNG THERE, unable to make their vessels move up or down, trying all they could to ease the simple machinery so that it did not detach itself from the tangled counterbalances and plunge them to their deaths, drowning in gallons of the most powerful potion known to the world. As Moonglum grew baffled and tired, Orlando Funk to calm him told a tale, speaking of his own reading of what he called *The Mykirian Epic*.

"I am, as you know, an adopted confederate of the Nihrain Brotherhood. We serve the same loyalties to forces that maintain the Great Balance through peaceful means, rather than any form of physical warfare. Violence breeds violence. Destruction leads to further destruction. Truth and history become the victims of such loss of cultural memory. We perform our function in several guises across a number of earthly planes, all closely associated with your own. Make no mistake, we fight. But always as last resort. I had no plan to trick you, Prince Elric, when we first met in the wood. I was already disguised to evade those jackals. I hoped only to warn you and, if I could, help you defend yourselves against those marauders and incidentally help you rescue the empress, and thus I hoped to begin a narrative useful to you both."

"And we should be grateful that you set us on a path which led us here?" Moonglum's somewhat muffled voice did not sound entirely sincere as he worked carefully at the cogs and wires.

"Well, sir, you were in a good position to meet the marauders I alerted you to!"

"It's said you helped some of them steal a flagon of mead . . ."

"I took it back, Duke Moonlight, from the thieves I followed. They in turn followed me with the intention of retrieving it. The rest, you know."

"Effectively, then," said Elric grimly, "you sent us into a trap."

"Out of which you gained access to the rulers of Kirinmoir, who in turn have the last piece of the map which will carry you home from here!"

"You know a great deal, sir. You offer a tale in retrospect which suggests you seek to control our destinies forever."

"Not so! I—"

"You tell us you manipulated events to achieve this end? So you are a seer, as well, Sir Orlando!" Moonglum continued to mock Funk as he tinkered with the machinery overhead.

"I benefit occasionally from a little foresight . . ."

"Perhaps you have some idea, in that case, how we escape from this impossible entanglement? We have gigantic Emerald Phoorn above. Below, a sorcerous amalgam of insect, reptile and mammals equipped with what I suspect must be a high concentration of lethal poison in their stingers. I fear the consequences once they discover we are not their hive-relatives!"

"We developed this colony."

Elric and Moonglum peered through the mist at Orlando Funk. The man was leaning on the rim of the bucket as it swayed back and forth. He seemed almost cheerful. "I believe I have fixed the mechanicals! Mine, at least!" And reaching behind him, he seized a lever, and very slowly the cauldron was raised. "A simple matter. I can get at yours now and free them, I hope."

Moonglum watched him ascend, trying not to see what lay further below.

"Colony?" Elric had caught the phrase uttered almost without thought by Funk. "We? You mean the Nihrain?"

"I mean my mighty cousins, aye. I was closer to them in an earlier time. Before it became my lot to wander the worlds in their service." Funk swung his vessel until, with his axe, he had grasped a part of the mechanicals over

Elric's head. "And serve other forces. However, I might redeem myself now I am returned from that nearby plane. Nihrain must flourish again!" He grinned mysteriously.

"With your help, Sir Orlando?" Elric kept scepticism from his voice.

"WITH YOUR HELP AND MINE, PERHAPS . . . ?"

Elric's first response was to clap his hands over his ears! He screamed as if the noise would blot out all he heard, all he saw, all that he perceived as rational and sane:

"NO!" cried the albino. And Moonglum saw clearly what Elric had seen, that huge saurian eye, so impossibly ancient, so pitiless as it glared down at his friend, a milky blue spread of spiralling stars and lightning flashes as if its orb held an entire plane of the multiverse in perpetual storm. As if its mind were on visual display. There was virtually no hint that this mighty millennia-old creature had slept for as long as it had. The flesh of his snout curled and wrinkled. Its cracked ivory teeth, stained blue near the gums and yellowing, were tall as Moonglum, as sharp and pointed, curved and cruel as they had ever been, while the green-and-silvery-blue scales patterning its lavender-coloured crest and neck gave no sign of its age. Only under and beside its eyes were there signs of its years. *FEAR NOT, LITTLE ARMOURED MAMMAL. I KNOW YOU ARE MY KIN, AND WHILE IN SOME SOCIETIES IT IS PERFECTLY NATURAL TO EAT ONE'S KIN, IN MINE IT IS CONSIDERED BOTH UNHEALTHY AND VULGAR! YOU ARE PRINCE ELRIC, AND YOU ADDRESS LADY GREATWING, YOUR ANCESTOR.*

"I am grateful that you told me, madam." Elric now understood that, although a few small sounds underlay his words in the form of almost inaudible clicks, purrs and squeaks, he and the ancient Phoorn were actually communicating mind to mind on a level so profound Elric had no means of explaining what was happening to them until he heard Funk murmur, "Is he speaking to you? Can you tell? Can you, Duke Moonlight, see if he speaks to the Phoorn? Or does the Phoorn speak to him?"

"We speak Old Phoorn together," said Elric. "Most of it is sub-vocal and subtly referential." He turned back to the ancient beast, Lady Greatwing, and, after staring for some time, apparently into the air, uttered a high-pitched sound that had a displeasing effect on his companions, causing them to curse and fall back into their vessels. Now it was their turn to cover their ears!

At length, with the huge dragon's head lingering in the misty shadows of a grotto, Elric explained that the Phoorn was his blood-ancestor, far older than any so far encountered. Aeons since, she had volunteered with others to take the long watch over the bees because she understood it to be her duty. Of late, she felt her duty to be long over. When, however, she tried to parley a release for herself or at least gain a pause for herself, with whatever powers there were who served the Temple and her bees, she would find herself falling back to sleep again. "They smoked me, I suspect, as they smoked my bee-kin to take their honey. As I smoked them to accommodate you three! We were no longer balanced comrades, each providing something the other required. We were effectively slaves. The priestesses began to steal too much honey in their moral imperatives. They began to destroy us through starvation. They did all they could to maintain their peculiar cultures and species and use them to maintain the great valley that is tranquil Kirinmoir. Aye, Lord Elric, they stole too great a share of our bounty with the best of intentions. And now my body dies. A crystallisation process neither uncomfortable nor even uneasy, but not of my choosing. I suspect that only those old women at the Well understand why they kill us so slowly. Or keep us alive so young. I understand the loneliness of being last to die. We all would choose death, would we not, if duty did not intervene?"

Elric was not entirely certain he agreed with this.

"THEY NEEDED ME TO KEEP MY KIN AWAKE AND WORKING. ALL OF US WORKED TOO HARD, AND SO WE DIED. WERE WE NOT THEIR CHARGES, WERE THEY NOT OUR STEWARDS, SWORN TO OUR WELL-BEING, AS THEY WERE SWORN TO MAINTAIN THE BALANCE IN KIRINMOIR. SOMEHOW THEY DECEIVED THE WITNESSES, DRUGGED US BUT KEPT THE PEOPLE TRANQUIL. NOW XIOMBARG IS ABROAD AGAIN AND UP TO HIS OLD TRICKS—"

Elric translated briefly.

"His?" Moonglum was confused. "Xiombarg is not female?"

"The Lords of Chance choose their identities at will," Elric told his friend. "Even the Lords of Law have been known to alter names and gender according to whatever whims of fashion prevail in the Higher Worlds."

"So," said the Elwheri in an altogether different tone. "So this is your prison. You did not create it all? How many—?"

"I am the LAST OF US."

The Phoorn, perhaps a little deaf, modified her tone and gave Elric an opportunity to translate and let the others join in.

"I did not create these conditions. The bees were already here, but hunters of many kinds were killing them to get at their honey. They had no care for the future. There were few here when we arrived to dissuade the hunters. Then came our relations—your folk, tumbling through time and space, down the planes of the multiverse, reality upon reality. Xiombarg, she—"

"The Queen of the Swords?" asked Elric. "Why is she taking this form? What part does she play? What does she want?"

"*She once had an entire constituency, remember, of your kinspeople! She led a nation—or what was more or less a nation—which was threatened only by Lord Arioch, who, as you know, was like her a great meddler in mortal business! Always desiring a part in your affairs. Savouring especially mortal pleasures. She relishes that identity almost more than anything else. But she relishes power most. She defies the Witnesses . . .*" The monster's eye closed slowly, and she took a vast breath. "*At very least, she breaks the bargain, the truce, the honourable agreement, which carries heavy punishment.*"

Elric nodded. "I understood something of that. The Sword Queen could never bear to be outshone in any way, especially by Arioch or Mabelode the Faceless."

"Or, indeed, by you, little worm." Did he hear a trace of irony in the she-Phoorn's response? "For these are the years in which demigods challenge gods and the final order be destroyed by the vicious and the vulgar who would obliterate all they do not understand!"

"How do the priestesses drug you, sister?"

"They are unaware that, by following ritual, ancient protocols and so on, they also follow many of the strongest of the so-called locking spells, which have a peculiar effect on Emerald Phoorn minds. Our strongest will cannot break them. We sleep, but we do not sleep. Only when the priestesses' minds are focused elsewhere or are given up to another, can we sleep naturally."

"We?"

"My wife lies dead at last in our roost. She lacked will, I fear, at the end. But, because she is distracted, the priestess's control weakens. I long for her to share the last of these strangely transmogrified days. I sense a powerful distraction for our captors! A shock! What goes on, young worm?"

Elric found that the dragon was echoing Funk's rather condescending tone and was irritated. "My Lady Greatwing—"

"I am Feemorninat Ke. You may address me as Lady Pheere, if you wish, boy!"

"I had heard 'Greatwing' in our dialect? I would appreciate it if—"

"Lad?"

This voice from behind him. He turned to address Orlando Funk. "I would appreciate it if I were addressed with more . . ." Elric regarded Funk's expressionless face, and he knew how pompous his voice sounded and pulled himself together, deciding to accept their mutual patronage and if possible co-opt it to his own use. He apologised.

"*You have my deepest respect, young Silverskin,*" said Lady Pheere very quietly, mind to mind. "*I respect you for the destiny you will fulfil and for the great sacrifices you will make, for you were born, Elric of Melniboné, to suffer all the world can do to make a mortal suffer, to lose what is most painful for a mortal to lose, and your reward for that will be unbearable loneliness, terrible grief and hopeless death; the death of memory and friendship. You will be remembered in your histories as a pale and nameless shadow and in your myths as one of many doomed heroes. With others of your ilk there will be none to remember you or your world. You will be remembered, Elric, by the better world your death will help create, but it will be as a dream, a vaguely recalled memory of your life and its actions. An uneasy play of dark upon light as mor-*"

tals settle the destinies of worlds and gods. Knowing this, you cannot resist your destiny. And that is why old dragons and young men must come together to help you achieve that destiny. Know it or not, Prince-Emperor, demigod you may or may not be, but you serve a great purpose. You will defend yourself and your world in the only way truly proper for you. Your narrative will renew the world and allow a renewal throughout the multiverse. And your story will give the world new energy, many new ideas and ways of seeing life. You will learn to free not only your own soul but—"

Steadying himself with his hand on the lip of his slowly warming cauldron, Elric interrupted. "Forgive my poor manners, Lady Pheere, but this talk of freedom without taking much action to achieve my freedom is making me impatient, for I know that the city above this mighty cavern is about to be destroyed. And almost certainly this place too, whatever the Queen of the Swords promised that crazed priestess."

"Might I put it to you, son," Orlando Funk called, having understood nothing, "that, while the bees are currently passive, they might yet be called upon to serve us. I doubt the stupefying smoke is planned to last for long and was never intended to aid us."

Elric explained all he could to his friends, how the Phoorn had made a plan, how he hoped to find something of immediate power which he might use against Xiombarg and Dyvim Marluc, but he was beginning to think that he faced overwhelming defeat, even with Lady Pheere on his side.

"Can you help us, Lady Pheere?" Moonglum was direct.

"*I am grateful for your visit, believe me.*" Lady Pheere's cold, ancient eyes closed, and a little smoke curled from her long, narrow nostrils.

Elric smiled. "*You* calmed the bees."

Her eyes confirmed this. "*I knew Xastera's plans. But whether or not I can find a means of resisting your greatest enemies, I am not sure.*" She and the albino continued to talk, mind to mind, with a few spoken words, while the other two looked on. "*I have given Kirinmoir everything. Flesh and blood. Bones and muscle and all my kin. There is little left, and soon my soul shall depart to join its brothers and sisters in those reaches of stars known as the*

Dragon Dances. Watch the picture for I weary of speech. I recall my wife, you understand."

Elric paused, then he passed the translation to the others.

"She is dying or fears so. Not, she says, 'herself.' She has reached the end of any warring days. Her spouse is dying, too, I think. Perhaps dead. She wanted vengeance against those who imprisoned her, who broke the original bargain with the mortals, demigods and so on, but even that desire, she says, is gone. All she desires is to redeem her kindred's honour."

"I would help you."

The dragon's breath was coming faster now, in fits and starts. Her eyelids were drooping, and her long mouth fell open.

The old dragon sighed.

"They have exhausted me. Complexity long since ceased to fascinate me. You are so wonderfully complex. When you are complex. You create so many stories. You do not deserve to die. You do not. Not the best of you. Mortals were never meant to be involved in this. Even Nihrain have no proper place in this story. I blame those bored, ambitious Lords and Ladies of the Higher Worlds. We should give them less harmful games to play. Of course, I know I am dying. We could be too late. Universes are lost in seconds . . ."

Elric translated this for his companions.

"By gad man, ye'll not talk that breed of poppycock around me." Funk's face grew red with anger. His red beard bristled, and his blue eyes blazed. "I've spent a century planning this and months enjoying the contemplation of my success. Getting you here alone took over two."

"Centuries?" Moonglum gaped.

"Almost." Retuning his attention to the dragon. "Ye'll stay alive, at least until ye're no needed and then—"

"I have limited choice in the matter." For an instant, Lady Pheere's eyes opened wide as she moved her long emerald-and-sapphire snout, indigo venom frothing still from scarlet gums. Her huge dark blue eyes became slits again as she kept them open with effort. "If I am to help thee—and thee aid me, as I know you plan, Sir Orlando, we had best begin."

"You schemed for this moment, and that requires revenge!" Elric, standing upright in his bronze cauldron, made in a stupefied way to pull his heavy blade from its scabbard. "Then I think I must slay you, Orlando Funk. Brother to the Nihrain." He nodded to Moonglum, who remained loyal if bewildered, blinking through smoke.

The Orkneyman shook his head. "By the gods of all the Jutes of Soombar, gentlemen! That would be unwise. My plan is to save us all. But it does require an element of civility and co-operation. I guessed Lady Pheere was here, and I have known that Xiombarg patronised a new warrior of your own race. But I could find out little more, so we both had nothing to speak of. There were references in many learned and obscure books. But the only mortal whom I knew carried a sword of Hell-forged iron and could speak ancient dragonish was a certain Lord Elric. I needed a translator who could interpret for us. That, Sir Emperor, was you and only you. I need to take instruction from your mighty ancestor!"

"You understood Xiombarg was coming and gave us no warning! You *knew* she was coming! Half the damned creatures in this plane knew. Yet you thought it better to manipulate me, rather than ask me directly for help!" Moonglum remained unmollified.

"Over the centuries of managing this world I have rather lost the knack of direct speech." Orlando Funk lowered his eyes. "I am sorry, gentlemen."

Elric looked down at the drugged workers and soldiers crawling over the mass of writhing grubs, at the pale queen with the hideously distorted body and patient, pale, martyr's face, staring into an oblivion painfully denied her. And he swore to himself that Dyvim Marluc should perish for his part in this and that if he had strength enough after that, he would challenge Xiombarg, Queen of the Swords, and, were it at all possible, kill her for her part in this attack on all that was sane and peaceful.

Could a goddess be killed?

"YOU *PLANNED* THIS!" Elric heard Moonglum say again, looking aghast at Orlando Funk, even as he continued to tinker with the machinery. Watching them, Elric felt an increasing urgency. "We have suffered all this because of your vile tricks!"

"That's a little melodramatic, sir, I think," mumbled the lanky Orkneyman. "I do not speak Phoorn. The priestesses became dumb when they suspected the point of my questions. I had little to bargain with. I had a complicated job to do involving the weavings of Fate and Justice, Law and Chaos. Well, sir, you know the vicissitudes of we who are doomed forever to sail the moonbeam seas . . . those seas of fate . . ."

"Your speech seems over-rehearsed, sir," said Elric sardonically. "We have been your pawns, I think. Acting in your interest instead of the commonality's!"

"Ah, there you are wrong, sir. I am your mentor, and protecting ye is ma charge. If I steered ye into danger, it was a danger easier to face than what was worse, which I steered ye awa' from!" As the islander's voice rose in outrage, his brogue grew thicker. "Surely, maisters, that's plain enough for ye tae ken."

Elric returned his attention to the Queen and her larvae, her workers and her drones crawling sleepily under the influence of the she-dragon's breath. Most of whom must be preparing for a further mating. What was it? She-Bee to Male, to maintain this extraordinary reproductive cycle. How many colonies sustained themselves in this way? Hundreds, at least, he thought. And how was each hive revived? What third or even fourth mating was required to produce a honey which was strong and rich enough to mix with dragon venom and make blue mead. Or had some other party already diverted that stream to a fellow thief? "There were too many flies clustered around this enchanted honey-pot," he said.

Orlando Funk, perhaps unwilling servant of the Runestaff, shifted in his swaying cauldron, his expression far more intent than usual.

"How else could I have brought you here in time?"

"In time for what?" Elric asked in exasperation. "To witness the death of a great and peaceful civilisation?"

"One based upon unconscious slavery? A cruel pretence of peace and liberty? Perhaps," said Funk. "I certainly hope not."

"Cruel?" Elric was puzzled.

"To rob an entire people of free will? For that is the purpose of manipulative lies," explained Moonglum.

And then Funk told them how he had not the stomach for a soldier or, indeed, anyone's job which took the life of a living creature but that he belonged to a Brotherhood which sought settlement of disputes between species and the resolution of all conflict between individuals and nations, at which Elric burst into laughter.

"You sound pious as a Pik' saint," he said. "Let's have no more lies or hypocritical manipulation, when we are all so close to the finish."

"I assure you, laddie, if I were not an old friend of Count Brass, I would be taking no interest in this plane, save that it happens to have his lordship's affections!" Although Funk's accent did not change, his idiom altered, giving him an officious air. "Moreover I cannot easily endure watching fools of mortals make further fools of themselves! I am brother to the Warrior in Jet and Gold, cousin to the Nihrain, which means I serve the Balance. Which means I serve the Runestaff, *as* I serve the Balance, to achieve fairness for all, equality between the powers of Law and the powers of Chaos. To do this on occasion I have hovered between reality and impossibility. Yes, I have manipulated others, including yourselves. I am Fate's tool, as are you! I use Fate's methods. And we should not all be here now were it not part of Fate's plan! But, believe me, this could be our last chance to hold this old world together, whichever Lord of the Higher Worlds you follow—or where you're from!"

"We cannot trust you, sir." Moonglum was green from the motion of the cauldron and the sight below.

"Would I leave ye hanging here in an identical situation as myself, gents?" cried Funk, as though stricken by something clawing at his eyes! He recovered himself. "I am not at my most stable, I'll admit. Here perhaps I'm no longer *persona grata*. Oh, dear. These fumes! Feeling helpless? I'll join thee in that, laddie." Reminiscently he drew a large bottle of the Macallan from within his gaudy clothing, uncorked it, and drank half of it off in one fluent draft! He leaned across, offering the bottle to Moonglum. The Elwheri, feeling queasy over the prospect of longer time where he was, took it and drank the rest and, not knowing what to do with the empty bottle, he lowered it slowly and sheepishly to the floor of the cauldron.

Elric found none of this amusing, dependent as he now was on the mead he carried.

"I have followed your progress for some time, hoping I might make an alliance," Funk began, coughing on the fumes from below. "I was commissioned by my brothers, or cousins, if ye will, to save the innocent as much bloodshed as could be." He glanced fearfully at the bees, which appeared to be stirring a little. "And then I followed these ancient writings, which you yourself have seen—here in Kirinmoir and elsewhere. In the same gallery as the larger piece of your map."

"Soon to be destroyed if we do not act!" Elric said, his voice full of impatience. "Clearly, I have no secrets. Not the barest privacy, it seems. Nor indeed discretion! Do you think I would not have listened? Why did you not risk it?"

"I could not," said Funk. "I do not know Phoorn. There is only one mortal in this world we know who does! We needed an interpreter. We still need you, Prince Elric. We knew Lady Greatwing and perhaps her spouse might still live or lie asleep here. We hoped to wake them both. Apparently she is dead. Mummified in a strange way—I did not exactly mean 'mummified.' This seemed a more positive function of the bees somehow. But for our purposes we must presume her dead.

"Usually my Nihrain brothers could find anyone in the world, but here they are mysteriously lost. Communication is difficult. Here are so few. She gave us the compass metal. It took my brothers some long time to discover your whereabouts and get myself some further time—not to mention certain temporal manipulations—to understand the somewhat dangerous circumstances in which you were tangled. Then there were directions and the usual manipulative sorceries and the gods know what else! *By the Staff, we were righteously coddled!* We could not reach ye except through the Southern Corridor which, if ye've seen it of late, is not an easy one to play. Chaos has some dirty business there, too."

"Sir." Elric glanced down at the writhing larvae and crawling insects in the glowing blue combs. "I fear I am not following either your reasoning or your language."

"Be that as it may, sir, I—ho, ho! What's this?" Bulging with pride, he demonstrated again that his mechanism was now working. "Are we too late?"

"For what?" Moonglum asked him bitterly. "For our inevitable defeat? This was our last hope, but we have found nothing at all to help us. Only more things to confound us! We are finished, Elric!"

Usually it was Elric who could see only gloom. Now he was also the realist. He could only agree. With growing dismay, he stared down at the slowly revitalising insects and the pure beauty of that one familiar alabaster human face staring at something beyond horror, beyond pain, beyond degradation, into an unchanging and relentlessly cruel future.

TWENTY-FOUR

Phoornspawn

DYVIM MARLUC, COUSIN to the greatest emperors his world ever knew, sat proudly in the howdah of his blond war-mammoth, whose brass-bound tusks curled at just the right angle to make them thoroughly efficient weapons for almost any occasion. His armour was of ivory and steel, with golden embellishments and a lattice of silk and thin bones. The white mammoth was a sign of rank, of his power over the conglomerate of tribes and nations, natural and supernatural, he had persuaded to march with him as their Great Captain, this golden stranger whose ally was the Red Queen of Chaos herself, carrying the mystical white sword Divergent as her sign of her power over Chaos, in the form of black, blazing Arioch, writhing in a cage of rustling, impenetrable roses and borne in triumph on a sturdy gallows carried between two elephants, whom Divergent and her inspired treachery had allowed her to capture.

Xiombarg was profoundly grateful to her priestesses, who stood beside her now, greeting the renegade supplicants arriving with the Blue Temple women and their leader from Kirinmoir! They had done what they could and now shared some honour with the other women. They had the prim piety of priestesses certain of the future. They were arranged around Arioch further to display Xiombarg's power. Kirinmoir rose proudly amidst her rapists, like a martyr preparing for the stake. And at this thought Xiombarg purred and sputtered with a delight which made her suppress what she now so desperately desired, to open her horrid lips and laugh like a maniac. Holding back her laughter made her seem all the more threatening. Even Ramada Sabaru, the Golden Warlord, the Chosen of Chaos, looked at his supernatural ally a little uncertainly. He could only remain suspicious. Cousin Marluc knew there was always the chance his ally would turn on him without warning! Chaos, after all, *was* Chaos.

Now the ranks of bizarre creatures and strangely armoured men, women and children, all craving to satisfy their blood-hungry sensibilities, cackled lustily and grinned with unnatural, drooling anticipation at all the foul things they would soon do to and in Kirinmoir.

The apish pikemen had already seen the treacherous priestesses, so knew what feminine prizes to expect as they breached the city's walls. Arrows had scant effect on city roofs sheltering the defending soldiers. They saw merely their appetites given free rein as they desired. There was no friend to warn these brutes that, once they were satisfied, they themselves would be disposed of quickly. They saw only a future in which they gulped blood and blue honey, fucked white long-eared maidens and forever ate rotting meat of doubtful provenance. The pikes at the front bore the brunt of the defenders' response. They had the highest death toll. Since their imagination could not anticipate their own deaths, they would fight mindlessly. Which was why the men above despised them. Some, even more mindless, such as the badly armed half-dogs and fatlings, did not despise anyone save themselves.

The stink of Chaos was almost visible. That Xiombarg and her mortal partner could achieve so much in a short time suggested that supernatural barriers had been removed. Ancient pacts had been destroyed. Ancient horrors were abroad once more! That was evident in the Chaos queen's army. *Unlimited Riches Forever*, a scarlet and gold banner proclaimed. A slogan well known to belong to Chaos disguised as Law. Others bore legends consistent with this such as *Morality is Money*, more like those Miggea of Law would carry into battle!

Arioch's appearance changed from old man to beautiful youth, to something with tendrils and mouths, to something with claws and eyes. The Duke of Hell knew despair, perhaps for the first time. His transformations lacked the familiar vitality those who followed him expected. His shapes were surrounded by dancing, angry auras of pink and green light, of parodies of his captors' appearance, to a tempting maiden, to a happy dog, and he flung his various shapes this way and that, screaming in pain and frustration, with the singular pleasure of anticipation, then despair, on the brink of begging his captor for release, while he sobbed his own name and that of his beloved mortal foil, over and over and over again! *ARIOCH! Arioch! Arioch! Fear me fear me fear me, Elric, my imperfect ward, for we are bound together by the strength of unchangeable narrative. Elric, myself made mortal! Elric, sweetest of my slaves! Fate has ordained the future! Fear me. Fear Arioch! Oh, are there none to be fearful, none to worship, none to follow . . . ?*"

Screaming her triumph, Xiombarg burned! She yelled like fire itself! She rose, mocking golden in her human form. Gold, too, for her ally, the Golden Warlord, who now led almost the whole male population out of the West to ensure the success of his invasion. Ramada Sabaru the Great, who rode in a gold-and-ivory howdah on his massive albino war-mammoth. Glowing gold for their standards, rising and ready for the march. She turned to address her ancient rival.

Now that Arioch was captured, fuming in his fiery cage, the other great Lords and Ladies of Entropy would soon be ready to fall to her standard. They would risk no further disruption.

"Who will help you now, Lord Arioch? Your favourite little boy? He lies buried with dead dragons! And many dead bees I suspect." She looked towards Xastera, High Priestess of the Temple Well. "You say they'll be boiled in their own juices?"

The High Priestess Xastera was eager for approval. For too long had she been forced to tell lies about fictional gods, but now here was a real goddess she could serve and, she knew, ultimately convert to goodness, to protect Kirinmoir as she had already promised. "Aye, my Lady Xiombarg. I deceived Prince Elric well, so that he thought I resisted his descent. I had adjusted certain machineries. They were soon trapped, unable to ascend to the top of the Well. The last dragons are dead! That trio of troublemakers will disturb my mistress no more! The angry bees will have stung them to death by now."

Xiombarg received this news very well. From her smooth body came the sound of a deep purr, like a leopard's. Again she directed her mockery at her brother. "Oh, Arioch," she bubbled, "is their nothing to save you from your degradation, from your coming tortures when you shall beg for the oblivion which all sentient beings secretly desire. And which I bring at last! My great gift to you, beloved brother! Thus subtlety shall be maintained in your long, slow inescapable journey to eternal limbo!"

She still suppressed her glee as she surveyed the army he had brought her. At a word from their captains, the army would progress foot by foot, destroying the outer wall by sheer weight, while the defenders, barely able to retaliate, watched. They had prepared for formal war, in battles for which they had trained, century upon unchanging century, and so found themselves using curving knives and slender lances against monsters armed with razor teeth and claws, flinging balls of flaming pitch or carrying long, cursed cutlasses and flame-hot spears, giggling for the sheer cruelty and pain of it all, which was what they lived for—confirmation of the painful miserableness of life, where only privileged demigods and Lords of Law and Chaos might live without pain or anxiety or drudging misery because that was what Fate decreed, and why the likes of Xiombarg had only contempt for their worshippers. Especially the priestesses who had brought her Divergent, believing she truly intended to deliver a millennium of tranquillity to both sides of the world and even those tall, old priestesses of the Blue Temple, who had destroyed Elric the Albino and brought him and Lady Greatwing, the last living Phoorn to protect the hive, to an unambiguous end!

Soon Xiombarg would return to the male form she occasionally favoured, but for the moment she had learned from Miggea how women were best manipulated by entities taking the shape of other women, and Xiombarg had sewn the seeds for this deception decades before, so that all Andra and Indra had ever known was her female role.

For now she savoured the delicious context in which she would enter Kirinmoir's gates! What plans she had for her conquered enemy! He would know infinite torture! Arioch, her archrival, whom she had tricked so easily while he still trusted the old protocols, imprisoned and humiliated him, disempowered him. She dreamed how she would fill virgins with blue honey and suck the sweet life-stuff from them as a delicious dessert. Satisfied that her enemies were killed or in the process of being killed, she was almost bored by the ease with which the great Western army advanced on Kirinmoir and the speed with which they would surely achieve their goal.

Dyvim Marluc also savoured his old enemy's death, though his emotion was tinged with sadness and curiosity. Would anything of Elric survive after an attack of huge killer bees? He had hoped to set the stuffed body in his throne room. The other two could be similarly embalmed and stand on either side of the humiliated hero, his useless sword sucked dry of Arioch's evil inspiration. Oh, how he would savour conquest and the building of a new Melniboné, here, on the other side of their world! He would revive the dragons. He would rebuild a civilisation and begin a fresh dynasty, recalling when fear ruled a great empire, whose sorcerers, wizards, mages and alchemists of every description gathered and explored all the experience they could find on the moonbeam roads and who ruled successfully by calculated fear. Even lowly mages once added to Melniboné's knowledge and power. New Melniboné would rise from the ruins of Kirinmoir. He would give his Melnibonéans silverskin wives and land, and soon the great empire would be restored. Not under the patronage of Arioch and the crude old spirits of nature, perhaps not under Xiombarg, either. Her presence on Earth was not assured. These were, after all, mortal lands. They were in the true order of things assigned exclusive to mortals by the Protocols of the Balance.

He might find himself struggling to negotiate the deadly traps his family would start to lay. His experience of war was useful to Xiombarg, but his experience of Court was scant, and he continued to believe her words which had still to be established as true or false. And in time, he thought, he would come to hold the Black Sword and show himself to be of the true blood of Sadric and

Martik, who had made Melniboné great as he would make her great again. Stormbringer, infused perhaps with Xiombarg's power, would lead his troops to war once more upon the upstart Young Kingdoms! So would both parts of the great world-egg be united as one, and Chaos and Melniboné would rule the whole as she was meant to do before that suicidal whining weakling had set about dismantling the greatest force of mortals, elementals and supernatural powers ever assembled upon Earth, which had ruled half the world for ten thousand years and, under the new Marluc dynasty, would rule for at least another ten thousand.

Nostalgia, desperation and a sense of unsatisfied yearning would no doubt help him there, especially if Xiombarg in male form made the occasional appearance before the troops. More so, if she displayed the caged and raging Duke of Hell, well known as Elric's greatest supernatural patron.

And so Cousin Marluc was permitted happily to relish a future which, Xiombarg knew, he would never enjoy. As she had first tempted Arioch with proposals of partnership, she would capture and destroy this self-styled Idramadahan Sanfgt Iru Iru Sab'n still more easily and any other rival challenging her power. Xiombarg of Chaos would dismiss the old laws and customs and, one by one, would rise to rule by lies and false promises, her entire sphere, with gods and godlings at her command. Then she would begin to destroy the walls between the worlds and let Chaos rule in all her wild glory!

But, if the rogue Melnibonéan had plans of his own to betray his patron Queen of Swords, he could himself likely provoke an endless war dragging in gods and mortals. Such warfare had almost destroyed both in the far-gone days, lost to memory or real historical record, when mortals, gods and Phoorn had fought each other across Time and Space.

Law had ultimately gained ascendancy. Then, in the name of the Balance, some unknown champion had claimed to serve the cause of Chaos. He came to restore the Cosmic Order.

A profound compact had been struck. All parties swore that, until some cosmic need should take precedence, the forces of Law and Chaos would be held in balance in Kirinmoir, where that great war ended. Only the Blue

Priestesses, of the little temple already over the lower spring, would guard the source of their power and the peace of the valley. No true supernatural agency could have power here. Ten thousand years ago all sides were exhausted. Time had eroded and altered the narratives as water does stone, but, if taking new shapes, the stories were still strong. Only a few of them remained.

That war had caused more than one great diaspora, not only of mankind but of dragons and demigods, too. There were observant eyes, however, who saw in repetition only exhaustion and decadence, folly and despotism, and some were in the Camp of Chaos, watching while a great Lord of Chaos howled and raged and struggled within his sorcerous cage, unable to help himself or save his servants.

So Xiombarg mocked him. His idiot pet mortal had fallen into the High Priestess's trap and descended with his foolish friends into a pit of infuriated bees of exceptional proportions, some of whom remained in a shaft leading to a cavern where more angry bees grew increasingly awake, increasingly alert and increasingly lethal.

Xiombarg, surveying all she had brought about, considered the diminishing threat to her army. She raised the White Sword, Divergent, to bring up archers and flying cavalry. She flicked the sword at her rival's blazing prison.

Arioch screamed. His cage flared scarlet, then shimmering green, then silver, then scarlet again as his hideous smoking fingers, no longer disguised by his failing will, grasped the white-hot bars. A stench came out of him, like foul meat roasting.

Laughing, Xiombarg savoured the moment, sharing it with the Melnibonéan upstart whom she planned to destroy once his army had proven useful. She mocked Arioch in all the languages of men and Hell; she relished the many torments to which she would put him and all his Court. She took particular relish in betraying those who trusted her. And especially those she herself had trusted, like that foolish High Priestess who had failed to bring her the Black Sword. Who had *forgotten*! Not that any power could be channelled through it while a certain *grand elemental* remained apart from it, unable to create that bridge between sentient souls and greedy limbo.

The invading army pressed forward once again, moving the sheer weight of its massive collective body against the outer walls, crushing its own numbers, filling the moat with the dead, dying and wounded and with enough rubble to make crossing to the inner wall much easier for the attackers and their huge war-beasts. The rubble ran red with the invaders' expendable blood! Meanwhile large predatory birds flew around the besiegers, their dwarf riders drawing bows to shoot at the defenders who shot back most of the arrows which landed harmlessly in the defences.

That moment held a certain stillness for Dyvim Marluc, another second or two in which to take pleasure.

Then, many things began to happen. Horses and elephants became uneasy.

Xiombarg drew a long breath. The ground shook violently, startling every beast, rider and foot soldier. They heard a high-pitched scream which became lower until it echoed the sound from Kirinmoir mountain. As if alive, the mountain voiced a deep, discontented rumbling.

Xiombarg's ugly mount began to sniff and lick its lips. A smell in the air. A familiar smell.

Another moment of stillness. A distant, whickering cry.

Far away, the blue dome of Kirinmoir's Temple Well lifted into the air with a growing roar. The Temple's many pillars fell crumbling outwards, and the dome shattered to glaring blue glass and granite, leaving massive stone blocks coated with fine blue glass, still falling. The air was filled with a million copper-, bronze- and brass-eyes glittering as shrapnel advanced to the ground. And an enormous shape began to struggle out of the ruins, sending earth, stone and ancient buildings tumbling, until, with gaping red jaws and stained ivory teeth, it sat panting on top of the ruins, its vast shadow seeming to spread across Kirinmoir Valley and the mighty tumble of rock they called the Witnesses, dwarfing the city of Kirinmoir. The massive Emerald Dragon, one of the first and most powerful of the great Phoorn race, which somehow had learned to mate with mortals in those long-gone days, blew a few clouds of smoke from her slender snout, causing Dyvim Marluc's great trumpeting war-mammoth to rear back. The Golden Warlord was forced to cling to the straps of his armoured howdah, roaring his anger and dismay, echoing that of his supernatural ally. With difficulty and in some pain, he hauled himself back to his feet. He was both furious and afraid. His golden sandals were scraped and dented.

The Emerald Phoorn appeared to grin as it saw what indignity it had caused the attackers. Yet it was still not entirely certain whether the dragon had killed the three men still trapped in the mountain or if the deadly bees had done their job as Xastera, the High Priestess, had promised.

Xiombarg turned to the priestesses, blazing: "You swore you would bring me the sword and failed! And you promised me that the dragons were dead!"

The High Priestess looked about her, as if an answer would present itself. She was speechless.

"You lied! Stupid old woman!"

Xastera saw all her old power waning at once. "This is impossible! We had a bargain made in mutual respect! I did what I promised. The Temple is destroyed. Your mortal enemies are slain. So much I have already done for you! I am beginning to fear, my lady, that you do not intend to honour our bargain!"

She folded her arms across her chest and offered the Queen of the Swords a virtuous and reproachful stare. She sternly awaited her answer.

The dragon, still some distance away, took no part in the action but looked mildly puzzled by the next events.

A bolt flew from Xiombarg's sword, Divergent, and struck the priestess directly in the face. Suddenly blind and tongueless, she held up her hands as she cast about for mercy that she knew could not come. She died, calling upon the dragons whom she had betrayed and manipulated, believing even as she died that she was a martyr, knowing that what she had done was for the good of all.

The other priestesses, always timid at best, cowered into the protection of Andra and Indra, and for a brief moment it seemed they were all about to die, pressing back dangerously close to the unnatural and hellish heat of Arioch's blazing cage, until Xiombarg, realising that her wild emotions, always hard to control, were to destroy all her allies before she had no more use of them, controlled herself and her restless mount and held the White Sword high. "The old, weak ways are finished. The old compacts no longer hold meaning. We are now more pragmatic." She preened as she surveyed her armies.

"Soon, not only shall I hold the White Sword of Law but the Black Sword of Chaos. I shall in effect *become* the Cosmic Balance! I shall control the Cosmic Balance, and Fate shall do the bidding of the Queen Emperor Xiombarg, who is now not merely the greatest power in Chaos but for all and all eternity shall be Queen of the Balance, King of Swords! All narratives shall spring from me, all speeches, all stories, all kinds and manner of people and creatures and things, the sole governor and creator of life. All reality! If I wish a tree to be a certain shape, so be it. If I want a man to be a certain shape, also so be it! I shall control the mountains and the oceans, but I shall also never fear death, for I shall be life's mistress and death's master. Thus I ensure my rule for eternity and watch feeble, weeping, snivelling Arioch, spitting like an angry little boy!

"Oh, I'll let you live, Arioch. I'll keep you in your cage like a seafarer's pelican. I shall take so much pleasure in your humiliation."

The Queen of the Swords raised the sword again. "Prepare your men, captains."

Bright, heavy banners were raised. An undulating whistling went from rank to rank as the captains and the lieutenants and the sergeants prepared to lead their men in a victory charge!

Traditions were trampled. Mandarin manners were disdained. Vulgarity was victorious! Chaos in all her old glory had come again to Kirinmoir.

In response to their captains' whistles and bugles, the men began to follow the thundering war-drums and press closer and closer together until the army resembled a single beast which drew its coils tighter and tighter before flinging its mass against the inner walls of Kirinmoir. It pressed its three sides against the city whose defences were not fully protected by those remaining long fingers of granite which cast deepening shadows even now mixing with late-afternoon air and misting stone dust mingling with growing twilight to make seeing exceptionally difficult.

But not the dragon on Kirinmoir's great citadel, spreading opaque emerald wings which had an unusual shimmer, a little like a mirage. Many called out to Xiombarg, begging her to explain why a dragon reared where all dragons were pronounced slain! Xiombarg immediately began the weaving of still another lie.

"She's no Lady Greatwing returned to save the city. She's a mere projection—a feeble illusion set upon you by your enemies! The explosion came from the bees in their hive resisting Elric! I stopped them! He and his friends planned to steal the secret of the people's mead!"

Again, silence.

With an ear-splitting bang, the Emerald Phoorn, eldest of all dragons in the caverns known to Man, flicked her gigantic wings. In a graceful movement, she flapped them again, knocking people and apparatus to the earth. There came a pause in the movements of soldiers as all watched the dragon leaving, taking all their work and aspiration with her, climbing in ever-decreasing circles. Had she carried a rider? Or perhaps two riders? Where had *skeffla'an* been found? Or were those horns on her head, near her neck, scales of some kind? The intense indigo of the dragon's parting colour made some watchers begin to cry from the profound, aching purity of it, forcing them to remember their deepest and most beautiful secrets.

Others thought she went for reinforcements and that the dragons had come to kill as many as possible, irrespective of their origins! More? Was she getting help? No! She was fleeing. Doubtless she had killed any mortals she found invading her domain. Panic rose and fell like a ragged tide.

"She flees! She has become a memory! An illusion. Nothing. She knows she has lost. She flees for all to see. She fears me. But have I the power?" Xiombarg mused, and many strained to hear. "I never courted the earth spirits as Arioch and Elric did. I shall need human slaves at first, employed to rebuild Kirinmoir and all her works in a greater, more magnificent form. Her towers will be taller, her walls more beautiful. Slowly I shall bring the great kings and queens of the natural world under my sway!"

Again Xiombarg enjoyed a warm moment of triumph. The decrepit old

Phoorn deserted them. Weak magic in play again. That was no more than the ghost of a dragon.

Then, suddenly, Xiombarg sensed a subtle attack! She jerked herself up with alarm. If her mind drifted, then the minds of her troops had been touched by deeper magic. It had a familiar taste but could easily be some local mage trying his last to destroy the city's enemies, or perhaps some pretty little sorceress thought she could strike down Chaos with a conjuring trick?

Here came another ragged remnant of Kirinmoir's finest flying cavalry, stepping from amongst his captured comrades, holding up an old sword, no doubt a family relic. Another attack? The hero was a young man, thin and crooked in the legs, like all Kirinmoir's feeble males, holding his wreck of a sword. His father's? Ah, no, she forgot! His father was some sort of wingless worm. Xiombarg could imagine the story he told himself. Oh, how they loved to be brave, to no purpose whatsoever, unless it was for the admiration of their peers. To give meaning, if this were meaning, to their lives? Here he came in his ragged mail, with strips of skin licked from his limbs by the tongues of monsters.

"Back! By the power of iron I command thee desist!" He croaked through cracked lips and a drying mouth. Xiombarg listened with a kind of relish. And in a moment the wretch was eliminated from the world without a trace.

Xiombarg chuckled, addressing the wounded prisoners they dragged up. "Iron? What am I, some savage? Titanium and platinum are ours to fashion without harm, and it has been millennia since we were allergic to silver. Your stories no longer tell the truth. Your weapons are out of date. Best join us and at least have some life under my folk. We are not always cruel."

She noticed a movement near the city.

Could it be that the giant stone fingers moved a little? Or was that an illusion also? Ah, yes. Clouds sailed upon the darkening horizon.

Then the granite, suddenly seeming subtle as molten steel, curved up like the fingers of a vast human hand. Silence. Then a faint groaning sound escaped it.

"YAAAH!!!"

Another piece of granite, like a forefinger, slowly raised its weight into the air until it was clear of the city, protecting it like a Titan's rising hand. If it had an owner, he must stand some seventy feet tall, at least. As tall as the old giants of epic and legend who had lived before. A giant left in the name of the Balance to protect the city they had favoured so thoroughly.

What great sorcery could make that long-buried mass of pale grey granite, grown with moss and lichen less than an hour ago, become this thing of alarming power and terrifying glory? A thing which she knew in her own old bones had been there before her birth as a boy-child in the booming sea-vaults of the cold-blooded *migagadinnom* she secretly adored as her monitor and her spiritual director. Encouraged to actions not even attractive to her. Could the casting of a certain spell create this movement or that movement? Another finger moved, and masses of earth, centuries of one layer upon another, were broken away with the rocks and dirt until an entire hand had emerged, and, as the granite fingers slowly closed, it was clear that some powerful force was either removing Kirinmoir from her foundations, threatening to crush all who lived within the city, or crushing the city as walls fell but houses remained standing. Some enormous counter-magic was at work, and all who observed it knew that they had invoked something which might destroy them all. A terrified scream from within the city. Were they being crushed? What would become of the Well? The spring? The honey? Were all the bees dead? If not, why so silent? Would the owner of the hand emerge?

And next there came the sound of excited soldiers and the anxious snort of beasts. Riders struggled with their mounts, tightening reins in a clank of metal and creak of leather while one weapon clattered against another, and officers bawled instructions.

When the noise of earth falling in thumps and thuds had been finally absorbed by a magical silence, there followed a stillness broken by the screams and bellows of frustrated beasts and men. This, too, subsided.

Within his flaming prison Arioch ranted and fumed and flung his hairy, misshapen body back and forth, grinding his teeth. He glared this way and that, his hands scarred by the rapid heating and cooling of the sorcerous bars.

"*STORMBRINGER COULD CUT THROUGH THESE IN SEC-ONDS!*" screamed the defiant Lord of the Higher Worlds. "*Elric is my willing slave. He needs my strength and the strength of the sword, for we are all three part of the same beast!*"

"But," taunted his old rival, "that sword is melted in Hell's heat and cannot cut butter now, let alone what *these* bars are made of, my Lord of the Black Metal and Deadly Stallions! That is existential *plietanium*! *You lack all power—now and for eternity! The blade cannot cut anything, for her runes are dissipated in a river of iron because she is drained of all that made her powerful!*"

Xiombarg found noisy pleasure in this constant provocation of he who once was most powerful amongst all the gods of instability! It made her spirit swirl and shudder. Words began to be touched by this same inner sorcery. Colours were changing, too. She was baffled, shaking her lion head to clear it. What was wrong? She knew she had deceived them all. He had risked much to follow Elric here. The other lords and ladies both of Law and Chaos were too weak to put an end to this, for in the Higher Worlds all was a-squabble. Only one or two of the lords and ladies were still not at odds. Having no alliances rooted in the nature spirits of this world, Elric knew he could rely on little else but his reputation, a flask of blue mead and a dying sword. Did any Lords of the Higher Worlds observe this struggle? If so, they shrugged and looked on in perpetual mockery as they provoked their colleagues. This was now true both in Chaos and in Law, so that the Great Balance swung almost out of control, this way and that, at random, like a many-decked but rudderless ship!

The calm priestesses Andra and Indra, survivors of that now-destroyed Temple Hive, their religion already doubted in the glare of Xiombarg's voluptuous narcissism, drew their frightened charges tighter around them and calmed them, telling them that Lady Greatwing would not harm her own, that the Emerald Phoorn was more frightened of them than they were of it, though indeed it should have died some centuries earlier. Its survival in any form was miraculous! The Phoorn were, after all, sworn to protect humanity, were they not? (They were not.) Those half-crazed gentle women continued to tremble until, in their beautiful peacock robes they seemed one single, exceptionally sweet-smelling shivering and gorgeous entity, an aspern-angel. Xiombarg yarked and snobbered in her frustrated fury, sending orange and green balls of fire in all directions, missing most of the people paused there and trying to guess the next move.

What had brought such unpredicted pause upon the battlefield?

For a while the various combatants stared at one another, listening to the silence. At that moment, they had lost all sense of what they were doing there. Soldiers had forgotten they were fighting, and war-beasts began to wander away. Louder and louder roared Xiombarg as she sought to drive the soldiers back to her charge. She screamed at her ally. "Melnibonéan! Take command of your forces, man!"

Within the great stone fist, all Xiombarg desired to see defeated lay sheltered. She would open that fist if she had to prise those stone fingers apart an inch at a time. And they would suffer for that, of course. Xiombarg was no modern goddess who plotted revenge for a thousand years ahead. Revenge for her was best when it was hot and salt and sweet as rich, fresh-drawn blood.

"All these little parlour magic tricks," she mumbled to herself, "are not enough to defeat me! I am neither mystified nor am I afraid. Wizards of the finest skills have challenged me and they have failed. They always fail, be they from Pan Tang, Kirinmoir or Melniboné. Their defeat is already determined. Soon only one queen shall reign over Law, Chaos and Limbo, too." She turned to the traitor Melnibonéan, Ramada Sabaru, the Golden, reluctantly consulting him. "It is your strategy to attack, also?"

"They cannot attack *us*, that's for certain!"

Ramada Sabaru fumed in his howdah. They needed a decisive leader. He began to modify his original scheme. He goaded his mammoth into the milling ranks, driving the beast closer to Arioch's sorcerous cage. He was nursing some half-formed plan to abandon Xiombarg and bargain with Arioch.

When she saw what her golden ally was doing, Xiombarg screamed until she had no more heads to scream. Everywhere soldiers' ears and eyes were bleeding as she raced towards Ramada Sabaru to cut him off and give their captains orders to reassemble the ranks of her armies. Thwarted for the moment, the Golden Hero let the mahout drive his mammoth back to the head of the army as it gathered itself. Then Queen Xiombarg lifted her sword Divergent and gave the order to press forward with what must be the final charge.

TWENTY-FIVE

Visions and Hallucinations

THE ENEMY CHARGE proved somewhat confused, dividing around various rocky and earthy promontories and making it harder to direct energies at the city's main gate. Since they had last moved, the gigantic stones had been still, hiding the city or sheltering it. Light did not fall out of it or into it. It had become self-contained within that protective fist. It required nothing of the outside save the sun's light, and that could be reproduced.

And so, for some fair amount of time, the armies continued to roar at one another, and by the dim firelight and candlelight inside the granite fingers they might occasionally see a defiantly brandished weapon. But now, it seemed, the inhabitants of Kirinmoir could in no way shoot or fling their missiles at the Chaos army, and the army had no targets at which to aim.

"They will want to treat with us!" sneered Xiombarg, settling into human form, a woman of brass and gilt.

"And us with them?" enquired Dyvim Marluc.

Xiombarg looked at him and sneered again.

She hardly recalled who her ally was. She had forgotten that they marched together. She was thinking how this would consolidate her empire, even if she simply kept that great irritating stone fist contained. Those inside it would eventually die, and meanwhile a great deal of their residual honey would leak out. When everyone in Kirinmoir was dead, there would be plenty to give the troops for years to come.

The last of her real enemies already lay dead inside that mountain, stung by a million bees or roasted by one of his own kin. With Phoorn fled and Elric dead, with even the remains of that Nihrain's lickspittle mixing with the flaming ashes of its kind, there were no more obstacles to her cosmic expansion. She had done what so many had sworn could not be done. She had overwhelmed the Cosmic Balance, the mechanism by which the whole of Law and Chaos kept the multiverse in motion, and now she would tell the multiverse how to function, how to determine what was just and unjust, fair and unfair; only from now it would be what was fair to Xiombarg and what brought justice to the Queen of the Swords or praised and insulted the Goddess made Great Again. Her rule would be remembered even after Law and Chaos were everywhere forgotten. The only name heard on Fate's chimes would be hers. For the Age-to-Come shall be the Age of Xiombarg . . .

Xiombarg licked her lush red lips and paused to taste a little of the wealth of souls which must soon come to her. *Oh, it will be good*, she thought. She watched, almost with patience, while their armies regrouped.

At that moment she was so beautifully at ease, her imagined future so sweet, that if she did not need to give her troops a show, she might have saved an enemy torture before killing them. She had already, she believed, shown considerable mercy and fairness to that foolish bee-keeping idealist of a High Priestess. Of course, Xiombarg had made all the usual empty promises. The valley was to become a peaceful paradise under her benign rule. Her sentimental dreams could be spread over the entire world! Xiombarg shook her heads. How could the woman think all she did was "useful"? What use was there to creating that ridiculous rural paradise for happy little humans? It had no ambition. No *size*!

Xiombarg was entirely baffled. Perhaps some perverse parental streak? She would not know it. She had all her own children in different forms and at different periods. In general, she had no feelings for her children, though she had eaten one or two when expedient. Perhaps she felt a little maternalism for captured Arioch, fuming and hissing his hatred in his impenetrable cage of fiery bars and sudden lattices of pain? Yes. Almost certainly it was neither hatred nor contempt. He, or at least the manner of his deception and capture, might have caused her a kind of—what?—contentment? Perhaps. Now her mood was uneasy again.

She had been told the last Phoorn was dead and then that the dragon she had seen was an illusion. Alarming? It involved no threat. It scarcely mattered, Queen Xiombarg thought. No single Phoorn or Melnibonéan, whatever their history, could threaten her great army combined with that of the finest mortal army ever gathered. They could take their time and saunter through those stone fingers at their leisure. She was assured the old Phoorn were dead or their bones so calcified they could not move. She had it on the authority of Xastera, the High Priestess of Kirinmoir, who had engineered the slow deaths of the dragons in her charge, saving only two females to continue making venom, though otherwise, she understood, incapable of flame. One female had died, it seemed. But there was now an alchemical means of producing venom. They no longer needed living dragons!

Of course, Greatwing would never fly again. She was little more than a head with an addled brain! Everything else had crystallised or corrupted. That image of Greatwing squatting on the temple ruins was a mere conjuring trick. A last attempt to frighten away the Queen of Chaos, her supernatural allies and her human armies! Xiombarg sneered. These mortals grew increasingly pathetic. Her heads blossomed, merged and re-formed as a glorious human face! And at that moment, without warning, she began to see obstacles! *Now there was little action to take aaah! Her brain her own brain tumbled and pounded like a crazy machine, images and ideas pouring one after another, seeming to leap from every part of her.* Defence had no place in her plans. Divergent flared silver. Only conquest filled her future! Conquest charged from her nostrils, blazed from her eyes, squealed and writhed in her ears. *What? What?* Lightning boomed in her several heads, and thunder crashed in her many eyes! The pain was intense. Sorcery? Where would this new attack come from? She growled with uncertainty. She had become a lion with the torso of a man, swinging her huge brass battle-axe, ready to make war on anything, man or monster! All her monstrous appetites were at war within her as the future she had imagined melted away to reveal a still more confused and contradictory ambition, more than she had known she desired.

She knew no entity unchained as powerful as herself! But it was as if she lacked the strength to contain so much power! She mumbled and twisted, putting her form through a multitude of shapes. Nothing, nothing, nothing they could do would confuse her, cause her to lose sight of her goal! She flung back her great leonine head, and a dreadful sound issued from it. That sound echoed for long moments up and down the valley, mournful, baffled, angry and threatening.

Was she thwarted? She shook her head.

She should not be concerned about the dying Phoorn! She repeated this vehemently to herself, gradually regaining control of her reeling senses. She assured herself that huge, fire-breathing, intelligent, vengeful Phoorn, creatures of ancient wisdom and well-tended imagination, were no more. What they saw was a memory. Its shimmering form proclaimed it a wizard's pretence. An illusion, a mirage, it had such poorly detailed outlines. Some trickster in the city, no doubt, hoping to scatter her armies! Well, her armies had held!

And, after all that, the illusion had failed and flown away. Fled. Disappeared. It had definitely had horns! The horned dragons belonged in the past. Their horns sprouted, perhaps to help them negotiate the unknown spaces in which they flew, beyond this plane in search of peace as she and her kind had fled before. Xiombarg's strange, supernatural brains speculated crazily between the natural and the fantastic. What she had anticipated and therefore assumed to be inevitable was not happening. The Phoorn's appearing had upset her. Those horns, around its crinkling neck! Could they be mistaken for a sign of renewed life? No! She tittered, a sound which startled the chimera on which she now seated herself. Diamonds melted in her hair. She peered towards where the departed Phoorn had last been seen. Gold encrusted her face, fell flaking across her shoulders. A wave of blood surged over the surfaces of her body. Xiombarg frowned. They were warts, to be sure. Something associated with extreme old age. She changed her ears to listen where she could. What did they think? Some of Xiombarg and Dyvim Marluc's generals believed the horns to be a condition of living for so long in those caverns. Others said there were figures on its back. Elric and Moonglum? Emerald Phoorn did not carry passengers! Not without a *skeffla'a*. No such thing had been found in thousands of her years, let alone mortal ones. Had that simpering priestess betrayed her? Ah! She should not have been so merciful.

Only three days earlier, Xastera, the High Priestess, unknown to her women, had sent Xiombarg a confirming portrait which was undeniably that of a dying Phoorn, whose venom sacs were bruised and prominent, whose eyes were rheumy and yellow and whose crests and scales flaked, drooped and were scraped, almost rusted, as she opened her transparent green wings and faltered, her outline fading and shivering with a faint, melancholy buzzing rather than any further growls. The creature was dying, as anyone could see! The effort of emergence had almost killed it. Or was that unstable outline simple proof of her being merely a fairly crude illusion, shimmering as mirages shimmered. A trick of the light. Elric and his Elwheri friend somehow alive, thinking to escape? Riding on an illusion? This amused her. Real men could not, whatever little sorcery they had left, ride upon the stuff of Faeyrie-Land! They had no *skeffla'an*. No—it had all been a crude illusion.

Illusion or reality, there was no escaping Xiombarg, and therefore there was no escaping justice. She *was* justice and could determine what rule they follow. She was every aspect and quality of this world, her vast mind stretching to encompass the multiverse and reconstruct it in her image.

She was disgusted by all tradition, whether mortal or immortal, its ridiculous games and needy, mindless, pointless rituals and values. Meaningless values which were contradicted on every side in reality. Perhaps they believed differently, but as she destroyed their beliefs, so would she destroy their realities. One came before the other and was as true as the other coming first, she told her uncertain self. "*Aaaaahiiiiii!*" Rage threatened to consume her again.

Oh, how she longed to crush them as she hoped that the grey Witnesses might yet crush the city it held in its gentle grip, balanced upon its palm. Of course she knew who he was and why he had been left there. She had believed him dead. Why had she not thought he would awaken after all these millennia?

These mortals and their legends and legendary allies infuriated her and made her itch to destroy even their ridiculous symbols. She failed entirely to come close to feeling what they felt. That was deeply frustrating to her. Empathy was not a quality she understood, and therefore she could not aspire to it. Of course, this enraged the barely stable or dispassionate Queen of the Swords even more! She was becoming the very personification of unchecked Chaos!

Xiombarg barely stopped herself from destroying everything. She deeply desired to wipe away all memory of them. *Every sight and stink of them.* She became a beautiful, green-skinned woman whose red eyes rivalled Elric's. Her plan, the plan in her head, carried here through all the planes of the cosmos, was thwarted as she had conceived it. The reality she had planned could not be imposed. She was determined, however, that her future would not be taken away from her! She had felt infuriated frustration in failing to make them lose their sad beliefs in the point of anything, especially of anything imaginary as well as everything they accepted as reality. Now—what had she said to herself? Senility? And they feared to tell her? The dragon in the citadel? A fantasy, of course. Law was defeated, no? Oh, she was expending all her energy in maintaining her battle plan. *What right had they to challenge her reality?*

Now reality was only Chaos and Limbo! Fated as always to perish, only Law stupidly resisting the inevitability of Entropy! No matter how distant the day before the multiverse exhaled her last gassy breath, Law was the final fart, she thought, of an old, used up, senile idea. Because her light travelled faster than their sound! Was there no audience for her wit any longer? Of course! She could hear its echoes even now. In her head she paced the halls of supreme power. Law and Chaos would kneel at the feet of the Queen of the Swords. Law resisted the actuality of Death. Was that Death's high-toned laughter?

Chaos accepted it and celebrated it and called for more pleasure for whomever sought pleasure, more enlightenment for those who desired it, more spiritual knowledge for those who sought it. Law proceeded and measured and rationed and took her time. Everything, all at the same moment, all in one glorious tumbling tornado of truth and revelation! That was what Chaos always brought. Glory! Glory! From the pit of her stomach—*Gloriana*! She juddered.

Could she *need* Law? She gnashed unhuman teeth, and her inhuman eyes threatened to destroy all. Law conserved and drew boundaries, carefully measured the heat death of their plane, calculating the existence and ultimately managing the end of all life. The end was coming, and everyone had to look after their own children, even those others had adopted. *Lewayly niyn a stae*, as they mocked High Melnibonéan. Oh, that hurtful tone. A war, so much larger than this, would consume first the World Above and then the World Below. No shelter from it. Was there no escaping the death of all? Chaos had gone mad in that quest for solace. Law had gone mad by refusing to accept solace.

Familiar landscapes warped and twisted upward into multicoloured shapes. NO! She sensed her power escaping her control! She feared all resources were exhausted sooner than she had estimated and that ultimate silence must inevitably come. Chaos hoped for better outcomes, although no truth persuaded the realists. She had broken all the old conventions, destroyed ancient agreements and shown only contempt for tradition in her refusal to accept inevitability. The new eyes found new paths to what remained of the ancient roads her soul now searched for if it could ever find peace in any world but this. "I followed so many paths to reach the portal to this plane. Yet I still had to persuade those stupid mortal women to invite me! They came to meet me, dragging that resisting child with them, only to lose it! *They said the White Sword Divergent is a map to ultimate rule. Strand upon strand. Blade upon blade. Splinter upon splinter. Which to follow?*" Much argument continued in invisible spheres, mortal to mortal and god to god. Xiombarg did all she could to hang on to what little she still understood of

Law's rationality as wrecked seamen cling to an enemy spar rising and falling in increasingly violent waves.

O, waking, darling Chaos, so profound, so sweet and strange in all her hallucinatory romantic towers, curling, round concrete trees or trees unsteady containing a golden beauty's bower or so it seemed, intended scenes and cruel nemesis tomorrow's lost domain, and mother's sweep the carrion ground of dusty bones as still they step in hesitant command of those Dilonic, authoritative tones. Those high, sweet flutes. Who now could fail to kneel? To gasp at sounds and opening salvos, suppressed groans and grinding teeth. *Pound pound pound.* The darling tones of grief! *O, cat! O, possum! Can anyone draw a chair up to the burning table?* A creative moment, was that? Or so they thought as the meaning gradually leached into mushed and mental mess. Self-pity or much worse. Don't weep! All weeping does is water the mould of memory. Its blood sweetens revenge! To bathe in blood, the blood of coward or hero. It is the same warm, salty stuff and never, never enough. *Spammer, please tell, is that pray how the bloodworm failed.* Is this all we receive by peering into the Abyss and considering oblivion? We cannot let ourselves die in a blaze that is merely gorgeous. That is how the Blood Giantess formed! O long ago and where the Worm? And Elric, was that wretched friend of elementals and other earthy scum his childhood wasted in its years what language is this? *She brought us almost to destruction! How can memory help us now? See!* Parting a curtain of confusion, her reason spent on the realisation of her impossible desires, Xiombarg lost human form and melded with her mount, opening her giant beak and screaming at the thwarting of her certainties.

Wobbling, swaying, rudderless and dizzy moving hands like broken ailerons in attempts to break first this fall, then that. Down, down she felt herself fall. A ship at seas. A dozen planes like ripples in a lake each spreading away from the centre like some Babylonian orrery, that middle road few could travel, if it were real at all. Swooning into harbour, just in time, blue as tranquil Adriatic evenings, a moment on the low- and middle-seas. Underground, amniotic, in the womb of the Earth, she had found and lost them more than

once. Unable to charm or otherwise persuade the Balance, she now understood her folly. And wished she were more intelligent.

The ancient, unsteady King of the Dead, frozen in Time forever, conscious
forever in that single woken moment before oblivion, no second chances
begged, at least, stiff as frozen chronons, too old to make the Sign of Chaos
with one hand, the Sign of Law with the other, ascending into the ramshackle
pulpit to conduct the few who live away from where the mourners hid, told
to remain at large but invisible. Not to stain the rocks with any fluid and to
be soundless. No farts, no sucking sounds. Instant combustion! Had they seen
the High Priestess? She was becoming a little spasmodic, she thought. They
were by now all encompassed by the orgasmic moment, eating them from the
inside gloriously *out*! *Ah! Ah! If commands ignored, then the full display of
Chaos will be with me!*

Black, mysterious, roiling distant, instant all of this, some—some terrifying holocaust? She baulked. Her brain was better than this! She had a finer
mind. But had she yet tested it to destruction? A great tripe, enholed, enlaced,
ensliced, stomach to stomach prepared for all. Oh, the gorgeous stink of it.
Vultures peck my living eyes as they stare knowingly, indestructibly into the
void. To share? With whom? Some sort of intimacy, held forever?

"*WHAT IS ALL THIS BLUE?*" Some foul presumption by the likes of
that trickster Jermays the Crooked?

"*He thinks I'm tame! Tamed at any rate. A man. Old, too. He deferred to
his detractors. Dead god forever dying. What's in sight? Nothing. Or very little
at any rate. This could well be Chaos's epiphany.*"

You could be sure Law's success was unlikely to follow now. *His name at
first was Karth, who served the Balance, then Dundane, perhaps. Were these
the earliest or the last of times?* His sorceries across the mysterious moonbeam roads cried out to Karol von Bek, the melancholy Duke of Wälden-
stein, to John Daker of London and to Urlik Skarsol of the Southern Ice,
and they selected Karol or perhaps his cousin, so poor were their powers of
communication across the planes. Vague? It could be so much worse! But

this was no plane on which Chaos should involve Law, as both forces more or less agreed. In the World Below there were already new disputes concerning the old protocols. All were certain that a great Event was coming, to change this plane forever. Law and Chaos struggled to be best positioned for it. There was some frustrating argument amongst the Lords and Ladies of the Higher Worlds concerning protocols, conventions and precedents that no longer functioned. Why could she not marshal uneasy thoughts? She had given herself up too much to unreason. She found common reality difficult to grasp.

She had always hated the human smell of sour wine and onions. No longer! Now she cultivated it! Xiombarg stretched and snorted, lapping at her teeth like a horse. *Again there was a smack of the convenient, a subtle containment, even. Still in rein, this superbrain split his chains and let the links fall where they could. Who was at the root of this plot? Elric? Impossible! Arioch? No. She had stolen his will with the sword. Long enough to weave his prison. She should have left him behind. But who could resist displaying a captured enemy? And who better a witness to her triumph!?*

Except, some tiny fragment told her, she had suited her strategy to a willed outcome, not to what was true . . . So she whined and grizzled again, a louder sort, and swore some power, her equal, was at work, but only smelled the stink of elementals, either listening or already summoned in waiting. No! This was the great white wolf, Elric, sent to thwart Chaos in coming times. But she was no expert in their theologies or even her own family history, especially that imaginary course which faeyrie-tale honey-women followed. Xiombarg paused to watch the fighting. Her victory was inevitable! *Aha! Those rich and revelatory smells of every kind. They overwhelmed the mind like some well-aimed pancake, covering it entirely and leaving no channel unfilled.* What had they planned to bake? An elemental poisoned pill plucked like some aerial shell to make the deadly black pearl, of which perhaps that demi-angel Gobseck perished so long ago. She must take control. She *must* take control. He had become too admiring of her own spectacle.

Our Queen of Chaos, as she began to style herself, laughed more fully and with so much more real pleasure than ever before, as she struck about her, breaking bones, sorting bodies or whatever else she needed for a comfortable chair, sitting amongst the squirming, dying bodies of the shrieking generals, which came close to soothing her several ears. This music was the only kind which relaxed her and brought her some kind of peace. She began to whistle. Five of her other mouths joined in. The tune was a merry one, a gathering of fifes. She tapped her tentacles, causing several minor earthquakes. She had become sanguine, she decided, very soon after that last pointless trick of the defenders. Xiombarg so suddenly could not understand why her brain no longer formed melancholy and logical connections. Her mind felt unmade. Even to her, in her uncertain triumph, Chaos had never seemed so all-consuming . . .

Certainly there was no "doom" for them and no punishment or ironic turn of events, no happy or even unhappy ending, for there was no going back. Why had she done this? Did it carry meaning? She controlled the Great Scales! (*Almost.*) Her goal. She turned her heads this way and that. So many enemies! Oh, she knew she broke their laws. New, simpler laws would soon replace them. A single law and a simple one. Absolute dedication of all living things to the worship of herself and her interests. But what then? She hesitated as she had never hesitated before. There was none to challenge her and survive! She looked towards the setting sun. She would see too little of her enemies by night, even if they lit the sky. Should she light a forest? Should she concern herself? Were there any enemies left? What conquests? What ambitions? She did all she could to rein in her twisting, racing thoughts. She would wait until morning before the sweet, subtle scents of fear could be fully relished. Not any fear of her own, nor of those who followed her. She settled herself in her chair, wondering why Dyvim Marluc stared at her open-mouthed. Her forked tongue moistened her eyeballs as, absently, she considered her reasons for keeping such daily accounts.

She remembered. Something she had needed. Something which mortals had.

Through the sky behind her a shadow rose, blue as the darkest possible shade of blue, solid, yet shimmering at the edges so that Dyvim Marluc, still somewhat bleary, wondered at the effect of the little blue honey he had consumed.

For Dyvim Marluc, whatever his ambitions, was no fool. He had begun to understand this Queen of Blades. She was also Mistress of Lies, the most cunning of all the aristocrats of Chaos. No agreement she made had substance. He had given her all his power. He had invited her to this plane against all. Where were her promised allies from the Higher Worlds? They should have ridden to her aid by now! She had led him to believe that Elric's painful death was her first priority, and he had shared that. Once that was achieved, she could summon allies from amongst the Dukes of Hell! Next, she spoke of leading the Chaos Lords in a crusade against Law, yet neither the Lords of Law nor those of Chaos had met them on the battlefield.

Like most of his family, Marluc was a scholar and something of a sorcerer. He had come to tell the difference between a truly cruel and unempathetic being with material ambitions and one so utterly lacking in any understanding of their world, so unable to project or interpret her loyalties and passions, not because she was an alien supernatural but because for all her complexity of character and birth, she had become irrational, pursuing inexplicable goals and impossible ambitions. He had read much of how a madness could fall like this on gods or men who were given more power than they were fit to bear. They were destroyed, quite literally, by their own ambition. Not much of an ally, he thought, sneering at his own gullibility. Her damned ivory sword, Divergent, had confused him.

With the protective closing of that giant granite fist and the appearance of that illusory dragon, their plans had faltered and the future become less distinct. The agency they had assumed withered into death was apparently alive! They still had a magnificent army but nothing to march against! Xiombarg, especially in her current condition, was barely capable of rational thought in that vast press of men, beasts, monsters and machinery, growing querulous and undisciplined as time wore on. For a moment, Dyvim Marluc was the man he had been before the fall of the Dreaming City: uncertain, unwilling to act. She was perhaps not entirely best able to lead so many. Why did not all her brothers and sisters support her? She had promised him they were simply waiting for them to reach the valley. As it was, he saw their supernatural ranks thinning a little as realisation of Xiombarg's lies or false promises came to them. Some disappeared into thin air. Mortal deserters had no such option. The frozen expressions on the Melnibonéans' faces had begun to change. Some were frowning and looking about them. What were they doing on the far side of the world? They had followed their blood-leader here. Should they have done?

Dyvim Marluc now seemed as mad as Xiombarg. His hatred for the albino had led him to make untenable compromises. These over-armoured Westerners and rabble of barbarians, they themselves had whipped into a disciplined army . . . Were they Melnibonéans' natural allies? The tall warriors, who had fought beside Elric in that far-off forest, had now seen Melaré's saurian cavalry and identified closely with Kirinmoir's pale women. Xiombarg's casual killing of High Priestess Xastera had brought sudden enlightenment to these survivors of the great betrayal. She was, as far as they knew, of their own blood. They had grown up with the Phoorn and saw them as friends or more—as beloved elders who protected and were protected by them. The dragons, surely, were their natural allies, whether they had Elric with them or not. They were becoming deeply uneasy. Had they already walked too far into this trap?

Sensing his warriors' uncertainty, Dyvim Marluc became convinced that Xiombarg was not only mad but had manipulated him into joining his army with hers and marrying her ambitions to his own. Or had *he* been mad all along? In some ways, certainly, she had somehow talked him into joining her madness. He sighed. Probably they had both been deceived by minds clouded by a need to be avenged on the albino.

Or was this a reward, a game for their unstable sister, to distract her? She had consorted with these creatures for too long! Was she simply the embodiment of mortal greed, unable to act in any other way? An element of their existence deliberately flawed, to produce change however change was resisted? Half her army was down; the other half was mostly his. He could withdraw it. He must not! Why had he and his been spared?

Brooding in his golden howdah, Dyvim Marluc wondered if this were more than a minor setback. There was to be no retreat, but all had been assured that Kirinmoir had no supernatural aid, was, indeed, forbidden to employ it. She had broken the great commandment almost the second that Dyvim Marluc had summoned her to his aid and helped her in turn entice Lord Arioch into her trap. But since their march to the East began, the Queen of the Swords had become increasingly unpredictable, and her several brains sometimes appeared to malfunction. They seemed at odds amongst themselves, even. In other words, part of her at least had always potentially been mad. Unable to deal with unpredictability, Xiombarg was an unpredictable god! If she made a plan, she did not expect that plan to be thwarted! A god gone mad was a dangerous god!

The Melnibonéan was not mad. He was by nature patient. He had long studied a dragon's capabilities for warfare, and his memory of charred bodies had been evidence of their considerable power, but even an Emerald Phoorn, flickering and shimmering, being old, must build her energy or find renewed energy, if she were ever to fly in battle again! In better days it could be hours or days before the Phoorn could replenish their flaming venom. Elric was no longer a threat, nor Moonglum. Roses must bloom in Melniboné, by the light of old Sadric's sun. There his spirit could sleep and her integrity keep where Stormbringer's deep pulse now drums.

There were none left to ride Phoorn, even if there were Phoorn left to be ridden!

Cousin Marluc had spotted the signs and was now about his business. Let her progress if she liked with her proscribed, inflexible clockwork-determined fantastic plans! He would not follow her into further nonsensical adventure! She might be a Lord of Law with her love of goals and charts! Elric was dead, and he had no quarrel with Kirinmoir. He would exact enough tribute to satisfy his men and then return with them as their king. If Xiombarg objected, she faced a force as great as her own on which to expend her power, and barely a single promise kept to her own people.

Thus, Dyvim Marluc, her only real ally, was wondering if he would have to kill Queen Xiombarg of Chaos as no doubt she considered killing him. This, as Elric had discovered, was part of the problem of making alliance with the Lords and Ladies of Entropy. She said what was convenient until it became convenient to say something else. She preferred her ostensible ally to die wondering and frightened, even if the Chaos she directed on others crashed down on her own head. Payment, at least, for so many of her fellows, so many burned alive or drowned in their own blood in consequence of being poorly taught, even incapable of learning.

Xiombarg was growing tired of her female garb. She had found it useful to pose as an older sister to her acolytes for the century or two in Ko during which she had made his plans. Women had a habit of trusting women, as she knew to her advantage. But the usefulness of this flesh and her costumes was almost over. With an irritable movement of her hand she turned her chair into gleaming rare woods, then did the same for the fresh seat she offered Dyvim Marluc, fashioned into a chair of exquisite workmanship, though it was still inclined to twitch a little as the Melnibonéan sat gingerly down.

He had been foolish, he supposed, to trust one of these scheming gods. In his lifetime only Sadric's line had direct access to the Lords of Chaos. He could have done better without allies from the Higher Worlds, if she were the only one. He had encouraged Xiombarg to march and now regretted it. He had seen himself destroying Elric and what he believed to be his cousin's adopted city. They were now more likely to attract unwelcome attention from greater powers! Her plan had been an illusion. His had been over-ambition. He cursed her, and he cursed the hatred which had clouded his judgement and let him waste his resources so recklessly.

He calmed himself. Elric, at least, was dead. Any new plan must account for that. He could not give up all he had done for nothing, but neither could he risk the lives of his soldiers.

He had been naïve. Fate had made him a leader, but he had not come naturally to leadership. Xiombarg, he now knew, was not a creature with whom to plot or against whom to plot. This, as her brothers and sisters of Chaos knew, was why they were wary of alliances with her, why so many already used discretion, knowing her to be a treacherous being, to fear and ignore. From whom to escape or to kill. A sudden moment of terror suddenly consumed him as he lowered his bony back into that fleshy throne, feeling it writhe and creak. His golden armour still throbbed and glared and half-blinded those who surrounded the goddess, whose scaly snout, imbedded with jewels, looked with more than mere approval at Xiombarg's rather comely human avatars. Beneath her needle-thin teeth foamed a sort of cream of favourites, while little, indiscriminate fledgelings she had saved from an unwholesome doom were angrily scattering, shrieking his name and begging him to stop this foul nonsense! They begged. Xiombarg could not make sense of their panic. *Are we alarming you, mortal?* Horror followed horror until it stopped for him at least, and sweet honeysuckle grew around a trellis on the other side of a red-and-white thatched cottage with a wide, high and fantastic roof and steeply gabled windows which made him shiver with fear of a vivid recollection of a terrifying childhood in which he was tested for non-existent diseases and unfashionable complaints. *He thought he would sleep. But not dream. Had his mother been so cruel? Those teeth!*

He had to decide whether to remain to take his chances with Xiombarg, a goddess gone mad, cut his losses, withdraw his army to beyond the mountains, or offer Kirinmoir a turncoat's alliance? He would be risking her attack as he retreated. He consulted his honour. Would retirement from the field be noble, practical, soldierly, or all three? He decided, as good soldiers will, to sleep on it while he could. Making her own plans for his murder, Xiombarg had no notion of her ally's decision to betray her. After discussing strategy which went nowhere, Dyvim Marluc succumbed to his real tiredness and made his excuses. She was barely aware of his disappearance as she dreamed how she would simplify her life.

Idramadahan Sanfgt Iru Iru Sab'n/Ramada Sabaru/Dyvim Marluc woke after an hour or two to see a moon-riven sky covered by an enormous black shape moving against it, almost walking or creeping over the horizon before it turned its terrible head, focused its huge red-and-yellow eyes, opened its vast red mouth and poured blue flame into the centre of the sleeping army behind it, doing nothing to the rest of that army except warm it a little. It roared again and ploughed another furrow of the dead. Row upon row of blackened corpses clutched at the nightling sky. Where, Cousin Marluc wondered absently, consulting his own experience, were the dragon's basslings, her little pink, wriggling snacks she loved so much? As if to answer him, involuntarily smacking her emerald lips, Greatwing apologetically coughed a little blue ichor.

"Impossible! 'Tis an illusion, nothing else, bereft of any flesh or power of flight!" Xiombarg's generals glared this way and that, confounded. Did their mistress still live?

"*Carrying two human passengers? No illusion could take that weight! Proven! And thus—ergo—merely an hallucination maintained by that destroyed false goddess to keep the population of Kirinmoir and her treasure under their sway! Eh?*"

Dyvim Marluc was blinded for a moment, lifting his golden arm against the deep blue glare, hearing behind it the growling roar, the deep, regular breathing of the eternal Emerald Phoorn! That she-dragon commanded the Dragon Master's respect returned across the waves of the spectrum, those resonating worlds sometimes called by seers multiplanes, where realities of so many kinds flourished and so many were disputed. They were in truth only completely real to those of the related Phoorn and Melnibonéan race, which had bred both between themselves and apart, as luck determined for millennia, who shared so much common blood almost since the first worlds cooled.

Then, with a single scream, a full third of the surviving army awoke and died! An enormous stench went up, for now many of their animals had caught fire, and tallow fat burned like candles putting black curling smoke into the air as the tallow rose with the sun and continued to clog the throats and nostrils of the living. A few who had not died immediately ran flaming through the startled camp. Dyvim Marluc did not leave but remained with whatever strength he had, to fight against this deadly illusion. Perhaps it was not. Perhaps he should retreat.

What was this fog? It filled the eyes of many a fire-stained man stumbling back down the hill to where Xiombarg wailed and howled and gnashed her many sets of teeth.

A further third of the remaining army fell back into shadow and was lost to the dragon's vivid indigo breath. Xiombarg's crazed and tireless eyes glittered with unstable forces. Now she was a true Queen of Chaos! Where was Greatwing, she of the slender figure and of the mighty width of wing, ridden only by queens and kings, possessed of her delicate wings, her extraordinary beauty in shimmering flight, a myriad of green from palest ivory to the deepest, thinnest slice of green sea-jade. Nurtured from the egg? Another deception? Perhaps not, since the midnight-blue dragon, the allegedly crystallised Phoorn, appeared to be separated, flesh to flesh, bone to bone and so on.

Xiombarg groaned without voice, and there was anguish in her eyes. The Nihrain, at the very least, were rehearsing something here, she suspected. Not one of her brains accepted the apparent reality of what had happened.

Cinders glowed everywhere.

The great Emerald Dragon rose slowly into the sky. Her lovely wings flapped once, creating an impossibly sharp wind, blowing the scent of the burning camp further and deeper in all directions and then, suddenly, she faltered.

Slowly the Phoorn flapped one wing and then another, and the great Queen of the Swords flung back her oddly articulated heads and smacked her unfortunate lips and closed her glittering orbs, hopping awkwardly from her chair and flapping her own wing and moving slowly, swaying, back and forth, unready to close until with a long sigh the Phoorn flew straight up into the air like a huge, startled gamebird. She came swooping to the ground again. Stumbled and fell forward, revealing on her back the two women whose city Xiombarg had sought to destroy and whom she had mistaken for Elric and Moonglum.

Those two women jumped from the collapsing dragon as the creature raised her sad, monstrous head, her long nostrils fluttering in death throes before her body began to disintegrate swiftly into ash and then dust, and the empress and her captain fell into the dust, landing on supple feet and running out of the cloud. Gasping through parched lips, they could barely form the words required to curse Xiombarg and Ramada Sabaru in seriously foul language. Almost incidentally they insisted to his forcing of innocent juveniles as bait, of allying himself with baby-killers and much worse. The dragon continued to disintegrate behind Melaré and Shirizha, until only glowing yellow-and-red eyes and blue, swirling dust and spiralling, murmuring dense, oddly moving clouds remained.

And the watchers began slowly to understand the dragon's collapse into components as the nature of those components became astonishingly clear. They were bees. Millions of bees. As dots make up a whole seen from a distance, so had the bees maintained the outline and innards of a dragon, Goldwing, who had been Greatwing's partner. Forming conical clouds and spreading wide, the bees now headed back towards the city. Lady Greatwing was still alive, if barely, within the mountain, which was safe for the moment within that gigantic clutching fist. She had somehow conspired with ancestral consent to reanimate the corpse of her noble wife, so recently dead and, like her, maintained in life by a symbiotic combination with the hive's billions of active bees, in certain ways the kin to those they came to save. The bees, blending their blood with the blood of mortal and dragon, had reanimated the great reptile and restored her power of flight! Sorcery enough, though not what Xiombarg and her allies had prepared for. The quasi-Phoorn had brought fairer odds to the battlefield.

There came a shout from near that enormous stone fist.

The fingers opened slightly, and figures could be seen in the shadows within. Perhaps a voice called? Then the sound, almost without doubt, of warbeasts' iron-shod feet clattering on hard earth. The growing rise of cries and Xiombarg shrilling. A further confusion of roars and shouts while the remains of the great army attempted to regroup under its captains.

She began to pace about snarling and rustling and letting her temper get the better of her again as the figures walked their massive, black Nihrain steeds out through a titan's grey fingers, preparing to duel for prizes which might be entire worlds. Xiombarg hissed in curiosity. Then Orlando Funk straddled his gigantic mule. Elric and Moonglum mounted their Nihrainian horses, and all three began to canter directly towards the Queen of Chaos!

Who grinned and growled and clasped her white sword Divergent and prepared for further combat.

TWENTY-SIX

The Battle Won and Lost

AS PLANNED, MELARÉ and Shirizha, standing on its back where the spine began, had ridden the semi-sentient quasi-Phoorn in an enormous arc, learning to fly again before resting, recovering and then returning to pour the last of this beast's blue fire into the enemy ranks. The Phoorn's outlines remained unsteady. Not an illusion as such, but the sisters were unsure if they could hold it together for much longer.

Now Elric and his companions bent flat over the necks of their mounts, galloping towards the still-considerable army assembled by their enemies. Although in disarray and scattered thinly, it stretched for miles across the sooted valley.

So astonished were Xiombarg and Dyvim Marluc that they barely knew to whom or what they should respond first. Their unthinking and incautious confidence in their plan of attack meant they had made no provision for change or failure. They had not prepared for any of this. The empress and her captain? Had they come to parley? The three yelling mortals who charged towards them? Had they some invisible army at their back? In their uncertainty the invaders had lost all advantage.

Her single face shifting from human to reptile, her steed now a great lion-headed horse with eagle foreclaws, Xiombarg raised her double-bladed battle-axe and screamed at her remaining generals to call their men to order. Dyvim Marluc hysterically called for his soldiers to form a wall, but they were too disorientated with half their captains down and the rest untrained against such enemies. Meanwhile there came a roar from behind them, and the fiery cage containing Arioch exploded with a million colours and all near him fell back blinded as the Lord of Chaos, a magnificent silver youth of angelic beauty, struggled from the flickering ruins clutching a black sword to him and screeched with glee before bursting upward and outward, the huge black cloud glittering with stars! As planned, the priestesses Andra and Indra had smuggled the sword from Elric to Arioch so that, while the enemy was distracted, the Lord of Chaos could infuse it with all its power again and use it to break the supernatural locks and chains with which his fellow Lord of Chaos had bound him! Knowing how disillusioned they had become, Elric had risked trusting them with this mission. They had comforted the other priestesses, drawing unnoticed, closer to Arioch's supernatural cage cursed by a powerful sword spell!

Now Elric raised himself in the stirrups of his black Nihrain stallion and lifted his sword of plain steel, the one he had carried into the Blue Well, over his head.

"*Arioch! Stormbringer!*" His voice, still half a mile away from his great patron, carried all the way to Lord Arioch.

And Arioch laughed with his old vibrant glee upon seeing his protégé, all triumphant scarlet and black flame, and he tossed Stormbringer high into the air! The world around them, the air between them, erupted with a blinding rainbow radiance which made all but the protagonists fall back screaming and covering their eyes.

"*Arioch! Stormbringer! To me, Stormbringer! To me!*"

And at last, like a hawk coming home, the familiar shagreen handle slipped into Elric's gauntleted hand and the Actorios in the pommel pulsed indigo and scarlet and the runes in the smoky black blade shimmered and writhed like ruby snakes within the cursed metal. And Stormbringer murmured. And Stormbringer moaned like a reunited lover. Stormbringer was ready to *feed*!

"*Arioch! Arioch! Stormbringer! To me! To me!*" That beautiful baritone voice carried over all the other sounds of the battlefield.

And then the sword began to sing! And the warriors, mortal and super-natural, shuddered at that primordial sound, many covering their ears as it came closer and closer, sung in harmony with a red-eyed albino devil who was at that moment invulnerable! Xiombarg had promised them that Elric the White Wolf was dead, and this clearly was their pale nemesis, more alive than ever! In the rear of Dyvim Marluc's army the ranks of cavalry and mounted engineers deserted their siege machines and began to canter discreetly back towards the tunnel, back to the outside world. No general saw them leave, for many generals were leading the retreat. Yet a big force of armed men and beasts still remained gathered either at the walls of Kirinmoir, having remained in the shallow gulches formed by the stone fingers, or in positions which had not moved forward since their arrival. A few had not yet left their positions in the rocky heights. Their sparser numbers, however, confounded them, for some did not recognise uniforms of others or even members of the same tribe, so quickly had Ramada Sabaru been raised to power by a naïve people. They had seen in their Golden King one who would lead them to their mythic glory of the kind every nation claimed, especially when attempting to establish itself or re-establish as a State! But Dyvim Marluc/Ramada Sabaru, powerful as he was in terms of what this people understood, had no real experience of leading so many and, now that he had known the responsibilities of Empire, decided he must abdicate as soon as possible.

"*STORMBRINGER!*"

He shuddered, turning to seek the source of the voice.

For a moment, he watched the black cloud drifting overhead, moving pur-posefully back to their hives, and then the sword hung above Elric's head. All ambivalence forgotten, the albino grinned and sighed with the pure pleasure of greeting an old friend. The more he longed to be free from the blade, the more he realised how he was bound for eternity to wield it and to suffer as a result.

The sword moaned like a favourite hound as it settled into his hand. There came a chill moment of real affection between two monsters while Arioch poured all his pent-up energy into him, and, invigorating him, filled him with enormous power. His eyes had grown dull. Now they blazed like rubies as the black Nihrain stallion reared, neighing and flailing his wild hoofs, eager for further battle. Through surprise and clever planning, and with considerable help from the traditional guardians and servants of Kirinmoir, the various strategic parts of the invading army had been wiped out. Yet the defenders still faced considerable odds against Xiombarg and her human allies on the open field.

The sword held overhead, he continued to call out his famous battle-cry. A battle-cry striking fear into all who heard it.

"Lord of the Seven Darks! Aid me now!"

Elric rode directly towards the Golden Warrior, killing casually, almost absently, any who attempted to stop him. And again the instincts of his Melnibonéan ancestors, the sustained savagery and recklessness of his attack, riding a horse which only *seemed* to gallop over the surface of this plane and was all but invulnerable, Elric was truly in his element, almost an element of his own devising. Immediate and rapid lusts and quenchings were his again! The albino laughed with the joy of it, and the song he sang was a song of delight, making his blood race and his body thrill with heightened sensation. With the muscular supernatural steed beneath him, he was fully himself again! If only Cymoril were here to celebrate and fight beside her mortal kin! A pang as he remembered Zarozinia. And Melaré. But only a pang. He would never entirely learn to feel guilt as humans felt it.

Stormbringer crooned with delight as she drank the sweet souls of mortal soldiers, while blood, bone and flesh flew in all directions and the albino's white face was streaked with the life-stuff of his enemies. His horse, harness and armour were equally smeared with the remains of those who had followed Dyvim Marluc or Xiombarg into this valley. Whether they struck from in front or behind, from land or air, Elric parried and killed, parried and killed. He was ready. He had waited too long. And his sword was very thirsty.

He called to all those with whom he and his forefathers had made compacts. But there was little response. Where were the great elementals? The supernatural remained banished from Kirinmoir, it seemed!

Elsewhere, Moonglum, Funk and the sword-wielding ex-priestesses of Xiombarg fought with the same wild courage as Elric, moving so swiftly from place to place that the army continued to be baffled, believing themselves attacked by a much larger force. And rank by rank the saurian-riding guards, the spindly generals and peasant-soldiers of Kirinmoir rode out to defend their strangely protected city. Slowly, one by one, the great elementals who still slumbered began to wake, but they did not join in this fight! Instead, they watched, wondered and decided.

Xiombarg and Dyvim Marluc remained dazed as they attempted to regroup. Many of their captains had no idea how to marshal panicking men and supply wagons whose teams were shrieking in terror as they struggled in their harness, some strangling, asphyxiated, kicking, dying in their reins. They had all relied far too much on the old methods to escape the building terror! Now they moved about the churned mud of the field seeking some means of stopping this unexpected attack from a dragon they supposed dead and a mortal the dragon should have killed.

Nearby, Moonglum kept to the safety of Arioch's shadow with the priestesses Andra and Indra, who now clearly served Arioch's cause, swinging their captured broadswords, so well-balanced they were easily held in one hand. Trained as all the priestesses at Ko were trained, they were proving to be skilled swordswomen and swift to learn. They fought in unison, with those same instincts which made Elric and his friend such effective fighters.

Elric swung the screaming sword this way and that, shouting in unison as Arioch, released from Xiombarg's prison by Xiombarg's own disenchanted priestesses, aided by Elric's and his own cunning, roared and rattled his fiery teeth, gibbering at his terrified enemies, gathering strength from their growing dismay, while Xiombarg and Dyvim Marluc, no longer focused on betrayal, but understanding they could only now hope to win as allies, tried to take control of their still-considerable, but now unruly, army. Two thirds of it lay grotesquely twisted and burned black upon the battleground. And meanwhile, the astonished citizens of Kirinmoir, having yet to take part in serious fighting, watched safe behind barriers of sentient granite.

The mysterious flight of the Phoorn had given Kirinmoir's defenders the advantage.

Elric, Moonglum and their immediate allies had the initiative and did not lose it as Orlando Funk on his mighty mule brought up the rear, his battle-axe swinging like a scythe. Xiombarg's own great battle-axe was now in her hands, going back and forth with clocklike precision as it kept her attackers at bay. Xiombarg's childlike, girlish human voice was stomach-turning as it issued from a head that was momentarily gigantic cat and long-snouted jackal, wearing the fiery armour of Chaos, which all those dark Higher Lords had on. Then she had adopted her favourite disguise, a green-skinned woman with a mass of auburn hair carrying a double-bladed bronze battle-axe and riding on something that was a cross between a goat, a lion, a wolf and an eagle, with enormous razor talons. All around her scattered in fear, and he saw Melaré and Shirizha burst from amongst their captors, laughing with crazy glee, ecstatically happy to be fighting Kirinmoir's enemies.

Xiombarg was momentarily calm as she faced her adversaries.

She was Elric's goal.

But she was Arioch's goal, too.

The squealing protests of terrified animals mingled with the shouts and roars of the stricken soldiers, the creaks and groans of war-engines and the bellowing of wounded beasts. This cacophony combined with the grunts and deafening roars of Xiombarg's remaining supernatural allies, drowning individual cries or screams. But Moonglum glimpsed Melaré and Shirizha turning captured horses back towards the city. Taking flight, after all! He had no more time to watch as a flying thing tried to grasp him with its talons. A single sweep of his left hand and Moonglum sliced his attacker's head while the beak still struck, missing him by a fraction as the rest of the warhawk's body fell heavily onto the field.

The Elwheri became wary of Stormbringer, keeping a distance between his red-eyed friend and himself, yet continuing to protect his back. He missed the help of the Kirinmoiris but fought on, with Funk taking up the women's position.

Moonglum's entire body ached from head to toe as he continued his expert attack on an army whose numbers were at least a hundred to one greater than the force still waiting in the protected city.

Would they come out to help or would they see their heroic defenders cut down at last when Xiombarg rallied? The bees were again nowhere to be seen as they fought on, but Xiombarg's dazed generals began to organise their army and isolate the albino and his friends who still wreaked such unholy havoc in their numbers. It could not be long before the little band, no matter how powerful Elric's battle-blade, would be overwhelmed . . .

"Arioch! Arioch! Lord of the Seven Darks. Aid me now!"

Arioch was gone again. Nowhere to be seen. Doubtless the Chaos Lord had given Elric all he could? He had been weakened. He needed to recuperate.

In the distance, a horn began to sound from Kirinmoir's battlements. A high, sharp sound at first, descending into deep sustained notes, echoed within the strange cavern formed by the granite fist of the one they called the Witness. Elric had not thought too deeply about a name so ancient it could mean almost anything. A passive word, he thought. Or a word corrupted by time. Was that the Mran of legend? The story was common to many, how an earth elemental was challenged first by Chaos, then Law, to fight a duel, take a bribe or believe a flattering lie, but who resisted and won the blessing of a goddess to stand guard over an enchanted city. An ancient tale designed to assure a people that some deity watched over them. The horn sounded again, half-heard under the shrill scream of a Byothic pikeman who fell before Elric's horse and, by some terrible alchemy, was trampled beneath hoofs from another dimension. When that screaming battlehorn sounded a third time, Elric pulled his horse to a halt and, standing in his stirrups, looked toward Kirinmoir.

Again the mighty stone fingers had parted, and through them streamed the mass Kirinmoiri army, ready to confront the invaders at last.

Brave banners now flew on tall standards as their strange cavalry, an odd combination of gigantic lizards, horses and llamas, rode to do battle with the Queen of Entropy and the Golden Emperor, both of whom had set out to take vengeance and wound up losing an empire. *So,* Elric thought, *we are pushed this way and that as the tides of history flow. Now it is Arioch's day and Kirin-moir's day. And it is my day, when Stormbringer has all her powers and we are complete! Let us pray, too, that this will be our victory day!*

He dragged a standard from a herald's hand, chopping the boy's hand off, then only slowly withdrawing his black, thirsty blade from the writhing corpse. The herald died pleading with Elric not to take his soul, not to steal the only precious immortal part of him. Elric scarcely heard him, it was such a familiar request. Again he threw back his wild, white head and laughed, his ruby eyes appearing to burn so brightly that men were struck down before them. He and the blade were in complete symbiosis. Possessed by its ancient evil, Elric had little patience with pleas for mercy. These people had looked forward, all of them, to profit in blue honey, slaves and loot from this war. They had expected to die in the attempt but not to lose those subtle parts of all mortals which are neither brain nor body but an elusive part of us we call the mind or life-force or soul, that small part held in common by all life, even if they denied its existence.

Elric and Stormbringer took that part and distilled it into demonic energy. The rest was dross. Sometimes the body went on living after a fashion. Elric knew by what terrible bargain with evil he lived. He hated his dependence on the sword. He had tried to be rid of it on countless occasions. Not now. Now he welcomed all the black blade could give him as he pressed on, urging his invulnerable stallion through the press to reach the creature he hated more, even, than treacherous Yyrkoon.

He took off his battle-helm to let his hair flow free, and he stuck it on the top of the staff so all could see it, and he cried, "*To me, Kirinmoir, to me.*" And he raised Stormbringer high, standing in the horse's heavy stirrups, and called the old, vibrant battle-cries which had announced his terrifying presence across two worlds! "*STORMBRINGER! Blood and souls for my Lord Arioch!*"

Elric guessed the sisters had fed their citizen-army with all the blue mead they could find. Every eye of every man and woman blazed with it as they ran behind the mounted guards. Now there was bloodlust in their once peaceful hearts.

At last they met, with Kirinmoir disciplined and efficient while the invaders remained disorganised but outnumbering their enemy by many thousands. Elric sought the enemy's golden leader and saw him at last, boxed in by his enemies and standing in the howdah of his white war-mammoth, a bow in his hands and full quiver of arrows on his back; he was shouting for Elric, but Elric galloped past him, deflecting showering arrows with his small shield and heading for Xiombarg, now some distance away. Elric could not remember killing a god before, but he was prepared to do it now even if she killed him in the process.

And if, when he had killed Xiombarg, he still lived, he would kill another treacherous cousin.

Xiombarg was now suddenly boyish again, almost as if she were deliberately lampooning the favourite guise of a golden mortal youth, generally adopted by her old enemy Arioch whenever he was invited to the earthly plane. But she was not mocking Arioch now. She was fighting for her future, her dream, for which she had broken the fundamental laws of the Higher Worlds. And if Elric had his chance, she was fighting for her life.

The embattled soldiers suddenly parted like a tide. Perhaps it was the shock of that great wave striking the host as army met army. It left a kind of tunnel of silence clear to Xiombarg, and Elric flung himself and his horse down it.

"*Arioch! Arioch! Blood and souls for Arioch!*"

Stormbringer blazed with black light, and the runes ran deep red up and down the length of the black steel.

Hearing the albino and her enemy's name, Xiombarg crouched down at first, licking her lips with a flickering forked tongue. The White Sword Divergent, which had given her the power to divide Chaos and thus entrap Arioch, flamed in a blaze of pale gold. Silence continued to encircle them so that the din of battle was muted. They knew a moment of uncalled armistice.

"You seek to destroy me, I think, Prince of Ruins." She swung the ivory gold sword hypnotically, back and forth. Elric sat upon his stallion with Stormbringer's pommel on his knee, waiting for her first aggressive movement.

"You may leave now with what remains of your allies, even Ramada Sa-baru. I seek only to serve this valley, as I swore I would, before my friend and I return to our own plane."

"The valley belongs to me," she said sullenly. "To Chaos. We conquered it. Chaos comes to claim her heritage. When she arrives, you had best be gone."

"Yet I heard that in the Higher Worlds the gods of Law *and* Chaos are at odds. Local people describe a so-called War Amongst the Angels, though perhaps they merely mean that you and Arioch are at odds. They squabble increasingly, sensing a coming war from which they can profit. They seek to position themselves favourably in the coming struggle for possession of my plane. And any other plane in the multiverse. It is where my particular ances-tors began. So therefore it is my land, settled by Phoorn and the descendant cousins to the Kirinmoiri. We call it the First Plane. Our legends speak of it."

"Legends!" Xiombarg rested carefully on her pommel, ready to kill him in a moment. "I know more of your history than you do, young Silverskin. I know how Phoorn in all their guises fled their nemesis through the planes, seeking sanctuary. At last dragons and mortal-kind, weary of flight, turned to fight their pursuers with such desperate physical and metaphysical ferocity they threatened the stability of the Cosmic Balance!

"The Black Nihrain, known for their neutrality in service of the Balance, formed a guard, and a truce was called. After so much destruction, both of men and knowledge, all contenders swore, in the name of the Cosmic Bal-ance, that this valley should be forever free from violence, while dragons, and the mortals they spawned and protected, should continue to live in harmony. Those kitchen bees, as well as our larger bees, were already settled here and were undisturbed. There was room for five Emerald Phoorn to roost easily within the mountain as over the centuries the city and her legends grew to-gether! Protected by the Witness, the city and all she protected flourished! I had patience in those days. One by one I watched from a distance, waiting for those dragons to die so that I could use Kirinmoir from which to begin an attack on your half of this world from this one! By then, I was sure, the makers of the old compact would be dead."

"You have waited centuries for this?" The albino had never suspected such a thing, despite all his old associations with Chaos.

"I have prepared for it, yes, as, upon my instructions, the dragons were kept in constant slumber by the priestesses supposed to tend to their needs. Year in and year out, they were maintained in hibernation, milked for their venom, which mixed with the honey and became part of their unconventional mating procedures. The High Priestess was long my secret worshipper and the others followed her orders. She believed I would guard Kirinmoir best, just as those fools brought me Divergent convinced I intended peace! They in turn advised the high-bred citizens as tradition demanded. The truth they understand is the truth I have been telling them for generations!" And the Queen of the Swords permitted herself a cackle.

Outside the tunnel of silence Elric heard a returned Arioch's gleeful roar as he slaughtered the soldiers of his enemy with new weapons forged by sorcery! Dyvim Marluc was out there, also, his own armour, silver, gold and gleaming steel, visible from below as his mighty war-mammoth tossed Kirinmoiris high into the cold air of morning.

Elric knew he must kill Dyvim Marluc first. He was not yet ready to kill a god. Although he carried Stormbringer again and the runesword had become his as a trained hawk returns to her master's gauntlet, he saw no reason why the ancient protocols should not stand. He knew what happened to worlds and peoples displaced by war. He served Chaos and would gladly continue his long relationship with Arioch if need be. But all depended upon the Balance and its constant monitoring of old compacts between earth and mortal, mortal and immortal and so on. If they were destroyed and their spirit denied, the nature of the Balance itself was threatened, resonating through all the planes of the multiverse, spreading like the branches of an immeasurable tree, affecting all sentient life, all spiritual and physical understanding. Millions of souls were at stake: all the souls, human and non-human, thrown like wagers upon the baize, their fates to be changed, perhaps for all time, by the battles and caprices of a few powerful gods and demigods.

"It is time to rip up the old compacts! If we do not, the world, decadent and doomed to destruction, shall soon fall into a bottomless abyss of her own devising!"

"You know much more than I." Elric was not entirely sarcastic. "Well, I have not come here to dispute with you, my Lord or Lady Xiombarg. Leave the field, with or without your forces, and you will not be stopped. My quarrel now is with Dyvim Marluc."

"Long, long ago, your Nihrain friends reached an agreement in the name of the Cosmic Balance and its witness, the earth giant Mran."

"I care not greatly for most ancient agreements. Merely those brokered between Melniboné and certain elementals."

"I, too, have no taste for useless bargains, as I have proven here." Xiombarg was yet to lower her guard. "Why serve that pouting fool Arioch when I am so much more powerful and intelligent? Surely you must admire my beauty over his? I can provide you with a far wider canvas for your talents."

Though he understood his danger, Elric found that he was fascinated by this encounter. Their ambitions were so different. Speaking to Xiombarg was unlike any conversation he had with any other being, even Arioch. "I am moved by curiosity, madam, not a lust for power. I was once the most powerful of all earthly princes. My nation, though still powerful, had fallen into decadence and complacency. My people expected me to make Melniboné great again, but such dreams are always empty. So many factors create an empire, and so many bring about its doom. Perhaps I should have tried to restore our power, as some wished. I learned that nations are no longer made great by force of arms but by trade and ingenuity."

"Well, White Wolf, I admire your old-fashioned loyalty—"

Elric was already turning in his saddle and wheeling his black horse about as Dyvim Marluc in his howdah drew back his bow, aiming an arrow at the albino's back, deflected by a black blade as Elric's instincts, becoming more sharply honed by the moment, sensed his cousin's intent. The Nihrain horse galloped straight up the line above the astonished mammoth's trunk and filled the howdah so that, bent backwards, Dyvim Marluc was forced against its rail, beating at the horse and Elric's body with his useless bow, grasping for his sword as the albino dismounted. Elric let his stallion trot back over an invisible hill and wait for him below. One in ivory, the other in jet, the Melnibonéans stood mere feet apart in glowering confrontation.

"You are aware I carry no special magical sword, cousin. Just simple steel, such as you carried against me a little while ago. If you could show me similar courtesy, I will—" And Dyvim Marluc's eyes opened wide as he looked down at his breast, at his armour sprouting scarlet, and saw Stormbringer pulsing there, her sorcerous steel sucking his soul so slowly from his body, her red runes glowing brighter and richer and the rare Actorios forming her pommel almost bursting with ruby light, red as his own pulsing blood, as Elric pressed the black blade inch by inch into Dyvim Marluc's gasping body. His black eyes stared into Elric's, begging him silently for release from the terrible truth of his finish, for some impossible reversal of fate.

Betrayed and betraying, impossibly compromised, the Melnibonéan died attempting to curse his cousin.

Elric, in turn, cursed Dyvim Marluc all the way to Hell, while that stolen energy was sucked into his being and he laughed as he cried—

"*Arioch! Arioch! Blood and souls for my lord Arioch!*"

Dragging his pulsing black blade from his treacherous cousin's drained corpse, he leapt from Dyvim Marluc's disorientated mammoth, remounted his stallion and slapped at the mammoth to send him lumbering back into his own forces, scattering them in any direction other than the one in which Xiombarg now screamed at them to follow! The other mammoths and elephants, without direction, panicked and began to stampede back over the soldiers behind them. In places, the very large invading force was pursued by a very small army of defenders led by Melaré, Shirizha and the generals under Mulxer Gash—full out on their racing lizards—trumpets blaring—bright steel glaring and the great, joyous hullabaloo rising from the ranks of the Kirinmoiris, which had a strong hint of disbelief as the defenders followed their enemies until they saw the first of them reach the great tunnel out of the valley and the other passages they had made for themselves, and creep into them without hesitation. The Slaughter in the Kirinmoir Caves would become an epic, often embellished and with several divergent versions.

Moonglum and Orlando Funk were bringing up the rear, warning the pursuers not to follow the invaders into the tunnels.

Elric rode to join his companions while behind him, Arioch and Xiombarg faced each other over the carnage for which only Elric and Melaré felt guilt.

Orlando Funk sat his great mule Munch with the ease of a man comfortable in a familiar saddle. Elric and Moonglum, too, found the Nihrain steeds easy to ride over long distances. They had no intention, however, of riding all the way to the tunnels. Elric and Moonglum had business in the more distant mountains and, beyond them, perhaps, the Weeping Waste and beyond that, perhaps, Ilmiora, Karlaak and Zarozinia, who loved him as he could not love himself.

The fight was, however, by no means over as Xiombarg, Divergent in hand and mounted on her lion-headed eagle, faced Arioch, as a glorious youth, preparing for a monumental battle which could yet destroy Kirinmoir, her army and all those left alive. Elric was not sure they still had strength enough to challenge the Chaos gods.

He had promises to keep. The restoration of a people to ensure. He prepared himself for a further fight as the ground around them began to shiver. Even the Nihrain stallion grew nervous. Swiftly shock wave followed shock wave almost flinging people to the ground. And now they knew the great stone hand carefully withdrew from under the city, leaving it with its walls and temple in ruins but all else otherwise still intact, its beautiful buildings still climbing the hill over the Well.

Then the animals all showed anxiety and had to be controlled as fissures began to appear around the stone, running like ratlines over the surface while first one great slab of earth was cast aside, then another, and another, until more masses of rounded granite were exposed, rising taller and taller, scattering earth and rocks in all directions, until Elric said—

"Greetings, Sir Witness. Greetings, patient Mran. I am Elric of the line of Sadric, which claims kinship with your brother Grome. We thank thee for thine aid!"

And the enormous naked elemental, a vision of perfect manhood, alive with rippling granite, shining like grey silk, stood astride the desolate field, full of blackened twisted corpses of men, women and beasts, and he frowned. Elric feared he was about to punish them, but then he saw that the monster was weeping. Yet, as he did so, Mran reached to pluck the glaring gods from the ground and growl his displeasure.

At that moment Elric realised to his surprise that the granite giant was more powerful than either Lord of Chaos who was now held writhing furiously in Mran's firm grip. He tried to hear what Mran whispered in the ears of those nobles of the Higher Worlds before he took one in each fist and passed them behind him. Then, with the air of a human conjuror, revealing his empty palm and offering the startled onlookers a gigantic and avuncular wink.

With a sense of resignation, Elric directed his horse towards Kirinmoir. The worst part of his adventure was still ahead.

EPILOGUE

Myth and Memory

ELRIC PLACED THE fragments of map into his inner pocket. If directions were accurate, and with some luck, they could be in Karlaak sooner than anticipated. He looked back at Kirinmoir, already reviving and restoring herself around surviving Phoorn, bees, mortals, and now Melnibonéan blood, in that strange, supernatural blend of biology and ancient magic. "Brought back to life by Grome and Mran, yet unlike Melaré, Lady Greatwing must still await a mate. There's a myth concerning a young Melnibonéan who comes riding on a wounded horse seeking his sister but mistaking one for the other. An opera was made of it, I believe."

Moonglum had more to regret. He had no woman awaiting him in far Karlaak. "Let's hope the new compact holds at least as long as the old!"

"They will need to reconsider and perhaps revise their myths," Elric said, settling in his pony's saddle and surveying the rebuilding of the city. Kirinmoir now seeming oddly naked since, promising to return when needed, Mran had trudged back into the realm of King Grome.

"Their realities, you mean?" Moonglum was unusually prim. He felt that Elric should feel as he did. He hated the secret he shared with his friend.

"A myth has no meaning if it isn't based in reality. A people without myths is a people without identity."

A shake of the reins, and Elric turned his pony towards the far mountains.

The sun was rising behind the tallest peak. With one regretful look backwards, Moonglum began to follow his friend out of the Kirinmoir Valley and up into the foothills which would lead them to the World Above, to fulfil their final destiny.

THE END

Parts of this novel, now substantially revised, first appeared in WEIRD TALES No. 349, *edited by Stephen H. Segal & Ann VanderMeer, March/April 2008,* and in Swords & Dark Magic: The New Sword And Sorcery, *edited by Jonathan Strahan & Lou Anders, Eos, 2010.*

ELRIC

MYYRRHN

TARKESH
The Plains of Toraunz

Banarva   · Nio

Vale of
Xanyaw

THE
PALE
SEA

Sequaloris   DHARIJOR
Gromoorva
The Hewn City
of Nihrain   JHARKOR   Nargesser

Cadsandria   Dhakos
Thokora·

SHAZAAR

Marshes of the
Mist

·Aflitain

THE
SILENT LAND   The Serpent's Teeth

STRAITS OF CHAOS

Nwamgaarl ·
The City of the
Screaming Statues

DA
TAM

THE DRAGON SEA

SORCERER'S ISLE

MELNIBONÈ
Isle of the
Imrryr,
The Dreaming

Hiding Place
of the
Sealord's Fleet

R'lin K'ren Aa   ·

THE BOILING SEA

Rama

Las

Dhoz-Kam·

ASHANELOON   OIN

YU   L
Ur River

N

W   E

S

to KANELO
and
WORLD'S E